Penguin Books
SPYSHIP

Tom Keene has worked with Thames Television and
Westward Television as both researcher and producer
of various current affairs programmes. In this capacity
he has travelled extensively in Europe, the Middle East
and the United States. He now writes full-time from his
home in Devon.

Brian Haynes spends part of the year living and
working in London making current affairs films for
ITV. The rest of the time he spends at a cottage in the
Malvern Hills flying kites and playing croquet.

Tom Keene with Brian Haynes

SPYSHIP

Penguin Books

Penguin Books Ltd, Harmondsworth, Middlesex, England
Penguin Books, 625 Madison Avenue, New York, New York 10022, U.S.A.
Penguin Books Australia Ltd, Ringwood, Victoria, Australia
Penguin Books Canada Ltd, 2801 John Street, Markham, Ontario, Canada L3R 1B4
Penguin Books (N.Z.) Ltd, 182–190 Wairau Road, Auckland 10, New Zealand

First published in the U.S.A. by Richard Marek Publishers 1890
First published in Great Britain by Allen Lane 1890
Published in Penguin Books 1981
Reprinted 1981 (twice), 1983

Made and printed in Great Britain by
Richard Clay (The Chaucer Press) Ltd, Bungay, Suffolk
Set in Linotype Juliana

For Joan, my mother, with my love.
You always said I would and I have.

Also for Sue and Toby.

AUTHOR'S NOTE

In 1974 the Hull trawler *Gaul*, 1,106 tons, disappeared off the north coast of Norway. Despite an exhaustive air and sea search, there were no survivors. A fine ship and thirty-six competent, professional seamen appeared to have been overwhelmed by heavy seas and sent to the bottom.

But rumours sweeping her home port began to suggest something quite different: that the *Gaul* had been used for Intelligence gathering; that she had been carrying Royal Navy personnel; that she had been boarded by the Soviet Navy and that her crew were now prisoners in some Soviet labour camp.

At that time Tom Keene and Brian Haynes were working as researchers for Thames Television's *This Week* programme. They spent more than a year investigating these and other rumours. Together with a detailed insight into the twilight world of electronic warfare, their factual discoveries resulted in an hour-long documentary, 'The Mystery of the *Gaul*', transmitted in October 1975. The reporter was Peter Williams. The programme was directed by Norman Fenton and produced by John Edwards and David Elstein.

The authors do not deny that the *Gaul*'s disappearance gave them the germ-seed for this book – but reality provided only the starting blocks for a novel that has drawn heavily upon both their imaginations and the facts and rumours surrounding several other sinkings, collisions and disappearances off Britain's shores and elsewhere: between 1965 and 1975, for example, American submarines, engaged in reconnaissance often close to the Soviet coast, were involved in at least nine collisions with hostile vessels.*

Spyship is not, therefore, a thinly disguised version of what the authors believe really happened to the *Gaul*. The *Gaul* was not a spyship; this book is fiction and the characters are fictitious – but the 'war' to which our vessel, the M T *Arctic Pilgrim*, sails, is not.

Tom Keene
Brian Haynes

ACKNOWLEDGEMENTS

Many sources have been consulted in the compilation of this novel. In particular, the authors would like to mention two excellent publications: *Jane's Fighting Ships* and *The Soviet Navy Today*, by Captain John E. Moore, R N.

Our thanks go also to Thames Television Ltd for allowing us, in the early days, to plant a small idea and watch it grow.

---

* Among these were:

1. A collision involving the U S S *Gato* on 14 or 17 November 1969;
2. A collision involving the U S S *Pintado* in May 1974. Both *Gato* and *Pintado* were carrying nuclear weapons at the time;
3. A collision involving a U S submarine and a Vietnamese minesweeper which later sank;
4. The surfacing of an American submarine *under* a Soviet vessel in a Soviet fleet naval exercise;
5. The grounding of an American submarine within Soviet territorial waters;
6. A collision with a Soviet submarine on 31 March 1971;
7. A collision between the American Polaris submarine *Benjamin Franklin* and a tugboat which later sank;
8. A collision between the American attack submarine *Tullibee* and a West German merchant ship on 6 October 1972;
9. A collision between the American nuclear attack submarine *Finback* and a submarine rescue ship on 8 January 1974.

CHAPTER ONE

For Norman Fullerton, 23 March 1969, was a special day. On that day, at the age of twenty-seven, he began to die.

True, his death was still some months away, swathed in the disguise of days yet to be lived, meals yet to be eaten, conversations yet to take place – but the events that culminated in a roar of stinking, icy grey-green water off the North Cape of Norway had their origins in that date.

As he shambled home from the pub, large fists thrust into parka pockets, shoulders hunched against the biting easterly that growled in low off the warehouse roofs, he was humming tunelessly to himself. He had come to a decision:

He would marry Sheila, settle down in that flat across the street from the garage where he worked and get on with his ambition of running the place himself by the time he was thirty. It was time he put down roots, started a family.

Had Norman Fullerton been able to couple clairvoyance with a happy aptitude for anything mechanical, that tune would have died on his lips. He would have seen a childless marriage batter itself to a standstill with cruel, blunt words used by a couple who shared little more than the room where they slept and the cursory, primordial use of each other's bodies; a marriage which, ultimately, would drive him back to sea and she to a mother who, with grim satisfaction, had always said he was not good for her daughter.

But bad marriages, however painful, are seldom fatal. The real significance of that date lay in the launching of a certain ship earlier that same afternoon in a Scottish shipyard.

It was never meant to be much of a ceremony.

The days of champagne over the bows and a prim little

9

speech from the chairman's wife were long gone, jettisoned for the harsher realities of completion on time every time. The sign in the manager's office on the quay said so. Launchings were supposed to be nothing more than a momentary hiccup in the tangled, rust-streaked life cycle of any yard racing for still more orders in the burgeoning North Sea market. Yet two hundred grimy dock workers had downed tools for a moment to wish this one Godspeed as she rumbled reluctantly down the slip at Gosforth Marine.

The thin, ragged cheers of her makers whipped away on the afternoon air, and the men turned back to their work, hiding their loss, for they had said kind things about *Arctic Pilgrim*: 'well found' was their tribute to her; a good ship on the slips.

She was designed by A. B. Anders Ltd, Marine Architects, of Gosport, Hants., to a specific requirement laid down by the eventual owners, Graveline Trawlers Ltd. Her name betrayed her destination, if not her role: she was to be an oceangoing, deep-water trawler – a hunter of fish. More prosaically, she was to be a single-screw factory filleter freezer vessel. A stern trawler. She was designed and built to take on some of the worst waters known to man, and her hunting grounds would be north of Norway, up in the Barents Sea and White Sea areas.

The men who designed and built *Arctic Pilgrim* were justly proud of her. From her duplicated radar arrays to the special carbon-dioxide-smothering arrangements built into her engine spaces, nothing was overlooked. The happy aura which surrounded her in the yard persisted through to her fitting out.

It soon became general knowledge that the ship's port of registration would be Hull. More importantly, it became clear that her crew would be picked from that town also. Once the news was out and the date of that first voyage became known, the conjecture and debate that flowed around the offices of Graveline Trawlers on St Andrew's Dock was intense.

The skipper too had yet to be chosen, and that uncertainty

gave rise to a good-natured sweepstake that involved not just the dock area but most of the shops and terraced homes for miles around. The local newspapers ran features on the vessel's progress, and soon the whole venture began to assume the proportions of a pageant : everyone wanted to touch some of the luck, the prosperity, that the new ship was sure to bring to the town.

The final interior cosmetics, the final loading of stores, the hanging of curtains, the laying of carpets, the final licks of blue and white paint went on as she lay alongside the quay in Hull late in July 1970. Old sailors from harsher times shook their heads as the word began to filter through, about the films that would be shown to the crew and about the video equipment someone's brother had seen being taken aboard, until 'going for an *Arctic Pilgrim*' became that town's synonym for having an easy time, a cushy number.

The date was set : *Arctic Pilgrim*, 1,146 tons, would sail for the fishing grounds on 4 August 1970, with a full complement of thirty-six hands.

The day dawned clear and fine.

By mid morning the ship was riding high to her new warps, gleaming white and huge in the sunlight as she lay to her own reflection in the still waters of the inner basin. Above, seagulls swooped and spun on lazy summer thermals, their cries of good fortune lost in the buzz of excited voices on the quay far below their outstretched wings.

The owners had cordoned off an area of the quay and erected an awning. There was shade there, and there were trestles with white tablecloths – and beer by the barrel. By lunchtime the dock police, perspiring in their shirtsleeves, were turning cars away while relatives of those who were about to sail jostled one another good-humouredly as they clutched their beer and free sandwiches and admired the ship that rose ever higher behind them on the rising tide, a new Blue Peter fluttering proudly at the crosstrees.

Martin Taylor parked his Mini in a narrow alley beside

the quay, tucked the square package firmly under his arm and strode briskly back towards the throng of well-wishers within the cordoned area. Of medium height, dark-haired and in his mid twenties, Martin carried himself with the easygoing grace of the athlete he had once been. He paused at the barrier to show his press pass to the policeman and then walked forward, twisting broad shoulders into the sea of shirtsleeves and summer dresses, scanning the hot and happy faces for one face in particular.

His press pass suggested he was here in a clinical, professional capacity, a spectator only, but that was untrue. Certainly he would cover the sailing, send in the story – but his presence owed more to selfishness than to the whim of some news editor. Martin now sighted the lined, familiar face over in the crowd, standing by the beer trestles. He grinned. Typical. The man had his profile to him. There was a pint in his hand and he was talking to another, younger seaman. Despite the weather both men wore the thick blue sweaters that singled them out as *Arctic Pilgrim* crew members. Martin approached unobserved and then hung back watching quietly, storing the moment.

The lines of strain around the mouth of the older man seemed softer, the pain that had haunted those dark eyes for so many weeks seemed dimmed. Martin read the signs hungrily and felt a shift in the weight of his concern.

A second observer watching Martin Taylor studying the older man would have immediately noticed the similarity between father and son. The slope of the forehead was the same, and the eyes – deep, striking grey flecked with brown and with an almost animal directness – the eyes, too, they shared. The father turned now, noticed his son and paused, pint mug half-way to his lips.

'What brings you here, Martin? That paper of yours still scratching around for a decent story?' he said gruffly, pleasure breaking through the old, worn gibe to reveal more clearly than it concealed the affection between father and son.

A quick, witty reply sprang to Martin's lips, but instead

he just nodded and said, 'Something like that. I thought I'd let you get me a drink.'

'Aye, seeing as I'm not paying.' The eyes twinkled behind the pint mug as John Taylor drank deeply. Then he handed his son his glass with a gusty sigh. 'Here, hold me pint – and don't you go drinking it, mind.' He turned and limped stiff-kneed towards the trestle.

Within weeks of the accident Martin had trained himself to ignore the limp and the tiny audible creak that accompanied each step, but the younger seaman standing next to him was less prepared. He stared openly, saw Martin watching him and took a swift gulp of beer to hide his confusion.

Martin rescued him. 'Sailing, too, are you?'

The other nodded gratefully and stuck out his hand. 'Aye. I'm Peter Anderson. Third engineer. I'll be working with your father. It's good to see him back on his feet –' He paused, aghast at his choice of words. 'Christ, man ... look ... I'm sorry, I didn't mean ...'

Martin smiled. 'That's O K. I know what you mean.'

Just then John Taylor returned, his face abeam with smiles. 'There you go. Down the hatch, son.'

'To your ship,' said Martin simply. 'To *Arctic Pilgrim*.'

'Aye, *Arctic Pilgrim*,' echoed the other two, drinking deeply.

Suddenly the chatter of the quay was rent by the deep, mournful bellow of *Arctic Pilgrim*'s foghorn. The sound rolled across the still air, reverberating around the solid buildings of the quay as suddenly, spontaneously, other hooters and sirens sounded elsewhere in the basin. The *whoop-whoop-whoop* of lesser craft dipping their skirts to *Arctic Pilgrim*'s imminent departure brought emotion pricking to the back of Martin's throat.

'That's us, then. Time we were off,' said John Taylor gruffly, finishing his beer.

His son remembered the package under his arm. 'This is for you, Dad,' he managed, thrusting the package forward suddenly.

'Get away.'

'Go on, take it,' Martin said impatiently as all the planned, easy words trickled away.

His father took the package reluctantly and weighed it in strong, heavy hands.

'Well, open the bloody thing,' said Martin roughly.

His father began to tear at the wrappings.

Thirteen months ago John Taylor had lost his leg when a trawl wire parted on another trawler. Six weeks after that and his wife, the woman he had loved since school days, died in hospital. Darkness. Long months of pain. Weeks, days and nights with despair and emptiness black as ashes. And then the long haul, the fight back, the struggle for this berth, the long climb that cost nothing but courage. And now he was back.

The last of the wrappings fell away, and a pewter tankard glittered brilliantly in the sunlight. John Taylor turned the tankard in his hands to catch the inscription.

The name of the ship was there and the day's date and, in smaller letters beneath the name John Taylor, one word: 'Fighter'.

He looked up and the tough, dark eyes moistened as he regarded his only son steadily. He reached out and grasped Martin's shoulder. 'She always said you had a way with words, lad. Your mother'd like that.'

Martin nodded, not trusting himself to speak.

Arctic Pilgrim sailed with the tide.

In the next few years she sailed with many tides to many seas. She sailed to winter gales and summer calms. She earned her keep and caught her catch – and she never lost a man.

It was a little after 4 p.m. two days before Christmas.

The dark streets of Hull were merry with Christmas lights as Martin Taylor picked his way carefully along the crowded pavements. Muffled to the ears in a thick scarf, he cradled a bottle of Scotch under one arm and clutched a heavy carton of groceries while trying to keep an eye on the young puppy that bounded and snuffled ahead on a length of lead that threatened to wrap itself round his legs at any moment. He paused, hitched the box higher and pressed on, homeward.

He moved away from the crowds down a side street and presently fumbled a key into the communal front door of a large Edwardian house that had been converted into flats. He lived alone on the second floor.

Now twenty-eight, he had left the newspaper he had been working on when *Arctic Pilgrim* first sailed and, after a year in Manchester working for a busy daily, had returned to the town of his birth to free-lance for the London papers. In recent months he had come to specialize increasingly in energy matters, and that, he sensed, might well be where his future lay. Meanwhile he wasn't rich, but there was money in the bank – enough, anyway, for a damn good Christmas and a couple of bottles with the Old Man. His father was home on leave while *Arctic Pilgrim* was in for routine repairs. Father and ship would sail together for the Norwegian fishing grounds in the New Year.

'Go on, boy. Up you go.'

Hercules, his six-month-old black Labrador puppy, scampered ahead up the stairs. His master floundered after him, clutching the carton of groceries.

Martin crossed the landing, climbed more stairs and keyed open his own front door. There was an ominous silence and a lack of scampering paws. He looked around for his dog.

'Jesus!' breathed Martin, dumping his groceries on the floor and pounding down to the landing.

Hercules was having a pee. Already the thin yellow trickle was seeping dangerously close to the gap under the door of one of the other flats.

'No, no, no,' Martin prayed savagely, picking up a startled Hercules by the scruff of his neck and charging upstairs for a cloth. He dumped Hercules in the kitchen sink, grabbed a handful of paper towels and rushed downstairs.

He was too late. Already Hercules' offering was disappearing with depressing swiftness beneath the door. Martin groaned and dropped to his knees, muttering promises of revenge under his breath.

The door opened.

Martin looked up.

'What's going on out here?'

'Ah,' supplied Martin helpfully.

'What does "Ah" mean? I've got a pool of water trickling into my hallway and –'

'It's not water, actually ...'

'Not water? Then what?'

'No. You see, my dog –'

'Your dog? Christ!' Martin saw irrelevantly that she was attractive, early twenties. Slim hands on blue-denimed hips, a fleck of rich brown hair falling across wide hazel eyes and – the girl vanished back into the flat, leaving the door open. She reappeared a second later with bucket and mop.

'Really, it's a bit much,' objected the girl, dropping to her knees with a cloth. 'Where is he?'

'Hercules? Er ... upstairs. In the sink.'

'In the sink. I should have guessed. Don't you have any control over him?'

'I can't understand it. Usually he's fine.' Martin held up a mass of sodden paper towels.

'Drop them in the bucket! They're dripping everywhere.'

Martin did so. 'Thanks. Look – I'm really very sorry.'

The girl looked about her. 'Forget it – no harm done.'

The damage was very slight. Another few seconds, a wipe with a clean cloth, and it was all over. They rose to their feet, disaster averted.

'How old is ... er ... Hercules?'

'Six months, give or take a week or so. He really should know better.'

The girl smiled. 'Well, don't be too hard on him.'

'We'll see. Thanks anyway.'

'O K.' The girl smiled again.

'Oh ... I'm Martin, by the way. Martin Taylor. I live just up there. Happy Christmas.'

'Suzy. Suzy Summerfield. Happy Christmas to you too.' She closed the door.

Hmm, thought Taylor as he closed his own front door,

wiped the dog's paws with a damp cloth and lifted him gently down to the floor.

'Nice one, Hercules,' he said quietly, stroking the glossy coat. 'A stroke of genius.'

In London that same afternoon Sir Peter Hillmore, head of British Secret Intelligence Service (SIS), threw the last of the biscuit crumbs onto the lime-stained ledge below the bay window and watched as the first of the pigeons clattered heavily towards him. He closed the window firmly, drew the heavy velvet curtains and plucked a silk handkerchief from a well-tailored cuff. He was wiping his fingers as the phone rang.

Crossing thick carpet to the wide mahogany desk still littered with the papers and signals of the day's traffic, he lifted the green receiver that connected him directly with his secretary in the outer office.

'Captain Miles Irving to see you, sir. Your five-fifteen appointment,' she said quietly.

Damn, thought Sir Peter. He'd quite forgotten there had been this late request for a meeting. He glanced irritably at the carriage clock on the marble mantelpiece. Hilary would be here soon.

'Show him in, please, Moira.'

Sir Peter crossed to the fire, where he busied himself with tongs and coal as the door opened. He glanced up over his shoulder. 'Ah, Irving — good to see you. Take a seat — I won't be a moment.' He balanced the coal carefully on the glowing embers as Captain Miles Irving, head of Intelligence (Royal Navy), positioned his knife-edged creases in one of the leather armchairs that flanked Sir Peter's desk.

Slim, grey-haired and immaculately uniformed, with the gold rings of his rank gleaming in the lamplight, Irving recalled that the coal fire at Christmas was as far as Sir Peter Hillmore was known to move towards a formal acknowledgement of the festivities. Occasionally there was a glass of pale sherry, but such an event was a rarity to be noted instantly and measured against the rigid slide rule of professional etiquette. At this height, at the slender apex of the service-career pyramid, whole futures could hang upon the misinter- pretation of such signs.

Sir Peter glanced sternly at the clock. The gesture was not lost on his subordinate. 'Now, then – this meeting you called for: you said it was important. I don't doubt it. Please proceed.'

'Very good, sir. If I go over old ground, please bear with me – it will help you get the general picture.'

'I understand.'

'As you'll be aware, in mid January Stanavforlant* go into the Squadex series of exercises up in the Barents Sea, Norwegian Sea area. With exercise duration at around twenty days, it's a major deployment. Naturally, we have already been anticipating the signals intelligence potential of that environment. You'll be aware also, sir, that in recent months our routine monitoring of Soviet countermeasures has yielded high dividends. There has been a growing and quite open reaction to the way we have deployed our own forces in all theatres – particularly on the northern flank. While they've been taking more risks to learn just what we've been up to, it follows that our own opportunities to discover just how good they are at reading our signals – following our electronic footprints, so to speak – have become greatly enhanced.'

Sir Peter Hillmore nodded absently at this array of old chestnuts. Sig-Int, the collection and analysis of hostile electronic emissions – the war of wits that never ended, because it had never officially started – absorbed much of his time. Captain Irving was just one of three Intelligence chiefs who hammered on his door with persuasive arguments for priority. And already it was 5.25 p.m. Hilary would arrive shortly, and tonight they were driving down to the Thorndike Theatre in Leatherhead.

'I asked for this meeting tonight, sir, because there appears every likelihood that the Russians are about to resume test firing of the new S S N-8. If our intelligence is correct, then

* Standing Naval Force Atlantic.

18

this could be our chance to determine whether those missiles carry single heads or M R Vs.'

'Is that hard information?' asked Sir Peter sharply, theatre forgotten.

'Pretty hard. Sosus endorsed by Illiac I V via satellite link. We don't think there's much chance of a slip.'

Sir Peter Hillmore nodded, satisfied. S O S U S was the chain of American underwater listening devices that littered the oceans' floor. Positioned at strategic 'choke points' like the Greenland–Iceland–United Kingdom gap, the Sea of Japan and, in this instance, the approaches to Murmansk and the twin headquarters of C-in-C Northern Fleet at Severo-morsk and the Soviet submarine base at Polyarny in Kola Bay, these seabed sonar fences acted as highly sophisticated microphones, picking up and recording the engine and signal transmissions of submarines and surface craft that passed in and out of Russia's largest military port complex. Vessels were thus logged in and out of base. These signals were flashed to Moffett Field, California, by communications satel-lite for identification and analysis. I L L I A C I V was the latest in the awesome family of American intelligence com-puters.

Now Sir Peter Hillmore pulled a notepad towards him, frowning at Irving's reminder of the S S N-8 missile. Since the 9,000-ton Delta-class Soviet submarine had first appeared in 1972 the characteristic of the S S N-8 missile load had remained unclear. There was a file about that somewhere in his safe.

Sceptical though he might be about some of the more lavish claims made by the Americans on behalf of their elec-tronic gadgetry, S O S U S was already, in Sir Peter's view, an element of proven value. That acoustical array had already pinpointed the firing frequency for the Russian nuclear mines that lay dormant in underwater silos around those same approaches to Kola Bay.

'So what you're suggesting, if I'm reading you aright, is ...'

'Trojan, sir – yes. I'd like to give Trojan a crack at it. See if those rumours are correct. We're presented with a golden opportunity. It's five months now since we –'

'I'll take the rest as read, Irving. You're preaching to the converted, you know,' rebuked Sir Peter Hillmore.

'Of course, sir. My apologies.'

Sir Peter nodded, pressed a buzzer on his desk and asked Moira for the Trojan file. He looked up sharply to stall the smile of victory. 'That isn't a yes or a no, Irving. It means simply that I am prepared to consider it. You still have to provide me with the usual safeguards and frequency. Ah, Moira – many thanks.'

She placed the file on his desk and left quietly. Sir Peter Hillmore flipped open the dossier and began reading.

Presently he looked up as Captain Irving said quietly, 'Weather considerations aside, Squadex deploys at the height of the deep-water fishing season. That's purely fortuitous, but it's one fact we can turn to our tactical advantage: there'll be a score of similar vessels in that part of the world providing the best sort of camouflage. I can't see it happening for a moment, but if things did get a little sticky Royal Navy ships already in the vicinity –'

Sir Peter had raised a sceptical eyebrow above the file. 'Cutlasses and a boarding party at dawn? Hardly.'

'Of course not, sir. I only wished to imply that ...'

Sir Peter returned to the file. Two trawlers did appear available for Admiralty secondment. *Wessex Wanderer* and this one – 'How long would Trojan need to be detached?'

'On task? Twelve hours, I should say, sir – fifteen at the very outside. I would plan that ...' Irving talked on.

After another three minutes of persuasive pleading Sir Peter glanced once more at the clock. He must move things on. 'Communications?' he interrupted abruptly.

'Standard procedure, sir. If you gave the go-ahead my people would make the usual contact with the skipper through the shipping line, and Operations would allocate a frigate to stand by for detachment for Squadex if needed. There would be unit-code contact between yourself and the detached captain R N only. There would be no need to go through the signal net after that. If you wished, we could –'

Once again the buzzer rang on Sir Peter's desk. 'Your daughter has just arrived, Sir Peter. She is waiting with me now,' said his secretary.

'Thank you, Moira.' Sir Peter smiled involuntarily and replaced the receiver with care, his mind aglow with a not unseasonal warmth. His daughter was the only family he had left now. She worked for U N E S C O as a bilingual translator in Geneva and was home for Christmas. These few days together, the theatres and the opera and the dinners he had planned were diamond-precious to the head of Britain's Secret Intelligence Service. He closed the file on his desk and looked up pleasantly.

'All right, Irving – you've made your case. I'll get my people to process your Trojan application right away. You're to take care of all the operational details and inform me again in due course.'

'That would be splendid, sir. Thank you very much indeed.' Captain Miles Irving tucked his cap under his arm and strode briskly to the door. He had his hand on the knob when Sir Peter Hillmore called him back.

'Oh, Miles.'

'Sir?'

'A happy Christmas to you and the family.'

Irving smiled with genuine pleasure. 'Thank you, sir. The same to you.' He closed the door softly behind him. Seasonal greetings and Christian names from the Old Man? It was the next best thing to a glass of palo sherry.

CHAPTER TWO

It was going wrong.

The captain of the *Arctic Pilgrim*, Harry Thomson, slipped off the headphones and patted the shoulder of his radio operator absently. Millar continued turning his dials, the frown deepening above the spectacles as his nimble fingers roamed up and down the wave bands. Thomson left him to it and climbed up the companionway to the wheelhouse.

He was worried. They were leaving it too late.

He glanced at the deckhead clock: 1509. He made a swift calculation. He had been told to remain on station another forty minutes. Steadying himself automatically against the ship's violent motion, he ducked through the hatchway, glanced over his shoulder, unlocked the door to his day cabin and slipped quickly inside. He went to a cabinet marked 'Do Not Open. Satellite Navigation Equipment in Active Mode.' Ignoring the lie, he turned the combination lock and swung back the heavy steel doors. Inside, the bank of electronic equipment hummed quietly. Digital display lamps winked busily, and coils of white perforated tapes spewed out of the machine and disappeared into the sealed units he had been instructed to take to London immediately he returned.

Thomson felt confused and angry. Unused to both emotions, he was torn now between the commercial desire to carry out his orders and his cautious instincts as a professional seaman.

Arctic Pilgrim heeled to a sudden wave, and Thomson made up his mind. He slammed shut the heavy metal doors. This was the last time. After this, they could stuff it. Mr bloody Harding could find another skipper to run cloak-and-dagger errands for the Admiralty.

Sitting at his radio, wedged against the pitch and roll of

the ship, Millar stabbed the red call-up button on his console. The peremptory buzzing was repeated on the bridge and in the captain's day cabin. Presently Thomson stood beside him once more. They exchanged glances.

'Same as before?' asked Thomson.

Millar shrugged and handed him the earphones. Thomson slipped them on and listened intently. He made a slight waving gesture with both hands. Millar shifted frequency up and down the wave band. The signal persisted.

'Right,' said Thomson decisively. 'Let's see what happens when we make it easy for them. Send back a quota signal to Hull. Strictly routine. Make it, say, forty tons deadweight up to twelve hundred hours today. Got that?'

Millar nodded, but within seconds he sat back, tugged off the headphones and laid them carefully aside. He took off his glasses and massaged the bridge of his nose between finger and thumb. 'I'm wasting my time, Skip. It's some kind of shore station, I reckon. The bastards are jamming right across the spectrum. I can't even raise an acknowledge.'

In the engine room amidships, Norman Fullerton, the duty engineer, wedged himself against the ventilation trunking, rescued the biscuit that was sliding across the table and popped it into his mouth. John Taylor, whose biscuit it had been, balled a huge fist and mouthed some cheerful obscenity in the language of mime adopted by men who work with noise as their constant companion. Fullerton grinned. Johno was all right, they reckoned, leg or no leg. All over the ship men who were officially off watch were asleep, reading or playing cards – but not John Taylor. For the last few hours he had stayed on, just to keep an eye on this engine of his. A real pro.

A half mile off Arctic Pilgrim's starboard side a thin, pencil-like object rose silently from the sea and knifed through the wave crests, dragging a plume of broken water in its wake. The attack periscope rotated instantly to Arctic Pilgrim's bearing, and the single eye regarded the plunging trawler implacably.

Forty feet below the periscope, Kapitan Leytenant Andrey

Gregor Griem, officer commanding the 4,400-ton Hotel II–class Soviet nuclear submarine settled into the attack saddle and twisted the periscope-focusing hand-grips impatiently. He completed the mandatory 360-degree sweep and then settled on the vessel they had been tracking for the last five hours. Sweaty and stale in the unvarnished confines of an operational submarine closed up to action stations, Griem had the usual dull ache from too little fresh air and too much concentration. For the last nine days he and his submarine had been on patrol, tracking up and down this particular parcel of ocean, listening to and analysing the electronic signatures of a score of different vessels as the men and machines of the enemy grouped and deployed for yet another major exercise on Russia's doorstep. Griem wiped greasy hands on the legs of his black dungarees and bent to the periscope. Yes, there she was, ploughing heavily eastward, course unchanged : a snooper.

The control-room party waited in tense stillness. Only the monotonous chant of the sonar and radar operators broke the trained silence as Kapitan Griem peered intently at the British trawler.

At that range Griem could read the ship's name with ease. He called sharply for the periscope camera, snapped it into its mountings and focused on the trawler's antenna array. Without taking his eyes away from the periscope for more than an instant, Griem began flicking through the plastic folder of photographs at his knee. It was an action born of practice; the photographs themselves represented something of a tally, a scoreboard of sightings frozen through the camera lens attached to his periscope. Griem turned to the section on British trawlers and began matching similarities between the picture at his knee and the plunging trawler off his beam. He had lost count of the number of times Western trawlers had strayed into Soviet waters hunting something other than fish, their radars and receivers teasing away at Soviet electronic secrets before they withdrew over the horizon to analyse and interpret those fragments of Sig-Int at their leisure. The camera whirred. Griem shifted focus, and now he could see the shadows behind the wheelhouse scuttles that were the men who commanded this British trawler so far from home.

For those men from a distant world who shared the same desert of sea and with whom, one day, he might share the same fate, Griem felt a sudden sad kinship.

The missile swooped in low.

Undetected, unseen by the unarmed British trawler, unsuspected among the deep troughs and crumbling wave crests, it swept in silently, trailing its whisp of evil, tell-tale smoke. It closed the last few yards and detonated with a terrible, awesome explosion of light on *Arctic Pilgrim's* fo'c'sle deck.

Nine men asleep off watch in their cabins directly below the point of impact ceased to exist. They were smeared and roasted, fused into the paintwork of their smashed and twisted cabins, mashed to slime in the pressure waves of the explosion that rolled on into a hideous rising thunder of sound.

Mortally wounded now and with a gaping hole lit by the flickering agony of fire below the waterline, *Arctic Pilgrim* was hurled violently through her centre of gravity towards the grey sea that began to batter against the starboard bridge scuttles already buckled and scorched down to bare base metal by the heat of the blast.

In the wheelhouse the wheel spun wildly into a glitter of brass spoke caps as the helmsman dropped away from his station to slither in his own pumping lifeblood down the canting deck towards the sea, his face blown away, a shard of jagged glass jutting from his neck. There was smoke, noise and blinding terror as those who survived the blast and the howl of glass fragments lost their balance and smashed viciously against the anchored equipment that blocked their wild tumble towards the scuppers.

In the engine room, John Taylor and Norman Fullerton were pitched to the deck. They lay sprawled on the metal gratings, their senses numbed from that hammer stroke of

25

sound, that dull, ominous boom that had torn the length of their vessel. Both now felt the ship begin to slide beneath them. The lights flickered and went out. Fullerton cried out in fear, and then the lights came on again. Taylor shook his head to clear the muzziness and watched incuriously as blood – his blood – dripped from a head wound onto the metal plates beneath him. He crawled to his knees with an effort.

'Norm – you O K? Norman?'

The figure stirred. When Fullerton looked up to brush long hair out of his eyes John Taylor saw the wide-eyed, staring look of a man close to panic.

'Christ, Johno – what happened?'

Taylor shook his head and began to crawl towards the telephone handset clipped to the bulkhead nearby. The phone connected him directly to the wheelhouse. It was dangling on its cord, swaying freely with the ship's motion. Taylor caught the handset and listened briefly above the roar of the engine room. He heard groans, screams, the rush of water and the crash of equipment breaking loose and smashing the width of the vessel. It sounded bad – as bad as could be. He jammed the phone back on its bracket and turned.

'Can't get through for present,' he said.

'Come off it, Johno – I heard that! We're sinking! We're sinking – aren't we? Come on, I'm off!' Fullerton scrambled to his feet and rushed forward.

Taylor paused. 'What about the ship? The engine? Better wait a while longer!' he shouted.

'Fuck the ship! Fuck the engines! She's going, I tell you!' Fullerton pushed past Taylor and swung onto the vertical metal ladder that led to the hatchway that gave onto a narrow passageway, the deck and safety. He began climbing in a frenzy of movement as Taylor turned and limped stiffly towards the engine control console.

Just then the deck beneath Taylor's feet gave a sudden lurch and there was a new sound, the steady thunder of rushing water that grew and grew like a train in a tunnel until it seemed to fill the narrow confines of the engine room. Taylor looked up as the truth dawned.

Fullerton was scrambling upward, actually knocking off the last of the retaining hatchway catches, oblivious to everything but the blinding need to escape. Taylor opened his mouth to shout a warning. The hatchway, freed from its catches, burst inwards. A solid column of icy grey-green water hit Fullerton in the chest, plucked him off the ladder and swept him away to fall with a thin cry into the battery store twenty feet below. The sea roared into the engine room in a cataract of sound and then slowed to a steady flow that swirled around Fullerton's limp body as the hatchway creaked open and closed to the motion of the ship as she wallowed lower in the water.

Soon the icy water in the engine room was ankle deep. Soaked through and shivering involuntarily, John Taylor pulled his way to the still body of his companion and touched his neck for pulse signs. Nothing. Fullerton had broken his back in the fall. Taylor stripped off his jacket and laid it carefully across the dead face before hobbling back towards the control console, the water tugging now at his calves as he limped away from the ladder that led to safety. He cranked the phone handle and lifted the receiver, steeling himself for more horrors. None came. The line was dead.

The ship lurched and groaned. Above the wild, unchecked pounding of the screw as it thrashed clear of the water, John Taylor could hear another sound. He cocked his head to one side and listened for a moment to the shouts of men, the sound of pounding boots as they abandoned ship.

Millar was still in the radio shack. He crawled out of the mountain of books and fittings, coats and crockery that had crashed with him into a corner. He was soaked, his trousers were torn and his face and hands were slimy with diesel. But his radio equipment was intact, anchored to the deck with stout bolts. He made for that equipment now, hauling himself with grim determination up the steep deck. Twice he slipped back among the sodden rubbish and half-submerged body of Captain Thomson lolling broken-necked in the deepening pool of debris.

Millar hooked an arm round the base of the radio table and pulled himself upright. He paused, panting. There was a low creaking, a body moan from the ship as she prepared, Millar knew, for the death plunge that must soon follow.

Millar shut everything else off, spun the dial to the International Distress Frequency, clapped an earphone to one ear and began to speak in clear, regulation Marconi to the world that would never hear him:

'Mayday ... Mayday ... Mayday. This is the Hull trawler *Arctic Pilgrim*. We are sinking. We are sinking. Our position is ...'

The ship gave another sickening lurch.

Millar banged out their position, tossed the earphones aside, grabbed his lifejacket and made a wild scramble for the companionway. He hauled himself upwards through a cataract of water and then flopped forward, exhausted, to slide headlong down a tilting passageway towards the door that opened onto the weather rail of the ship. He slid forward and fetched up against the padded bulk of another seaman's lifejacket. The man in front hesitated before stepping out from shelter. Millar banged him impatiently on the shoulder: 'Go on, mate – move!' he commanded, thumping again on the man's lifejacket. The wet head rolled back incuriously, and Millar recoiled in horror. The man had been whipped across the upper half of his face by a trailing length of wire cable. Both eyes were gone, smeared into a bloody tramline washed clean by the sheets of salt spray that crashed into the passageway past the splintered door. The man was dead. Millar pushed him away with revulsion, lost his footing and sprawled full-length on the exposed deck. He slid forward towards the sea and scrabbled furiously for a handhold as his glasses fell off his nose, bounced across the deck and slid over the side.

Millar wrapped both arms round a stanchion and clung on with desperation. He hauled himself to his knees and stayed there for a long moment gathering his strength and watching

with horrid fascination as the corpse he had pushed roughly
aside slid sluggishly across the deck towards him, paused
with a toe caught against the decking and then, with a
grisly half-wave from a dead, flopping hand, rolled in-
graciously over the side into the waiting sea.

Sobbing for breath, Millar struggled to his knees and
looked wildly about him with nearsighted eyes, his thinning
hair blown into wet spikes by the spray, his orange lifejacket
hunched above his shoulders like some malignant marine
growth.

The wind ripped gleefully at his sodden, fluttering clothing; sights and sounds tore at his battered senses: smoke and
flame came from somewhere up for'ard; the stench of an
electrical fire; the batter and clang from somewhere above
and behind him as huge sheets of the funnel's metal skin
flogged against the wheelhouse top; here and there a splash
of bright orange as other survivors moved dazedly about the
ship's superstructure.

Millar stared around for the lifeboats, the liferafts, but
there were none, just a few sticks of wood that banged
futilely against the side of the ship on the end of their retaining cables. Over there, beside the wheelhouse door,
another cluster of orange lifejackets as two or three crew
members huddled together in deceptive security. Millar
moved to join them and then hesitated. Safety, rescue, did
not lie there. His mind spinning with the pace of events,
Millar jerked round to face seaward as the thin cry came
again :

'Millar ! Millar !' He searched the heaving wave crests desperately, rubbed a hand over his blasted weak eyes and tried
again. There ! Twenty, thirty feet off from the side of the
ship – three men clutching at the remains of a carley float :
'Come on – jump for it !' The words drifted down towards
him, yet still he hesitated. Other orange blobs seemed to be
making for the wreckage also. He'd have to be quick. He
lifted his eyes beyond the men by the floating wreckage and
saw with a start – was it for only the first time? – that already two other vessels were nearby, manoeuvring to pick

up survivors. There was a submarine on the surface eighty, perhaps a hundred, yards away and, beyond the submarine, another larger vessel that seemed to drift in and out of the mists of rain. Millar was aware also of the mournful wail of the foghorn and the shouts of men in the water. It would be no distance to the submarine, he calculated swiftly. No distance at all.

Pilgrim gave another lurch, and this time Millar heard equipment start to break loose below and batter against weakened bulkheads. Once those began to go ... He turned, irresolute, and peered again towards the men in the water. It was time to be off. He kicked off his shoes, stepped forward, balanced against the lip of the deck and fell clumsily forward. He seemed to fall a long, long way, arms wind-milling, before he hit the water with a dull thud that drove all the breath from his body.

Aided by the massive positive buoyancy of his lifejacket, Millar bobbed to the surface immediately. Already he was twenty, thirty feet out from the side of the stricken vessel. He looked for the men and the wreckage he had seen from the deck, but down here he could see nothing beyond the next heaving wave crest. He tried shouting but there was no reply, his voice lost on the wind like confetti thrown from a car window. Millar swallowed more water, gagged on its saltiness and, swept high on the next wave crest, made out the huge bulk of the submarine lying directly in front of him, waiting.

It looked no distance, no distance at all. He would make for that, he decided. He struck out strongly as the cold began to strike upward through his thin clothing like sullen steel daggers, crushing his lungs, flattening his chest, piercing his vitals.

Millar swam on. Presently the sea seemed to fall quiet around him until he was alone in his efforts and there had never been a ship, or a sinking, or a group of friends shouting at him from floating wreckage.

Millar smashed on through the grey waves, kicking out with bare numb feet and hauling overhand with leaden arms, his body twisting high out of the water as he moved doggedly away from the sinking ship towards the warmth and safety of the submarine that must lie beyond the next wave crest – beyond *that* wave crest, surely, because he was tired and already he had swum ... Millar stopped swimming for a moment and trod water as again he imagined he heard the screech and saw of tortured metal and the sudden bellow of sirens and foghorns as though there had been a collision. He shook his head in sudden fear : he must be weaker than he thought, he realized, to be imagining things like that. Then realization dawned – they were beckoning him on, that's what it was – although why they couldn't work their ships just a little bit closer ... He shook his head and determined to finish the last few yards in fine style. He must be almost there now, he told himself, with a warm glow of accomplishment. It had really been no distance, he thought happily. No distance at ...

Slowly and methodically John Taylor began shutting down the engine. Then and only then, when the last fuel cock was tightened down, the last key turned, did he begin to drag himself hand over hand through the waist-high icy water and up the steeply tilted deck towards safety. Other men might panic, abandon their posts while there was still a job to be done. John Taylor was not among them.

He had almost reached the metal ladder when the lights failed for the last time and the flow of water built to a torrent against which no man could climb.

John Taylor died alone and in darkness.

At 1528 there was a sudden increase in the volume of urgent, high-grade radio traffic coming out of the Soviet Navy's Northern Fleet Headquarters at Severomorsk.

The sudden increase in locally originated one-timers was noted and logged by the duty watch eighty miles away in the CIA-manned COMINT station at Vadsø, northern Norway.

The Soviet ciphers were intercepted and then beamed by

communications satellite to the National Security Agency's cryptanalysts in their computer complex at Fort Meade off the Baltimore–Washington Parkway, Maryland.

While N S A's decoding experts pored over their calculators, their rolls of green-striped paper and the endless lists of figures and letters, the American and British naval attachés in Oslo received an exploratory diplomatic phone call from the Soviet Embassy. There should, perhaps, be a meeting.

Another top-secret coded signal was flashed to the Soviet Embassy in London's Notting Hill Gate. Marked 'For Information Only', it was passed to Stefan Rokoff, a senior member of the Political Group attached to that embassy.

There are five main groups behind the façade of any Eastern Bloc embassy. Each works autonomously. These are the Political, Counterintelligence, Scientific-Technical, Economic and Internal groups. With the exception of the last of these, each is primarily concerned with gleaning intelligence and placing contacts within the host nation's bureaucracy.

The Political Group at the Soviet Embassy in London works under cover of overt diplomatic functions and targets its attentions on the equally overt activities of the House of Commons, the House of Lords, the Conservative, Labour and Liberal parties, the trade unions and, just lately, the National Council for Civil Liberties.

The Counterintelligence Group – usually of ten or twelve men – is based on the Consular Section and directs its operations at MI6, MI5, the Northern Ireland Office and the Metropolitan Police, with particular regard for the S P G, the Special Patrol Group. The embassy drivers – all professional surveillance specialists – form a part of this group.

The Scientific-Technical Group works under the aegis of the scientific attaché: it pays regular attention to government research organizations and private companies engaged in military research. The first leak on Chobham tank armour came from this source in the autumn of '72.

The Economic Group sifts through mounds of 'clean' intelligence spewed out by the Department of Trade and

Industry, the Treasury and the Ministry of Agriculture and Fisheries. It also monitors East–West liaison on financial matters.

The Internal Group is assigned to defence of the building and the residents of the embassy against physical and technical (electronic) penetration. It services the network of field agents in the host country by the performance of 'good services' – by obtaining passports, birth certificates, driver permits, government forms, customs and duty documents, maps and city plans. The Internal Group also attends to the safety of couriers to and from airports, wraps and seals diplomatic mail, and transmits and receives coded messages for the embassy.

Stefan Rokoff decoded the message and read of *Arctic Pilgrim's* sinking, frowning in annoyance. After much careful preparation he had finally succeeded in placing a man aboard *Arctic Pilgrim*. Now presumably he was lost. All that work wasted.

It had begun several years ago when Jonathan Silvers had been thirty-two. Short, balding and overweight, Silvers had been a full-time marine electrician working on the docks at Hull, where he had also been branch secretary of one of the electrical trade unions. That summer he had been invited to London to attend one of the union's conferences. Nothing too onerous was involved, Head Office hinted, and most of the work would take place with a glass in his hand. Flattered, he accepted.

The conference lasted two days. He drank a good deal and, surrounded for once not by political apathy but by the animation of others of a like political persuasion, he talked a good deal, too.

On the afternoon of the first day he found himself in earnest conversation with a man called Husak who, he gathered over a series of drinks, was some kind of minor labour attaché at the Czechoslovakian Embassy.

The two seemed to have a great deal in common – Husak with his detailed knowledge of practical socialism, Jonathan

33

Silvers with what Husak admiringly referred to as his 'street smell', his practical grasp of the grass roots.

They bought each other drinks and parted as friends. Silvers returned to work as an electrician in Hull.

Six weeks later he was summoned to London once more, this time for a conference on industrial democracy.

He was pleasantly surprised, checking into the modest Bayswater hotel where he was to stay, to find Husak reading a newspaper in the lounge.

Over dinner in a small Knightsbridge restaurant after the serious business of the afternoon had been concluded, the two men grew expansive. Waistcoats were unbuttoned and tongues began to loosen. Husak poured more of the excellent Yugoslav Riesling and bemoaned the political canyons that still divided their two societies. The Cold War was over; détente was the thing of the present, the hope for the future; there was a spirit of new trust abroad in both their lands ...

Silvers, aglow with the wine and swept along on the crest of Husak's rhetoric, shifted in his seat and wished there was something ordinary people like him could do. After all, it was the ordinary people, not the politicians, who could ...

Husak fidgeted with his cutlery and weighed Silvers over the rim of his glass. Would he really like to help? Would he? No, no forget it – it was unfair; he was taking advantage of their friendship; he had no right even to ask.

No, no – go on, Silvers had insisted.

Well, began Husak, embarrassed now by the whole thing – it really was too silly for words: what his people needed was some help in the organization of local labour pools into party branches. He, Husak, had been listening to Silvers describe the way he had set things up in Hull, and, well, if it really wasn't too much trouble, could Silvers do a report which he could submit to his people in Prague and say, 'There – that's how it should be done!'

Silvers brought the carefully typed report with him to London a month later. Husak was delighted. It was exactly what he wanted! He offered to pay Silvers – not for the report, you understand, but for all the time it had taken.

Silvers refused – he was glad to have been able to help, that was all. Very well, then, insisted Husak, he must at least let him attend to his train fare and expenses. That was only fair, yes? Silvers eventually agreed. Where was the harm in that?

'So, if you could just sign here ... and here ... and here ... just for my people, you understand. Mean lot of schmucks! Zero inflation and still they count every koruna!'

Silvers signed and returned to Hull.

His report went into the wastepaper basket.

The receipt with his signature upon it went into the file.

Ten more months, two more reports – and then suddenly, inexplicably, Husak's attitude hardened. Now he would like information on any military activity in the dock areas of Hull, Grimsby and Fleetwood.

Silvers was appalled. He couldn't possibly agree to a thing like that – why, it was tantamount to ... to spying! Husak readily agreed and showed him some of the receipts he had signed.

Silvers had turned ashen as the trap yawned open before him. Husak had sat back patiently. It usually took them like this. Finally:

'What ... what sort of information?' Silvers had said.

Stefan Rokoff laid aside the report on *Pilgrim*'s sinking, deep in thought. Then he reached for the phone and placed a call to the Deputy Director of Britain's Secret Intelligence Service. Three hours later he was conferring earnestly with Colonel Francis Mann-Quartermain over drinks in the Lansdowne Club, Berkeley Square.

The British public would have been surprised to learn it was not the first occasion upon which the Deputy Director of SIS had bought drinks for a man he knew to be one of the most effective clandestine representatives of a major power whose declared aim was the overthrow of capitalism. But the British public was not alerted to this strange meeting of interests, and thus Francis Mann-Quartermain and

Stefan Rokoff were able to work out the perimeters of their departments' future interest in the *Arctic Pilgrim* business without interruption.

Had Jonathan Silvers been present at the meeting in the Lansdowne Club he would have found it all very confusing, for he had known Rokoff by a different name; he had known him as Husak and he thought he came from the Czechoslovakian, not the Soviet, Embassy. But as the two men ordered another round of drinks, Jonathan Silvers, Norman Fullerton, John Taylor and the other thirty-three members of *Arctic Pilgrim*'s crew had been dead four hours.

CHAPTER THREE

Martin Taylor was in bed. He swung his feet down to the ground and reached for his spectacles. Yawning, he padded barefoot across to the living room and drew back the curtains, a hand clapped across his eyes. He and Suzy had been out for dinner the night before and he had crawled back to his own bed just a few short hours ago. The phone rang again and he groaned, the wine still with him.

It was a pay phone. When the pips stopped, the voice came on. It sounded breathless, nervous. It struck a chord from somewhere: 'Mr Taylor? Martin Taylor?'

'Speaking.'

'Remember me, Mr Taylor? Tibbett's the name – Peter Tibbett. We met down at the docks. I'm a friend of your father's.'

'Oh yes, Mr Tibbett – I do remember.' The voice took on a face. Greying, fortyish, plump. 'What can I do for you?'

The voice paused now, suddenly awkward. 'It's ... it's about *Arctic Pilgrim*, see.'

'What about her?'

'Well ... I don't know how else to say this, mind, but she's ... well ... she's missing, like.'

Martin snapped fully awake. 'What do you mean, missing?'

'It's like I said: missing. She's not kept her sched, and blokes down 'ere are getting dead worried.'

'Plenty of ships are late in reporting in. Nothing special about that.'

'Yeah? Not for days on end, they aren't. And why's there all this brass down here, looking like tomorrer's been cancelled? Anyway, it's up to you. I reckon it's worth a phone call, myself. Your dad's a mate of mine. I just thought I'd pass it on, like – you know, for Johno. He's got a lot of mates down 'ere.'

'Sure. Thanks,' muttered Martin abstractedly, a cold chill in his guts as he pictured the creased, battered face and their nonchalant parting on the quayside. A playful punch, a slap on the shoulder and that tough, limping figure had turned up the gangway without a backward glance.

It might be worth a phone call, at that.

Martin dialled Graveline Trawlers Ltd and got the busy signal. He dressed hurriedly and dialled again. Busy again. He looked at his watch and frowned: 6.55 a.m. He dialled another number, and this time the call rang in and was answered. It was Suzy in the flat downstairs.

'Hi,' said Martin briefly.

'Hello, you,' said Suzy drowsily from the warmth of her pillows. Her voice suddenly sharpened. 'Martin? Do you know what time this is? It's not seven yet! You promised me you'd –'

'Yeah, I know.'

'Martin? What's wrong?' said Suzy, picking up the edge to his voice.

'Maybe something, maybe nothing. It's Johno. I just got a call from a friend of his. Says Dad's ship is missing.'

'No! Oh, Martin.' He heard the bed creak and the rustle of sheets as she sat up. The night before Johno had sailed she had cooked dinner for the three of them downstairs. The evening had been an immediate success, an occasion of warm amusement and easy-flowing intimacy. Martin's loss would be her loss also.

'Now, hang on, Suzy,' warned Martin: 'It may be nothing – probably just a missed sched.' I hope so, he thought. Oh, Christ, I hope so. 'I've tried calling, but the office line is engaged. I'm going down there now – I'll let you know if I hear anything.'

With Hercules in the back, Martin swung the Renault into a wide curve on the wet granite and brought it to rest within two feet of a long, unprotected drop into the black, oily waters of St Andrew's Dock. Leaving Hercules to frighten himself with misty patterns on the back window, Martin got out, tugged on an anorak and bent to lock the door. Towering over him brooded gaunt warehouses, and hanging like a greasy cloak over the grey, dripping buildings lay the stench of fish, the smack of money.

Two sides of the dock were packed with the rust- and salt-streaked hulks of oceangoing trawlers. There was a rumble above as a conveyor poured ice into the forward fish hold of one of the nearby sidewinders. In the drab half-light of early morning the ice glistened and shone as it tumbled from sight. The tinny sound of a transistor came from one of the trawlers moored nearby.

Lights shone from the bay windows of the Graveline offices.

In the pale backwash of illumination beneath these windows, he could see the dark-coated figures of a group of women standing together in a huddle, waiting in the thin rain.

His heels rang on the cobbles, and faces turned sharply towards him. An impression of drabness: pinched cheeks, head scarves over rollers, the glitter of cheap jewellery pinned to stout bosoms, synthetic raincoats from Woolie's – and overall a keen anxiety, a gnawing hunger of concern as decent women waited for news of their men.

'You with the company, are you?' 'Any news, then?' 'What's happened to Pilgrim?' 'Aye – where's our fellers?' The barrage of questions broke around his ears as he stood silent among them. Then a voice that stilled the questions: 'Leave off – that's Johno Taylor's lad. He's one of us.' The shoulders slumped fractionally, and the women fell silent.

Martin: 'Have you been here long?'

'Hour. Hour and a half, near enough,' answered a short stout woman in her early forties, their natural spokesman.

'What have you been told?'

'Told? Nothing. Jean 'ere got a phone call sayin' something was up from one of the lads. But we ain't 'eard nothing.

39

Nothing official like – and you'll get no joy from them, neither,' she said bitterly, jerking a thumb at the office windows above. 'Though God knows we've a right to know what's going on. Disgusting, I call it.' There was a low murmur of agreement.

Martin crossed the quay, flat-handed his way past the double green doors and took the stone stairs two at a time.

There is an aura about tragedy – a certain something that strikes the senses as suspended, breathless, unnatural. It hung around the terminal buildings at Heathrow Airport after British Airways' Trident Papa India went down; it lurks, always, in the homes of those left behind after a fatal accident. It was in the offices of Graveline Trawlers that wet chilly morning.

The secretary was crying. She looked up miserably as Martin Taylor walked in – a red-eyed, raw-cheeked eighteen-year-old with huge bangle earrings that went with the tears like party balloons at a funeral.

'Mr Harding's in, is he?' asked Martin softly.

The girl nodded, sniffing into a Kleenex.

Martin knocked at the oak doors, paused and then entered on a muffled, impatient command from within.

It was a wide, spacious boardroom with a bay window overlooking the docks. The room was hot, crowded and wreathed in tobacco smoke. In the centre was a table strewn with papers. A powerful radio transmitter-receiver stood over in the corner.

Men in shirtsleeves, their jackets slung over the backs of their chairs, turned curiously towards him as he strode across the carpet taking in the tired faces, the unshaven chins, the stack of empty coffee cups and the brimming ashtrays.

'What do you want?' snapped the florid, harassed-looking man in the unbuttoned waistcoat, hairy arms supporting his weight in a welter of papers and charts. 'Who let you in here?'

'You did. I knocked, you answered, I came in.'

'I gave strict instructions I was not to be disturbed. I will not be disturbed when I am in conference.' He paused. 'Don't

I know you?' Suspicion hardened to certainty as Martin nodded.

'I'm Martin Taylor. We met a month or so back, Mr Harding. I came to see you about a story on those trawler heating units. I'm a reporter. A journalist.'

A stillness dropped into the room.

Harding recovered quickly. 'Yes, yes – I remember, but I can't talk to you about that now, I'm far too busy. If you'll –'

'I didn't come to talk to you about heating units,' said Martin quietly. 'I came here to ask you about my father.'

'Your father?' Harding looked puzzled.

'My father. He's one of your employees, Mr Harding. An engineer. On *Arctic Pilgrim*.' Glances were exchanged as Martin added, 'Where is she? Where is *Arctic Pilgrim*?'

'Why d'you ask?' cut in one of the men seated beside Harding.

'Because someone told me she was missing.'

'That's preposterous!' exclaimed Harding heartily. 'Who told you –'

'Look, Mr Harding,' cut in Martin impatiently. 'There are twelve women standing outside your office right now. They've been there for more than an hour. It's cold and it's raining and all they've had is a rumour. They're waiting for a word from *you* about your ship with their men on board. If *Arctic Pilgrim* isn't missing, if everything's fine, O K: you can have the pleasure of telling them. If she *is* missing, then you can tell them that too. And you can tell me, for a start.'

'Mr Taylor, I really think –' began another man at the table.

Martin turned on him swiftly

'I'm not talking to you – I'm talking to your boss, Mr Harding here. My question stands: Where is *Arctic Pilgrim*?'

Harding picked up a cigarette and lit it with hands that shook. He inhaled deeply. 'We aren't absolutely sure,' he said finally, studying his cigarette.

Martin waited, certain there was more. Nothing came.

'And that's it?' he demanded finally, incredulously.

'I'm afraid so. We don't know exactly where she is. Not exactly. We haven't heard from her for ... for some little time.'

'How little?' snapped Martin.

'A few days.'

'A few days? What about radio messages, that sort of thing?'

Another silence got under way.

'When did you last hear from her?' Martin asked again.

'Thursday. Last Thursday. She reported in at ten hundred hours. We haven't been in contact since.'

'Last Thursday? Jesus! That's – what – that's four days ago!' For the first time Martin felt exasperation give way to the stirrings of real alarm. What the hell were they playing at?

Harding dragged a tired hand through his hair and drew heavily on his cigarette. He looked exhausted, and the strain gave the lie to his next words of hollow reassurance: 'It is a little premature for that sort of reaction, Mr Taylor. We're anxious, shall we say, that's all. There is almost certainly a simple explanation for *Pilgrim's* silence. Directly contact is reestablished you will be informed. Perhaps, if you leave your number with that secretary of mine –'

'And what about those women waiting outside?' said Martin, standing his ground. 'What will you tell them?'

Harding sighed and reached for his jacket. 'I'll come down with you.'

He followed Martin down the stairs and stood on the steps in his shirtsleeves, his jacket slung over one shoulder in the rain. They *had* lost contact with *Arctic Pilgrim*. She had missed her scheds. Relatives would be informed directly radio contact was reestablished. Meanwhile, there was no immediate cause for concern. He had nothing else to say.

The words fell onto a silent cobbled sea of wet upturned faces. Harding turned on his heel and vanished upstairs, and the door closed firmly behind him. Martin Taylor stood with the women, gazing up at the office lights. Harding's departure was greeted with a buzz of pathetic, fearful speculation.

'Sounds as if it could just be something with the radio,' suggested a woman's voice timidly.

'Not like *Pilgrim* to miss her sched. Not like her at all,' chipped in another.

'Don't talk daft,' said the stout woman roughly. 'She'd enough radios to run Radio One. Something must be up. They wouldn't be making all this fuss, else.'

'She's never been in any trouble before,' piped up another woman lamely, as if the only ships that sank were those that had sunk before.

Other women stood and listened silently to the feeble words, the weak and slender barriers erected hastily in the path of shock and terrible possibility. Presently one and then another of the women began sobbing quietly. Neighbours comforted them as Martin turned to a woman standing beside him.

'Is your husband aboard?'

'Might say he's my husband. Leaves his boots under my bed most nights when he's home, any road.' A tired smile, and a brief cackle of laughter from others in the gloom.

'What's your name?' asked Martin.

'Cathy. Cathy Silvers.'

'Husband been at sea long?'

'That's the joke, I suppose.' The voice was not smiling. 'It was Jon's first trip. He's not even a seaman, see. He's a marine electrician by trade, down on the wharf there. Comes home a month or so ago and says he wants to see what it's like – going to sea and that. Week or so later and he's wangled himself a trip on *Pilgrim*.' She paused. 'I only hope the silly bugger's all right,' she ended, almost in a whisper.

One of the women who had been crying now burst into a fresh flood of tears, her voice rising with her grief. 'Something's happened, it has, I just know it! I can feel it!' she sobbed.

Martin turned to see a girl in her late teens with a thin, pinched little face and a large pregnancy barely contained beneath a short tight coat that gaped at the buttons. The girls' raw tears brought a stirring of response:

'Something must have happened ...'

'There can't just be silence, like ...'

'It's the Russians! You mark my words – the Russians have a hand in this, and it won't be the first time, neither!' The voice was strident, harsh, commanding. Martin peered through the crowd at a strong dark-haired woman in her late thirties.

'Go on with you, Jean,' called another. 'You've been seeing Russians under that bed of yours for years.'

'Yeah? What do you reckon, then?'

'I reckon she's hit a spot of bad weather. She's laid in out of the storm in some fjord somewhere, snug as can be. She'll turn up again, don't you fret. Old *Pilgrim* will be all right.'

The women talked on, clutching at straws, hanging on rumours, comforting one another. Soon they began to drift away from the docks back to their factories, their shops and their homes, where they sat by their telephones and their transistors, waiting for news. *Pilgrim* would be all right – she'd turn up.

Martin drove home via Hull University and caught Suzy just as she was turning into her laboratory. Suzy was an industrial chemist on loan to the university. She saw him coming through the throng of her students and ran lightly towards him, brown hair fanning out in the wind, a pile of books and papers tucked beneath her arms.

'What did they say?' she asked gently, reading the signs in his face.

Martin shrugged. 'Hard to say. They haven't been in contact with *Pilgrim* for four days – and that's unusual. But that's all there is, just the silence. Could be just radio failure, a breakdown of some sort. Could mean anything.'

Suzy nodded, her coat collar buttoned high against the February cold. 'But you don't think so?'

'Honestly? No, no I don't. It's just a feeling I have but ... no, I don't. And I'll tell you something else, Suzy: I don't think Harding does, either.'

The story was picked up by a local reporter and put out on Radio Humberside at ten-thirty. New to the role of consumer rather than reporter of news, Martin caught himself listening avidly, curiously incapable, at this moment, of turning private concern into a source of professional income. The news flash told him little he did not know already : the owners were still expressing 'concern' at the lack of radio contact. Sea conditions were bad, but *Arctic Pilgrim* was supremely capable of riding out the prevailing storm. Freak atmospherics would probably account for the radio silence, etc., etc.

At 1 p.m. B.B.C. national news took up the story. *World at One* carried the item second from the end and then went on to discuss the sporting results.

Martin, unable to concentrate, tossed aside the feature he was writing and began making a few inquiries himself.

By 3 p.m. the story had moved into fourth position and news editors were dispatching reporters to catch the 5.10 p.m. train from King's Cross.

A little later Martin slipped down the road to buy the afternoon papers. There it was : a double-column front-page story under the headline 'ARCTIC PILGRIM SILENT — WHY?' Below the headline was a picture of the ship taken when first she sailed. A list of crew members was not published. Traditionally this is not done until there is no hope of survival.

The town began to worry.

Events moved swiftly now as concern mounted. In mid afternoon the Ministry of Agriculture and Fisheries announced that a search of the area had already commenced. The Ministry of Defence had diverted several vessels to the area, the Norwegian Navy was standing by, and foreign and British shipping had been asked to report any sighting of the missing trawler.

A Norwegian long-range Orion search aircraft was already over *Arctic Pilgrim*'s last reported position. Hunched over their glowing instruments, warm in their zipped flying suits and bulky green lifejackets, the airmen flew a wrist flick away from the brutal Arctic. The flight engineer finished his neat calculations and slipped a fresh fuel-state card into the metal slot above the control yoke. Litres of fuel used, litres of fuel remaining. Turn-back time at present height and speed. The captain raised a gloved fist, thumb extended. His lips moved soundlessly as he spoke into his headset to the tactical navigator at the computerized chart table aft: it was time they climbed and gave the radar men in their tiny curtained cubicles the chance to put their equipment through its paces. The nose of the aircraft lifted, and the second pilot relaxed, his hands dropping away from the duplicated controls as the altimeter needle began to rotate away from red towards safety. The aircraft rose away from the angry sea and the scattering of tiny searching ships that were all but lost in the vastness of the heaving Arctic.

Behind the scarred and battered Clearview screens of those searching trawlers the tired faces of watching seamen took on a cold, ferocious anger. It was an anger that stemmed, in part, from fear.

They had been searching now for twenty-seven hours.

It was not right, or just, that such vigilance, such effort, should go so totally unrewarded, be so utterly, contemptuously frustrated. Surely to God there must be *some* trace, something to pick up, even, to mark the vessel's passing? There had been improvements over the years, many inventions. Gradually and at great cost man had made the sea a safer work-place. Many of those inventions and improvements had been incorporated into this new vessel they believed more seaworthy than their own, so that by her very design she had earned more than this ignominious dismissal.

In Hull, Suzy cooked dinner for them both in Martin Taylor's flat. It was a silent, miserable meal. With the television turned up loud in the living room, Martin suddenly banged down his knife and fork.

'What the hell are they *doing* out there?' he snarled with exasperation. 'She can't have fallen through a hole in the bloody ocean!'

Suzy, wisely, said nothing. They took their coffees through and hunched down on the sofa in front of the television to wait for the nine-o'clock news.

Second lead story this time – and those who waited for

46

news at home in Hull were referred to not as relatives but as something else: next of kin.

In the hours since the news had first leaked out, the British press had been busy piecing together *Pilgrim's* last voyage.

She had sailed from Hull in the early hours of 22 January, bound for the North Cape fishing grounds. The trip was to last five weeks. On board were thirty-six hands all told. By 23 January the ship was halfway between Aberdeen and Bergen; the following day she was off Norway's southwest coast and moving steadily northward. All that next day *Arctic Pilgrim* followed the sweep of Norway's western coastline in favourable sea conditions, good visibility and a rising wind.

The following morning the mate, Peter Fielding, missed his footing on a metal ladder, crashed twenty feet to the deck below and broke three ribs. *Arctic Pilgrim* sent a radio message back to Hull and was ordered to proceed directly to Tromsø, where she would pick up a replacement mate. The vessel arrived at Tromsø, and Fielding was put ashore. His condition was not serious and arrangements were made for him to be flown home the next day.

On 27 January *Arctic Pilgrim* moved on to the fishing grounds. For the next eight days she fished off North Bank in steadily worsening conditions. She was in visual and radio contact with a number of other British trawlers, and she made at least two radio contacts each day to her owners in Hull. In the morning she would report her position and later she would send back coded details of the day's catch and tonnage.

At 1000 hours on 7 February she reported she was trawling at position 71°49′ N 28°58′ E. That same afternoon the mate of another trawler, John Ryder of the *Midnight Sun*, reported *Arctic Pilgrim* three miles off his starboard bow. She appeared to be steaming eastward. He had watched from *Midnight Sun's* bridge before *Pilgrim* was swallowed up in the mists of rain.

She had not been seen since.

With unintentional callousness the newsreader shuffled his notes and launched immediately into a story about Rhodesia.

Martin Taylor got to his feet and paced restlessly up and down the room. 'You can't just *lose* a ship that size – not these days. What about her Mayday? Her distress flares? And all those life rafts? She can't just *vanish* – it isn't possible.'

'She could still turn up,' offered Suzy from the sofa.

Martin turned. 'But she won't, don't you see? Not now.'

'Why do you – ?'

'Look, Suzy,' he said suddenly. 'If you don't mind I'll just go out and walk a bit. Get a drink somewhere. There's no use my staying in here, I'll drive you round the bend.'

'Like some company? Want me to come with you?'

Martin shook his head. 'Thanks, but I'd rather ... you know ... just be alone. Clear my thoughts.'

Suzy nodded.

At five past ten that night the King's Arms was crowded and hot, the air fighting for space with the cigarette smoke that hung in a haze above the wide brown bar that dominated the length of one wall.

It had been one of Johno's favourites, and Martin waved at familiar faces as he pressed through the throng for a drink, catching his reflection in the speckled Bass mirror behind the inverted spirit bottles.

While he waited for his change he looked over his shoulder at the men who crowded round him – men in sharp suits and greased haircuts, the sailors on leave, flush with money; old men, old sailors, nursing their drinks, putting off the lonely shamble home; a group of noisy youngsters, flushed with drink, playing bar billiards – and somewhere, amid all the noise and the boasting, the conjecture and the argument, a radio vied for the ear of anyone who would listen.

'Quiet. Quiet, please. Ladies and gentlemen, silence for a moment, if you please.' The barman, a stout, balding man in a knitted cardigan, held up his arms importantly. He turned to the radio and fiddled with the volume while an unaccustomed silence settled on the bar. A billiard ball rolled unheeded across the floor as the voice of the newsreader filled the room:

'... missing since Thursday. Earlier today the Minister for Agriculture and Fisheries announced that ...' It was all there, except the news they waited to hear. *Arctic Pilgrim* was still missing.

The barman moved across to the radio and turned down the volume with deliberate, time-consuming movements, embarrassed by the gusto with which he had heralded what, in the absence of anything else, turned out to be bad news. He faced his customers and began to polish his spirit glasses furiously. 'Not so rosy, I must say. Still, there's always to-morrow, as they say. Now then, gents: what's your fancy?'

That same evening at 2250 the following signal was trans-mitted from the vessel coordinating the sea search for *Arctic Pilgrim* and jotted down in the twisting, heaving radio cabin of the Boston trawler *Midnight Sun*:

HERMES TO MIDNIGHT SUN ONPASS ALL SHIPS. SEARCH ABANDONED. MANY THANKS TO YOU IN THIS DOGGED SEARCH. MOST IMPRESSED YOUR HANDLING TRAWLER FLEET AND BY DETERMINATION IN EX-TREME CONDITIONS. GOD SPEED AND SAFE RETURN HOME PORTS. ENDS.

More sinister than any tolling bell, more final than any letter of condolence, they published a list of missing crew members late the following afternoon.

There were thirty-six names. All but three of these came from Hull.

Loud men and braggarts, quiet men and good providers. Family men and the town's lovers. Drinking men and men who owed money. Men who were loved and those who were not. Local men. Now, only now, Hull was waking up to her loss, and it was not a pretty awakening.

That day also it was announced that the formal inquiry into the loss of the motor trawler *Arctic Pilgrim* would take place at the Victoria Gallery, City Hall, Hull, on Monday,

6 May. A Commissioner of Wreck had still to be appointed.

And, a postscript: with the agreement of both the Soviet and the Norwegian authorities, a temporary and localized international fishing ban would be imposed on that area to the east of Vardø, northern Norway. It was purely a temporary measure until the cause of *Arctic Pilgrim*'s mystery disappearance could be established. With the weather building to its peak of seasonal savagery, it was considered a sensible precaution.

In a timber-framed house in the tiny fishing village of Kiberg, near Vadsø, northern Norway, Piers Iversen leaned his clammy forehead against the cool tiles of the bathroom wall and waited for the latest bout of nausea to recede.

It was shortly after 1 a.m. Twenty minutes ago he had stumbled urgently from his bed to vomit into the toilet. When the spasm finally passed he tugged out the light switch and felt his way unsteadily back to the bedroom. He slipped beneath the warm quilting to stare unseeing up at the ceiling. Ever since they had returned from the fishing three days ago he had suffered from nausea, vomiting and diarrhoea. Tonight, however, the vomit was laced with blood, and now Iversen, a tough, practical seaman not given to morbid hypochondria, wondered if he should take his wife's advice and visit the doctor. He pondered that. *Nijdar*, the sixty-foot fishing vessel he shared with Horst Elvaag, Jan Scroeter and Jacob Borgssen, was in for routine maintenance. He could be spared for a few hours. Perhaps he would go and see the young doctor and ask for something to settle his stomach. Presently he fell asleep until shortly after 6 a.m., when he awoke suddenly to vomit once more.

His arrival at the tiny village clinic deeply worried the young doctor. Now as they chatted cheerfully, he asked the big, gruff Norwegian to roll up his sleeve. It might be as well to take a blood test, he said casually. Just to be on the safe side.

CHAPTER FOUR

The rain had started just after dawn, falling with monotonous determination out of a dull, leaden sky.

It was still raining at a few minutes after ten that Tuesday morning, 19 February, as thirty-nine-year-old Thomas Silvers, his skinny frame wrapped in a heavy, unfashionable overcoat, ducked in out of the rain at the offices of the *Hull Daily News*.

There were two young girls behind the counter, talking. One was filing her nails. They looked up for a moment, took in Silvers's thin face with the lank hair plastered wetly over the balding scalp and resumed their conversation. Silvers waited. He was often kept waiting.

'Yes?' Finally.

'Er ... Good morning. I'd like to talk to one of your reporters, please. Someone who's been dealing with the story about the *Arctic Pilgrim*, I think.'

The girl dialled a number and sat staring into space, drumming her nails. Silvers wandered away to plan what he was going to stay. He felt nervous.

Presently the girl replaced the receiver and beckoned Silvers forward. 'Mr Nott will be down in a minute or two. You can wait over there.' She gestured at a small glass cubicle.

Silvers went inside. There were three chairs, a table, a company calendar and a Bass ashtray. He sat down and waited, fingers nibbling at the button of his overcoat.

Ten minutes passed. Then the door opened and a young man walked in. 'Mr Silvers? You wanted to see me?'

'Er ... yes. Yes, I did. My name is Tom Silvers. I live in Milton Road, just up the way here. My younger brother, Jonathan, was on *Arctic Pilgrim*.' He paused.

'Yes, Mr Silvers – go on.'

He drew another breath. 'Well, I've read all the reports about the disappearance, the search and so forth, about how they never found anything from her, and I think ... I think I've worked out why.'

Nott looked up. 'Why's that, then?'

'I think they must have been searching at the wrong time. I mean – they must have been, not to get anything, anything at all.' Silvers gathered himself. 'I work here in Hull with the Meteorological Office.' He fished a visiting card from his breast pocket.

Nott studied the meagre credentials of a clerk in that office's shipping department. He nodded politely. Silvers scrabbled in an inner pocket and dragged out a battered notebook, which he consulted.

'Now – it's twelve days since *Pilgrim* last made contact. If we assume she went down roughly where she was last seen by the *Midnight Sun* – then, in those conditions and with that wind, tide, current and so forth, it's only now that wreckage would begin to break off, float to the surface and get blown ashore. It's only *now*, now when there's no one out there looking for it ! The search was called off days ago !' Silvers sat back.

'O K – tell me slowly : Why should there suddenly be wreckage to find now?'

Silvers leaned forward. 'First of all, consider the conditions at sea at the time. One ...' He talked on, explaining his theories with desperate eagerness.

Presently Nott interrupted him. 'Have you told all this to anyone else – officially, that is?'

Silvers shook his head. 'Doesn't seem much point. They're not going to start another search just to find a few bits of driftwood, are they? Not on the say-so of an obscure civil servant like myself.'

'So what's your next move, Mr Silvers?' asked Nott idly.

Silvers clasped both hands together on the table.

'I want to mount an expedition to go and *find* that wreck-age. I want to get up a party to go and scour the likely coastline until we find proof that the ship has sunk. Proof for all the families.' Silvers studied Nott's face intently. 'I want you to write a story about it. Say I'm looking for volunteers and funds to back the expedition – would you do that? I thought I'd call it *Pilgrim* Search or something like that.'

Nott winced. It sounded more like a holiday exhibition. Nott had not been with the paper long. He was not about to commit professional suicide by taking at face value every eccentric who walked in at the front office. Besides, Silvers did not look the type to lead an expedition to the public library, far less the Arctic Circle. Yet if it stood up its very strangeness could make a good human-interest story: Clerk Returns With Proof Navy Could Not Find. Exclusive by John Nott. Byline in eighteen point Ludlow medium condensed. Why not?

'You and your brother must have been very close,' suggested Nott, playing with his pen, weighing his man across the table.

'Yes. We were. Very close,' agreed Silvers, dropping his voice to a suitable pitch as one does when talking about the dearly loved and sadly missed.

Close? He had hated his younger brother. Hated him because all his life he, Tom Silvers, had been upstaged by a Jonathan who was more successful than he. It was Tom Silvers who had first summoned the courage to talk to Cathy at the Methodist Hall all those years ago, but it was Jonathan who stepped in with the wide smile and easy manner, stepped in, asked her out and later married her.

It was Jonathan. Always, always Jonathan. Jonathan the marine electrician, the union organizer who somehow managed to save enough for a little shop of his own. And now he was gone, drowned at sea, all because he 'wanted to see what it was like'. A bit of spice, an adventure, while he, Tom Silvers, caught the bus to work as he always did. Well, now it was his turn to grab the limelight.

'Will you do the story, then?' he asked, he pleaded.

The story made front-page news the following day.

Six days later a slim manila folder containing clippings on

the proposed search for the *Arctic Pilgrim* landed on the drab metal desk of Colonel Francis Mann-Quartermain, M C (Retd.), Deputy Director, S I S.

A little earlier in the morning Sir Peter Hillmore had been on the confidential line. In the brief, crisp sentences Colonel Mann-Quartermain had come to resent, he had sketched out the department's policy – the actions he expected his subordinate to take, the need for caution, for subtlety, for discretion out of the public eye. Now Mann-Quartermain skimmed through the clippings rapidly, referring constantly to the attached closely typed pages of confidential information relating to one Thomas Eric Silvers.

The Deputy Director of one of the least-publicized departments of the Ministry of Defence swore under his breath.

All security matters in Britain come under the aegis of the Secret Intelligence Service, whose Director works out of the Cabinet offices in Whitehall. Intelligence matters overseas are dealt with by M I 6 under the direct control of the Ministry of Defence and the Foreign Office. British internal security is coordinated between M I 5 and Special Branch. Mann-Quartermain, in a process that had taken many years of careful nurturing, had established himself in the grey middle-ground between the two rival departments. The position of his office off Berkeley Square placed him conveniently close to the M I 6 offices in Curzon Street and his club, the Lansdowne. Less convenient, however, was the location of M I 5 in Century House, Lambeth, across the Thames. That, as Mann-Quartermain constantly reminded his armed driver each time they threaded their way through the rush-hour traffic for the weekly security meeting, was a bind.

Colonel Mann-Quartermain had won his Military Cross at Cassino, leading a frontal assault on a *Fallschirmjäger* machine-gun nest with a pistol in one hand and a bayonet in the other. He was used, therefore, to reacting directly to his problems. 'Damn,' he muttered now, slowly and with great feeling, as he read the report on Thomas Silvers. 'Damn, damn, damn.'

He primed his pipe, lit it and wiped the shards of tobacco

off the report in front of him. When the pipe was drawing to his satisfaction he waved the match to extinction, leaned forward and pressed the intercom beside the blotter. Presently the door into the adjoining office opened.

'Yes, sir?'

'Ah, Simon,' began Colonel Mann-Quartermain, waving him forward with the report. 'You've had a squint at this, I take it, from our chap in the north-east?'

'Yes, sir.'

'Comments?'

'Not so good, sir. Could be rather embarrassing if the search ever gets off the ground. Seems unlikely, though. That last paragraph does seem pretty definite.'

'What? Oh, yes. Yes – it does.' Mann-Quartermain flipped open the folder once more and searched briefly through the text. He read aloud: ' "In view of the subject's almost total lack of any personal charisma and the absence of any real powers of organization and leadership, it appears extremely unlikely that the proposed operation will move beyond the initial planning stages." ' Mann-Quartermain closed the file and locked it in a desk drawer with a little key he fished from his waistcoat pocket.

'Neatly put, I must say,' he said, straightening up. He puffed gently on his pipe, sending feathers of smoke spiralling gently towards the ceiling. 'If things should, indeed, move "beyond the planning stages" we should perhaps have something in reserve. Leave that to me. In the meantime, Simon, see if you can't persuade someone over in the Department of Trade and Industry to drop a hint of discreet discouragement in the right circles over in Norway. You know the sort of thing: free-lance operation without proper backing, shady motives, embassy not asking for any special facilities, that sort of thing. Sir Peter's been on the blower again about this one, already.'

'Very well, sir – I'll get on to it.'

'Good. That's all. Oh, Simon – one other thing.'

Simon paused and turned, his hand on the door handle. 'Yes, sir?'

'This whole Hull thing is strictly confidential. No carbons, no crumpled paper into wastepaper baskets, not even your secretary to see the origins of any signals, right?'

'Right, sir.'

'Good man.'

The door closed softly.

The bearded young Kiberg doctor patted the shoulder of the elderly fishmonger and steered him gently towards the door of the clinic. Everything would be fine. It was just a simple stomach infection; there was nothing to worry about. The doctor's smile snapped off the instant the door closed behind his elderly patient. He slipped behind the glass partition and spent several minutes deep in thought pondering the little row of glass phials. He was building up quite a collection of blood samples: Piers Iversen, Horst Elvaag, Jan Scroeter and Jacob Borgssen – the crew of the fishing boat *Nijdar*; the entire crew. And now Uls Tunmst, the fishmonger. The doctor moved back to his desk and picked up the phone. It was time Vadsø Medical Centre came up with some conclusions.

By Wednesday, 27 February, a week after the story had been published, there had been fifty-four phone calls from volunteers. In addition, £2,828 in cash, cheques and postal orders – much of it anonymous – had been handed in at the newspaper's front office. Journalist John Nott got his by-line.

In London, Colonel Mann-Quartermain got another collection of press clippings. He read them and then sat in thought for a long while, smoking his pipe. He was interrupted by the peremptory buzzing of the black phone on his desk. It was the line that connected him directly to the office of Sir Peter Hillmore. Mann-Quartermain sighed.

'Sir Peter wishes to see you in one hour's time, Colonel. His office, if you please – and bring your file on the Trojan business with you.'

'Very well – one hour,' replied Mann-Quartermain brusquely, irritated by the interest from above which he interpreted as interference and, not least, by the prospect of another armed drive through the nation's capital.

One hour later he was seated before Sir Peter, his Trojan file lying unopened on the desk. Sir Peter rose and paced the carpet, his highly polished shoes sinking deeply into Wilton pile. He perched on the edge of his desk, crossed one glossy shoe over another and folded his arms.

'Piece in the *Telegraph* this morning about the Hull business, Francis. Only a paragraph, but it seemed to suggest the search and the appeal for funds were getting off the ground. What's your evaluation?' The head jutted forward as he regarded his Deputy over the top of his glasses.

'Three-day wonder it looks like to us, sir. It's extremely doubtful if it'll ever come to anything, in my opinion. It's all there, sir – in the file.'

'Yes.' Sir Peter reached behind him and weighed the buff folder with its double green star in his hand. 'Keep on top of this one, Francis. The P M is expecting a surveillance digest at Cabinet tomorrow. Trojan is bound to come up.'

'Leave it to me, sir. Would you like us to get any ... further involved?'

Sir Peter's eyebrows rose a well-groomed fraction. 'I think not, Francis – not at this stage. Just a watching brief, don't you agree?'

Mann-Quartermain did not. 'Indeed, sir,' he said, a decision already taken in his own mind that would have earned Sir Peter's wholehearted disapproval.

Back in his office, Mann-Quartermain reached for his phone, asked for an unsecured outside line and dialled a private, unlisted number in Newcastle. It was the number of his northeastern operative, Paul Evans.

'See him? The man crossing the zebra now?'

'Him? The feller in the overcoat?' asked the schoolboy, leaning down to talk to the man through the open window of the yellow Scimitar.

'That's the one. Off you go, then – and remember: he must touch it.'

'O K.' The boy trotted off across the busy road. He picked his way through the crowds, closing up on the man from behind.

'Excuse me, mister.' He had to tug at the back of the unfashionable overcoat to attract the man's attention.

'What? Yes? What do you want?' demanded the man, raising his voice above the roar of the traffic and peering down at the boy who had stopped him so abruptly.

'Are you the man who's leading the *Pilgrim* expedition?'

'Well, yes. I am, although ...'

'Smashing. Could you do me a favour?' The boy held out the atlas in the shiny new cover. 'Could you just show me where you're going? It's for me geography, see.'

'Well, yes, all right,' replied Mr Silvers, mollified by the attention. 'Let's go back into this doorway away from the crowd, shall we?'

Mr Silvers took the atlas and began turning the pages. 'I think we shall probably start looking up here somewhere ... and here ... and then ...'

'O K, mister – thanks a lot.' The boy grabbed the atlas and darted away.

'Look here ...' Mr Silvers started after him as he vanished into the crowd.

The boy was back beside the car within a minute. 'Here you are, then, mister. That's a quid you owe me.'

Evans held out the pound but retained control of the note between thumb and finger. 'And he did hold it? You're certain of that?'

'Yeah – 'course he did. Just like you said.'

'And you didn't hold it there?'

'Naw.'

'Show me where he touched the cover.'

'I just told yer –'

'Show me!'

'Well, here ... an' here ... an' ...'

'Don't touch it, just point. Right. Drop the book in here.' Evans held out a large brown envelope.

The boy did as he was told.

'Right. That's fine.'

The boy took the money and sauntered off. Money for jam. The tricks grown men get up to just because it's someone's birthday.

Evans placed the large envelope on the passenger seat, wound up the driver's window and then drove slowly round to the car park behind the bus station. He locked the car door and checked that the blanket covered the object in the cargo space at the rear of the car. Satisfied, he locked the boot, pocketed the keys and walked briskly back to the shopping centre.

He went into one shop and bought a tradesman's white working coat and a pair of cheap flexible imitation-leather driving gloves. Then he walked next door to the newsagent and bought a wide roll of Sellotape, a pair of scissors and a two-ounce tin of tobacco.

He drove round to his hotel in Paragon Street, parked in the side road running beside the Berni Inn and took his carrier bag, together with the brown envelope containing the atlas, up to his room.

He had not completed the theft of the stereo equipment that now lay in his boot much before 4 a.m., and he had missed breakfast by sleeping late. He ate a quick meal now and set to work.

Pulling on the driving gloves, he tipped the atlas out of its envelope onto the bedspread. Lifting the book gingerly by the bottom right-hand corner, he placed it gently on the vanity table and prised open the tobacco tin. Then he walked through to the bathroom and emptied two ounces of Players tobacco into the toilet bowl.

Holding the book up to the light, watching carefully for the smudges of Mr Silvers's fingerprints, he noted precisely where they lay, cut three four-inch lengths of Sellotape from the roll and pressed these firmly over the greasy smudges.

He peeled the tape gently away from the book's shiny cover and inspected the result against the light. Not perfect, but it would do.

Taking the pieces of tape one at a time, he carefully drew

them across the open – and now empty – bottom half of the tobacco tin, making sure the ends of the tape stuck securely to the rim. Finally, he pressed on the airtight lid and slipped the sealed tobacco tin, with the three sets of fingerprints intact and protected, into the pocket of the white workman's coat. The job was done.

Evans waited until 3 p.m. and then went down to the reception desk with his luggage and the plastic carrier bag with all his recent purchases. He apologized to the pretty receptionist. Something had cropped up and he would not be staying the night after all.

Half an hour later all but two of the contents of the carrier bag – together with the carrier bag itself – were scattered in various waste bins and refuse dumps across the city. When the car drew near Milton Road at 3.50 p.m., the casual passer by might have noticed that the driver was wearing a white salesman's coat and black plastic driving gloves.

Careful reconnaissance a week earlier had revealed that Mrs Silvers was a creature of habit. She left the house shortly before 4 p.m. to fetch the child home from school. She was usually away eleven and a half minutes. Evans, sitting in the car, was banking on that.

He waited until he saw Mrs Silvers disappear around the corner, waited a minute longer and then drove round the corner and parked in a nearby side road. He waited two more minutes. Then he stepped from the car, moved round to the boot and unlocked it. Twitching the blanket aside, he pulled the heavy stereo equipment towards him. He closed the boot with his hip and crossed the road, carrying the equipment in front of him. No one gave the repair delivery man a second glance.

Six minutes left. He turned confidently in at the gate and walked round the concrete path to the rear.

Four minutes later and he was out again, turning back into the road without a backward glance. He crossed to the car, stripped off the white coat and climbed behind the wheel. He drove back into the main road, stopping courteously at a zebra crossing to allow a woman and a child to cross the road in safety. Mrs Silvers raised a hand to thank him. He smiled.

Half an hour later, the coat, the tobacco tin and the driving gloves hidden a mile behind him in a thicket beside a small stream, Evans pulled in beside a phone box and made a call.

One hour later, Hull Criminal Investigation Department found a quantity of stolen stereo equipment under the stairs of a house in Milton Road. They apprehended Thomas Eric Silvers on his way home from work. He denied all knowledge of the stuff ever being in his home. Didn't they all? Open-and-shut case, the sergeant said. The bloke's fingerprints were plastered all over the stuff.

CHAPTER FIVE

'... for that reason should never have been allowed to take place.' The Minister was making a meal of the simplest of statements. Yet, as usual, the Prime Minister did not interrupt.

The Cabinet meeting on the first floor of the brown stone building on the corner of Whitehall and Downing Street had been going on for fifty-five minutes already. Far too much time had been wasted discussing the constituency implications of a recent hospital scandal in County Durham. The Prime Minister now coughed and rapped his pipe gently against the edge of one of the crystal ashtrays presented to the nation by a grateful American ambassador forty years earlier. The Minister glanced to the head of the table and then gradually fell silent.

'Sir John?' The Prime Minister nodded to the Secretary, who consulted a neatly typed agenda. The Secretary to the Cabinet does not, contrary to popular belief, record Cabinet decisions and debates verbatim but records in longhand merely a résumé of each subject and the decisions that are taken.

'Prime Minister – I feel we should call Sir Peter Hillmore, who is at present waiting outside this chamber. You will recall you asked for him to be present at any discussion which might border upon our intent regarding the current Trojan surveillance programme. In view of recent unfortunate ... ah ... developments, I feel that might now be wise.'

There were nods of assent from both the Home Secretary and the Minister for Defence. Other senior ministers flanked the Prime Minister in an arrangement of his choosing, while junior ministers faced their seniors across the leather-topped table. Three private secretaries sat stiffly in elegant chairs along the far wall. One of these now walked to the door and summoned Sir Peter in a soft voice.

He entered, nodded gravely to the Prime Minister. 'Prime Minister. Ministers. Gentlemen.' He sat down.

'Good morning, Sir Peter – I shan't keep you long : this Trojan business. We discussed the matter briefly some days ago, as you know. I expressed myself satisfied that there was little risk of embarrassment to Her Majesty's Government and that, crudely put, gentlemen, we were more or less flameproof. You will remember?' Heads nodded in agreement.

'However, there seems to be a possible fly in the ointment with this chap ...'

'Silvers, Prime Minister,' supplied Sir John promptly.

'... Silvers we've all been reading about. Does he and his crackpot scheme represent something of a threat and, if it does, what should we do about it? Sir Peter?'

'Yes, indeed, Prime Minister.' Sir Peter smiled his assured smile, the one that said that everything was under control. It was the smile they expected to see, and he gave it to them. But the smile, the assurance, hid thoughts that would not have found favour with a single member of Cabinet now assembled.

Sir Peter's appointment dated back two years and was to run for five. It was one of the few appointments in government that remained untainted by the smear of party politics, and his had been made as a personal recommendation by the former Conservative Prime Minister in the twilight days, Sir Peter always fancied, of political courage and straight-dealing. Sir Peter now believed he had witnessed a profound change in the moral calibre of the Cabinet he was supposed to serve. Everything, it appeared, was now weighed in the scale of party advantage, while the national good was lost in the boggy ground of votes and what three of the Cabinet always referred to as 'the element of C I' – of Constituency Impact, of the effect upon the dozen or so by-elections that plagued a government clinging to power without a clear mandate from the people to do so. In his short time in office, Sir Peter fancied he had seen this lack of political maturity manifest itself in the most disturbing of ways: information given in Cabinet by one minister was promptly leaked to the press by another; petty bickering and secular interest dogged the simplest of decisions. Surrounded by small men fighting smaller battles, Sir Peter had unconsciously begun to select that information which he was prepared to place before superiors he neither respected nor trusted. Now, almost out of habit, he told them what he believed they could stomach. The unpleasant nuts and bolts of truth that clattered across his desk he kept to himself and passed only to one other – the former Conservative Prime Minister, whose photograph hung in his office as a flag of loyalty, a simple badge of faith. And so now here he was, facing these politicians with information which would, if properly divulged, condemn the Trojan programme to immediate extinction and lay half the Cabinet low with palpitations while the other half reached with trembling hands for the meagre figures of their constituency majorities. He would, he decided once more, simply spare them the inconvenience. He reached into an inside pocket and drew forth a sheet of folded paper.

'This is a photostat of the court list of Hull Magistrates this very morning. It came over the wire not two hours ago.' He paused and looked down. 'Thomas Eric Silvers is to appear before Hull Magistrates this morning charged with theft – some two hundred pounds' worth of stereo equipment, so I believe.' There was a stirring around the table, and Sir Peter looked up. 'If you will permit me to say so, Prime Minister, the man you have been worrying about is nothing but an opportunist, a common thief. He should be appearing before the bench –' Sir Peter glanced at his watch – 'about now. I suspect his trial and conviction will undermine whatever tenuous credibility he may have built –'

'You assume his guilt with a refreshing disregard for the basic tenets of our legal system, Sir Peter – or did you arrange that too? Do you really expect us to accept his appearance in court today?' The left-wing Minister for Industry was on to one of his favourite hobby-horses.

'In view of what the Secretary for Industry has said, I feel I must first of all state categorically that this man Silvers's appearance in court has nothing whatever to do with S I S,' Sir Peter said with a conviction he genuinely felt. 'For once it would appear that the laws of coincidence, of pure chance, have worked in our favour.' He looked up at the Secretary of State for Industry and allowed himself a tight smile at the enemy. 'As to the threat he and his expedition pose, I believe that ...' Sir Peter Hillmore talked on smoothly, confidently, reviewing past actions and future intentions. He most certainly did not tell the whole truth. When he had finished:

'I'm a trifle concerned about our handling vis-à-vis the Soviet end of things, Sir Peter,' confessed the Prime Minister. 'Do you feel there is need for a sterner, more formal protest than we have given at present?' The Prime Minister's tone was less than enthusiastic.

'Not in the least, Prime Minister. Whatever implications may arise now can be more than adequately handled by our people at my end. I'd suggest we leave it at that.'

The Prime Minister lit his pipe and glanced quizzically to left and right. 'Very well. We will leave the matter there. Sir Peter is confident there is no need for further action, and the subject is therefore closed. I do not want to hear the *Arctic Pilgrim* business mentioned again. Sir Peter – thank you for your attendance.'

'Thank you, Prime Minister. Good day.' Sir Peter rose and left.

Thomas Eric Silvers appeared before Hull Magistrates at ten o'clock that same morning.

He was charged with theft of a stereo set and released on bail until 4 June in the sum of £200. He put up his own bail, and, after murmured consultation, this was accepted by the court.

Thomas Silvers left the court buildings hunched in shame,

battered by an ordeal for which he had been totally unprepared.

He hurried across the road to the blare of angry traffic, turned down a side street and darted into the first shop he came to. Pressing into the gloom, he tried to shrink away from the imagined hard, staring eyes of strangers.

Catching sight of his own drawn reflection in the bookshop window, he started. None of this was happening to him – none of it : the smell of the cells overnight; the distempered walls, the rough blankets that smelled of vomit; the evil bucket beneath the window; the beige and drab browns of the courtroom. Another Thomas Silvers had just stumbled out of there, out of that nightmare of statements, signatures and questions.

He ran a trembling hand through his hair and studied the shelves of books with sightless eyes, his mind fluttering after the logic that would explain the mistake that had swept his life into chaos with such terrifying swiftness.

The bearded young doctor of Kiberg had qualified in medicine six years ago at the Pasteur Institute, Bergen. He had moved north with his young family because he sought the challenge and responsibility that inevitably came with a remote, isolated practice.

In the last few days he had taken on all the challenge, all the responsibility, he could handle.

First it was the four crewmen of the trawler *Nijdar*; then it was the fishmonger. And now? Now he had nine more patients – and two were critically ill with fever, hair loss and livid skin spots. Yet when he had phoned Vadsø for medical prognosis they appeared vague : they'd send him the results of his blood samples as soon as they could. Well, it had gone on long enough.

He swept his coat off the hook, shut up shop and backed his car noisily out of the garage. He would go to Vadsø; he would make them see sense if it took all year. Firstly, because these were his people, his responsibility; secondly, because those first four men had been fishing together, the fish-

66

monger had bought the fish they had caught, and the nine patients who had become his latest concern had all bought fish from the fishmonger's slab. Fourthly? Well, because, fourthly, you didn't need to be Einstein to recognize the symptoms of radiation sickness. Not really.

'Cheers, then, Martin.' Barry Shotter, chairman of the Hull Trawler Officers' Guild, raised his glass and drank deeply.

'Cheers,' echoed Martin.

Shotter had been an old friend of his father. Martin was having a lunchtime drink in the Guild buildings, a ramshackle set of stone offices full of wood panelling and wooden chairs with a potbellied, coke-burning stove in one corner. It was a cosy place to pick up gossip.

'You're not writing anything on that expedition lark, are you? Daftest thing I've ever heard, that is.' It was a common line among Hull's professional seamen. The ship was gone. Let that be an end to it.

Martin shook his head. 'That bloke Silvers? No – not my line of country.'

'Good. There's been quite enough said – and written, mind – about old *Pilgrim* as it is. Let her rest in peace. 'S truth, you've only got to mutter under your breath and half the town's got a new theory about what happened.' Shotter paused, considering. 'I ... suppose you've heard about that letter Pete Fielding's supposed to have brought home with him?'

Martin paused, glass halfway to his lips. 'Letter? What letter's that?'

'Letter he's said to have brought back with him after that fall. From one of the crew to his missus. Talk is he wasn't too happy about something or other. It's only talk, mind...'

Martin braked to a halt outside the address Shotter had given him in Parkfield Way, Newington. The house was small but well cared for: coloured paving stones led to the front door past a small windmill standing sentinel over the front garden. Lace curtains at the windows, smoke from the chimney.

Martin rang the bell. Presently a woman opened the door.

'Mrs Fielding? Is your husband in? My name is Taylor – Martin Taylor.'

'You'd best come in. He's in the back. We weren't expecting visitors,' she warned, and Martin walked down a long dark hall into the rear room.

A large balding man running to fat was lying full length on the sofa in a white vest, trousers and carpet slippers. He was watching horseracing on TV, and there was a pile of beer cans beside him.

'Who're you?' demanded the man suspiciously, bringing his feet slowly off the sofa, a hand held to his side.

'Martin Taylor. Johno Taylor's son.'

'Oh, aye? Pleased to meet you.' The hand went out.

'I'm also a reporter.'

The hand hesitated. 'Oh, are you? Another one.' They shook hands cautiously.

'I'd like to ask you about that letter you brought back with you after your fall.'

'What of it?'

'Who gave you the letter to post, d'you remember?'

''Course I do. Bloke by the name of Millar. Harry Millar. The sparks. Our usual oppo stayed ashore – I dunno, some problem or other. Harry got roped in at the last moment. Good bloke, he was. Bloody shame.'

'D'you remember the address? On the letter?'

Fielding thought for a moment. 'I wouldn't swear to it, mind, but I recall it was somewhere over in Egton Street.'

'Thanks.' Martin turned to go. 'How're the ribs?'

'Painful as 'ell, but the doc says they're mending.'

'You got off lightly.'

Fielding grimaced. 'That's what they all say.'

'That's what I keep telling him, but he doesn't see it that way,' agreed Mrs Fielding from the doorway.

'What does she mean?' Martin asked Fielding.

Fielding shrugged awkwardly. 'I dunno. It's hard to put

68

into words. I was mate. I'd chosen a lot of those lads myself – the deckies, the spare hands and so on.'

'And you feel you should have gone down with them, you mean?'

'I suppose – something like that. Anyway, skipper'd given me a free hand. Just before we sailed a young lad, Frankie Nelson, he came to me, here in this house, asking for the trip. Well, first I said no and then later, when he kept on, like, I said O K. Now he's gone. Can't have been more than seventeen. Only lived round the corner.'

'One last question, then I'll be off,' promised Martin. 'If she did flounder in heavy seas, as they're saying, why wasn't there time to send out a distress signal?'

Fielding shrugged. 'Search me. There should have been.'

'Who would have been in the wheelhouse at the time?'

'Any number. The skipper and the helmsman. And Mr Farmer, I shouldn't wonder, the bloke who replaced me as mate. Two or three lookouts, maybe more.'

'You read about some ships without lookouts.'

'Not on a ship where I've been mate. And not on *Pilgrim*. Especially not in those conditions. No one's that tired of living.'

Martin drove to Egton Street and stopped at the corner newsagent. Newsagents deliver newspapers. They keep accounts. And addresses.

'Mrs Millar? She's moved, love. Used to live up at number eighty-eight.' A heavy ledger was opened, a finger traced across the page. '*Daily Mirror* delivered regular for the last five months or so. Came in only last week to cancel the order. Said she was moving away. Didn't say where. Very upset she was, you know, what with her husband being drowned.'

Martin tried the neighbours. No, there was no forwarding address. Dead end. He drove slowly homeward through the rush hour.

Early that evening Thomas Silvers sat in stony silence in front of the television. He was not alone in the room – his wife sat opposite. They had eaten supper together in strained silence. Now only the television bridged the emptiness stretching between them with its bright, brittle chatter.

Silvers opened a newspaper and scanned the pages with unseeing eyes. She didn't believe him, either. It had been in her eyes as he tried to explain, tried to make her understand the incomprehensible; it was the same look he had encountered on the face of Nott, the young reporter – the one who had been so friendly earlier on. Now he didn't want to know, either. Silvers had conned him, let him down. Taken him for a ride. He would talk to the editor and get in touch later. Maybe.

Silvers glanced furtively at his silent, disapproving wife. She had failed him. Whatever it was that had once held them together had proved insufficient to match the need of the moment. Her mute disbelief earlier as he tried to explain, make her understand, and then that dead feeling inside as she had begun to talk, haltingly at first and then in a bitter torrent, about the shame and the court case and the newspaper reports and about the neighbours, the neighbours, the neighbours.

He turned the page of his newspaper, and the noise broke like gunfire in the laden room. He laid the paper carefully aside and walked into the hall for his overcoat.

As Thomas Silvers walked the wet, empty streets alone, Martin Taylor told Suzy about the day's mystery letter. They were sitting over their menus in the expensive restaurant beneath Hull's Central Hotel. Halfway through Martin's long and involved description of his visit to Fielding, Suzy laid her knife aside and dabbed at her lips with a crisp napkin.

'Martin, can I ask you something?'

'Sure,' he said cheerfully.

'Why keep on about it? Why can't you accept the ship's gone? That it's over. You talk about nothing else: about the radio messages that were never sent, about the weather, the search and now about this letter business. It's ... it's almost like a hobby.'

'Like stamp collecting? Needlework, perhaps?' asked Martin quietly, dangerously.

'I don't mean like that, no.'

'Then what do you mean? A bit boring, is it?'

'Stop it, Martin. I don't mean like that.' Suzy reached out and laid a hand on his impulsively. 'What I meant was: I *know* how important it is to you – but you're not going to bring Johno back. He's gone.'

'I can accept that he is dead,' said Martin calmly. 'What I can't accept is ... I'll try and explain: I'm a journalist, right? A reporter, an investigator? That's my trade, my profession, yes? Six months ago, before I met you, I wrote a piece about three blokes, here in Hull, who were running a bent garage. I wrote a story about what they were doing. The police followed up, the men were charged and convicted. Now they're doing time. You with me?'

'I didn't know –' began Suzy as Martin shrugged.

'No reason why you should. It's not important. What I'm talking about is cause and effect. I felt useful, *effective*. There was something happening that was wrong. I changed that. Are you with me?' Suzy nodded: 'OK. What happens? The biggest ship in my town goes missing, that's all. She sails off into the wide blue yonder without leaving so much as a paper plate floating on the water and, as if *that* wasn't enough, my father's one of the crew – so I'm involved, yes?'

'Yes, but I don't see how you could –'

'Hang on: so what do I do? *Actually do?* Oh, I write up the story.' The voice was heavy with sarcasm. 'I ask all the right questions, make all the phone calls and file down to the London papers for all I'm worth – it's their money that's paying for this meal, incidentally.' Martin shook his head impatiently. 'But all that's just gloss, journalistic sleight of hand, if you like. Nothing, not a single, solitary word that's been written, has been of use, has been *effective*.' He sighed and sipped his wine. 'That's OK for the others, I suppose, they're not involved. It's just another story: a car crash, a pit collapse, a train disaster. But that won't do for me. I ... I owe him *more*, d'you see that?' He leaned forward, knuckles white against the tablecloth.

'But what more can you do? What can anyone do? You can't start dredging the oceans. The fishermen are right: these things *do* happen; ships *do* go down.'

'Yes, but not –'

The French waiter who had been attending their table bustled through the serving doors and made for Martin's side importantly: 'Pardon, monsieur,' he said, bending low over their table. 'I could not but hear you are talking about this ship, your *Arctic Pilgrim*, no?' Martin nodded. 'There, in the kitchens, we have the radio, yes? We have jus' heard – they at last have found somethings. They have found the – how do you say? – the –' he flapped his hands in agitation – 'in French we say *ceinture de sauvetage* ... the ... the life belts. It is good, no?'

CHAPTER SIX

They heard the details on the car radio during the drive home.

Just after first light that morning a fishing boat, *Kingflud II*, had spotted a round plastic ring floating in deep water off the north coast of Norway in roughly the same position as *Pilgrim*'s last reported position. Arnt Jacobssen, the skipper of *Kingflud II*, had killed her engines, drifted alongside and taken the lifebuoy aboard.

Flagging public interest in Silvers's proposed expedition to tramp over Norway's sensitive coastline looking for any trace of the *Arctic Pilgrim*, dealt a near-fatal blow by his arrest and release on bail pending trial, now received the coup de grâce.

The people of Hull had all the proof they needed.

Slowly, in a trickle at first and then a flood, contributors approached the *Hull Daily News*. They wanted their money back. They wanted out.

Nott did arrange a meeting between Tom Silvers and the editor. It lasted four and a half minutes. When it was over Silvers was out in the street again, his dreams demolished.

The next morning's papers announced that, in view of the discovery, the formal inquiry into the loss would be put back from Monday, 6 May, to Monday, 3 June.

Colonel Mann-Quartermain shrugged into his fawn overcoat, reached for his brown leather gloves and stabbed the button on his intercom. 'Simon?'

'Yes, Colonel.'

'I'm out the remainder of the afternoon. If I'm needed you can reach me at the club, right?'

'Yes, sir.'

Mann-Quartermain patted his pockets for pipe and tobacco and then took the private lift to the ground floor, where he acknowledged with a touch of gloves to an imagined cap rim the respectful salute of the elderly master-at-arms at the door.

It was cold and raw outside as the Colonel hailed a taxi and ordered the driver to drop him at the corner of Oxford Street and Great Portland Street. As the taxi scythed through the traffic, Mann-Quartermain glanced at his watch. A quarter past four. He was going to be early. Which was as it should be, he mused, craning his neck past Horseguards. Punctuality, he believed, established an ascendancy in such matters.

He paid off the taxi, tipping with an imagined generosity that was four years out of date, and crossed hurriedly into the Torino Continental Café.

The place was almost empty, caught between the late lunchers and the after-work crowd. He acknowledged the bobs of welcome from the Italian waiters with their frilly white shirts and starched aprons and irritably waved away the attentions of the young manager. Bloody Wops. (It was a measure of the man that his prejudice was thirty years old.)

He walked almost the entire length of the counter and then chose one of the marble-topped tables over in a corner away from the large windows that look out on to Great Portland Street. He draped his coat over a vacant chair, ordered toast and a pot of tea for two and settled down to wait.

Rokoff the Russian arrived exactly on time.

'My dear Francis.' Rokoff advanced towards him, arm raised in salutation, impeccable overcoat hanging open, revealing with each step a slash of silk scarf, a three-piece suit of exquisite cut, pale-blue shirt and silk tie.

Mann-Quartermain rose to greet him, and the two shook hands warmly like old friends, which, in a way, they were.

'I've ordered tea and toast already,' said Mann-Quartermain as Stefan Rokoff added his coat to the one on the chair and smoothed a hand over his mane of silver hair.

74

'Excellent, excellent,' approved the Russian. He peered a little closer. 'You look a little under the weather, Francis.'

'Bit of a cold,' admitted Mann-Quartermain shortly, irritated as usual by the man's fluent, idiomatic use of a foreign tongue. Damn it all, the man was on the other side. He held out the plate of toast. Rokoff smiled and helped himself.

The social baubles that went with the job amused the chemist's son from Podolsk who had risen through the ranks to command a troop of ill-equipped Russian tanks against Guderian's panzers at Kazaki during the savage struggle for Moscow in August 1941. Surviving that mauling, decorated and transferred to Intelligence and the Kirov field office of the N K V D, he was in Berlin for May 1945. He remained there until shortly after the American–British airlift which broke the Soviet blockade of that divided city in 1949. Then, promoted to the First Chief Directorate of the newly formed K G B responsible for foreign affairs, he served in Yugoslavia, Turkey and Sweden. He came to London in 1968 as junior trade attaché, on indefinite attachment to Knightsbridge Section operating out of the Soviet Embassy building in Notting Hill, which is protected so obligingly by uniformed members of the Metropolitan Police. He was one of the few K G B officers who survived the expulsion of 104 Soviet 'diplomats' by Foreign Secretary Sir Alec Douglas Home in 1969.

Now, sipping tea and munching toast with the British ex-colonel about whom he knew so very much, it amused Stefan Rokoff to delay coming to the point of their meeting. Predictably, it was Mann-Quartermain who spoke first.

'It ... er ... it all seems to have gone down rather well, I must say.'

'Really? You've heard?'

'Just before luncheon.'

'Ah! And?'

'Come, now, Stefan, old chap – you don't mean you haven't been told?' chided Mann-Quartermain, tugging his pipe from his pocket and regarding the Russian tolerantly.

Rokoff smiled blandly. Told? Of course he had been *told*.

Mann-Quartermain rapped his pipe gently against the

table in time with his words. 'Cancelled. Indefinitely. And that means forever. With the discovery of the lifebuoy the Hull newspaper has dropped the expedition idea like a bag of snakes, and the chap who was trying to get it off the ground can't even get credit for his groceries.'

'Excellent. Excellent. If the idea had caught on it could have become most embarrassing. Intolerable for you to be under that sort of pressure – quite intolerable.'

'And you, Stefan – aren't you also under pressure?'

'Myself?' Rokoff smiled deprecatingly. 'We are all under pressure of one sort or another, of course.'

'Hurrumph,' snorted Mann-Quartermain. He considered the ploy with the lifebuoy quite unnecessary, a dangerous overreaction, like calling the fire brigade after setting the toast on fire. Still, *his* yardarm was clear. His message to Sir Peter expressing 'considerable reserve' saw to that without putting him beyond the pale if the thing did come off. That was the worst of these joint efforts: too many hands in the brew. And Russian hands at that. 'It should never have been necessary, if your people hadn't –'

'And your people are so efficient?' countered Rokoff swiftly. 'Look at that ridiculous Holystone* mission of yours before you talk to me about what is necessary and what is not.'

* The Holystone project, code name OPPO-099U, under the command of Captain Jack B. Richard, commander of Naval Intelligence, United States Navy, was a series of deep-penetration submarine missions sanctioned each month by the 40 Committee of Congress to gather electronic intelligence from within Soviet territorial waters. The programme was hallmarked by a series of incidents: in 1969–70 an American nuclear submarine was beached for several hours at low tide on the Soviet Pacific coast. The submarine later escaped undetected. In March '71 there was a collision between an American and a Soviet nuclear submarine seventeen miles off the coast near Murmansk. That same year an American nuclear submarine scraped the bottom of a Soviet submarine inside Vladivostok harbour. Damaged, the American submarine made its escape without further incident. In late '73 there was an underwater collision between the Holy Loch-based US submarine *James Madison* and a Soviet submarine in the North Sea. *James Madison* was carrying nuclear weapons at the time of the incident.

'That was the Americans, not the –'

'Does a wolf need a first name to be dangerous?' countered Rokoff.

'Don't you go using your peasant folklore on me.'

'How dare you?'

'I'm sorry – that was inexcusable,' apologized Mann-Quartermain instantly. That would not do at all. He had almost lost his temper with the fellow.

Rokoff held up a hand. 'I too was at fault.'

After a moment's uncomfortable silence Mann-Quartermain leaned forward and said quietly over the clatter of teacups nearby, 'There is a lot of common ground over this thing, Stefan. It is in neither your people's interest nor mine for this matter to be pushed further into the public eye.'

Rokoff nodded. 'I have no quarrel with you on that.' He paused. 'I suppose there is no way in which a public inquiry can be avoided?'

Mann-Quartermain shook his head. 'I am afraid not – it's the first thing the public expects.'

'And who will be the – what is the phrase? – the Commissioner of Wreck?'

'That is in the hands of our people at the moment. I'll be in touch again when we have found the right ... er ... candidate.'

'I should be most grateful. Is there anything else you wish to tell me, Francis?' Rokoff added, glancing at his watch.

'There's a small question mark about some sort of letter that's supposed to have been written by the radio operator and posted back to England by that mate who cracked a few ribs, but we've nothing firm on that yet.'

'If we can be of any assistance, Francis, you have only to –'

'No, no – it's quite all right. One of my chaps is looking into that. I don't anticipate any problems.'

With that the two men rose, put on their coats with each other's help and then, after the usual good-natured squabble over the bill, shook hands and turned their different ways down Oxford Street – Stefan Rokoff back to Knightsbridge to make his report, and Mann-Quartermain to his club for a swim before dinner and a game of billiards with that peppery colonel from Signals.

The lifebuoy, carefully wrapped in lightweight polythene sheeting, cushioned on wood shavings and packed in a large heavy-duty container, duly arrived at London Heathrow shortly before noon on Thursday, 7 March. It was taken off the scheduled SAS Oslo–London flight, loaded onto a cargo trailer and then driven, together with other cargo, to the line of sheds which flank Runway One Zero Eight, where it was put in a corner and ignored.

Twenty-seven hours and twelve phone calls later, it was unearthed beneath a pair of skis and a crate of machine parts.

It was then 3.30 p.m. on Friday. A young driver with more dash than common sense rushed the package to the Department of Trade and Industry's Civil Aviation and Shipping Division offices at Shell-Mex House, Piccadilly. An hour passed before the mistake was realized and the package rerouted to the Marine Division Headquarters, Sunley House, Holborn. Records show it arrived there at 5.24 p.m.

There are few things more sacred than the Civil Service weekend and the lifebuoy did not appear before department officials until a little before 10 a.m. on Monday, 11 March.

It was opened and examined in one of the first-floor laboratories before two senior scientific officers, a secretary and an official photographer. The purpose at this stage was merely to log the find and its condition, note any obvious or glaring irregularities and then pass the lifebuoy down the bureaucratic pipeline to the Admiralty Materials Laboratory at Holton Heath, Dorset. The Ministry of Defence has an arrangement with the Department of Trade (D T I) whereby the A M L undertakes most of the country's major civil marine forensic investigations.

The senior officer present, Professor James M. Conway, first identified the lifebuoy's make and dimensions and had it weighed and photographed. He and his colleagues studied the lifebuoy for some while and from many angles, peering at this, stooping to examine that, all the while murmuring in their exclusive dialect of specialization while the secretary made notes.

The following day, Tuesday, the lifebuoy was packed up again and taken, by messenger, to the Admiralty Materials Laboratory for analysis. The driver took with him a letter from Professor Conway, who had scribbled in red ink on a fresh sheet of DTI-headed note-paper :

The objective of your task is to establish four things :
1. If the lifebuoy was attached to the sunken *Arctic Pilgrim* and, if possible, for how long and at what depth.
2. If the buoy has been drifting and, conceivably, for how long.
3. Any other information that will be of value in giving some indication of where, how and why the *Arctic Pilgrim* sank. It would be much appreciated if this investigation could be expedited with all dispatch. The formal inquiry will commence on June 3rd.

Down at Holton Heath the security officer signed for the letter at the gate and sent it across to the reception area. The technician on duty there read the note, glanced at the calendar and muttered under his breath. He had seldom known a time when those brown envelopes from Sunley House with the spidery red writing had *not* contained that time-honoured phrase from Nelson's day, 'Expedite with all dispatch'.

But despite the irritation of being asked, as usual, to tackle an intricate task at a fast gallop, those quiet, highly skilled men at Holton Heath with their white coats and powerful microscopes, unapproached and unapproachable by Mann-Quartermain, would do their job thoroughly, properly, painstakingly and in as long a time as it took. They had all read about the disaster, talked about it in the canteen, spared more than a passing thought for the drowned men and their families left behind. Now, here in this very building, downstairs in the laboratory, lay the one piece of wreckage which just might hold the clue to the disaster. The lifebuoy deserved their highest attention. If there was an answer, their microscopes would find it. If it took all month, they would find it.

Professor Conway's letter was passed to the Senior Director (Projects and Research), Dr Martin Isaacs. Dr Isaacs read Professor Conway's letter slowly, and then he too sighed. He had met the man on two separate occasions, and at both functions Conway had pressed without preamble for further favours, quicker results, more elaborate tests.

Dr Isaacs considered for a moment and then reached for the phone. 'Get me Dr Dowdall at his home, please,' he told the switchboard operator.

Later that same night the switchboard operator at Radio Humberside had a little trouble with a caller. That eccentric who'd been conning money for an expedition to Norway had been on again – you'd think that now, with the lifebuoy and everything, he'd give it a rest. She'd been polite but firm to begin with, and then, when firmness failed, she simply disconnected the call in mid sentence and turned back to her magazine.

In a phone box across town, Silvers slammed down the receiver with a cry that was torn from somewhere deep within him.

Dr Dowdall lived quite alone in Polperro, Cornwall. When the phone rang in his quiet little cottage perched high above the wheeling gulls and tumbling hills that surround one of the prettiest villages in England, the semi-retired microscopist was asleep in a wickerwork chair in the conservatory.

The old man gave a start. Pale, blue-washed eyes fluttered open, staring myopically. He roused himself, fumbled around for his spectacles and then went through to the living room and into the hall, pulling his worn cardigan into some sort of shape as he shuffled along, as though telephones now brought pictures too. Since his wife had died he seldom saw anyone, preferring to communicate with his professional colleagues by letter. Now he picked up the receiver as though it were something unpleasant. Perhaps it was.

'Yes? Who is it?' he asked carefully.

*

Although he had never heard of Dr Dowdall, Mann-Quartermain was also on the telephone that day, making arrangements that would directly affect the doctor, who was now fussing around his slides and phials of sea-water samples in the little wooden laboratory at the bottom of his garden. The lifebuoy, the doctor had been told, would be with him by morning.

Unaware that the lifebuoy had any further role to play in the *Arctic Pilgrim* story, unaware, more importantly, that the lifebuoy, even now, had passed out of his reach, Mann-Quartermain studied the list of names he was jotting down on a notepad as they came to him over the telephone.

'... N ... E. E for echo. Got it. What? ... Are you sure that's the lot? No ... No ... Much obliged. Thanks very much indeed. Goodbye.' He replaced the receiver and frowned at the names in front of him. This commissioner business was proving harder than he had imagined.

He had never bothered to consider just *how* a Commissioner of Wreck was appointed. He had assumed, he supposed, that there was some ever-ready pool of grey, anonymous experts who could, when the need arose, be suborned for Queen and Country. It came as something of a surprise, therefore, to discover through a helpful aide at the Lord Chancellor's office in Romney House that Commissioners of Wreck were about as plentiful as hangmen in Sweden. Invariably, Mann-Quartermain discovered, the men he sought were Admiralty Division Queen's Counsel silks – highly skilled, highly paid and much revered pillars of support at the temples of Truth and Justice. He discovered, too, that at that particular time there were just five Commissioners of Wreck covering the entire British Isles.

Inquiries into loss at sea, added the helpful aide, were presided over by a Wreck Commissioner whenever there was loss of life or the merest suggestion of maritime incompetence. Then the Wreck Commissioners took over and became a virtual law unto themselves. They not only *knew* the law, they seemed to have learned the only copy of the legislation by heart and then thrown the book overboard. Representing

Her Majesty herself, they were usually quite prepared to accept the paltry government fee awarded on these occasions in exchange for the ephemeral and temporary trappings of majesty.

A brief glimpse at Who's Who convinced even the direct and not overly sensitive Deputy Director (SIS) that these five men were of a calibre unlikely to be wooed by anything as tawdry as the kind of bribe he could drum up at a moment's notice. No, no – something altogether more discreet was needed to match this situation.

Presently he began to regret his earlier promise of swift action to Stefan Rokoff.

He sat in deep thought for a long while, rising only once, as the short afternoon drew to a close, to pull the velvet curtains and light the lamp on his desk. Then he sat again, smoking his pipe and sending little puffs of smoke spiralling into the darkness above. The clock showed a few minutes before six when he pressed the intercom and summoned Simon once more.

Simon was caught buttoning his overcoat, about to leave. He was going to his Knightsbridge flat to change for the theatre. He studied his watch. Trust the Old Man to want him now after leaving him alone all day. Still, he could just make it if he didn't keep him long. He peeled off his overcoat, checked the knot of his tie and then turned the handle on the door into the Colonel's office.

The Colonel was sitting in almost total darkness with his face in shadow. Only a pair of dismembered hands lay in the soft pool of lamplight, toying with a cigarette lighter.

'Ah, Simon.' A voice from the shadows.

'Colonel?'

There was a short pause. Mann-Quartermain began tapping what looked like a short list of names with the tip of an expensive fountain pen. 'We've run into a spot of bother with the Pilgrim operation, I'm afraid.'

'Sorry to hear that, Colonel,' responded Simon neutrally. If the old fox was about to dump the mess on his plate – and all the signs suggested that he was – then he could damn well make a formal job of it. 'Trouble for the department, Colonel?'

'Hardly that. More a matter of ... ah ... suitability.' Mann-Quartermain studied the jaws of the lighter intently. 'Just a matter of getting hold of the right sort of chap for Sir Peter to head the inquiry. Sort of fellow who'll handle the whole thing discreetly without raising needless questions.' He paused. Simon stood before him, waiting. Mann-Quartermain sat for a moment, weighing invisible odds. Then he leaned forward. 'I want you to take a look at these names here.' He turned the sheet of paper round with the tip of his pen and shovelled the note across the desk to his aide.

Simon studied it. A line had been drawn under the first five names, and there were another eight or so below the line. Each of the eight was followed by a question mark.

Mann-Quartermain made a throwaway gesture with his free hand. 'Forget about those first five. Concentrate on the others. To the best of my knowledge those eight or so are in the same line of country as the other five but have not enjoyed the same measure of success. They might, therefore, be more amenable to our ... ah ... suggestion. Dig into their backgrounds, Simon. Start with Records and then go on to the Civil List. If you draw a blank there, have a chat with that fellow Michaels over in the Treasury Solicitors Department. They're handling marine inquiries all the time.'

'And when I've found this ... this mythical man of ours, Colonel, what then?'

'Oh, he exists. Be sure about that – he exists. More important than just the man, Simon – find a lever : a lever we can use. Walpole said it first : "Every man has his price." I want you to find a man with the kind of price we can reach without too much fuss or complication.'

'Very good, Colonel. I'll get on to it first thing in the morning.' Simon turned away and so missed the frown of annoyance on Mann-Quartermain's forehead.

'That won't be soon enough, I'm afraid. We have to persuade the Minister, the Minister himself, mark you, to play along with us while a renegade takes over one of *his* precious

inquiries. I have to meet him soon. I have to see him in –'
the Colonel glanced at his watch – 'twenty-one hours exactly.
I would like to take with me our short list of probables which
we – or, rather, you – will whittle down to one in the next
four days or so.'

Nine working days were to slip by before the Colonel's
weary, suit-rumpled aide was able to drop the single slim
manila folder on Mann-Quartermain's desk, turn his back
on the hateful camp bed with its issue blankets in the corner
of his office and crawl home to an exhausted sleep between
clean sheets.

Of the eight names on that list, one had died a year earlier
(where had the Colonel found *his* name?), one had moved
abroad and two were on holiday and so would be out of the
country until well after 3 June. Of the remaining four, three
had withstood detailed research carried out by Simon
personally with the unwitting help of one of the larger
consumer-credit vetting agencies, but only one, Marcus
Armstrong-Carpenter, a recently retired civil servant from
Chalfont St Giles, had passed the final acid test in the twin
crucibles of greed and thwarted ambition.

It was early afternoon and Dr Dowdall was working on
the lifebuoy in his laboratory at the bottom of his garden.
He had been there from early morning until late evening for
the last four days – an unusual dedication, you might think,
for an elderly man who was semi-retired. As usual, he had
forgotten all about lunch.

He had scraped from the lifebuoy a sample of green slime
containing plankton. He had spun it in a centrifuge, separat-
ing the material. From the top of the solution he pipetted off
the surface plankton, put this sample on a microscope slide
and became instantly absorbed in the images that swam in
and out of focus as he adjusted his microscope on the work
bench before him. Presently he sat back for a moment,
rubbed his weak eyes and eased his aching back. Interesting.
It really was most interesting.

The doctor got to his feet and moved slowly to the cord hanging by the wooden door. It was chilly in the hut and he needed the extra bar from the electric fire above the door. He held up his hands for a moment and then resumed his seat on the high stool that was padded with a mass of old newspapers. He tilted his lamp to one side and held up the sheaf of papers. He read slowly through the requirements of the letter from Dr Isaacs at the A M L. Yes, yes, there was no mistake.

The letter stated quite clearly that the lifebuoy – now resting, in two carefully bisected sections, against the far wall – had been picked up on 28 February and packed, *uncleaned*, into a packing case for direct delivery to London. Yet...

He sighed and rummaged once more through the pages from Holton Heath. Maybe he was already too old for this sort of thing. Betty had wanted him to quit years ago. His eyes focused on the second paragraph of the letter: '... found eighteen miles off the coast of Norway in position ...' He read no further but turned impatiently to his microscope, needing to find the mistake which would account for the conclusion he could not otherwise avoid.

Now, added to his confusion and impatience, was born a nagging germ of worry. It was not in his nature to make mistakes. More than that, his work with the D T I left no margin for error, and (he admitted to himself for perhaps the first time) it was the work he lived for now.

The doctor spent a further hour in his laboratory and then, getting nowhere, turned off the light and picked his way back to the house, head bowed in thought. Tomorrow he must telephone Norway and speak to whoever had taken charge of the lifebuoy immediately it had been found. He sighed. The prospect of initiating such a miracle in the unfamiliar world beyond the prism of his microscope depressed Dr Dowdall profoundly.

In the morning he made his call, getting through to the obscure northern fishing station just before lunchtime. Half an hour's discussion merely confirmed his worst suspicions, and he replaced the receiver exhausted by the delays, the repetitions and the strange procedures of an international telephone conversation.

He lowered himself wearily into an armchair for a few minutes and then went through to the kitchen, where he made himself a thermos of tea. Then, clutching the thermos and his pages of scribbled notes, he returned to the laboratory to compile and conclude his report for the busy men at Holton Heath. He wondered bleakly if, after this, they would ever use him again.

CHAPTER SEVEN

It was Sunday, 2 June, and the sky had grown overcast just before dawn, the black cloaks of cloud scudding in low from the north-east to rain on the streets below. Now, at a little before eleven, the rain cascaded steadily off parked cars and bounced into gutters, wetting few save the faithful as they hurried on their way to worship and the less devout as they scoured the newsagents' for the Sunday papers.

Martin Taylor was still in bed. He lay there drowsily, listening to the wind as it moaned between the buildings. Somewhere in the distance a church bell tolled the hour as he turned towards the voice by the door.

'Breakfast is served – I've even brought the papers, though by this time of day they're practically out of date,' pronounced Suzy as she padded barefoot towards the bed. She placed the loaded tray on the bedside table, threw the papers onto the bed and stood, hands on hips, as an agreeable aroma of fried bacon, hot toast and coffee rose into the room.

'God, just look at you.' She smiled.

'Me?'

'The arrogance of the male written all over you in letters –'

'All over me? You're sure about that?' offered Martin generously, sweeping back a corner of the blankets with a regal gesture. Suzy tried to look modest, failed, leaned forward to pull back the blankets and then dumped the breakfast tray into Martin's lap with a cruel thump and an inaccurate assessment of Martin's immediate priorities.

'Come on, you – eat. Your eggs will be getting cold.'

'No chance,' muttered Martin. Suzy was wearing a loosely tied dressing gown. Martin found his eyes drawn to the delicate gold chain around her neck and from there to the deep divide of her cleavage. As far as he was concerned, eggs could freeze over forever.

'Martin – you're staring again,' warned Suzy with a grin, tugging the gown tighter around her full bust. Which helped not at all. The doorbell rang.

'Shit!' exploded Martin as they sat for a moment, frozen by the intrusion. He reached for his dressing gown, padded across the flat and threw open the front door.

Male, middle-aged, wearing a damp, heavy overcoat. As Martin stood there waiting, the man wiped a hand across his damp, balding head and stepped forward hesitantly.

'Mr Taylor?' he asked. Martin nodded suspiciously. 'Oh ...' The eyes darted nervously, taking in the unshaven jaw, the dressing gown. 'I'm sorry. I didn't think you'd still –'

'What can I do for you?' asked Martin shortly.

'Well ... er ... that is ... I'd like your help,' the visitor blurted out.

'I'm sorry? Help you? I don't know who –'

'Silvers. Thomas Silvers.' The man held out a hand and Martin shook it reluctantly. 'I've read what you've written about *Pilgrim* these ... these last few weeks, and what with your father and everything, I thought perhaps –'

'Silvers. You're the bloke who was running that expedition to Norway until the law picked you up for – what was it? – possession, right?'

Silvers swallowed and then nodded uncertainly. He looked so unlikely that Martin's curiosity was aroused.

'You'd better come in,' said Martin wearily.

'This is good of you, Mr Taylor – very good. I ... I won't keep you long.' The warmth of the flat made Silvers's spectacles mist up. He took them off and began polishing industriously. Martin took his coat and guided him to an armchair. Silvers looked ill, wasted.

'Now – Mr Silvers. Why come and see me?'

Silvers took a deep, shuddering breath. 'It ... it isn't easy to explain. Even now ... even now it all seems like a ... a nightmare. My mind's a blur – I still can't grasp. I mean ...' The words choked off. Silvers fished a handkerchief from his pocket, blew his nose noisily and leaned forward. He was close to tears: 'I'm a civil servant, Mr Taylor. I earn thirty-one hundred pounds a year. I've lived in Hull all my life and I've never, *never* been in any trouble with the police. Yet ... yet suddenly, on my way home from work a few weeks ago, I'm arrested, my house is searched and stolen goods are found in *my* home, under my own roof ... I'm at my wits' end.' The voice cracked.

'Take it easy, take it easy.'

There was silence while Thomas Silvers collected himself.

'That stereo equipment they discovered under my stairs. I'd never seen it before! Yet the police said my fingerprints were all over it, Mr Taylor – my fingerprints!' Silvers held up shaking hands. 'Yet I've never seen the equipment before – never touched it! I've never stolen a thing in my life, Mr Taylor, I swear it!'

'Forgive me, Mr Silvers, but I still don't see what any of this has to do with me.'

'It's something to do with the expedition – it must be. I ... I can't think of anything else. And yet –'

'O K,' sighed Martin. 'O K – say the stereo *was* planted. Someone put it there so it would be found and you would be blamed. Why would they bother? And how d'you account for the fingerprints?'

'You believe me, then?' grasped Silvers hungrily.

'I don't know if I believe you or not – but a name or two might help, O K?'

'But I can't think of anyone, anyone at all!'

'No one? Someone goes to such elaborate steps to set you up and you say you haven't an enemy in the world?'

'I've been trying, believe me. I've been lying awake, trying to work things out, trying to come up with something Nothing comes. Night after night – nothing. Even Grace, even she's come to think of me as a criminal – that I'm guilty, that I did it. Thirteen years we've been married, Mr Taylor. Thirteen years and –'

'Hold on a minute, Mr Silvers, just hold on. Let's look at this rationally.'

'Rationally!'

'Calmly, then. You come to me for help because you reckon this gear – this stereo equipment – has been planted on you and you think maybe I can help you in some way, yes?' Silvers nodded. 'But you can't think of anyone who'd do that to you and you can't think of a reason except that maybe it's got something to do with your plans to take an expedition to Norway to look for wreckage – and the only reason you tie *those* two events together, the stereo equipment and the expedition, is that they happened at roughly the same time, am I right?'

Silvers nodded miserably. Jesus, thought Martin, come on, old man, give me something, anything. He began to feel annoyed at the other's helplessness. 'Well, how about someone at work? Or a neighbour? Someone at your club?'

Silvers rose shakily to his feet and looked about him for his coat. 'It's been kind of you to see me,' he stumbled. 'To spare me so much time.'

'Now, hang on. I didn't mean –'

'No, no – really, I must be off,' floundered Silvers, looking suddenly very old. 'Things ... things to do.' He gathered up his overcoat and retreated rapidly out the front door.

'Aaaah!' exclaimed Martin in exasperation, pushing a hand through tousled hair. He walked through to the bedroom and pushed open the door. Suzy was sitting up in bed, Martin's breakfast congealing cold beside her. 'Did you hear all that?'

Suzy nodded through a mouthful of toast. She swallowed hurriedly. 'How did he look?'

'Silvers?' Martin reflected. 'Worn out, haggard, battered – nervous as hell.'

'Are you going to help him?'

'On what he told me? How?'

'Well, did you believe him?'

'About that stuff being planted in his house? I'm not sure. *He* certainly believes it – he thinks it was planted; that there's some kind of plot against him.'

'Which means one of two things,' Suzy continued for him. 'Either there *is* a plot against him –'

'Or he's off his trolley. A nutter with a persecution complex the size of *Arctic Pilgrim*.'

'And yet,' Suzy added thoughtfully, 'when you offered him all sorts of enemies – neighbours, men at work, people at his club and so on – he didn't jump at any of them. Which suggests that whatever else your Mr Silvers may be, he's probably *not* off his trolley. Not in that sense, anyway.'

'Right. And that brings us back to his idea of some kind of a conspiracy.'

'Except for one thing: even he admitted his fingerprints were on the stolen goods. So how did they get there?'

'You're right,' Martin decided after a pause. 'Maybe he is off his trolley after all.'

'Anyway,' said Suzy, her mind slipping to pleasanter thoughts, 'I think it's time you concentrated on something else. Breakfast always gives me an appetite.'

She slid sensuously out of her dressing gown, arched her full breasts and lay back among the pillows, waiting.

Two hours later, Silvers forgotten, Martin and Suzy were enjoying lunch in a country pub with Hercules at their feet. Martin had just returned from the bar with their drinks when they touched on the subject both had skirted around since late the night before when Suzy had announced she had to return to London tomorrow. Now tomorrow had turned into today, Sunday.

'Will you be away long?' Martin asked.

'Couple of days or so back by Wednesday at the latest, I should imagine. Will you be busy next week?'

'Should be. The *Pilgrim* inquiry gets under way tomorrow. I'll be covering that for a couple of London papers. That should see me through to – Christ! Look at those – they're bloody low!'

Suzy followed the line of Martin's outstretched arm and saw two aircraft, flying at zero feet, flash between a clump of trees and disappear with a waggle of wings down a shallow valley to the south. A few seconds passed and then the bellowing roar of their engines crashed against their ears,

a hello and farewell of derision from aircraft that had broken
the sound barrier with effortless ease.

'Buccaneers – late back for lunch at Scampton, probably,'
Martin pronounced knowledgeably.

In the event, those aircraft were Phantoms, not Buccaneers,
outbound from A Flight, 141 Squadron, based at R A F
Scampton, Lincolnshire, sixty miles to the south. They were
carrying out – on orders – a low-level radar-evasion exercise
that had taken them in a jagged dog-leg over York and the
North Sea. Then they had turned west again, grazed over
the deserted sand dunes of Skegness and swept inland at
hedge-top height like twin marauding sharks prowling just
above the ocean floor.

A further turn to port had had them streaking steadily
southward, four seconds ahead of the noise of their engines.
Three minutes later they passed over Taylor and Suzy; two
minutes after that and they turned slightly to port again,
picked up the ruler-straight line of the main London–Hull
railway and then, on the leader's curt 'Executive', lifted their
noses and climbed, effortlessly, smoothly and with great
power, away from damp Mother Earth. A second later they
were lost from sight, swallowed up into the murk at nine
hundred feet. Few people saw them vanish into the clouds.

One of those who did was Mr Marcus Armstrong-
Carpenter, retired civil servant, chairman elect for the mor-
row's D T I board of inquiry and a first-class passenger on
the afternoon's train from King's Cross to Hull Central, now
thirty miles south of its final destination.

Thousands of Armstrong-Carpenters leave middle-echelon
business each year, happy to hand the pace and the challenge of business to younger men, content to stand aside for
the more able, opting instead for the contentment of retirement and a dig in the garden in clement weather.

But Marcus Belvedere Armstrong-Carpenter was not content, and he hated gardening. More than that, he recognized
and despised the cards which fate had dealt him, seeing in his
own dull competence the boot-print of other, younger men

as they swept past him up the ladder of advancement to the rewards of high office. Rewards which had always eluded him.

After forty years at his chosen profession, first with the Board of Trade and then, after reorganization in 1969, with the Department of Trade and Industry, he had never once advanced beyond that level awarded by length of service alone. He had passed exams, but promotion, when it came, always carried with it the slur of formality.

But he *had* risen: from clerical officer to executive officer to higher executive officer. Transferring in 1956 to the Marine (Loss and Recovery) Office, he rose to become Senior Collations Officer for Commissioners (Wreck) at the time of the *Torrey Canyon* disaster. In the last few years he had served as personal assistant to three of the five serving Commissioners of Wreck. In his scrap of a study at home he had letters of thanks and photographs to prove it, if anyone had ever asked. No one ever had.

Always the blooming bridesmaid ...

Even his marriage had become, in time, the funeral pyre of his domestic happiness. His fiancée's father had been his immediate departmental superior back in the late 1930s. That had seemed the way to get on. God, the hope, the blind hope and optimism, of those days! Armstrong-Carpenter frowned at his reflection in the carriage window, but then, as he remembered what had brought him on this journey, the frown faded. His father-in-law had approved of him, he knew that. Why, he had even hinted at grand plans for his son in law. But those plans, like the laughter of those early married days, had evaporated as morning mist when the Great Man – the *one* man who had believed in him – had, with spectacular selfishness, drowned one summer while fishing on a Scottish loch.

His daughter's marriage had survived him in name only. Fifteen years ago it had been in grave danger of structural collapse. The childless façade had been saved, but its heart had been ripped out. Propped up by a wife's lack of interest in the emotions and thwarted ambitions of her disappointing

93

husband, the best that could be said for the Armstrong-Carpenter marriage was that, like the concrete air-raid shelter at the bottom of their garden, it had once served a purpose but would no longer stand close examination.

Armstrong-Carpenter smiled slowly.

All was not yet lost, the end was not yet in sight. Not quite.

His fat fingers stole involuntarily to his breast pocket, feeling beneath the cloth of his new grey suit the letter formalizing his appointment to this most important inquiry. He was to preside (he pictured the wording exactly, set half-way down the cream paper with the Minister's personal seal and crest positioned discreetly upon the top right-hand corner) with all 'might, moment and dispatch' over his own court of inquiry.

Vindication. Vindication at last. Vindication, exoneration and recognition rolled into those four short sentences above the Minister's own signature, brought to him in the last closing moments of a lifetime's dedicated service, calling him, Marcus Armstrong-Carpenter, out of retirement to perform this one last, vital duty. For Queen and Country.

He sighed contentedly, recalling in loving detail that Colonel's solemn promise that, by the time the House sat once more after the summer recess, one more name would have been added to the roll of select personages who were permitted to write after the name they had carried since birth 'Member of the Order of the British Empire'.

Presently the train began to slow down as it slid through the built-up outskirts of Hull. Armstrong-Carpenter roused himself from pleasant thoughts, put on his heavy overcoat and wrestled his suitcase down from the rack. He gathered up his papers and placed them carefully in the new leather dispatch case with the freshly engraved gold initials beneath the handle.

Taylor walked with Suzy to the ticket barrier, carrying her case.

'Now, you're sure you've got everything?' he said.

'Quite sure.'

'Positive? Nothing forgotten?'

'Nothing. Honestly, Martin, you're worse than an old woman.'

'That's not what you said last night. You said – and I recall your words quite clearly – you said –'

'Sshhh – not so loud.'

They waited a few moments while the last few passengers pressed through the barrier and surged onto the main concourse of the station. One of the last through the gate was a portly gentleman with a black leather dispatch case.

CHAPTER EIGHT

Martin parked in Dock Street and threaded through narrow side roads towards the Victoria Gallery.

He showed his press pass to the uniformed constable at the entrance lobby and was waved through into a wide stone-flagged hall and up a short flight of stairs into a world of lofty ceilings and marble pillars.

His heels ringing on polished stone, Martin followed the wooden finger beneath the legend 'INQUIRY: MT ARCTIC PILGRIM' and presently found himself in a long rectangular room at the western end of the huge old building. The chamber had a high-domed glass roof that was rimmed with dirt and stained with bird droppings. Canvas-backed stacking chairs filled the rear of the hall and were divided by a narrow companionway. An elderly retainer in black was now walking carefully between the rows, dropping an ashtray onto every fifth chair. A short space in front of these chairs and set at right angles to the main body of the chamber was the press table. Two other journalists were there already, while a third was carefully trailing microphone wires back from the raised dais at the head of the chamber.

Between the dais and the place where Martin was sitting were three rows of trestles, each covered with green baize. These tables were already piled high with files and documents bound with the pink ribbon of the legal profession. Martin counted eight separate clusters of papers, eight different areas of professional interest. There would sit solicitors for the vessel's owners and solicitors for the marine architects; solicitors for the next of kin and solicitors representing the Trawler Officers' Guild, the Department of Trade and Industry and the shipyard that had built her. For them all, an inquiry was a big occasion, a crucial period of investigation. A finding of technical fault in the design could result in the immediate recall of dozens of vessels now afloat.

Such a finding, backed by the verdict of law, could wreck half the careers represented in the room.

Presently the looped rope across the hall entrance was removed and members of the public began to file into the chamber.

Martin twisted round in his chair to watch them arrive. Women mainly, many with children and babies they had been unable or unwilling to leave behind; clusters of relatives sharing the burden of bereavement; here and there a seaman on leave in his best suit, hair shiny with Brylcreem under the bright lights. The public, such as it was, took its seat among much scraping of chairs and exchanges of opinion in the hushed tones of the uninitiated.

Three minutes later the senior clerk walked to the raised dais, and, conscious that every eye was upon him rapped his gavel twice and with great solemnity. He bent to the microphone.

'Ladies and gentlemen – the inquiry is about to commence. Will you please rise and stand silent for the chairman of this inquiry, Mr Marcus Armstrong-Carpenter.'

Chairs scraped back. People duly rose and stood.

There was a pause, and then a small door at the side of the chamber opened and out trooped two figures dressed in sombre dark lounge suits. The first, a youngish man in his mid thirties with lank brown hair and the harassed air of a small-town clerk, took his place at a wide desk directly in front of and a little below the raised throne of the chairman.

Martin felt a sense of anticlimax. So these were the experts who would investigate the loss of *Arctic Pilgrim*, the deaths of his father and thirty-five other men. But they looked so ordinary, so nondescript: routine little men doing a routine little chore – except that lives were involved, and deaths, and the presumed loss of a great ship. It seemed inadequate, somehow.

The chairman looked about him, adjusted his spectacles,

coughed and then tapped lightly on the microphone to see if it was in working order. It was. The muffled boom sounded like thunder in the still room. It startled the two official shorthand writers who were sitting, pencils poised, directly beneath the loudspeakers.

It also startled the chairman, who pulled back as though stung, cleared his throat and then bent again to the microphone. 'Mr ... er –' he bent to consult his papers – 'Travis, I believe. Will you please address this court?'

A tall young man in pinstripe suit and waistcoat with gold watch chain bobbed to his feet, bowed gravely to the chairman and then, gathering up a sheaf of papers, walked confidently to the witness stand. He smoothed a hand over his glossy hair, patted his papers into a neat block and then began in a smooth, well-modulated voice:

'May it please you, sir, I will now read the order for the formal investigation under the Merchant Shipping Act of 1894.' He paused, consulting his notes. ' "Whereas, on or about the eighth day of February 1974, the British motor trawler *Arctic Pilgrim*, official number 433875, was lost in approximate position 71°49′ N, 28°58′ E with the loss of all hands, and whereas a shipping casualty has occurred, the Secretary of State for Trade, in pursuance of the powers vested in him by Section 466 of the Merchant Shipping Act of 1894, hereby directs that a formal inquiry shall be held into the said shipping casualty." '

The court listened in silence. Opposite Mr Travis, the shorthand writers were scribbling furiously.

Travis talked on quietly, rapidly covering the events leading up to the missed sched and the first quiverings of alarm. He spoke about the normality of that passage up to the fishing grounds and about Fielding's accident and the arrival of the new mate; he skimmed over the steady routine reports from *Arctic Pilgrim* culminating in her last report to Hull at 1000 hours on 7 February. He described at some length the last visual sighting by John Ryder aboard *Midnight Sun* when she was 'heading easterly running before the weather ...'

Finally Travis turned over the last page of his initial outline, slipped it back into its manila folder and looked up. 'Sir, in this formal investigation I appear, instructed by the Treasury solicitors, on behalf of the Department of Trade. Before you also are seated the representatives of those parties intimately concerned in the outcome of this inquiry into the tragic loss of the M T *Arctic Pilgrim*. As this inquiry takes its course, sir, these several persons will make their interests known to you. I thank you, sir, for your attention.'

The young man bowed to the dais and walked back to join his colleagues.

Behind the seniority of his office, Marcus Armstrong-Carpenter felt a twinge of alarm. He knew that no one had told this Mr Travis just what was expected from this inquiry, and he suspected that, had he been told, he would not have co-operated. Now, faced with the competence and sangfroid of the younger man, Armstrong-Carpenter was suddenly not at all sure that he could maintain that tight grasp on the direction of proceedings he had so often admired and taken for granted at someone else's inquiry. Now he and he alone was charged with the satisfactory conduct and conclusion of this inquiry, and he did not feel up to the task. It had all seemed so simple on the train – I must stop this, he thought suddenly. He took off his glasses and polished them carefully. The court of inquiry hung on his words.

'Thank you, Mr Travis, for so lucid an opening address.' Marcus Armstrong-Carpenter's voice took on a firmer note as he got into his stride. 'You have heard just now from the reading of the Statement of Case the circumstances leading up to the loss of the *Arctic Pilgrim*. Later this inquiry will hear of the discovery of a single lifebuoy from the vessel in question. Despite exhaustive efforts, nothing else has been found which might shed some light onto the reason for the disappearance. This inquiry is therefore faced with the task of determining circumstance and cause of loss with only this one piece of evidence. Indeed, we may conclude, after hearing all the evidence, that the precise cause of loss can never be determined with any degree of certainty ...'

'Long-winded bugger's hedging his bets a bit, isn't he?' murmured one of the reporters.

Martin shrugged. It was unusual to hear the chairman of an inquiry begin his investigation with a statement that sounded like a series of conclusions. Martin leaned forward to catch a glimpse of Mr Travis. He was regarding the chairman impassively, and, whatever he was thinking, his eyes gave away nothing beyond a polite attentiveness.

Now Travis rose once more. 'Sir, may I call Mr Thomas Ernest Adams, marine architect with the Gosport firm of A. B. Anders Limited.'

A short, dumpy little man in dark-brown suit stood up from the front row of the hall, collected a heavy folder of notes and drawings from the empty chair beside him and took his place at the witness stand. As he did so a junior clerk began distributing rolls of architects' drawings to the chairman.

Presently the court settled again and Mr Adams stood in the witness box surrounded by his notes and charts.

'Mr Adams, I believe you're forty-eight years old and that you are currently employed by A. B. Anders Limited of Gosport as a marine architect?'

Mr Adams swallowed visibly. 'That is correct.'

'And how long have you held that position?'

'Fifteen years.'

'And as senior architect?'

'Eight years.'

'And you were, I believe, intimately concerned in the design of the motor trawler *Arctic Pilgrim*?'

'Yes, indeed.' Mr Adams cleared his throat importantly. 'The company with whom I am employed was awarded the design contract in –' he consulted his notes – 'the late spring of 1967. M T *Arctic Pilgrim* was to be a single-screw factory filleter freezer vessel designed for stern trawling. She was of all welded steel construction. You will see from the general arrangement plan – that's the top chart before you, sir – that the vessel's frame numbers, indicated on the bottom of that profile, run from aft to stem of the vessel from zero to ninety-two. If I may deal with those frames first, sir ...'

Mr Adams's evidence took the rest of the morning. Much of it was delivered in that peculiar professional dialect that left most of the public with a glazed look of incomprehension.

At 1 p.m. exactly Mr Marcus Armstrong-Carpenter adjourned the inquiry for lunch. The court rose with some relief. If Mr Adams was the man who set the pace, then it was going to be a long inquiry.

Fifteen hundred miles to the north-east, another inquiry was drawing to a close. Separated by distance and the flag of another nation, the two shared a common bond that neither of them could or ever would formally acknowledge.

It was the waiting he found hardest to take. Already he had been sitting on the hard wooden chair for almost four hours. Bleakly, he wondered why it was taking them so long.

Suddenly the warning light above the president's chambers turned to red, and Kapitan Leytenant Andrey Gregor Griem felt his muscles quiver involuntarily as he snapped smartly to attention, damp palms pressed tightly down the seams of his best uniform. The door opened and the three-man Tribunal of the People's Marine Court Judiciary, sitting in private session, strode grimly into the high vaulted chamber deep beneath the city streets and took their places once more at the head of the wide green baize table. Above them on the high walls the stern faces of party comrades looked down impassively, waiting for justice.

For a moment there was silence save for the hum of the air-conditioning as Griem stood before the table, a tall, solitary figure awaiting the verdict of his superiors. Far, far above the pictures on the wall and Griem's closely cropped head, the people of Murmansk hurried about their business, picking their way through the maze of drab, dun-coloured buildings, unaware that below their feet one of their countrymen was about to pay the immutable, age-old price of command.

'Andrey Gregor Griem,' intoned the president, domed head

tipping forward slightly as he steepled his fingers, eyes down-cast to the papers before him. He looked up, weighing his words carefully. 'We have considered the evidence placed before us and have weighed most carefully what you have told us and what has been submitted in written evidence by your advocate. However, it is the unanimous verdict of this court that you are guilty : guilty as charged in all respects.'

Griem felt the despair wash over him like acid. That was it. Finish.

The president looked up sharply. Griem stared impassively ahead.

'Therefore, be it recorded that this court-martial finds you guilty in that you needlessly endangered the safety of your vessel, together with the lives of your crew, on the eighth of February this year. Your actions regarding the British intruder on that date reveal a series of tactical errors that, taken together, made that which ensued almost inevitable. The people have a right to expect that those who have the honour to command ships at the spear-point of this great nation's maritime defence are men of the soundest judge-ment, the utmost integrity, the highest possible skill. Nothing less will be asked, nothing less will be accepted.

'We find that your initial reaction to the developing situa-tion was slow; that your subsequent actions – as recorded by your own hand in your personal action log – reveal, in the opinion of this tribunal, that the people's faith and trust in you were misplaced. That, you will be aware, is a most serious finding.

'This Tribunal of the People's Marine Court Judiciary, however, finds that your decision to ignore those seamen who were still alive in the seas around your ship was tactically correct. That fact, that one fact alone, will be reflected as generously as the law permits in the findings and recom-mendations of this court.

'Kapitan Leytenant Andrey Gregor Griem, this is our sentence : One, that your temporary relief of command be confirmed. Two, that you be downrated four hundred places in seniority. Three, that your service record bear formal witness to the findings of this court-martial and that you serve the next four years of your service ashore before being reconsidered for sea duty. Four, that seagoing command in the future will not be reconsidered.

'You may appeal against this last decision not less than five years from this date, should you so wish. Do you have any questions?'

'No, Comrade President,' replied Griem, his voice almost a whisper, his eyes fixed at a spot three inches above the president's head.

'Very well. Then that is all. This court-martial is concluded.'

There was a scraping of chairs as the three men gathered up their papers and left with a curt nod towards Griem's rigid salute.

In Hull, Mr Adams was still giving evidence:

'... to the V P P – the variable-pitch propeller. The bridge was equipped with pitch indicator, Pneumaflex clutch control and an emergency clutch disengage. All these items, of course, were in addition to the traditional electronic and Navad equipment carried on a vessel of this class and were, for the most part, duplicated below on the engine-room console.'

'Indeed,' agreed Armstrong-Carpenter dryly.

'The engine-room console,' continued the speaker portentously, 'was limited, in addition to the above, to temperature and pressure fault indicators which . . .' The voice droned on.

The second day of the formal inquiry into the loss of the Arctic Pilgrim was well into its stride. If the gentlemen of the press were hanging with rather less than razor-edged keenness on the marine architect's every word, then the same and more could be said for the public. Mr Adams's dry, technical broadsides had thinned out the sensation-seekers like grapeshot. The morning lengthened, and gradually, very gradually, Mr Adams worked his way through his pile of notes and jottings.

Finally, on a point few would later remember, he concluded his evidence.

In the sudden silence that followed he gathered up his

papers, bobbed a little bow at the bench and returned to sink back into the sea of anonymous grey-clad solicitors, clerks and witnesses.

Marcus Armstrong-Carpenter laid his fountain pen aside with some relief. He removed his spectacles and placed them carefully in an inside pocket. The thing seemed to be going satisfactorily. Time for a spot of lunch and a small sherry. He tugged a pocket watch from his waistcoat pocket and consulted it long-sightedly.

'This inquiry will now adjourn for one and one half hours for luncheon.' He closed the watch case with a snap, and the court rose.

'Here you are, then, sir – one Ploughman's and a pint of best.'

Martin took a deep, appreciative pull at his beer. After the stuffy legalities of the inquiry it tasted good. He looked around as voices rose in anger.

Over in a corner a middle-aged man was arguing querulously with one of the barmen, his back to Martin Taylor. He was swaying on his feet, and his voice was slurred with drink. In the universal manner adopted by the tolerant clientele of such places, the other lunchtime drinkers merely gave him enough room to sway comfortably and resumed their conversations. The man stumbled, swung round in a complete circle, slopped beer down the front of his overcoat, and peered hazily in the general direction of the bar.

'Oh, God,' Martin muttered, turning away as the drunk tottered towards him.

Martin's arm was jogged violently from behind. He saved his drink, recovered and turned in annoyance, to be met by a blast of beer fumes from Thomas Silvers. His tie was askew as he pawed feebly at Martin's elbow.

'Mr Taylor, isn't it? Fancy seeing you!' he slurred, cocky with drink. 'Here – let me get you something. Barman! Must get my friend a drink. Leas' I can do in return.' Even through the haze of alcohol the bitterness was unmistakable.

'Hello, Mr Silvers. Been to a party, have you?' said Martin, resigning himself to a scene. He noted the once-clean shirt and crumpled suit beneath the overcoat.

'Party? A party? Funeral, more like – *my* funeral. D'you know what they did to me this morning, Mr Taylor?' Silvers swayed closer. 'Two years they gave me, two years suspended – that's what they gave me. Said I was guilty, guilty as hell! No one would listen to me. Said I was guilty.' Bleary eyes focused suddenly. He fumbled some money onto the counter and waved vaguely at the barman. 'Can't remember being drunk before,' he admitted conversationally. 'Long time ago – long time ...'

The barman ignored Silvers's money on the counter. Instead he stepped round to the customers' side of the bar and took Silvers firmly by the elbow. 'Come on, you – outside. You'll cost me my licence, else.'

Silvers tried to wriggle free. His weak mutterings faded as the barman propelled him gently but firmly towards the door.

Marcus Armstrong-Carpenter did not waste much time after lunch. Within minutes he was announcing his intention to call Peter Harold Fielding, formerly mate of the *Arctic Pilgrim*.

Fielding stepped up to the witness stand smartly enough, but he looked awkward, ill at ease in a suit that was too tight and a pair of pale-grey socks that only emphasized the gap between trouser and ankle and the even wider gulf between the sailor and the tailor cut sleekness of the solicitor who rose to examine him : a fisherman out of water, thought Martin.

Travis walked around the solicitors' tables and folded over the top sheet of a file of papers. 'Are you Peter Harold Fielding?'

'That's right.'

'And do you reside at number forty-seven, Parkfield Way, Newington, Hull?'

Fielding nodded.

'I'm sorry?' queried Travis.

'That's where I live. Yes.'

'And you had, I am given to understand, been serving as mate of the M T *Arctic Pilgrim* between January 1973 until the time of your repatriation from Norway in January of this year.'

'Correct.'

'Tell me, Mr Fielding – what certificates do you hold?'

'Skipper's and mate's, both.'

'And when did you first get your mate's certificate, can you tell us that?'

'Nineteen fifty-seven or thereabouts.'

'And you've been at sea how long?'

'Twenty-six, twenty-seven years, near enough.'

'I want to come now directly to that last voyage from Hull. Is it correct that you sailed from Hull at 0600 hours on the morning of January twenty-second this year?'

'That is correct.'

'And you were bound for the Norwegian fishing grounds?'

'Yes. We was going up to the Barents Sea.'

'Was this quite normal? Did you often go to the Barents Sea – in winter?'

'Yeah. On and off. It depended, really. On what the skipper thinks – where the fish are.'

'But you'd been up there before?'

'Oh yeah ...'

'Many times?'

'Lots of times.'

'I am right in saying, am I not, Mr Fielding, that you had some experience of how the *Arctic Pilgrim* behaved in rough weather? Would you be kind enough to tell this court something about this vessel's capability at sea?'

Fielding brushed a strand of lank hair out of his eyes and looked directly across the court at Mr Travis. 'She was a fine ship. To me and to most of the lads, *Pilgrim* was one of the finest ships we had ever signed with.'

The press too began to fill their notebooks with that 'human interest' that had eluded them for so long, while at the head of the chamber Marcus Armstrong-Carpenter, fortified and somewhat mellowed by an excellent lunch washed down by half a bottle of claret, sat back in his high-backed chair, content to let the able Mr Travis guide this simple fisherman where he would. His inquiry, once again, was steering a safe course.

Fielding gave the first clear picture of what it had been like to live and work on the *Arctic Pilgrim* and of how their vessel had operated in some of the least hospitable waters known to man. He gave life to the memory of the *Arctic Pilgrim*. He told a good story that was simple and unvarnished, a story of a happy ship. It should not have been the epitaph to a major casualty in the Lloyds Shipping Register.

Travis let Fielding pick his own words, tell his own story; he sank skilfully into the background as the mate of the *Arctic Pilgrim* plucked the public out of their canvas-backed chairs and took them on a tour of the vessel they had all come to love.

The driver of the station-wagon swerved violently to avoid the drunk who suddenly tottered into the road almost beneath his wheels.

Silvers was walking home. More accurately, he was staggering in roughly the direction of Milton Road.

The drunken assurance of the Brown Bear at lunchtime had been replaced by a haze of alcoholic self-pity as he relived, again and again, the indignity of his court appearance. The charge of theft had been dropped in favour of receiving, and his plea of not guilty had been summarily dismissed in just thirteen minutes. Thirteen minutes, and his hopes and meagre prospects were reduced to a mean legal slur that would stay with him as long as he lived. They had listened attentively to what he had said and then pronounced their verdict: guilty.

He had lost his job, of course: Matthews had called him in for a little chat a fortnight ago to 'explain the position'. Should the case go against him – highly unlikely, of course, but these things had been known to happen – then, regrettably, the department would have no alternative but to ask for his resignation. He understood the delicacy of such matters. A government department must remain above reproach, free of the merest breath of suspicion. A lamb to the last, Silvers had merely nodded.

Grace hadn't been there. Thirteen years they'd been together, but she hadn't been there when it mattered. In court. That was where the greatest pain lay. Thirteen years, thirteen minutes. Thirteen years, thirteen minutes – the pattern made a soundless little tune inside his buzzing head. He thought of all they'd shared, all they'd been through : the money he had saved; the holidays they'd never really been able to afford; the dresses and the little luxuries *he'd* provided while he had gone without. And she hadn't been there.

He'd tell her what he thought of *that*, God yes ! He'd tell her in a moment – when he got home ...

'And what are the worst conditions you have appreciated on the working deck as far as the amount of water coming inboard is concerned?' queried Travis, returning to the point once again.

'During working conditions, d'you mean?'

'Not necessarily. The worst you have ever seen on any one occasion, at any one time?'

'I should think the worst was in seven or eight ...'

'And during that time, Mr Fielding, how much water do you estimate came onto the working deck, the trawl deck, d'you suppose?'

'Hard to say. I –'

'A great deal of water?'

'Not a great deal of water, no. I reckon about ... about three or four feet of water, not more. That's only a guess, mind.'

'Quite so. Was there ever any difficulty in clearing this volume of water from the trawl deck, Mr Fielding?'

'Not that I know of, no. It just sort of ran up the deck and away through the freeing ports.'

'On every occasion? Was there never any blockage, no gear in the way, nothing like that? Think back carefully.'

'No, no there wasn't. I'm sure of that. Not when I was mate, anyway. Part of my job was to keep the trawl deck clear, to make sure there was no loose gear –'

'To prevent just such a blockage, perhaps, Mr Fielding?' Travis interrupted neatly, pencil poised over his notes.

'Nah. I keep telling you – nothing like that. It was just part of the job – proper seamanship. It doesn't do to have gear banging about loose. It can get washed away or do someone an injury.'

'Quite so, Mr Fielding, quite so. No one here is disputing your ability or the manner in which you carried out your many tasks. But let us suppose – purely for the sake of argument – that something did impede the proper flow of water through the freeing ports. Now, if that were to happen, what I am getting at is this: would that heavy envelope of trapped water, that extra weight, would that affect the trim of the vessel and therefore impair her ability to respond to a helm order?'

In the pause before Fielding could reply a woman's voice rang out from the very back of the chamber. The voice was high-pitched, charged with emotion. 'Stop talking bloody rubbish and ask some of the questions *we* want answers to! Freeing ports this and freeing ports that! It's the Russians you want to be asking questions to, the bloody Russians, not that poor sod up there ...' The rest of her outburst was lost in uproar.

Armstrong-Carpenter banged his gavel for order while those seated in front of the woman twisted round or stood up to see who had caused all the trouble. Those beside her, her friends, clapped, called encouragement and, catching her mood of frustration, began calling questions of their own.

Fielding stood forgotten at the witness stand.

Martin and others at the press table rose and tried to catch a glimpse of the troublemaker. It was the spokeswoman of the wives whom Martin had spoken to outside the Graveline offices all those days ago. Other women, familiar faces on the quayside, were clustered nearby. Some were grinning, enjoying the outrage.

'You tell him, love!'

'We're right with you, Jean!'

At the other end of the hall, Marcus Armstrong-Carpenter felt as though he had walked from a Buckingham Palace investiture into a slaughterhouse. It was a nightmare.

In a daze of disbelief he hammered ineffectually with his gavel, calling for order. He had forgotten to switch on the microphone, and his words were lost in the bedlam of sound that had suddenly crashed around him with no more warning than summer thunder. Above the rumble of sound Jean Williams's voice floated strident and clarion clear: 'Why don't you give us wives a chance? Why don't you ask us what *we* bloody think instead of us sitting here listening hour after bloody hour –'

'Order! Order, I say!'

'– or about that letter he brought back with him. You don't want to know about that either, do you, you ... ?'

'Will that woman *sit down*. Ushers – *do something*,' boomed Armstrong-Carpenter, the words magnified at last by the microphone. Black-frocked ushers scurried towards this new disturbance. A sound like machine-gun fire followed Armstrong-Carpenter's last words as, caught in a frenzy of frustration, he hammered close to the microphone with his gavel.

As suddenly as it had begun, the storm that had been Jean Williams blew itself out. She sat down angrily. The ushers hung back, uncertain. The gunfire stopped.

There was silence.

Every eye was drawn to the dais. With an effort Armstrong-Carpenter controlled the wild thumping of his heart and laid the gavel carefully to one side. A tumbler of water appeared suddenly beside him, handed up by the attentive clerk. The chairman raised the glass of water with a hand that shook slightly. He drank and then placed the tumbler carefully beside him, patted his thin lips with a neatly folded handkerchief and tucked the handkerchief back into his pocket. He gained a little time with his little actions. Then:

'In all my years as servant of the Crown, I have *never*,

never before been party to such an outrage. While I am willing to make certain allowances in a case such as this, I will not, I simply cannot, tolerate behaviour which is calculated to undermine the formality of these proceedings. This inquiry stands adjourned for one hour.' His voice ended in a high undignified squeak. He gathered up his papers, rose to his feet and, in unbroken silence, led the way off the dais.

It was quite an exit.

As soon as the party had left, dozens of voices broke out – some raised in anger, others muted in gossip, a few asking questions to the inquiry at large. The press were on their feet, converging on Mrs Williams or heading for the phones at the end of the corridor. With luck they would make the late editions.

It was quiet in the anteroom as the clerk closed the door carefully behind them. Armstrong-Carpenter walked directly to the chair where he had left his briefcase and began putting away his papers. He looked up:

'We will meet here again in –' he consulted his watch – 'forty five minutes.'

'But, sir,' began the clerk, 'might I suggest that in view of –'

'Forty-five minutes,' repeated Armstrong-Carpenter brusquely, snapping shut the lock on his briefcase. He walked rapidly down the private corridor and out into the street.

He must return to the hotel.

He saw nothing of the short walk back to the Central Hotel, and the fact that the sun was shining passed unnoticed. His mind was a blur of questions. What had gone wrong? How had he *allowed* that to happen? In vain he tried to recall the closing moments of Travis's examination, to salvage some clue as to what had triggered off that internal woman's outburst.

Good God, he thought, appalled: she could have wrecked everything – perhaps she still could. He should never have agreed to take the job in the first place. But then ... but then ... he quelled a feeling of near-panic as the vision of that altogether pleasant investiture later in the summer shivered and seemed to fade. No sooner had he fought that fear to near-extinction than another rose to take its place. What, he wondered bleakly, what would the press make out of the disruption? What if it was reported on the radio? Or on television? Surely, surely not on television. His steps clipped faster along the pavement, and presently he pushed through the revolving glass doors at the entrance to his hotel.

Brushing away the smiles and good afternoons of the hotel staff, he took the lift and went to his room deep in thought, his feet hurrying soundlessly along the carpeted corridor. He placed his briefcase on the chair by the window and unbuttoned his jacket. God, how weary he felt! He hung his jacket behind the door and, in shirtsleeves and braces, walked through to the bathroom, where he ran cold water into the hand basin. While the basin filled he looked long and thoughtfully at his own reflection in the mirror. The face he saw looked pale, drawn and startled. The eyes were bloodshot. He turned off the tap and buried his face in the cold water for a long moment. Then he dried his face carefully and returned to his bedroom. With a creak of protesting springs he got up onto the bed and lay full length, hands linked behind his head. He stared unblinking at the ceiling and tried to think clearly and calmly, planning what he should say.

Five minutes later he crossed to the wardrobe and, panting with the exertion, tugged down his heavy suitcase. In one of the elasticized pockets at the back he found the scrap of paper he had placed there three days earlier in the certainty that it would never be needed. He sat on the edge of his bed and stared for a moment at the old-fashioned black telephone on the bedside table. He lifted the receiver.

'Yes, sir? May I help you?'

'I'd like a London number, please,' he said heavily.

'One moment, please, sir.' A moment passed. 'What number would you like, sir?' asked the girl's voice.

'Er ... 01-246 8026.'

'One moment, sir, and I'll connect you.'

The switchboard digested the number with the usual clicks, whirrs and pauses. Presently these gave way to a soft ringing tone.

'Yes?' A man's voice – neutral, businesslike, unwelcoming.

'It's Armstrong-Carpenter calling from Hull. I want to –'

'Wait one –'

'Yes?' Another male voice came on the line almost instantly.

'Hello? It's Armstrong-Carpenter here, in Hull.'

'Yes, Mr Armstrong-Carpenter. What can we do for you?' said the voice with just a suggestion of frost.

'We ... er ... we seem to have hit a bit of a snag, I'm afraid.'

'What sort of snag?' asked the voice sharply.

Armstrong-Carpenter took a deep breath. 'I've had to adjourn the inquiry.'

'You've *what*?'

'I've had to adjourn the inquiry,' he repeated. 'For an hour or so, that's all. I'm sure there's no real problem,' he lied hastily. 'I just felt that, in view of our meeting, I should keep you informed.' There was no response. 'Hello? Are you still there?'

'Yes. Yes – of course I'm still here. It was quite right of you to phone. Quite correct. Why did you adjourn?'

'I didn't have any choice,' explained Armstrong-Carpenter hurriedly. 'It seemed the best thing to do. Everything seemed to be going along smoothly when suddenly one of the women started heckling from the rear of the hall about the Russians.'

'What about the Russians?' asked the voice sharply.

'That they'd been responsible for the sinking or some such and –'

'What nonsense. What utter nonsense,' scoffed the Colonel. 'Tell me exactly what happened.'

Relieved, Armstrong-Carpenter did his best to recollect what he had gathered above the din of interruption. He concluded: 'She kept asking what had happened to some letter from the radio operator which the mate had brought back with him from the vessel. I couldn't catch it all. By that time the thing had got so ... noisy that I judged it prudent to adjourn.'

The voice on the other end of the telephone thanked Armstrong-Carpenter for keeping him informed.

'The thing is, though,' persisted the chairman of the Inquiry, 'what am I going to do now? It would appear that unless those women are given the opportunity to testify there are going to be more ugly scenes, more disturbances. I can't very well ban them *all* from open court. That in itself would only draw attention –'

'All right, then, *let* them give evidence! Let them tell their silly little stories. Not one will stand the light of day on the witness stand.'

'Do you think that's absolutely wise?' queried Armstrong-Carpenter doubtfully. 'What about this letter they keep talking about?'

'Don't you worry – we'll take care of that.'

'But what if –?'

'While you're on the line there's something else I'd like to raise with you. Can you spare a moment?' Mann-Quartermain thought back to the previous afternoon when a classified preview of Dr Dowdall's report on the lifebuoy had landed on his desk. It made disturbing reading. The confounded man had been a little too thorough, had raised too many questions. He'd sent someone down to see him, of course, but still it was all rather awkward. 'In a day or so I expect you'll be turning to the Department's report on that lifebuoy?'

'Yes, indeed. I thought I'd start with –'

'Before you start with anything,' said Mann-Quartermain sharply, 'I'd like you to listen to me for a moment. We've had a glimpse at the report down here, and there are one or two little points I'd like to raise with you ...'

Four minutes later Armstrong-Carpenter replaced the receiver and reached for his jacket. For the second time that day he felt the stirrings of alarm. Already the thing was rolling away from him. Perhaps even now it was beyond his reach.

Mann-Quartermain put down his telephone and gestured to Simon to do the same with the extension. He began filling his pipe with nimble, practised fingers.

'I'm not happy,' he announced. 'The man sounded breathless, jumpy, rattled.'

'I shouldn't worry, sir. He'll settle down again. And he did do the right thing. Phoning.'

'I suppose you're right. Meanwhile, find out about this letter business. And then get hold of our chap in Newcastle – priority.'

A quarter of an hour later the Colonel unlocked a bottom drawer and lifted the dark-blue telephone onto his desk. From the little tray clipped to the underside of the phone he took a Chubb key and unlocked the security clamp on the phone jack-point hidden by the curtain behind his left shoulder. He made the connection, lifted the receiver and then waited for the peremptory 'Line through and checked, sir' from Security two floors below. Then he dialled the Knightsbridge number. He did so with some reluctance.

As usual it took time for the call to be connected internally. It was one of the jokes they had between them. Mann-Quartermain waited, imagining the spools of tape spinning, the computers whirring into action, the voice sensors calibrating and confirming.

'May we talk now?'

'But of course we may talk,' said Stefan Rokoff. 'Always a pleasure, you know that. How may I help you?'

Mann-Quartermain cleared his throat. 'A minor embarrassment up at the inquiry, I'm afraid. One of the women, one of the wives, I believe, started shouting that you people are to blame. An emotional, illogical outburst. Quite unpredictable, I'm afraid. Our man's taken care of it now, of course. I just thought I would keep you informed.'

'Most considerate of you, Francis.' Rokoff sounded quite unperturbed. 'Such things are to be expected at times like these.'

'Bound to be something in the morning papers, I shouldn't wonder.'

Rokoff gave a dry laugh. 'I should be most disappointed if

there wasn't.' He paused. 'Perhaps we should meet to-morrow?'

'I think that would be wise. I might have some more information for you by then.'

'Excellent. Shall we say seven-thirty p.m.? Would that be convenient?'

Mann-Quartermain consulted a slim leather-bound diary. 'I think I can manage that.'

'Fine.' They made their arrangements and then terminated the conversation.

Rokoff pressed the intercom buzzer and spoke briefly to the duty officer of I G(3) and asked for the file on the Northeast to be sent to his desk immediately.

Armstrong-Carpenter resumed his seat in an air of tense expectancy and raked the rows of canvas-backed chairs with what he hoped would be taken as the stern, implacable eye of authority. A cluster of ushers stood like marker buoys near the back rows, ready to pounce at the slightest sign of even a breath drawn in protest.

'Ladies and gentlemen: a short while ago there were those among you who demonstrated that you wished to have the opportunity to address this court – an opportunity that you felt, for some reason, was being withheld from you. Very well. I have decided to afford you that opportunity.'

A ripple ran through the court. A few heads turned to look at the back of the chamber. Armstrong-Carpenter rapped sharply with his gavel, and the noise ran away.

'Those persons wishing to give *evidence* relating to this inquiry – and I emphasize the word "evidence", not hearsay or rumour – will please give their particulars to the court ushers at the termination of today's evidence. It will be my intention to hear that additional business at the outset of tomorrow's hearing. Now –' he hunched forward briskly, administration attended to – 'I am anxious that there should be no further delay. Mr Travis, if you would like to resume your examination of the last witness, should he still be with us, I would be grateful if we could proceed.'

'Indeed, sir,' replied Mr Travis. 'May I recall to the stand Peter Harold Fielding . . .'

Silvers was home.

For the first time in his life he slammed the front door noisily behind him and bawled incoherently for his wife.

There was no answer.

He stood in the hall for a long moment, digesting the silence. Then he struggled out of his heavy overcoat, tried to hook it on its peg, missed, and stepped uncaring over the mound of material into the living room, where he collapsed onto the sofa. Surprisingly, he did not sleep but sat for a long while, marshalling his thoughts and listening to the tick of the clock on the mantelpiece and the silence that proclaimed the absence of the uncaring woman he lived with.

Shortly afterwards he remembered the bottle of sherry in the dining-room cabinet. The sherry they kept for best. For special occasions. Like this one. He chuckled.

An hour later the sherry was finished and he was still alone. His frustration, fuelled by the sherry and the half bottle of vodka he discovered at the back of the cabinet, had built into a towering anger.

Suddenly, a thought struck him – a beautiful, simple thought, dazzling in the brilliance of its simplicity.

He struggled up from his seat and blundered up the narrow staircase to rummage about in the bedside table for his wife's sleeping tablets. There were quite a few in the bottle, he discovered – quite enough to give Grace the fright of her life when she returned home shortly . . .

It was 8 p.m. before Grace Silvers turned the key in the latch. She was later than she had expected to be, much later. She had left their daughter with friends for a few days until all the fuss died down, and Maureen had insisted she stay for supper. Mrs Silvers carried her shopping through to the kitchen, where she saw the note she had left for her husband where she had left it, propped against the tea caddy on the table.

She made herself a pot of tea and carried it through to the living room, where she sat with her feet up for half an hour, watching television. It was 9 p.m. before she went upstairs and found her husband's body sprawled inelegantly across the nylon bedspread, and by then he had been dead one and a quarter hours.

CHAPTER NINE

In Newcastle, Paul Evans glanced at his wristwatch and decided it was time to make a move.

He had just replaced the receiver at the conclusion of the short but explicit conversation with his superior in London, the man he knew simply as 'the Colonel'. That phone call had ordered him south until further notice. Already he had worked out the shortest, most direct route to his target.

Evans drained his coffee at a gulp, dragged a battered suitcase from the top of the wardrobe and began packing. He lived alone in a neat terraced house in the middle of one of the impersonal new developments on the outskirts of Newcastle. It never took him long to prepare and pack for a job. He was a man of few possessions, and his rented house reflected that austerity which, in the services, is taken for efficiency.

Evans was, it is true, a civilian. He was employed and paid, through devious and well-laundered routes, by Consumer Census Surveys Ltd, by the Home Office and, ultimately, by SIS itself. Yet he retained a soldier's contempt for what he still thought of as a 'cushy number', and, if you can ever judge a man by his home and by the books he reads, then Evans also was cold and clinical and empty.

He was a tall, rawboned man going prematurely bald. He kept fit by jogging round the development in a track suit every morning. And if any of his neighbours felt his performance in all weathers a trifle unusual for a man they understood to be a civil servant, they kept their doubts to themselves. The little children did not go near him, either. They found him frightening. There was something about his cold-blooded dedication that discouraged intimacy from children and adults alike.

Evans came downstairs. A few paperbacks littered the living room, and there was a regimental plaque on the wall above the plain three-piece suite. A television set stood alone in the corner. Not much of a home, really – more, almost, a headquarters.

Number 47 Brecon Gardens, Newcastle upon Tyne, was one of SIS's secret operational centres camouflaged from prying eyes not by twigs, bracken and a lick of brown paint but by the trappings of a dull and uniform suburbia. Those operational centres were the brainchild of Colonel Mann-Quartermain himself. In the eighteen months it had taken to establish the 'clinics' (as he called them) he had come to view their existence with a certain proprietorial pride.

The men who worked out of those unremarkable little houses had been chosen by, and were answerable to, Mann-Quartermain alone; their existence was known to very few, their exact location to none save the Colonel and his aide.

Sir Peter Hillmore was unaware of their existence.

Their control and use rested with Mann-Quartermain entirely, and, once he had managed to lose costs and administration elsewhere in the department, they had come to signify a force, an arm of private muscle, which he could flex with rare autonomy.

In the last year he had used his team for a variety of covert and highly illegal purposes within the United Kingdom. In each case work had been carried out with efficiency and without detection – a simple piece of industrial infiltration in Coventry, the arrangement of compromising evidence just prior to a trade-union election in Clydebank, the tracing of the I R A Active Service Unit in Southampton,* the planting of evidence, the disruption of harmful work programmes in Northampton and Filton, the frustration of two quite separate investigations by a Sunday newspaper – all these

* This information was fed back through MI5 and on into the Special Air Service for disposal. The incident of the executed informer found in a Surrey lane had been the nearest Mann-Quartermain's programme had ever come to detection.

activities fell within the Colonel's self-appointed ambit. At the time of the *Arctic Pilgrim* operation there were, in addition to Newcastle, five such bases scattered up and down the country. The others were in Greenock, Manchester, London (Ealing), Cardiff and Salisbury.

Evans's recent interference with the plans and ambitions of Thomas Silvers had been a particularly neat example of the work coming out of the Newcastle 'clinic'.

Paul Maurice Evans was born on 3 September 1939 – a fitting start for a man whose interest, profession, vocation even, was violence, force and persuasion.

His father had been a paratrooper, killed with so many others of Lieutenant-Colonel John Frost's Second Battalion defending the bridge at Arnhem in September 1944, awaiting the help that never came. His father died a hero. The son was to leave the same regiment under rather different circumstances.

Young Evans enlisted in the Parachute Regiment on his twentieth birthday and saw active service in Cyprus. He was commissioned three months after his twenty-third birthday.

An expert shot with both rifle and pistol, Evans was rated an intelligent, efficient platoon commander, outstanding in a competitive and aggressive regiment. Softness, compassion and the tender treatment of prisoners were not among his weaknesses. In 1971 he was posted to Northern Ireland with the rest of the battalion.

Lord Widgery's exhaustive investigation into the less than heroic activities of the First Battalion, the Parachute Regiment, on what later became known as 'Bloody Sunday', 30 January 1972, led to the identification of Evans as one of those whose reckless use of a high-velocity rifle in Glenfada Park could not be excused, far less overlooked. Thirteen civilians died that day. No fewer than four carried rounds fired from Captain Evans's S L R. In each of these four, paraffin tests proved negative. At the inquiry his identity had been protected from outsiders, but that was all. His commanding officer thought he was lucky to escape charges of murder and said so at the court-martial. Evans was quietly discharged, Services No Longer Required.

Civilian life has little use for a man who can jump out of planes and drop a man in his tracks at six hundred metres. Eight months passed in a haze of odd jobs and dead ends. Then he heard over a drink with another ex-soldier that the Home Office was looking for special messengers. Evans went along for an interview. Much to his surprise he went forward on a short-list of four, and a little later he was on the pay-roll.

Evans began to dust himself off. He put himself through a gruelling period of training; he lost weight and smartened up, throwing himself into his new work with a zest that surprised and pleased his employers and did something to wipe away the slur of dismissal from the Army. At the end of six months his position was confirmed, and six months after that Colonel Mann-Quartermain's people caught up with him.

It was the only time the circumstances of his dismissal actually worked in his favour.

By June 1974 Evans had been working for Colonel Mann-Quartermain for a little over a year.

Evans took a final look around his front room, picked up his suitcase, walked round to the garage and unlocked the door. It rolled back with a loud, hollow rumble.

A neighbour in a brown cardigan looked up from his digging. 'Off again, then?'

Evans nodded curtly.

'They don't give you much rest, do they?' said the neighbour.

'It's all go,' replied Evans neutrally, disappearing into the gloom of the garage.

'You know what they say – no peace for the wicked,' said the little man happily, returning to his digging.

Evans slung his case into the back of the car and slid behind the wheel. Two minutes later the lean snout of his yellow Scimitar was nosing hungrily towards Gateshead and the new stretch of motorway that would put him well on his way towards Selby, his destination.

*

Martin awoke refreshed. He had gone to bed early after sending out a few routine letters chasing payment. After taking the dog for a walk and reading the papers, he was one of the first reporters to take his place in the Victoria Gallery. He awaited the morning's hearing with curiosity. It would be interesting to hear just what the redoubtable Mrs Jean Williams would make of her unexpected opportunity to give evidence; nothing Johno had said in any of their innumerable conversations suggested that there was any truth behind Mrs Williams's outburst.

The Gallery filled slowly, and the inquiry started late. When it did it was not Mrs Williams who was called to give evidence by Mr Travis but the mate, Mr Fielding. Martin caught sight of Jean Williams at the back of the court, arms folded across her bosom.

Shortly after twelve-thirty Peter Fielding was dismissed from the witness stand. Mr Marcus Armstrong-Carpenter peered over his spectacles at Mr Travis, the Treasury solicitor, who, so far, had monopolized the proceedings.

'And who is your next witness?' asked Armstrong-Carpenter rhetorically. The list of witnesses had been posted up on a notice board in the Gallery entrance since early morning.

'May it please you, sir,' began Travis, always the correct, strictly formal solicitor, 'I would like now to call upon the wife of one of *Arctic Pilgrim*'s crew – Mrs Jean Hilda Williams. Mrs Williams, will you take the stand, please.'

With much scraping of chairs and 'excuse me's', Jean Williams struggled out of the depths of the closely packed rows and walked briskly to the witness stand, her heels ringing firmly on the parquet floor.

'Are you Jean Hilda Williams?'

'Aye.'

'And do you live at twenty-seven Monkton Drive, Hull?'

'Aye, I do.'

'And how old are you, Mrs Williams?'

There was a short pause. 'Thirty-two.' She looked older.

'And you are, as I understand it, a relative of one of those

123

who sailed on the *Arctic Pilgrim* on January the twenty-second last – is that correct?'

'That's right. Me husband Martin. He sailed as a spare hand aboard *Pilgrim*.'

'Relax, Mrs Williams – no one's here to eat you,' reassured Travis unexpectedly.

Mrs Williams gave a fixed, frozen smile.

'Mrs Williams,' Travis began briskly, 'by your very behaviour yesterday, here in this court, you indicated that there were things you wanted most strongly to say. What information, what evidence, do you have that should, you feel, be properly placed before the attention of this inquiry?'

Armstrong-Carpenter took a slow sip of water without taking his eyes off the witness stand. The two official shorthand writers paused and looked up, pencils poised. The crowded press table was silent and still, eyes and ears straining to catch the syllables that must come soon. A silence lengthened.

'Well. I ...' Mrs Williams faltered, floundering for a moment in the sea of waiting, staring faces. 'I've ... I've heard things, haven't I?' she managed.

'I don't know, Mrs Williams – have you?' countered Travis, eyebrows raised.

'I'm telling you I have, see.'

'What sort of things have you heard, Mrs Williams?'

'About what goes on when our lads go to sea. About our blokes having to carry Royal Navy fellers. Officers and that, for spying on the Russians, and how ...'

There was a murmur in the court. Here was something new, something to write about. The reporters started scribbling.

But Travis, for one, was not about to accept anything at face value, much less the empty ravings of a disturbed and uninformed housewife. 'Now, then, Mrs Williams – just hold on one second. Let's just take all that a little at a time, shall we? Let's start again. What *does* go on when our ... er ... lads go to sea?'

'Well, apart from the fishing and that, they get up to all

sorts, spying for the Russians ... er ... spying on the Russians, I should say ...'

'Spying on the Russians, you say,' repeated Mr Travis, scepticism barely concealed.

Seated in front and a little above the solicitor, Armstrong-Carpenter surreptitiously wiped a shaking hand across a damp forehead. Why, oh why had he ever agreed to allow the woman to give evidence? It had been madness, folly. He had *known* it was unwise, he should never have agreed, never.

'Let me get this quite clear in my mind, Mrs Williams,' Travis was saying. 'You maintain that *our* trawlers – fishing vessels from Britain's merchant navy – are used for intelligence gathering, spying, snooping, call it what you will. Am I hearing you correctly?'

'That's what I'm saying, aye.'

'Why?'

'Pardon me?'

'I asked you why, Mrs Williams? Why? Do you seriously ask this inquiry to accept that our Lords of the Admiralty would entrust matters of naval intelligence into the hands of our merchant fishermen? Do you?'

Mrs Williams's fingers twisted together nervously. 'I wouldn't know about that, I'm sure. I only know what I've been told.'

'Which brings me to my next question, Mrs Williams: Where did you hear this ... this story?'

'The fellers on the quay. On the boats and that ... it's common knowledge.'

'Which men on which vessels, Mrs Williams?'

'I never was one for names ...' she tried.

'I don't need them all, Mrs Williams. Just give me one or two. Who told you that British trawlers were used for spying?'

Mrs Williams's gaze wavered and then dropped to her hands.

'Come, now, Mrs Williams,' insisted Travis as, with growing confidence, he stepped closer, 'you said just now that it was common knowledge down on the docks. "Common knowledge" – those were your very words. I need hardly remind you that Hull is a fish town. I would presume therefore that such a thing would be common knowledge all over town in a matter of hours. Good Lord – one of our trawlers used for spying! It would spread like wildfire! Yet you are unable to give me one name? One solitary name?'

There was a heavy silence.

'All right, then, Mrs Williams – let me make it easy for you: give me the name of one *vessel* whose crew can endorse what you have just said.'

Mrs Williams was still looking down at her hands, fingers twisting together nervously.

Armstrong-Carpenter began to feel a faint stirring of hope, a feeling mingled with gratitude and not a little admiration for the way Travis was discrediting the witness. It might still be all right, it just might.

Travis stepped closer and rested a hand on the walnut rail of the witness stand. 'Mrs Williams, what you have said at this inquiry, both yesterday and today in formal evidence, is extremely serious. You can see that, can't you? It could have the gravest consequences. In simple fairness those allegations must not be left hanging in thin air. They must be authenticated beyond any reasonable doubt or they must be dismissed as hearsay and rumour.'

'I'm telling you the truth! Don't you go calling me a liar!' snapped Mrs Williams.

'It is not a question of lying, Mrs Williams. We have to be *sure*,' insisted Travis wearily. 'This is a factual inquiry. It is concerned with the truth. To arrive at that truth we must deal in facts, Mrs Williams, hard facts. I am afraid that, unless your "evidence" – and I use the term advisedly – unless your *"evidence"* can be authenticated through corroboration by a third party, it must remain invalid. Do I make myself plain?'

Mrs Williams's head lifted, and she looked slowly across the bench of solicitors and their clerks, across the rows of chairs and back, finally, to Mr Travis. Fastening her eyes on a point of his waistcoat, she said, 'I told you – I can't remember the names. All I know is that some of the lads were talking about how they were sick to death of carting the Navy around as if they hadn't got any boats of their own. They said they were sick of being used like a ferry service and it was about bloody time they stopped chasing the Russians and did a bit of fishing instead. That was it – it was about bloody time they stopped chasing the Russians and started after the fish instead. That's what they said,' she concluded.

'They said that, did they?'

'Aye – I'm telling you.'

'But you can't remember who said it or where it was said, I suppose?'

'No, I ... it was in a pub. The King and Crown down by the docks. I remember now.'

'You're sure of that?'

'Aye.'

'But you can't remember anything else? Who was doing the talking? When it was? What vessel he was off, that sort of thing?'

'I'm sorry, no,' she concluded ineffectually.

'I see. Mrs Williams – is there anything else, any other *evidence* you would like to place before this inquiry?' There was an unmistakable air of finality about the way Travis asked the question and folded over his notepad. The message was clear. If Mrs Williams could do no better than that, then she had wasted enough time already.

She shook her head.

Travis turned round to face Armstrong-Carpenter. 'Sir, unless there are any questions you feel ...'

'This inquiry will now adjourn for one hour for luncheon,' announced Armstrong-Carpenter, his voice cracking with relief. He rapped loudly several times with his gavel. Splendid, oh splendid!

Travis turned and walked slowly back to his place while around him the court erupted as the public, solicitors, clerks and reporters poured once more towards the exits. Few spared a glance for the wife of one of *Arctic Pilgrim*'s deckhands. If they had, they might have noticed she was crying.

On the way back from lunch, Martin stopped at the corner for a newspaper. The front page was full of the morning's early evidence.

He was about to throw the paper into a wastebasket when another story caught his eye. Tucked away at the foot of a side column on the front page was a short story headlined 'Fire Death'.

The body of a young woman had been removed by firemen following a blaze in a flat in Parsons Road, Selby. The woman's name was given as Millar – Mrs Frances Millar.

CHAPTER TEN

Martin swung the car off the main road, the village sign slid past the window and he was in Howden, twenty-two miles due west of Hull and the inquiry he had so suddenly left behind.

No one had ever bothered to print postcards of Howden. It was flat, drab and very small – the kind of place you drive through on the way to somewhere else. Martin's somewhere else was Selby. He was going to the scene of a fire, of Mrs Millar's death.

He stopped at the crossroads and bought a map of the surrounding area from the post office. He found Parsons Road on the map and drove on. Presently the first drops of rain began to mottle the windscreen.

Martin parked, got out and looked up and down the road. Fifty yards away a policeman was standing under one of the porches, hands clasped behind his back. Martin pulled his coat closer around him and walked over wetly.

'Afternoon,' he offered, stepping under the porch.

'If you say so,' replied the policeman, the rain dripping off the rim of his helmet in a thin, miserable trickle. He snifted and dabbed at his nose with a damp, miserable handkerchief.

'Nasty old business,' Martin said conversationally.

'Show me one of these that isn't.'

'Been on long, have you?'

The policeman sighed. 'Come on at one. On till eight. Been raining like this since just gone two.' He stood a little straighter, mindful of his weighty responsibilities. 'Can I help you, sir?'

'Press,' replied Martin, groping in an inside pocket for his card. He offered the cellophane envelope to the policeman, who studied it long-sightedly.

'Missed the boat a bit, haven't you? Your lot were here hours ago.'

'Came in from Hull. What happened, anyway?'

'Better check that at the station.'

'Mind if I take a look around? Won't be a moment.'

'Against regulations. No one's allowed in there. Not without the super's say-so.' The policeman stamped his boots and shifted his weight from one foot to another. There was a lot of it to shift.

'Won't take a second – I'll be in and out before you know it,' tried Martin.

The policeman dabbed at his nose with the damp handkerchief and said nothing.

A schoolboy walked alone along the pavement. He glanced curiously over the hedge and ambled down the concrete path towards the two men.

'O K, then – only just you be sharp about it,' said the policeman hurriedly, stepping out into the drizzle to intercept the onlooker. 'Now, then, son – what d'you think you're after?'

The words receded as Martin walked to the front door. He stepped into a small, narrow hallway which gave almost immediately onto a steep staircase. A woman's mauve sweater still hung from a hook on the coatstand, but the glass above was smeared with a film of soot. Martin reached out and the smoke smear came away on his fingers.

The patterned wallpaper, once a garish motif of ducks and windmills, was gashed and torn in places, and three of the black banister rails were splintered; the red carpet on the stairs was stained beyond repair, branded with the tread of heavy, grimy boots. Firemen are not trained to wipe their feet before entering a blazing building.

Martin reached out automatically for the light switch and then stopped the gesture in mid air – there were less stupid ways to risk electrocution. Casting around for a way to sever the gloom, he discovered a small flashlight on the shelf below the coatstand. It still worked. He took the stairs gingerly one at a time.

It was still hot, and Martin started to sweat. He wiped his forehead with a grimy hand and loosened his tie.

He was standing, he reckoned, about halfway down the length of the narrow flat. Ahead he could see the living room, with a small kitchen beyond a pair of frosted-glass doors. Both these rooms seemed to have escaped serious damage. Across the landing was a narrow bathroom. A pair of panty hose was still drying over the bath.

He spent a moment or two confirming the obvious: the fire had been contained almost entirely in the front half of the flat. Specifically, in one room and that part of the hall nearest the road.

The flashlight wavered over the scorched wall and the sticks of burnt, worthless furniture as Martin walked forward, picking his steps with care. To his straining ears the crunch of his footfalls sounded like gunshot, his breathing unnaturally loud in the parched, crackling stillness of this, a charnelhouse.

Martin stepped over the remains of a carpet and entered the front room. This was where the fire had burned at its most incandescent.

Here it was still hotter. The reason was apparent as soon as his flashlight played on the windows: the salvage people had nailed corrugated iron over the opening, trapping the hot air within the room. Martin let the beam sweep round. The light faltered, flickered. He banged the flashlight against his leg with a feeling of sudden panic. He did not need darkness. Not here. The light shone forth with renewed intensity, and Martin let the beam flicker over the room at random.

Ashes, always, everywhere, ashes. A small chest of drawers wrecked by flames, its drawers upended in a corner; a wooden wardrobe badly burned, dresses strewn across the room like leftover fancy-dress rags; tatters of what might once have been curtains dangling forlorn from a buckled strip of plastic curtain rail.

He scattered a pile of debris with his toe and unearthed a

charred paperback. He tossed it aside with a whirr of scorched pages. Over in a corner there was a tray of cosmetics and, over there, part of a dressing gown.

It was eerie and a little frightening to be alone in a hot dark room where someone had just died. Martin began to back towards the door. For a second his thoughts flipped to Suzy, hunched over a nice clean microscope surrounded by pools of warm, friendly light. What would she think if she could see him now, picking over a dead stranger's belongings like some scavenger, looking for ... looking for what?

He had been backing towards the door, with his eyes and the flashlight on the floor at his feet. Just then his toe had caught in something and sent it skimming across the floor in a cloud of ashes. The light caught it again. He bent, and dusted the worst of the filth and soot off the plastic writing case.

He cradled the torch under his arm and flipped the case open.

There was a block of cheap ruled writing paper on one side and the usual two or three sleeves for envelopes on the other. The notepad was blank. Turning to the other side, he poked his fingers into the pocket, and his fingers felt paper. He bent closer. A greeting card of some sort, a bill for the electricity and a postcard from someone in Scotland. He stuffed the bill and the postcard back into the writing case and turned with quickening interest to the greeting card. It was about six inches by five. He turned it over in his hand. By the light of the torch he could just make out the words at the bottom : 'Et Ekte Kort Norge'. Norge! That, at least, he could understand. 'Norge' was for Norway, the *Arctic Pilgrim*'s last landfall.

Martin heard a soft noise.

He froze. There it was again, a slow creaking. Someone was coming up the stairs behind him.

He fumbled guiltily with the writing case, pushed the card deep into a jacket pocket and tossed the writing case aside.

'Oi – you. What're you doing up there? Come on out of

there – you've taken enough liberties with my patience for one afternoon.'

Martin leaned back against the wall, knees trembling like tuning forks. This wandering around in the dark had to stop. He swallowed and then called out loudly, his voice cracking with relief, 'Coming.' He turned the flashlight on again and stepped out into the hall and down the stairs.

He found a Wimpy Bar at the corner of the High Street and ordered some food. He took a bite of his bun and dug out the greeting card from an inside pocket. He smoothed out the corners and placed the card carefully in front of him.

Harry Millar, thought Martin with sudden certainty. Harry Millar had sent this home – Harry Millar, the *Arctic Pilgrim's* efficient radio operator, the 'sparks', the man who had stepped in at a moment's notice.

Martin opened the card. On the right-hand side was a large colourful map of Norway, and on the other the start of a letter.

Martin peered closer at the blocks of neat capitals that ran across the top of the paper. Regulation Marconi.

MY DARLING FRANCES,
   What do you make of this then, pet? I thought maybe Mike's youngest might like it – her Uncle Harry living it up with the Eskimos! Some hope! I only popped ashore for a moment while the medico straps up one of the lads who took a nasty fall. Weather's so-so (*they* say) although I can't say I was sorry to get ashore – I've been throwing everything up ever since we left Hull. One of the blokes has given me some pills he says will do the

The page ended and Martin turned it over impatiently, anxious to read more. Only there was no more. What had happened to the rest of the letter? Martin cast his mind back: it had not been in the writing case, he was sure of it. It had been dark and the flashlight none too bright, certainly, but he was looking specifically for letters, for papers. It was inconceivable that he had missed it; besides, people who bother to keep a writing case at all usually keep the rest of their letters there, too, he reasoned. And she had been a tidy little woman.

A tidy little woman.

The phrase set off a nagging tremor of worry at the back of his mind. Yes, she had been tidy, hadn't she? Table in the kitchen nice and clean and bare, plates and cutlery stacked on the drainer, bathroom towels hung neatly over the rail. A tidy little woman. So what was it that ...?

Martin tried to think. Something was wrong, something was missing, out of place. His eyes were trying to tell his brain they had seen something, if only his pudding of a brain could catch up. Now – think! He'd walked in at the door – and then what? What had he seen? Right – I'm in the hall. Up the stairs. Then what? He had paused and then turned to the right. To the right, yes. That's it, to the right...

He rose, crammed the rest of his cream cake into his mouth, paid at the till and made for the door. Outside he asked the way to the fire station.

It was a modern red brick building set off a ribbon of dual carriageway on the outskirts of the town. Martin pulled in to the side of the wide tarmac forecourt.

At the rear of the yard beside the practice tower he could see a fireman in bright yellow waterproof trousers washing down a pump escape. He walked through the deserted appliance shed.

'Afternoon.'

The fireman looked up from his work. 'Afternoon, Squire.' He bent down again and continued with sponge and bucket, a thickset man in his middle thirties.

'I wonder if you can help ...'

'What's your problem? Cat caught in the trees again?' He shot Martin a gap-toothed smile.

'I'm a reporter – doing a story on that fire over in Parsons Road, the one where the woman was killed.'

'What about it?'

'I'd like a word with one of the firemen who went over there.'

'Which one?'

'Doesn't matter – anyone will do.'

The fireman wiped a bare arm across his forehead. 'I went along, as it happens. Me and my mate were two of the first inside.' He picked up his bucket and sponge and moved round to the front bumper.

Martin moved after him. 'You and your mate: were you the ones who found the body?'

The fireman polished busily. 'That's about the strength of it.'

'I've been inside. Not much left now.'

'Seen worse. She can't have known much about it, anyway.'

'Oh?'

'Nah. Bags of smoke and filth. We had to go in there on our hands and knees. Found her flaked out beside the bed with the room blazing away all round her. First thing we did, of course, was whip her out. Didn't do any good, though. Ambulance said she was a goner before they even loaded her into the vehicle.'

'Was she badly burned?'

'Wouldn't want her mother to see her, if that's what you're getting at. Face and neck, mostly. Poor bugger must have toppled into the flames soon after she passed out.' The fireman concentrated on his work.

'Then what did you do?'

'Me?' The face peered round the orange indicator lamp. 'Went back inside with Tommy and the hose. It was all over in about fifteen minutes. Funny thing, that – the fire was raging away inside her bedroom and down that end of the hall, but the rest of the place was hardly touched.'

'Did you shift things around much – inside the flat and the bedroom, I mean?' asked Martin casually.

Something about his tone made the fireman stop polishing. He stuck his head round the bonnet. 'Not that I know of.' He decided he had said enough. 'Look, chum – I've got work to do, so if it's all the same to you . . .' The head ducked out of sight.

'Yeah. Sure. Many thanks.' Martin sauntered out of the yard.

So if the firemen hadn't upended that dressing table's drawers and scattered Mrs Millar's dresses all over the furniture, who had?

CHAPTER ELEVEN

The 3.38 from King's Cross ran under the dirty glass roof of Hull Central Station two minutes behind schedule. Whistles blew, doors swung open and passengers surged down the platform and out through the ticket barrier until only the old and the laden were left to trickle out of the station and across the forecourt.

One of the laden was a slim, attractive girl with brown eyes, wearing a blue parka and faded jeans.

Suzy looked disappointed, as though she had been looking forward to meeting someone. Bending down, she lifted her heavy suitcase and set off down the platform, the case banging awkwardly against her legs.

Martin Taylor was still four miles west of Hull, and he had known for half an hour that there was not the slightest chance of meeting Suzy off that train.

It was the delay at the police station which had screwed things up, he remembered, taking the Renault into a tight bend at an imprudent fifty-five. Traffic slashed by and there was the blare of a horn as he swerved, straightened up and raced on.

They had kept him hanging about for forty minutes before one of them had deigned to come across and tell him there would be 'no comment' about the fire death, possibly until after the P M was completed but probably – here the sergeant had leaned comfortably across the station counter – probably until after the inquest itself.

Sod them – sod the lot of them, he thought. Because this time he knew he had something. What, he wasn't sure, but it was a lead. And it was all he had been waiting for.

Martin glanced at his watch again, muttered under his breath and bore down on the accelerator.

*

It was not the lateness of the hour that was causing Colonel Mann-Quartermain to frown but the notes he was studying on his desk. He had made them a few short minutes ago, listening intently as Evans reported in by phone.

Sitting there alone in the darkened room, Mann-Quartermain drummed a pencil against the edge of his desk and pondered.

He had learned by experience that it did not do to pry too closely into the activities of his operatives – particularly on an external line. Need-to-know was the rule. Although he had gone along with Evans's sparse, offhand explanation of the accident with Mrs Millar at Selby, the Colonel was not totally satisfied. The good news was that it had been success-ful – they had the letter; the bad news was that the opera-tion had been necessary at all. Mann-Quartermain looked down at his notes and felt again that faint fluttering of unease. Evans disturbed him.

He rose, crossed to the metal filing cabinet by the window and twirled the combination lock with practised fingers. He withdrew a green folder, returned to his desk and settled back to refresh his memory.

If you want to understand a man, then discover his limits, his tolerances, his weaknesses – watch him under pressure. The folder was marked 'Confidential : Evans, Paul Maurice. Psychiatric Evaluation Under Stress'.

Soon after he found Evans the Colonel had sent him on the interrogation phase of the Special Air Service selection course at the foot of the Brecon Beacons at Hereford, on the Welsh border. Although the S A S specializes in such evalua-tions, the Colonel learned very little.

The interrogation phase of the course lasted for an indefi-nite period. Recruits were given one simple instruction : to say and sign nothing. 'Name, rank and serial number' went out with the bolt-action rifle.

It was January. Evans was stripped naked and left alone in a barren Nissen hut. He was denied all sleep and subjected to continuous loud noise and bright light. He lost all sense of time. Half-way through the third day a civilian doctor entered his hut and asked Evans to sign for his kit issue. Evans completely ignored the first person he had seen for three days; in other huts elsewhere in the compound nineteen recruits signed in a blur of relief and exhaustion. They failed the course.

Evans was forced to stand now for hours at a time, his legs spread, his fingertips pressed against the wall, his head hooded. When he moved he was kicked until he stood up. Another day passed.

He was told it was not an exercise at all, that they knew all about *him* and that if he did not sign they would most certainly arrange another of their 'accidents' which would be explained away by the Ministry in due course. That was the only time Evans uttered a sound. From within the black muslin bag came a harsh, muffled laugh.

On the eighth day he was buried underground in a ventilated coffin for twenty-four hours. The coffin was filled with human excrement. Sign, they said when they dug him up, just sign. Sign and it will all stop and the noise, the debasement and the abuse will be replaced by warm clothes, hot food and no hard feelings.

Evans did not sign and he did not speak. He passed the course. Together with a thin, wiry little sergeant from the Royal Ulster Constabulary, he was the only man who did.

The papers that accompanied Evans back to London were sparing in their praise. The subject was 'notably more intro verted' than others on the course, with a highly developed sense of self-reliance and an ability to distance himself from the immediacy of his surroundings. A quiet man, a remorseless man, a dangerous man.

Mann-Quartermain closed the file, reached into his waistcoat for his lighter and stroked the flame into life. His reading of the Evans file had not given him the reassurance he had hoped to find. The man was too ... too ... There was *something* there, something that was not quite right about the man and about this particular operation. Too many loose ends, for one thing. Why had the fire been necessary, necessary at all? He'd been told to get the letter, not litter corpses all over the landscape. But what to do? The Colonel tapped impatiently with his lighter. He could always shift responsibility upwards, of course, call in Sir Peter, tell him what he had been up to, lay his cards on the table.

But what cards, exactly? He answered his own question: cards that would show he had a tiny private army that existed without the knowledge of the head of S I S and that was paid for by the taxpayer; that he had a highly illegal method of operation; that on occasions too numerous to mention he had carefully and with calculated intent diverted funds, manipulated people and orchestrated events in such a manner that the concept of obedience to the orders of a superior had become increasingly blurred. Never mind that he saw it as duty to the England that promptly vanished up its own arsehole along with short hair and National Service – he would be out, out on his ear. So – tell Sir Peter? Cry on his shoulder? With the Retirement Review Board coming up next spring? Hardly.

So what if, even within his own broad terms of reference, this chap Evans was a little ... well ... unorthodox? If it came right down to it, Evans could look after his interests, too.

Mann-Quartermain held the half page of notes over the ashtray and watched it curl into ashes. He tapped the crisp flakes with the bowl of his pipe, and the evidence of the phone call from Evans disintegrated. Completely.

Mann-Quartermain paid for the two drinks and carried them over to their table. He raised his glass to Stefan Rokoff.

'Cheers.' He smiled and rubbed his hands together. 'To business, eh? First – a spot of good news.' Mann-Quartermain pulled his chair a little closer. 'Remember Silvers, the chappie organizing that expedition we'd both find so awkward? Well, he's dead, Stefan – stiff as mutton. An accident, it appears. Silly bugger killed himself last night with an overdose. Body found this morning.'

Rokoff pursed his lips together and nodded silently. His

own people had not been inactive. The information had been in his hands four and a half hours ago.

Mann-Quartermain leaned closer still and lowered his voice. Instinctively Rokoff eased back a little further in his chair.

'Our man at the inquiry's been on the blower again. No problems there either, by all accounts. On my advice he let that woman who'd been on about your lot give evidence this morning.' Mann-Quartermain rubbed his hands together and began patting his pockets for pipe and tobacco. He beamed. 'Did I say "evidence"? Made a bloody fool of herself – a *bloody* fool. Turned out she knew nothing at all.'

Martin drove into the suburbs of Hull and found a welcome in the necklace of amber street lights that beckoned towards the centre of town.

He was tired, his eyes ached, he needed a shave and his clothes reeked of smoke – but there was another sensation too, one he welcomed: that urgent, steady, professional excitement that came with the scent of a good story. He ticked the clues off in his mind: the mystery letter, Mrs Millar and her sudden death in suspicious circumstances just when the chairman of the inquiry had invited wives to give evidence. The ingredients were all there. Now his engine was running and the cogs were beginning to mesh. And, besides, this was personal.

As soon as Suzy heard movement in the flat above she was up the stairs, a newspaper clutched under her arm. They kissed hungrily and then Martin pulled away, placed his hands on her shoulders and steered her towards a chair, his eyes gleaming with excitement. Suzy noticed the smell and the stains on his jacket. He looked awfully tired, she thought.

'Guess what?' he said 'Pilgrim. I think I've found something. Remember that letter I told you about? The one –'

'I've got something, too,' interrupted Suzy.

'Hang on. That letter to a Mrs Millar – what do you mean, you've got something, too?'

Suzy brandished the newspaper that had been crushed between them. 'Have a look at that. Back page.'

'Red Scare Demolished', ran the headline. Beneath this the paper gave brief details of Mrs Williams's testimony and the manner of her dismissal as a witness of any consequence. It was exactly what Martin had expected. He might have written the story himself.

'I know. I was there,' he began impatiently. 'I've just –'

'Not there, stupid. *There* – lower down.'

Martin followed Suzy's pointing finger. 'Holy shit,' he whispered softly.

Hilton Park runs along the western side of Sutton Park Municipal Golf Course, and some of its neat three-bedroom semi-detached houses look across this golf course to Hull Royal Infirmary half a mile away over the pleasant slopes and greens where the wealthy make their deals and take their leisure.

Number 55 was one of these. Martin rang the doorbell and waited, the evening paper held down by his side as the two-tone chimes echoed within. The curtains were drawn, but he could hear the sound of a television from the front room.

A shadow crossed the hall and walked towards the frosted glass of the front door. A dark-haired girl in school uniform opened the door cautiously. She looked about fourteen.

'Yes?' The girl leaned against the door jamb and inspected the visitor. Martin felt uncomfortably aware of his creased parka and scuffed shoes.

'Is your mum in?' he asked.

'Who wants her?'

Martin told her.

'She's having her tea. We're all having our tea.' The words carried reproach.

'Yes, well ... I'm sorry to call at such a bad time, but it is important. Will you tell her that? That it's important?'

The girl left the door and stuck her head inside the sitting room. Presently a large woman in a pink cardigan came out into the hall. She peered nervously at the man on the porch and wiped her hands on her apron.

'What d'you want?' she demanded.

'Mrs Nora Franklin?'

'Yes. That's me. Who are you?'

'Martin Taylor, Mrs Franklin. I'm a reporter. I'd just like to ask you a few –'

'I'm sorry, I've got nothing more to say.' The door began to close.

'Mrs Franklin – please – I wasn't at the inquiry this afternoon, so I don't know anything about how things went or about what you did or didn't say in there. I only know what I've read here this evening.' He held up his folded newspaper. 'All I'm after at this hour of the night is a little background information, a few answers to a few questions. Then I can get off home to my tea too.' He tried a smile that looked as tired as he felt. It struck a chord somewhere.

Mrs Franklin sighed and pushed a hand through her hair. 'You'd better come along in. No use catching your death out there.'

'Many thanks. I won't keep you a moment.' Martin stepped inside and wiped his feet carefully on the doormat.

'Come in here,' she said, holding wide the kitchen door. 'Now, then – what were those questions I wasn't going to let you ask?' Mrs Franklin permitted herself a tight smile.

Martin cleared a space on the kitchen table and smoothed out the newspaper.

'Well, to begin with – how did things go in there this afternoon? At the inquiry?'

'For me, you mean?' Taylor nodded. 'They made me look a right bloody fool if that's what you mean. Jean and me both – a right couple of Charlies.' She gave a harsh little laugh. 'That'll teach me to go putting my oar in.'

'Why did you?'

'Very good question. Why did I? I've been asking myself that ever since I got in. I don't really know. It's just that they made such a job of poor Jean that –'

'You know Jean, then?'

'On and off, so to speak. We're not exactly good friends, but we say hello to each other, that sort of thing.'

'What made you decide to get up there and give evidence? After seeing what happened to Jean you must have known there was a chance you'd get the same sort of treatment.'

The woman made a grimace. 'You were at the inquiry this morning? You saw what happened to Jean? That bloke laid into her with everything but his bare hands. It just didn't seem right, that's all. It could have been any one of a dozen of us up there. She was made to look stupid.'

'He made a fair meal out of you too,' Martin observed candidly. 'Didn't you have anything better than that to go on?' He ran a finger along the printed page. ' " ... no useful purpose served ... a repetition of rumour and half-truth" – that's the chairman speaking – "Mrs Nora Franklin ... blah blah ... another proponent of the kind of disruptive wishful thinking that should never have been allowed to progress as far as the witness stand." Et cetera, et cetera, et cetera. Was it all like that?'

She shrugged. 'Pretty much. All I tried to do was show that Jean wasn't making it all up. There *have* been rumours about the Russians and our blokes and so forth. Now, I wasn't saying, "Come to me and I'll give you chapter and verse." I never said that. What I did say was that someone should look into all these kind of things. There's a lot of naval activity up where *Arctic Pilgrim* vanished. They hold exercises – like the one on at the same time *Arctic Pilgrim* disappeared. Why, the fellas say they can be fishing one minute and then up pop submarines – up and down like whales only yards away.'

Martin pulled the newspaper towards him.

'There's a bit here that does interest me. You're reported as saying, "We've heard stories of blokes carrying stuff aboard – interceptor receivers and such ..." ' He paused and looked up. 'Did you say that?'

The woman stirred uncomfortably.

'I might have done. Why?'

'I'm curious, that's all. Is that what you said?'

'Yes, if you must know.'

'You talked about interceptor receivers?'

'Intercept receivers – yes,' she corrected him.

'O K – intercept receivers. You mentioned them specifically? By name?'

'I told you.'

'Yes – I know. What I'm getting at is, where did *you* get the name from? It's not something you'd pick off the back of a packet of cornflakes.'

She shrugged but said nothing.

'Can you tell me what made you use that name? What are they? I've never heard of them before. Were you asked about that at the inquiry this afternoon?'

'No. No, I wasn't,' she said, turning back to the table. 'I wasn't asked about that, now you come to mention it.'

'Why d'you think that was?' asked Martin.

'Soon as I got up and started in where Jean left off they didn't want to know, did they? I mean, no one was really listening – not really. I was another nutter, wasn't I?'

'Where did you get them from, these intercept receivers?' he asked. 'Did you read about them somewhere?'

She shook her head. 'I think Frank got talking about them one evening when we were chatting to a few of his mates down one of the pubs somewhere. The name just stuck in my mind – it's unusual, like.'

Martin hunched closer. 'Do you ... d'you remember who else was there that night?' he tried.

'I don't know if I should. I mean, what would Frank say? He'd think ...'

Finally, Martin got a name. One name.

It was past eight-thirty before he found Sam Spalding. He had gone to the man's home in Sissons Street, a quiet two-up two-down terrace of cottages that nestled in the shadow of the gas works off Clough Road. There Martin had met Old World courtesy in the shape of a little old lady in worn carpet slippers who had led him into the front room, sat him down in an armchair and given him a cup of sweet

145

tea before he realized Mr Spalding was 'away at the pub'.

With her guest thus anchored, Mrs Enid Spalding had been free to show off a glass cabinet stuffed with badly made Airfix models of ships and galleons with the glue hanging off the spars and decking like gossamer rigging. They had been made by her son, she explained. Before he left home. Martin had admired them greatly, gulped his tea and made for the Three Mariners.

He captured Sam Spalding's attention by the simple ploy of buying him a pint and then steering him away into a quiet corner.

Sam was past retiring age. He had red-rimmed eyes, a bulbous nose and the kind of throat a pint slides down without touching the sides. Martin watched this in awe. He refilled Sam's glass and pulled his chair a little closer.

'I've just come from Sissons Street,' he began.

'Oh aye? You met the wife, then?'

'She told me I'd find you here. Showed me your son's models.'

'She did, did she? Can't stand the bloody things myself – not like the real things at all.' Sam leaned forward. 'Now, when I was a lad, me and my mates used to *carve* them out of wood and whalebone – just like them French buggers used to do a hundred years ago. Now, *there* were models you could be proud of.' He peered into his glass, discovered it was almost full and took a deep swallow. He wiped a hand across his lips and let out a gusty sigh. 'Now, then – what's on your mind?'

Martin leaned his elbows on the table. 'I've been talking to Nora Franklin. Her husband's a friend of yours.'

'Oh, aye,' agreed Sam. 'Old Frankie. Known him since he was a nipper. Good bloke, Frankie. Fine seaman.'

'Did you ever sail with him?'

Sam nodded. 'Back in the late fifties, early sixties, it was. In those days I was mate on any number of boats out of here. I recall he must have shipped with me ... oh, four or five times over the years. Maybe more.'

'Why did you pack it in?'

'Me age, mostly. That and the missus. When the lad left home, like.'

'When was that?'

'A while back. Five or six years, must be. I'm a night watchman down St Andrew's now, four nights a week.'

Both men took another drink.

'I've been covering the *Arctic Pilgrim* inquiry,' said Martin.

Sam nodded. 'Oh, aye?'

'I'm doing a piece on the kind of electronic gear that goes onto some of the fishing boats,' Martin said vaguely. 'Nora told me you and Frank were talking last time you met about some of the stuff you'd seen – intercept receivers I think she called them. Ring a bell?'

Sam drained his glass and set it down carefully on the table. Martin could take a hint along with the best of them.

'Same again?'

'Ta.'

Another trip to the bar. Back Martin came, weaving his way between the crowded tables in the smoke-filled room.

'Cheers.'

'All the best.' Martin set his glass carefully on the table. 'What about those receivers, then, Sam?'

There was a silence while Sam stroked the dry runnel of his throat and stared off into space for a long moment.

'We were having a jar – me, Frankie and a few others. About a year or so back it must have been. In here, too, as it happens. Well, we got chatting about this and that. Frankie had just got back from a trip with Jacko Grogan on *Tinkerbell*. They'd been up Iceland way, near as I recall. Winter it was, too. Not the time to be up there in a –'

'Sam,' Martin interrupted with an impatience born of tiredness, 'you were going to tell me about those receivers.'

'Aye – so I was. Well, I was jawing away with Frankie about this and that, as I say. He told me about his trip, like, so I thought I'd pass on my bit of news.' There was a twinkle in Sam's eye as he tapped the side of his nose with a stained finger. 'I'd been working down the docks, right? Doing just the usual, patrolling the boats that's tied up alongside waiting for a cargo or whatever. Not a lot to do – just make sure there's no one skylarkin' about where they're not supposed to be, you with me?'

Martin nodded.

'Well, pissin' like hell it was that night. I was ducked in out of the rain under a scrap of canvas aboard one of the ships alongside the jetty – *Sovereign* I think her name was. Deep-water boat. Anyway, I was all right there – I could look down on most of the dock and see who was coming and going without getting soaked for me pains. I'd got me torch and a thermos and I was just settling down when this lorry rolls to a stop not twenty yards away beside the gangway to the next ship up the line. Bloke hops out, looks about him a bit furtive like and then signals to his mate who's still in the cab. 'Course, by this time I've killed the old torch and I'm watching to see what happens next.'

'Why were you suspicious?' asked Martin. 'Maybe they –'

'At a quarter past fucking three in the morning? Stroll on ! Besides –' Sam tapped his nose again – 'you get a feeling for things in this game.' He took a pull at his beer. 'And besides all that, I knows it isn't regular : I get *told* if there's to be a special delivery or anything like that. And no one had told me anything. Not a dicky bird ... Where had I got to? ... Anyway, blow me down if *another* bloke doesn't get out, too. They drop the tailboard and all start heavin' and pullin' at this crate they've got up there in the back. It's still pissin' like hell, mind, and those blokes – all dolled up in smart raincoats and that – start struggling up the gangway with that crate for all they're worth. Like the Marx brothers, it was.'

'What'd you do?'

'Me? I waited around a bit and then, when I saw a light up the bridge, I walked across, softly like, and went aboard. I didn't use me torch or anything – I was after a look to see what their game was. I had a squint through the bridge-house windows, and there's these two blokes knocking open this crate and inside there's all this electrical stuff, wiring and that. That's when I heard them talking about these receivers and such – anyway, that's when they had me.'

'What d'you mean?'

'I only saw two blokes inside, right? The crafty buggers had left the third one outside, hadn't they? He got behind me and got me in there so fast me feet didn't touch. Gave the other two a helluva shock. They asked me what the hell I thought I was doing and I asked them the same right off, said I was in charge of dock security and if they didn't have some good answers I'd be calling the police. That set 'em back a bit. They made me wait outside while they had a little natter. Then they had me back inside and told me I was to take their word that it was all on the level: legit. I wasn't to worry, they said.' He snorted.

'What did you say?'

'I called them a bunch of cunts. I needed papers, manifests and such 'fore I'd go along with that – I mean, at half past sodding three in the morning, what would you think?'

'So?'

'So then they had another little natter. This time one of them took me back to the phone at the docks' entrance and made me ring the boss at home.' Sam made a grimace.

'How did that go?'

'He sounded dead rattled. Called me all sorts for getting him up. Then he said I was to do as I was told and that if I wanted to keep my job I wasn't to ask no questions. I didn't know what to make of it.'

'What did you think?'

Sam shrugged. 'Well, I just let 'em get on with it, didn't I?'

'How long did they stay on board after that?' asked Martin.

Sam thought for a while. 'All that day. Most of the next.'

'What did you reckon they were up to?'

'Buggered if I know. I'll tell you one thing, though: that boat belonged to the same people as owned *Pilgrim* – Graveline Trawlers.'

'Did she,' breathed Martin. 'What was she called?'

'*Venturer*. Nine hundred tons, thereabouts.' Sam Spalding looked for a reaction he didn't find. He looked disappointed. 'You know what happened to *Venturer*, don't you?'

'No. No, I don't.'

'Stone me. And you're a reporter? Every time she went anywhere near Norway or wherever, she ran into trouble. Every time. First the Norwegians boarded her, and then it was the Russians – claimed she was infringing fish quotas and such. Yet when they got on board they didn't make for the fish holds or the nets and stuff to check on her catches – they made straight for the bridge and started taking photographs.'

'You're sure about all this?'

'Sure I'm sure. I knew a lot of the lads who worked her. Tell you something else too. Know those blokes I was telling you about on *Venturer*?' Martin nodded. 'Well, early the next morning – about six it was – I thought I'd just see if there's anything they wanted. Know what? When I looked inside the bridge they were all curled up on sleeping bags. And you know something else? The clothes they'd taken off were uniforms. Royal Navy uniforms.'

CHAPTER TWELVE

Martin drove slowly home, his mind full of the day's discoveries. Hercules ambushed him joyfully from behind the kitchen door.

He crouched down and fussed over his puppy as Hercules slobbered enthusiastically down the front of his parka. Martin doled out the usual over-generous helping of meat and biscuits and then, with Hercules snuffling greedily over in a corner, walked through to the bathroom.

Five minutes later, clean-shaven, he was luxuriating in a hot tub. He could feel the tension ooze away. He lay back for a long time and closed his eyes. It hadn't been a bad day, all told. The day's activities ran before his closed eyes like a sequence of photographs: Jean Williams in that hideous coat; Travis, always fiddling with that pencil; Mrs Williams again with her pathetic 'Well, I've heard things, haven't I?'

The fire. The flat. The bedroom and that writing case. The funny little card. The missing pages from inside. Images crowded in: the smell and the feel of the place; Police Constable Plod and the fireman; those rods at the police station; Mrs Nora Franklin and the hunch that had taken him round there; old Sam Spalding and *his* little story. Not a bad day's work, he conceded. Not a bad day's work at all.

The images stayed with him, like a series of photographs. Like a series of photographs. The phrase stayed with him. He stopped scrubbing his toes. A photograph. A photograph. One would exist, for certain. Maybe *Arctic Pilgrim's* radios and antenna gave the game away if you knew what to look for. Martin scrubbed furiously, his thoughts racing ahead and back again to something he had to remember.

He erupted from the bath in a shower of spray and soap-suds, wrapped a towel around his middle and strode through to the living room, leaving a trail of damp footprints. He tossed papers aside on his desk. There'd been something in the ... Here. He had it. He squatted down on the carpet with the newspaper that had first carried the news of *Arctic Pilgrim*'s disappearance. ' "Arctic Pilgrim" Silent: Why?' ran the headline. The paper was dated 11 February, with *Pilgrim* four days behind sched. The front page carried a photograph of the vessel taken on the day she first sailed from Hull decked overall with flags and bunting. A happy photograph taken on a happy day.

He bent low over the newspaper and studied the photograph intently. Now, he thought exultantly, let's be having you ... Thirty seconds later he sat back on his heels in disappointment. Without a comparison it was inconclusive. Sure, he could make out the shape of the various radio masts and antennae on the roof of the bridge superstructure – bright as day, they were. Only where did all that get him? Without some sort of training he would not recognize anything out of the ordinary if he fell over it.

He read the front-page story again. Automatically he turned to the feature on page five and began to read about the 'Floating Hotel'. He remembered reading the story before, and his eyes began to wander down the page.

A short story further down the page excited his interest – a short feature about eleven-year-old twins who had just compiled a photographic record of dockside life as part of their school project.

Martin's mind leaped at the possibilities. Maybe there was a chance after all – an outside chance. He towelled himself dry, ran a comb through his damp hair and pulled on jeans and a polo-neck sweater. He reached for his notebook and made a note of the boys' address.

Martin's luck was beginning to turn.

It had stopped raining, for one thing. The stars had come out and no one was slamming doors in his face. Little things like that always helped, and besides, they don't go in for that sort of thing in the Bonham Terraces of this world.

The twins lived half-way along a pleasant tree-lined avenue of proud, prosperous four-square detached homes in Risholme Carr – the kind that really do put the second garage to proper use. Daddy came to the door smoking a pipe and looked comfortable in an expensive cardigan and carpet slippers.

Martin told him he was doing a follow-up on the project story for the newspaper.

'You'd better come inside,' said Mr Newell in his quiet way, leading the reporter into a spacious drawing room with French windows at one end that presumably overlooked something a trifle more pleasing than the municipal refuse dump.

'This is Mr Taylor, my dear. Mr Taylor – my wife, Amanda.'

She nodded at him.

'Mr Taylor is a reporter, dear. He's come about the boys' project – you know, the one for the school.'

Mrs Newell smiled approvingly.

'Tell me – what exactly do you have in mind?' asked Mr Newell.

'I'm looking for a particular photograph. It just occurred to me that your sons, Richard and Charles, might have the photograph I'm looking for.'

'They take photographs, they don't collect them,' offered Mrs Newell as one explaining the blindingly obvious to a village idiot.

'Indeed . . .' began Martin.

'You must be a little more . . . specific,' said Mr Newell, moving over to stand beside his wife. 'What exactly are you looking for?'

'I'm looking for a photograph of a ship – one ship in particular. I think there's a good chance your sons might have photographed the vessel I'm looking for here in Hull sometime during the past eighteen months.'

'Which ship are you looking for?'

'*Arctic Pilgrim*. The one that's disappeared.'

Mr Newell looked puzzled. 'I've seen her picture a dozen times in the papers since she disappeared. Can't they help you out?'

'The newspapers? All they can come up with is that one picture of *Arctic Pilgrim* taken when she first arrived in Hull back in June 1970. I'm looking for something a little more ... recent.'

'I see. And that picture won't do?'

'I'm afraid not, no.' There was a little pause. 'I wonder – would it be possible to have a brief word with the boys themselves? If I could just –'

'George? They're in bed. It really is a little late for this sort of thing.' Mrs Newell looked up at her husband with maternal concern, and Martin wished her daggers.

Mr Newell took another puff at his pipe and considered. Then, to Martin's surprise, he smiled. 'Oh, I don't see it would do any harm, dear. They'll skin me alive if I tell them someone came round after their precious photographs and I didn't wake them. Would you wait here a second, Mr Taylor? I'll go and dig them out.'

Presently there was the chatter of excited voices and the hurried scuffle of bedroom slippers on the stair carpet.

Two youngsters erupted into the room. Mr Newell made the introductions. 'Mr Taylor – this is Richard. This one here is Charles. Boys, say hello to Mr Taylor.' The two boys stepped forward and shook hands gravely:

'How do you do?' they said, almost in unison.

'Hello,' replied Martin. They looked, as twins often do, almost identical.

It was Charles, the taller and slighter of the two, who spoke first. 'Daddy says you're going to use one of our photographs, is that true?'

'Sssh – he didn't say that,' whispered Richard. 'He only said he *might*, silly.'

'Now, boys, stop that,' ordered Mrs Newell from her throne beside the television. 'Mr Taylor wants to ask you a few simple questions and then you're to go straight back to bed, is that clear?'

The twins pulled faces and dumped themselves on the sofa.

'It struck me that, with all the work you two have done down at the docks, you've probably got a pretty good record of what goes on down there – you know, which ships come and go and so on.'

Charles was nodding rapidly. 'We spent hours and hours down there – at weekends, mostly. Mummy wouldn't let us stay down there after dark because *she* says –'

'Charles!' warned Mrs Newell darkly.

The boy sat back on the sofa and stared at a fixed point somewhere beyond Martin's left ear.

Martin judged it prudent to continue. 'Anyway, I'm working on a special project, too, only mine's about that ship that vanished off the north coast of Norway.'

'The *Arctic Pilgrim*,' piped in Richard promptly. 'She went missing weeks and weeks ago and they haven't found any bodies. Not one. They all drowned together – she sank with all hands.' The words rolled off his tongue with relish.

'That's right – more or less. Only they did find a lifebuoy, didn't they? But you're right – so far no one's been found.' Martin leaned a little closer. 'What I'm looking for, and the reason I've come to see you, is this: I'm looking for a photograph of *Arctic Pilgrim* – one that was taken between the time of her commissioning and her disappearance in February. D'you think you can help?'

The boys looked at each other. Richard gnawed furiously at a fingernail.

'I can't remember,' Richard began. 'You see …'

'Can we show him the Hole, Daddy?' asked Charles.

'Oh, yes, can we? Please?' implored Richard.

Charles turned to Martin with the air of a conspirator. 'That's where we keep all our pictures and the camera and things.' Both boys looked towards their father, the ally of the evening.

'I think that would be all right,' said Mr Newell carefully.

The two boys scrambled off the sofa and raced towards the door. Martin excused himself and followed the twins upstairs. They were waiting for him on the landing.

'It's down here,' directed Charles, darting off down a passage. Martin followed and the boys led him into their bedroom. The beds were rumpled, the walls plastered with photographs of tanks, footballers and warships torn from various magazines. There was a fort in the corner, and toy soldiers lay about in heaps. Martin ducked under a couple of plastic aircraft dangling improbably from lengths of string and followed the two boys to the back of the room.

They stopped outside a small door that had once led to a walk-in cupboard. The door of the cupboard was now daubed with the words 'Private. Keep Out. Trespassers will be Electrocuted.'

'This is the Hole?'

Richard nodded, pushed open the door and turned on a light.

The boys had turned the wardrobe into a tiny darkroom. They had dragged a basin in from somewhere, pushed a hose through a hole in the door and installed makeshift shelves and a work surface round the walls at waist height. There was an antiquated enlarger over by the far wall, and trays for chemicals were laid out neatly to the left of the door.

Richard took down a large blue exercise book from a shelf, and the three of them backed out of the Hole and sat down on one of the rumpled beds. Richard flicked through an index at the back of the book and began reading aloud: ' "*Ancestor* ... *Anvil* ... *Arctic Buzzard* ... *Arctic Tern* ..." ' He stopped. 'Here it is – "*Arctic Pilgrim*" !' he exulted. 'I knew we'd got it. I knew we had !'

'Where? Where? Let me see,' pleaded his brother, bouncing up and down on the bed.

Richard handed over the book and darted into the Hole again. He emerged a moment later clutching a shoebox. 'This is where we keep all the negatives at the moment,' he explained: 'When it's all really finished we're going to mount them properly.' He sat down, lifted the lid and began riffling through the negatives. 'What number was it, Charles?' he asked.

'Two one nine. Thirty-five mill.'

Richard worked one of the little cellophane envelopes out of the box and held it up against the light. 'Here you are,' he said, matter-of-factly. '*Arctic Pilgrim*.'

Martin took the envelope.

'When was this taken, d'you remember?'

Richard leaned across his brother's shoulder and consulted the exercise book. 'October the fifteenth, 1973.'

'You're sure?'

''Course we are,' said Charles, his voice pitched high in indignation. 'It's down in the docket.'

'Do you have a print of this?' asked Martin.

The boys nodded and Richard ducked back into the Hole. 'Here you are.'

Martin bent for a long moment over the glossy print. When finally he straightened up he smiled at the twins. 'Super. Fantastic.'

CHAPTER THIRTEEN

'Straight home, driver – Number Ten,' ordered the Prime Minister as he stepped swiftly into the waiting Rover beside the cloistered entrance to the House of Commons.

'Right away, Prime Minister.' Sid Marran closed the door smartly and bustled round to slip behind the wheel. Now was not the moment to dawdle. Driving for the Prime Minister for the last three years, he had come to recognize the signs : it was Sid this and how's the wife and kids in Poplar? when the Old Man was in a good mood, and Driver this and Driver that when he was not.

The armed police officer seated beside Marran sat a little straighter, adjusted the weight in the holster under his arm and began scanning cars and faces with the intensity of a sergeant of detectives who wants to make inspector. It was just after 3 a.m. and the roads, almost empty of traffic, gleamed slick with rain. As the car swept into Parliament Square Sid Marran heard the whine of the window going up behind him. The Old Man was going to make a phone call.

'Get me Sir Peter Hillmore at his home,' rapped the Prime Minister as the car gathered speed and turned down Parliament Street past the Treasury and the Department of the Environment. God, what a balls-up ! If word got out that Britain and the Soviet Union were co-operating to keep a mutual scandal out of the newspapers, they'd be Going to the Country before the summer was out. Christ, what a shambles ! That was what happened when you let someone who –

'Good morning, Prime Minister,' said Sir Peter, a trifle languidly. He stifled a yawn. Resplendent in turquoise dressing gown, silver hair awry, he had taken the call in the study of his elegant Tudor home outside Dorking. It was not the first time he had been roused from his sleep, but if this call merited the interruption it would be the first time the Prime Minister had troubled him with something that could not properly have waited until a more acceptable hour. Mentally Sir Peter shrugged. It was just another symptom of the disease. Now the tone, if not the yawn, was calculated. The dislike of two powerful men one for the other lay there just below the surface of their professional exchanges, like tin beneath granite.

'I've just this minute left the House. Earlier there was an interesting question from one of the Honourable Members for Hull – I'll read it to you.' There was a pause and Sir Peter could hear the rattle of notes above the surge of an engine. ' "Is there any truth in recent suggestions that Royal Navy personnel have been carried aboard British merchant vessels for covert purposes?" That was the question, Sir Peter.'

There was silence.

'Hello? Are you still there?' demanded the Prime Minister sharply.

'Still here, sir. I was just thinking that –'

'What the hell is happening? I told you to take care of that *Pilgrim* business days ago! Do you have any *idea* of the harm something like this could do?' The most powerful voice in Britain rose to a yelp.

'A fair idea actually, Prime Minister, yes.'

'What? What's that you say?'

'I said –'

'Never mind, never mind. I don't recall asking you for a written report on that trawler business, and that was remiss of me – most remiss. I would like an operations report from you, Sir Peter, at your earliest convenience. Your very earliest.'

'Just as you wish, Prime Minister.' The line went dead. Sir Peter replaced the receiver slowly and glanced at his watch. He sighed. No time like the present. Crossing to the SIS-installed wall safe, he fiddled with the combination, withdrew a bulky folder, sat at his desk and began to compose the report.

He worked on until dawn began to lighten the fine view beyond his study windows. When it was finished, the report emphasized the strategic importance of the Trojan programme and the pressing need for hard intelligence on the SSN-8 missile. Sir Peter harped, too, on the need to stifle public interest in anything as inflammatory as an expedition to search for wreckage, and, lastly, he touched lightly upon the sinking and Soviet involvement. By 6 a.m. he had completed his task. He read it for the third time and then locked it away in his briefcase. He was satisfied. It told the right story. Not the whole story, not even the true story, but a story that would, he felt sure, satisfy the political needs of the Prime Minister.

He frowned. The business of writing the report had focused his attention, not on the irksome foibles of the Prime Minister, but upon the recent actions of his own subordinate, Francis Mann-Quartermain. It was time to do a little checking of his own.

Suzy left early for the university. Martin awoke late and lay alone in bed, catching up with the papers and their coverage of the inquiry while he had been in Selby the previous afternoon.

He turned to the *Hull Daily News*. The lead story was about a row over school meals. The Department of Trade and Industry's inquiry into the loss of the MT *Arctic Pilgrim* had a single column on the front page, and he had to turn inside to pick up details of the day's evidence.

Mrs Jean Williams had been given short shrift by the newspaper. Her allegations, together with those of Mrs Nora Franklin, had been summarily dismissed with just four single-column inches. Maybe, thought Martin, maybe if he could have persuaded old Sam Spalding to give *his* evidence ...

There was, surprisingly, a follow-up – a sequel to the story. One of the Hull MPs, Frank Turpin, had picked up the allegations and repeated them as a parliamentary question that evening in the Commons.

Was there any truth, Turpin had asked, in allegations made at a public inquiry in Hull that Royal Navy personnel had been carried aboard merchant navy trawlers for covert purposes?

In reply [ran the story from the News lobby correspondent in Westminster] the Under Secretary for Defence (Navy), Sir Forbes Pym-Smith, said Royal Navy personnel had been carried aboard Merchant Navy vessels but never for any clandestine purpose. They had been carried, he said, on two separate occasions: once in July 1972 and again in October 1973. On both occasions Junior Officers in the Navigating and Engineering Branches of that Service had been seconded for duty aboard the trawlers to complete complicated testing procedures with Satellite Navigation Equipment for the Admiralty's Hydrographic Department. The duration of each attachment lasted from four to eight weeks.

Martin tossed the paper aside, pulled the phone towards him and dialled the direct number that would carry him through to the new suite of MP offices along the Victoria Embankment, a few paces downstream from Big Ben.

The phone rang just once before it was answered by a gruff male voice. Only the more senior MPs have private secretaries in the new building. Most share a modern office with at least one other member.

'Mr Turpin?'

'Speaking,' confirmed the gruff voice.

Martin introduced himself: '... we met recently over that divers' charter you're working on. I came along to your home one Sunday morning,' he said, blowing hard on the embers of an earlier meeting.

'Oh, aye – I've got you. You're the free-lance laddie. What's on your mind? It'll be a few weeks yet before there's any move on that, you know. These people take their time.'

'I realize that, Mr Turpin. I'm calling about something

161

else. It's to do with the inquiry into the *Arctic Pilgrim*.'
Martin waited.

'What about it?'

'Well ... about your question in the House yesterday, the one you asked Forbes Pym-Smith ...'

'I remember.'

'I was at the inquiry when those allegations were made. Can you tell me –'

'Bloody nonsense,' snorted Turpin.

'Sorry?'

'I said, load of bloody rubbish,' Turpin said bluntly. 'Not a grain o' truth in any of them.'

'Oh?' managed Martin, thinking hard. 'Then why did you ask the question?'

Turpin passed. 'An MP has certain responsibilities towards the people he represents. He must fulfil certain ... ah ... expectations,' he managed, slipping unconsciously into the Westminster dialect of obfuscation. 'I couldn't leave that sort of rumour just ... lying around, not when I had the chance to take it straight to the horse's mouth, so to speak.'

'Pym-Smith?' Martin supplied.

Turpin grunted.

'You did well to get a question in at such short notice,' observed the reporter.

'Luck, laddie – pure luck. I – what do they call it down here? – I "caught the Speaker's eye".' Turpin, Martin recalled, had not been an MP for long.

'Did he say anything else? About those Navy men, I mean?'

'Like what?'

'Oh, I don't know,' replied Martin vaguely. 'Anything. Where they picked up the ship, where they went to exactly – that sort of thing.'

'Only what's in the papers: they went aboard to do tests for the Hydrographic Department – been going on for quite some time too, so I gather.'

'Really? Did he say why they were using trawlers in the first place?'

'I told you. To do tests.'

'Sorry – I meant: why trawlers? Why not minesweepers? Or those Fishery Protection vessels up at Rosyth?'

'Maybe the Navy's running short of boats, I don't know. It seems this gear, this satellite stuff, it has to be tested for long, continuous periods in heavy weather. It's got to be really bad. Place for that? Ask any fisherman – up past the Arctic Circle, where the fish are, you with me? Blows for weeks at a time up there, sometimes months. Cheaper to stick the gear on a boat that's going that way anyway.'

'What is this satellite navigation equipment, anyway?' Martin asked.

'I haven't an idea,' crackled the voice on the phone. 'Some sort of receiver, I shouldn't wonder.'

'Did he say which port they'd used or which companies they'd got to agree to –'

'Look, Mr Taylor. No offence, but if you'll take a piece of friendly advice, why don't you drop it? The sooner these people settle down and forget all about *Pilgrim*, the better for them. I've lived in Hull all me life – that's fifty-five years, near enough. I *know* these people. We've had ships go down before and they'll be going down again – aye, and bigger'n *Pilgrim* they'll be, too. Better for everyone concerned if we just scrub it and look to the future. You try working this up into something it isn't and no one'll thank you. Why don't you just let it go at that, eh?'

Martin chatted for a minute longer, asked a question or two about the divers' charter and then rang off.

He sat looking at his notes while the coffee grew cold at his elbow. Presently he reached for the phone once more.

'Which town, please?'

'Taunton, Somerset.'

'And the name of the people?'

'The Admiralty Hydrographic Department.'

'Wait a moment, please.' There was a short delay. Martin made a note of the number, looked up the exchange and dialled the number. In some office a couple of hundred miles away, a phone began to ring.

'Seven nine hundred.'

'Is that the Admiralty Hydrographic Department?'

'It is. Can I help you?'

'I'd like to speak to someone regarding satellite navigation,' Martin said simply, remembering the time he had worked on a story about C I A activity in London. He had got the information he needed not by digging in dustbins or lurking on street corners but simply by phoning the listed C I A number in Washington and asking for it.

'Is your query private or commercial?' asked the receptionist.

'Er ... commercial.'

'Can you hold on a moment, sir?' There was another short pause.

'Can I help you?' inquired a male voice.

'I'm sure you can. My name is Martin Taylor. I'm a journalist and I'm doing a piece on satellite navigation equipment.'

There was a pause.

'Oh. I'm not at all sure we're supposed to talk to the press directly,' the man began doubtfully. 'These sort of requests should go through the Admiralty in London. Have you been through to them?'

'It's all right,' Martin assured him breezily. 'I'm not after state secrets. As you probably saw in the morning's papers, the Under Secretary talked about the system yesterday in Parliament.'

'Well, no, actually, I ...'

'All I'd really like is a little simple clarification,' Martin explained reasonably. 'I wouldn't be bothering you at all if Pym-Smith hadn't mentioned it.'

'Well ... what is it you want to know?'

'I won't keep you more than a moment or two. I'd just like the chance to catch up on a bit of background.'

'And you're Mr ... ?'

'Taylor. Martin Taylor.'

'Martin ... Taylor ...' Martin could almost see him writing out the letters in neat block capitals.

'What's the stuff supposed to do – is it a new concept?'

'Here at the AHD we don't actually *refer* to it as "stuff", Mr Taylor,' the man rebuked frostily.

'No, of course,' Martin corrected himself. 'What I meant –'

'But, yes, in some ways it *is* a new concept – or at least we like to think so,' continued the man in Taunton. 'I myself helped design the test programme, actually.'

'So you can tell me what it's supposed to do?'

'Well ...' The man paused, considering. 'How familiar are you with the standard computer-based navigational systems currently in general use?'

'You can assume you're talking to a technological idiot,' warned Martin candidly.

The man in far-off Taunton laughed a thin little laugh. 'I see. Well, in a way, that helps. A little knowledge, as they say, is dangerous. Especially in our field, Mr Taylor – especially in computers.' Intellectual superiority thus comfortably established, the man paused, coughed and settled himself, as one about to give a lecture. Perhaps he was.

'In the past, ships' navigators have relied upon a regular series of read-outs relating to the vessel's speed and heading, the wind and the tide and so forth, to determine their position. These reports have, in recent years, taken the shape of regular reports from a simple computer on the ship's bridge. That read-out is readily available at any given moment, but the information it contains is updated only every four, five or six hours – say for argument's sake four or five times in any twenty-four-hour cycle. That system, obviously, has two distinct disadvantages.'

'It has?'

'It has. Firstly, it is a wasteful system in that the navigator has to make a corresponding number of sequential course alterations during that twenty-four-hour period if he is to keep the ship to an accurate course. That is the first consideration. You can readily appreciate, incidentally, that, with the recent increase in the cost of Arab oil and its derivatives, the cost element alone assumes increasing importance.

'Secondly, at the very time when a "fix" is most crucial – at night, during heavy seas, a storm or poor visibility – that traditional method of plotting such information often breaks down in the face of the very conditions it should help overcome and, to some extent, sidestep. Do I make myself clear?'

'So far,' Martin muttered, listening hard.

'Good. Now, then, with the SM-Five Hundred – Satnav – we're hoping to avoid the necessity of a course change after each positional "fix" by a new, integrated system which *continually* reads out the corrected Great Circle course to any selected location.' He can't be making this up, Martin thought bleakly. He has to be telling the truth. 'With this information, beamed off a slave satellite and with a continuous, updated display on the bridge monitor, set and drift can be measured in such a way that automatic compensatory procedures can be fed into the standard navigational package, not just four times a day but continuously, twenty-four hours a day, in all weather conditions, providing a positional notation accurate to within two one-hundredths NM – depending on the ship's latitude, of course.'

'NM?' asked Martin. Perhaps this was what Sam Spalding had seen. Or thought he had seen.

'NM? Nautical miles, of course.'

'Of course. Stupid of me.' Back to the bottom of the class. Martin began to nourish a worm of dislike for the smug dismembered voice on the end of the phone. 'I'm surprised no one thought it up sooner,' he said deliberately.

'Sooner? Do you realize, Mr Taylor, just how *long* it has taken to perfect such a system?' The voice climbed to a satisfying squeak.

'I'm afraid I don't. Not my field, you see. When do you think the tests will be over?'

'Impossible to say,' rapped the man impatiently. He had wasted enough time with this caller. The man had no grasp of the complexities involved, no grasp at all. 'It's quite impossible. At a conservative estimate – two years, two and a half, something of that magnitude. Now, if you don't mind –'

'As long as that?' interrupted Martin, genuinely surprised.

The voice sighed. 'You have to understand what's involved. We're talking about a very exact science. Fox Electronics would consider it their major project, not just of the year but quite possibly of the decade. The sort of slapdash standards that pass muster in other professions simply won't do in this kind of highly specialized scientific work.'

'But a five-year period of tests? Isn't that a little –'

'What five-year period?'

Martin went very still.

'I ... I rather gathered tests had already been going on for quite some time.'

'Your information, like so much the press chooses to print, Mr Taylor, is wrong, quite wrong. As I believe I already mentioned, I have been responsible for much of the test programme for the Admiralty, and ... let me see ...' Pages were turned over. 'Yes, here we are – I completed outline programme proposals on ... March the eighteenth of this year.'

Martin scribbled furiously. 'So the tests would only have started, what – three months ago? At the outside?' he coaxed.

'They started on April the tenth.'

'Are many ships involved with this testing?' asked Martin, racing against the clock of the man's patience.

'At the moment there's just the one attached to Coastal Survey,' the voice admitted. 'Look – I really think all these questions could be better answered by the Admiralty. I'm not supposed to –'

'That would be H M S *Discovery*, I suppose?' Martin hazarded, pressing on with a name plucked at random from his memory.

The corny old ruse worked. '*Discovery*? I don't believe so. H M S *Beagle* is –'

'Oh, yes, *Beagle*,' Martin corrected. 'Has she –'

But this time it was he who was interrupted. 'I'm sorry – I can't talk to you any longer, Mr Taylor. I really must get on. Good morning.'

'Fine. Can you just confirm that only Royal Navy –'

Click.

Martin replaced the receiver slowly and called the man a name which had precious little to do with positional notations. He leaned back in his chair, linked his hands behind his head and stared at the ceiling.

He dialled Westminster once more.

'Mr Turpin?'

'Speaking.'

'Me again, Mr Turpin – Martin Taylor.'

'Oh, aye?'

'Sorry to trouble you again, but there's something I forgot to check with you.' Martin took a deep breath. 'Did Pym-Smith actually *say* the Royal Navy had been doing those tests on trawlers for quite a while, or am I imagining things?' He kept his voice deliberately casual. He waited an age for Turpin to reply: 'Mr Turpin?'

'Aye, that's what he said, more or less.' Turpin paused. 'You're not still chasing around after that, for God's sake?'

'Please, Mr Turpin – do you remember *exactly* what was said?'

'Hang on a moment – I've got it written down here some-where.' The phone went down with a crash. Martin could hear a faint banging about in the background. 'Here we are – found it. Now, then: I asked him how long they've been doing this going to sea on trawlers, and he said a couple of years. He said the Royal Navy brought in commercial Satnav sets from just the one source, Fox Electronics, and they'd been testing them for a couple of years or so.'

'Thanks very much indeed, Mr Turpin. I'm very grateful. I'll ... er ... get back to you on that divers' thing before too long.'

'Aye – you do that.'

'Fine. So long for now.'

Now Martin went through the directory inquiries again and then to Fox Electronics. The call put the matter beyond doubt. The Royal Navy had taken delivery of Satnav equipment for the very first time on 10 April.

Sir Forbes Pym-Smith, Under Secretary for Defence (Navy), had been lying.

CHAPTER FOURTEEN

At the top of the curve of stone stairs Martin turned to his right, crossed a small landing and pushed open two heavy oak doors.

The annexe to Hull's modern Reference Library is not, strictly speaking, a room at all. It is a chamber – a high, graceful place with a domed ceiling and an ornate gallery which runs above head height almost the entire circumference of the library.

Martin walked softly towards the woman at the inquiries counter, his eyes sweeping along the loaded shelves and the long polished refectory tables with their comfortable, worn leather-backed chairs. Someone, he noticed, had placed a vase of wild roses where they would catch the light from the high windows, and the place smelled agreeably of old books and furniture polish.

The place was almost deserted. An old man sat hunched over the library's bound edition of the morning's papers, and two girls in school uniform were working together at another table over by the window.

The elderly librarian looked up at his approach. 'May I help you?' she inquired pleasantly. The rose-picker for a certainty, Martin guessed.

'You run a beautiful library.'

The woman's cheeks dimpled with pleasure. 'Isn't it lovely? Early Victorian, you know.'

'Really? Someone knew his business.'

The woman smiled again. 'I rather think he did. What can I do for you?'

Martin cleared his throat. 'I'm not sure you'll be able to help me,' he began. 'I'm after something on warfare – electronic warfare.'

'Electronic warfare,' said the gentle lady naturally. 'Let me see, now.' She bent over a little tray of index cards and began flicking through them with nimble, practised fingers. 'No, I'm sorry – nothing on that specifically.' She tapped the tip of her finger against pearly white teeth. 'Have you tried looking under *Jane's*, *SIPRI* or *Brassey's Defence Yearbook*?'

'*SIPRI*?'

She took pity on him. 'Come along with me – I'll show you.' She edged from behind her counter and led Martin away into the depths of the reference section.

Presently he smiled his thanks and carried a pile of books over to one of the old oak tables and began reading:

When the Second World War drew to a close the Russian Navy had virtually ceased to exist. It had been decimated. Half her surface ships had been sunk, many of her submarines had been lost, her shipyards and building slips were smouldering ruins and 400,000 of her ratings had been swallowed up fighting the costly land battles that should have been left to the infantry.

The Navy that survived was poorly officered, badly trained and ill-equipped.

Yet, Phoenix-like, it was to rise from the ashes. The Architect of that resurrection was Rear Admiral, soon to be Admiral-of-the-Fleet, Sergei Gorshkov. He was appointed Commander-in-Chief, Soviet Fleet, on January 5th, 1956. He holds that position today.

Under his Command the Soviet Navy embarked on a programme of rapid expansion …

While the Western World consigned the distasteful weapons of war to the junk yard, the Russians built …

Martin tugged his notebook out of his pocket and patted his jacket for a pencil. He failed to find one. He walked across to the two schoolgirls and, amid much blushing and giggling, borrowed one from them. He returned to his seat and began making notes.

… Slowly the Soviet Navy changed from being a puny, coast defence force into an ocean-going attack fleet of awesome size.

The Soviet Navy of the 1950s stayed in home waters. By 1960 it was venturing occasionally into the Norwegian Sea and Arctic Ocean; by the mid 1960s – shortly after the Cuban fiasco – its flag was a commonplace in the western Atlantic and by 1968 this was coupled to a strong Soviet presence in the Mediterranean. Today that presence is worldwide.

Gorshkov still commands all five Soviet fleets – the Caspian Flotilla and the ships of the Pacific, Black Sea, Baltic and Northern Fleets.

This last, the Northern Fleet, is the most important. Based around the ice-free inland port of Murmansk, it is the only one with unrestricted access to the vastness of the Atlantic Ocean.

On impulse Martin borrowed an atlas and turned to the map of northern Europe. He spent some minutes poring over that, estimating distance by measuring the end of his borrowed pencil against the scale in the margin.

Presently he replaced the atlas and turned back to his reading:

... whereas at the end of World War II the Northern Fleet was the weakest, today it is Russia's strongest – the point of her sabre.

Under Admiral of the Fleet Yegorov's direct command lie eight hundred warships – three quarters of Russia's Second Strike capability.

Sailing out of Severomorsk, the Fleet HQ on the eastern side of the Kola Peninsula, and Polyarny, the submarine base on the opposite western bank, come seventy-five nuclear-missile-firing submarines,* eighty-three conventional submarines, ten Cruisers, twenty-five Destroyers and fifty-seven Escorts of various sizes. These are protected in turn by three hundred and forty combat aircraft dispersed among sixteen hard-surfaced, all-weather airfields together with two Mechanised Divisions and one Naval Infantry Brigade of Marines with, on permanent stand-by, seven combat-ready Airborne Divisions of seven thousand men each.

* One new nuclear submarine is launched from the yards of Severodvinsk, Leningrad, Sudomekh and Gorki each month.

The Headquarters of the Russian Northern Fleet and the growing number of 'defensive' land forces deployed on the Kola Peninsula lie no more than seventy miles to the east of the northernmost member of NATO – Norway.

'Excuse me ...'

Martin looked up, startled. 'Er ... yes? What is it?'

It was the taller of the two girls who had been working over by the window. 'We've got to go now. Have you finished with my pencil?'

'Oh. Yes – of course.'

It was obvious that he hadn't. The girl hesitated.

'Doesn't matter – you can keep it.' She smiled brightly, turned on her heel in a spray of rich chestnut hair and hurried after her friend.

While western eyes have watched with alarm the growth of Soviet military strength on the northern flank, any scenario of a Russian land invasion which began in northern Europe has remained unchanged; it has always included the assumption that Norway alone would never be able to halt a Russian advance.

Consequently, Norway's internal Defence Policy, formulated over twenty years, ago, has been two-fold – on the one hand active, defensive, on the other passive, diplomatic.

Militarily, Norway has prepared for a guerilla war in which her 330,000 Home Guard and Reservists working in six-man cells and armed with conventional weapons augmented by hand-held anti-tank and anti-aircraft missiles, harass and slow down the Russian advance until help arrives from her NATO partners.

On the diplomatic front she has evolved a policy of co-existence towards the USSR aimed at ensuring that nothing which happens in Norway can give Russia the reason – or the excuse – to mount an invasion. To this end Norway has refused to allow NATO troops or nuclear weapons to be stationed permanently on her soil.

It has been left to Russia's Northern Fleet to personify what NATO sees as the New Russian Threat but it has been Norway's dogged refusal to allow outside help in time of peace that has forced NATO commanders to concern themselves less with the line-up of conventional forces on the flat tank plains of Central Europe and more with the balance of power to the east of Norway's northern frontier.

Martin stretched, sat back and stared at the window in front of him, trying to absorb what he was flicking through so rapidly. The old man had put the papers away, and Martin was alone at the tables. The lights had been switched on since he had last looked up.

Will Norway be able to contain a Russian advance if and when it comes? Can she hold the line or has she, as Edward Heath suggested in 1971, already begun to 'lapse into neutrality'? A neutrality in which even her kind of mountainous hit-and-run warfare becomes invalidated by the tactical and numerical superiority of a well-prepared enemy? It is questions like these which have brought NATO's Commanders back to the numbers game with a new and a feverish intensity.

Today the business of counting heads, gauging strengths, plotting movement and deployment has assumed critical importance.

In Nelson's day they looked for the masts, counted the guns, the lines of advancing infantry. Then, as the paraphernalia of war moved back over the curve of the horizon, they relied on the spyglass, the telescope. In the Second World War the radio transmitter sent messages over the horizon to warn of enemy strengths and intentions; radar plotted the movement of ships and aircraft far beyond the sight of man. Since those relatively simple times Electronics – and thus Electronic Warfare – have moved out of their infancy. Those tell-tale signs of movement and deployment which just might be the prelude to invasion are likely to be detected not by the eyes of the lookout but by the ears of the highly trained technicians who man the listening stations contained within those low, grey little huts that litter a dozen different frontiers with the Soviet Union.

Instead of looking for masts, guns and smoke these men listen for the diadidah of Soviet Army radiograms in code or in clear; a careless voice report about ration strengths from Company to Battalion; the buzzing of air-defence radar and the bleeps of missile telemetry. The weapons of war rely on electronic pulses for initiation, control and, in the case of missiles, alteration to course in flight. The use of those electronics to one's own advantage, the degrading of hostile radar, the disruption, distortion, interception and 'bending' of enemy communications, the decoying of enemy aircraft and missiles – all this has become the battlefield currency of the 1970s.

In 1974, the West spent £900m on Electronic Warfare ...

'The library closes in ten minutes.'
Martin looked up once more.
'Ten minutes. I'm closing the library in ten minutes.'
'Fine.'

Electronic Warfare can be divided into three phases: Electronic Support Measures, known as ESM; Electronic Counter Measures, ECM; and Electronic Counter-Counter Measures, ECCM.

ESM can be taken to include all actions taken to search for, intercept, locate and record, enemy communications – known as COMINT – and also the gathering together of electronic information relating to enemy sensors and weapons' systems which in turn go towards the compilation of a computer-fed 'library' of identified enemy signals, call-signs, radar emissions and missile-initiation pulse widths upon which the initiator can mount a programme of effective counter measures ...

Martin ran his fingers through his hair and flicked through the pages he had yet to read. They went on and on. He looked at his notes, rubbed his eyes, stretched and yawned. Missile initiation, ELINT, COMINT, measure, countermeasure, counter-countermeasure ... He flipped the book open again and read a little more at random:

ECM is the action taken to prevent or reduce an enemy's effective use of the electro-magnetic spectrum. This can be done by imitation, by deception or by jamming. Jamming takes three main forms – Broadband, Spot and Deception Jamming. Broadband Jamming can be described as the 'brute force' method whereby the Operator jams over a wide frequency and thus creates an abundance of traffic which clutters the opposition's electronic picture and so makes it difficult if not impossible to pick up the relevant echo ...

His eyes began to wander over the page. This wasn't a subject for tired, underpaid reporters – it was a religion, a cult, a subterranean civilization all of its own. He leaned forward, and then his eyes were caught suddenly by a few lines of copy beside a small photograph on a page he had yet to read properly.

... the prime requirements of ELINT fall into three main functional categories ... receives a broadband response by the use of broadly-tuned circuits ... the simplest is the wide open or 'furrow' Intercept Receiver (see picture right) which can only be used when the telemetry ...

Martin's heart pounded against his ribs.

The density of the electromagnetic environment on the modern battlefield has greatly increased in recent years. The large warship of today is acutely vulnerable to surface-to-surface missiles; its survival depends upon the timely detection of impending attack. The need therefore for a passive tactical warner is paramount. Priorities are high intercept probability coupled to minimum time loss between detection and identification. The build-up of such Intelligence is now considered a strategic necessity; Intelligence thus gained may be the only method of ascertaining the likely weapons systems used by a potential hostile. The planning of effective counter-measures, therefore, depends upon this tactical warning system.

He studied the picture closely, his excitement mounting. So – maybe old Sam Spalding hadn't been making it all up after all. And if *Venturer* had been carrying these things, these intercept receivers, then why not *Arctic Pilgrim*? They were owned by the same firm, they sailed to the same sensitive areas. Martin sat back, thinking furiously. Johno.

Johno hadn't told him because Johno, tucked away in his engine room – Johno hadn't known! No one knew! Oh, the skipper, sure – he'd have to know – and the owners, of course. But not the crew, not the other thirty-five poor sods who got roped in to Harding's fun and games without the option. Martin thought suddenly of that crowded dockside office early that first morning, and of the stale, crowded atmosphere and a harassed Mr Harding leaning on his papers and barking at Martin's unwelcome arrival. He'd known then, the bastard! Right. And if Sam Spalding wouldn't go out in front of that bloody inquiry and ask a few straight questions about *Pilgrim*'s antenna array, there was nothing stopping *him* from – Wait a minute! Antenna array. That missing letter! What was it Shotter had said? 'Talk is he wasn't too happy about something or other' – isn't that what he'd said? And Millar had been the radio operator! A new hand – the one man who ...

Martin started banging random thoughts down on paper in an urgent, untidy squiggle. Then he began taking a series of photocopies of various E W equipment. He paid for the copies and walked rapidly homeward. Supper first, and then another little chat with Sam Spalding.

And after that – Harding. Mr bloody Harding.

CHAPTER FIFTEEN

Back in the flat Martin kicked off his shoes, loosened his tie, padded over to the bed and lay down.

Linking his hands behind his head, he closed his eyes and forced himself to think rationally and dispassionately about the sequence of events he had stumbled into since he walked out of the inquiry and discovered that Frances Millar had died in a fire.

Fifteen minutes later, as his thoughts began to coalesce, he went over to his desk by the window and pulled the typewriter towards him. He loaded the machine automatically and sat for a moment, fingers poised above the keys as though reluctant to turn suspicion into the reality of cold print.

Then, slowly, he began to type:

1. There *was* a letter from the radio operator, Harry Millar. How important that was is now uncertain because:
   (a) the recipient is dead, killed in a fire;
   (b) relevant page of letter is missing.

But Millar was the new man. He would have had little choice but to go along with E W mission. Maybe he didn't want to. Maybe he hinted at same to wife in letter?

Martin paused before adding another line: 'Flat could have been searched before fire took hold.'

There was another, longer, pause.

Martin reread what he had typed, took the paper out of the machine and then sat over it a while longer. Finally he took a fountain pen from the top drawer and wrote in longhand: 'About to give evidence at inquiry???' He drew a circle around this and linked it to the word 'recipient'. He did the same with 'Top floor front mainly : too localized?' linking that to the one word 'fire'. 'Was fire started deliberately as cover? Does this make Frances Millar's death murder ? ? ?'

He laid that sheet of paper aside and reached for another.

2. Between commissioning in 1970 and January 1974 antenna configuration changes on bridge superstructure. Photographs. Change in role – a change in use?

3. Jean Williams and Nora Franklin said RN had been on trawlers. Correct.

Ministry of Defence has admitted RN have been embarked but only in July 1972 and October 1973 and only for 'civil and peaceful purposes', i.e. to complete SATNAV tests.

Untrue. SATNAV not off Government workbench. Major MOD cock-up. Too structured to be simple mistake.

Nightwatchman saw RN loading cases onto *Pilgrim*'s sister ship while in employ of same company. That was in February–March 1973. Sworn to secrecy by Managing Director who authorized late-night loading of stores, overheard phrase 'Intercept Receiver'. Later picked out Intercept Receiver pix from Library photostats.

Jane's lists Intercept Receiver as suitable Electronic Warfare recording device; own superficial research shows suitable Electronic Warfare climate exists off Northern Norway. Therefore hard evidence to suggest trawlers *have* carried electronic equipment for intelligence-gathering purposes.

Martin pushed the typewriter away, took his notes over to the bed, sat down on a corner and read through them once more.

They were fine – as far as they went. But, he realized, he was still no nearer finding out what had happened to the *Arctic Pilgrim*. Suppositions and clever deductions gave rise to tantalizing possibilities, but that was all. He still had no hard *facts*.

He mashed his neatly typed notes into a ball and lobbed them into the wastepaper basket. His eyes flicked to the clock on the kitchen wall. Enough time wasted. He had done his thinking, his browsing in the library. Now he tugged on his shoes, scooped up the photocopies and the photo of *Arctic Pilgrim*, reached for his coat and slammed the front door behind him with a crash.

Martin drove past the Hessle Road post office, turned down West Dock Avenue and right again into West Dock Street, with Hercules sitting beside him on the passenger seat. Then down the awkward narrow road that led to the underpass beneath the railway line and up to the mini-roundabout on the other side.

He drove round to the car park behind Graveline Trawlers, reversed neatly in to a small gap between a Rover 2000 and a yellow Scimitar and strode briskly round to the front of the building with more confidence in each step than he actually felt. Reality in these surroundings had to do with the price of cod, with fishing quotas – not intercept receivers and the Russian Menace. Martin gripped his photographs, his evidence, a little harder.

Sandra Harris was sitting at her desk, typing. She looked up as the door opened and for a moment or two failed to recognize Martin as he stepped towards her. He noticed a tall, rawboned man in his early thirties with unfashionably short hair sitting on a chair beside Harding's office. Martin nodded pleasantly to him and then turned his smile on the girl.

'Hello. How're you?'

'Fine now, thanks.' She managed a smile. Her cheeks looked rounder, less pinched.

'Good. I'm glad to hear it. The boss in?'

'He's tied up at the moment.'

'Will you buzz through and tell him I'm here? I've got some photographs I'd like him to look at.'

'Mr Harding did say –'

Martin felt his patience slipping away. 'Just do it, will you? It's important.' The girl looked startled. Martin remembered the man by the door. 'Look, I hope you don't mind waiting. It *is* important.'

'Help yourself.' The man shrugged.

The girl paused and then bent to the intercom.

'Yes, Sandra?'

'Sorry to trouble you, Mr Harding. There's a gentleman here, a Mr Taylor. He says he must talk to you.'

'I can't talk to him now, Sandra. Tell him to make –'

'I know, sir. Only he's most insistent. He says it's urgent. About some photographs he wants you to see.'

'I don't care. I'm busy. Tell him to call back and make an appointment like anyone else,' snapped the voice. The line went dead.

Sandra Harris turned towards Martin and shrugged. 'You heard what he said. If you'd like to –' But she was talking to herself. Martin was moving past her towards Harding's office.

'You can't go in there –' began the girl, jumping to her feet as Martin turned the heavy handle and pushed into the room.

Harding was sitting at his desk in his shirtsleeves, working on some papers. 'What the hell d'you think you're – ?'

'I'm sorry, Mr Harding – I couldn't stop him. He just –'

'Sorry to burst in on you like this, Mr Harding,' Martin began evenly, 'but if I waited until you were ready to see me I'd be waiting at Christmas. I've got to talk to you today – now. It's to do with *Arctic Pilgrim.*'

Harding glowered and stubbed out his cigarette, grinding it to shreds against the side of the glass ashtray. 'Bit old hat, that, isn't it? All right, Sandra, you can leave him with me. We won't be long.'

'Why doesn't she stay? After all, she's involved – we're all involved.'

Harding glared up at him from under thick eyebrows. 'Don't bugger me about, lad – get to the point. You've wasted enough time already.'

Martin took a deep breath. 'Now, there,' he said, 'there I agree with you. About five months in all, I should think, what with the search and everything.'

Harding reached across his desk for the phone. 'I never did like riddles,' he remarked. 'This has gone on long enough. I'm calling up a few of the lads. I wouldn't advise you to be around when they arrive.' Fat fingers worked at the face of the phone.

Martin stepped up to the desk and stood over Harding. 'The reason for all this pissing about, Mr Harding, is this,' he said softly. He dug under his coat for the twins' photograph of *Arctic Pilgrim*. 'I'd like you to tell me, if you can spare the time, just what the hell one of *your* ships – one of your trawlers – was doing carrying *this* little lot.' He slid the glossy photograph onto Harding's desk and pushed it under his nose. '*That's* what I'm on about, Mr Harding – intercept receivers. Intercept bloody receivers.'

Harding's fingers forgot about dialling.

He reached out slowly for the photograph, and his head sank closer to the desk. Martin reached out, plucked the phone from his limp hand and slammed it back onto the cradle.

'Where the hell did you get this?' whispered Harding, his head sunk over the photograph.

Martin pushed another photograph under the nose of the managing director of Graveline Trawlers; it had been taken in June 1970 by the local paper. 'Now you see it – now you don't,' he murmured conversationally. 'What I'd like to know, Mr Harding, is, what made you go in for a spot of the old intelligence gathering in the first place? A generous grant from the Min. of Ag. and Fish? A little help with the bills when things got a bit rough?'

Harding moved the photographs this way and that. 'Where did you get all this –' He paused. 'Where did you get all this fucking stuff?'

'Mr Harding? What's he saying? What was *Pilgrim* –'

'Shut up,' snarled Harding. 'Go on – get back to your work.'

The girl backed reluctantly towards the door.

'The top photograph I'm not so pleased with,' Martin admitted candidly, as though addressing the local Photographic Society. 'The definition isn't so good: the outline of that aerial ... there ... isn't so easy to make out, you'll agree. It was taken in October, by the way. The other one, that one there – that was taken ... oh ... about four years ago. See the difference? Unmistakable. Now, if I can just –'

'Difference? What difference?' Harding looked up slowly. 'I don't even see any photographs, Mr Taylor. Do you?' With that he ripped up the photographs and let the pieces flutter into his ashtray. He set fire to the corners with his lighter and looked up with a humourless grin.

Martin made no move to stop him. Inside he felt a fierce exultation. 'I was hoping for a signed statement, but I'll settle for that. I still have the negatives. There'll be another set of prints in the post tomorrow morning. I'll call round and see you again then, and then we'll get down to a few facts, Mr Harding – a few fucking *facts*!' He turned on his heel and walked to the door.

Harding slumped back in his chair and lit another cigarette with shaking hands. Christ Almighty.

The door opened again and Harding looked up. It was the man he knew as Connors.

'You heard?' managed Harding, puffing nervously on his cigarette.

'Enough,' replied Evans shortly. 'What else does he know?'

'Well ... he said ...'

'Think!' Evans snapped. 'What else does he know?'

Harding gulped. 'Everything – practically. He must. Almost everything, I think.'

Evans stabbed a finger into the smoking mess in Harding's ashtray. 'These?'

'Er ... photographs. He showed me some photographs.'

'Photographs? What photographs?'

'Of ... of *Arctic Pilgrim*. Before and after we fitted for role. Her antenna array.'

'That's all we need. Right – this is what you do,' said Evans softly. 'You stay here, right here – you don't move. Got it? I'll be back shortly.'

Harding nodded gratefully. 'Oh ... there's one more thing you should know about that man Taylor. He's tenacious – and he's not just a reporter. His father was one of the crew.'

'Then you've got yourself a problem, old son, wouldn't

you say?' Evans turned and moved towards the door on silent feet. He dropped downstairs and sprinted to his car.

Martin was angry. I handled that all wrong, he told himself as he turned into West Dock Avenue; I blew it. I lost my temper with the bastard and that was stupid. I should have been sweet as pie; I should have led him on, asked a couple of innocent little questions about the radio and *Pilgrim*'s antenna and then, *after* he trapped himself, *that* was the time I should have hit him with the photographs.

As it was, Harding was alerted now. He would be careful in the future, cagey as hell. Martin had seen he was frightened then, but it would not take him long to recover.

He parked outside his flat and went inside. A minute later Evans cruised past, drew in to the kerb and killed the engine. He got out, locked the car, entered the building and began climbing the stairs, reading the door plaques as he climbed.

Martin chucked his coat on the bed and reached for the phone. Evans moved forward gingerly onto the landing and pressed an ear to the door. He could hear Martin speaking.

'Is that Mr Harding's secretary? This is Martin Taylor.'

'Oh,' said Sandra Harris. Her voice dropped. 'Did you mean what you said back there about *Pilgrim*? Was all that true?'

'Yes. Listen – I need to talk to Harding again. Right now. Can you put me through?'

'No. No, I can't. There's been several calls, you know, business calls, but he won't take any of them. What did you mean when you said –'

'His home address, then. Have you his home address?'

'I don't know if I –'

'Please. It's very important.'

Her voice dropped to a whisper. 'He lives out on Anlaby Road, I think. Somewhere down there, anyway. We all went to a party there once a year or so back and –'

'Isn't it written down somewhere, then?'

'I thought it was. Wait a moment.' He heard papers being

moved. 'Here we are – Clearmont View, Forest Drive, Anlaby.'

'Thanks a million.'

'Mr Taylor . . .'

'What is it?'

'You know what you said?' she began hesitantly. 'About the money and such – and about being helped out of a sticky patch?'

'I remember.'

'Well, after you left I got to thinking. I had a look at the diary, just to make sure, like.'

'What did you find?'

'I'm coming to that. I hadn't noticed it before. I mean – I'd no reason to, see. It had all been set up before I joined, know what I mean? But when you . . .'

Martin cradled the phone against his shoulder and began scribbling furiously.

Presently he interrupted the steady flow of information. 'And you'd show me those records? Talk me through the books? Can you meet me for a drink somewhere, tonight? . . . Fine . . . How about the Plume of Feathers, out on the main road about three miles on towards Selby? O K, fine. About seven-thirty then? Oh – one last thing: be careful. If Harding even suspects you're about to drop the curtain on his little act, well, I needn't spell it out. Just take care, O K? I'll see you.'

Forty minutes later Martin snapped a lead onto Hercules' collar and allowed his young and straining puppy to drag him downstairs. On the way he stopped at Suzy's flat to tell her what had happened. He hammered on the door, but there was no reply. He hammered again and a door opened on the floor below.

''Ere – you! What's all that bangin' about? There's others live 'ere besides you, you know. Besides – she's not in.'

Martin leaned over the stairwell and spied the querulous Mr Hoskins, one of the older tenants, peering up at him through the banister rails.

'Sorry, Mr Hoskins,' Martin whispered. 'Only way. Bell doesn't work.'

'Neither will you if that row goes on. Just you be quiet about it.'

Martin went out to the car, Hercules ranging ahead like a black, gleaming Geiger counter.

Sitting in his Scimitar a little farther up the road, Evans watched him drive past. He gave him another two minutes and then slipped back into the building and up the stairs. Using a set of keys the Colonel had acquired on his behalf, he let himself quietly into Martin's flat.

One of the first things he did was examine the contents of Martin's wastepaper basket.

Evans turned down the side road and parked. He pushed into the phone booth and dialled a London number. The call was picked up almost immediately. He gave the code and asked for Simon's extension.

'Put me through to the Colonel, will you?'

'Why are you calling from –'

'Not to hear your voice, sonny. Put me through. To the Colonel.'

'Hold.' There was the shortest of delays and then Mann-Quartermain came on the line.

'This is an unsecured line, so I'll be brief. Bad news, Colonel – the worst. A reporter up here is on to what's happened. Name of Taylor. Martin Taylor. Free-lance operator, far as I can gather. I was staking out H as per your instructions and ...' Briefly Evans reported what had happened.

As Mann-Quartermain listened bleakly his mind went back to the mid-morning call from Sir Peter. The Director of SIS had ordered Mann-Quartermain to report to him at 1900. It was a prospect he did not relish. And now this reporter business. He sighed. There was a line of action, of course, that although extreme did hold the promise of finality.

'You'd like the Sanction, I take it?' he asked quietly as Evans finished.

'Correct, Colonel – I'd like the Sanction.'

Mann-Quartermain paused again, reviewing the options. There weren't any. 'You have it. Reestablish contact when Sanction is completed, clear?'

'Got it, Colonel.' Evans replaced the receiver quietly.

Mann-Quartermain took out his fountain pen, made a few careful entries in the *Arctic Pilgrim* file that did *not* go to Sir Peter and locked it away carefully in the drawer of his desk. Good. That should take care of that rather nicely – and Sir Peter need never be any the wiser. He glanced at his watch. There was just time for a drink in the lounge downstairs before that meeting with Sir Peter Hillmore.

Ten minutes later, he sensed there was something wrong the moment he stepped out of the lift and walked along the corridor back towards his office. The door was ajar and an unfamiliar man was standing in the centre of his secretary's office, arms folded. Like a sentry. There was no sign of his secretary or of Simon, his aide.

'Who're you? What are you doing here? This is a restricted area.'

'Your name, sir?' Unimpressed.

'Show me your ID.'

'That's hardly necessary, sir.' The man showed Mann-Quartermain a small cellophane identity card. A9.

'Internal Security? What the hell's going on? This is my office.'

'In that case, sir, you best go in there.' The man jerked a thumb over his shoulder.

Through the crack in the door Mann-Quartermain could see figures moving around his private office. He pushed past the burly sergeant and stopped in his tracks. His safe was open, his filing cabinets had been emptied and plainclothes men were stacking his papers in neat piles on the carpet. Someone was sitting at his desk, rifling through his drawers.

It was Sir Peter Hillmore.

The *Arctic Pilgrim* file was open on the desk, and Sir Peter was not smiling.

'OK, you two – leave that for now and wait outside. I'll call if I need you,' he said quietly.

The two men working on the carpet rose and left the room, closing the door softly behind them.

'It's been a bad twenty-four hours,' Sir Peter began conversationally. 'First the PM gets hot under the collar, then the Under Secretary for Defence starts making unauthorized statements in the House without going through SIS, and then ... this.' He held up Mann-Quartermain's *Pilgrim* file. ' "Clinics" ... Newcastle ... Greenock ... the Lennon business ... secret funds: what the hell have you been up to? I knew nothing about all this.'

Mann-Quartermain realized it was all over. Finished. He managed a shrug of the shoulders. 'You know the rule, sir: need-to-know, and all that.'

'Twaddle,' said Sir Peter briefly. 'You had no possible authorization to mount something like this behind my back. It amounts to ... to a private army. How long have these "clinics" of yours been operational?'

'A couple of years, sir – perhaps a little longer.' Perversely, Mann-Quartermain found he almost enjoyed compounding his errors. Go out with a bang. 'Something of that order, anyway.'

'A couple of *years*? Christ in heaven!' Sir Peter ran a hand through his hair. The man was off his trolley. He studied the file again. 'And this ... this Evans character, and this other man – Taylor.' He stabbed at the notes Mann-Quartermain had added to the file less than an hour ago. 'Where does he fit in?'

'Taylor, sir? Oh – he's a journalist. A reporter. Bit of a snooper, really.'

'And your man Evans is *working* with him? With a journalist?'

'Oh, no, sir – not working with him, exactly.'

'Well, man, what then?'

'Don't you see? He's going to kill him. Sir.'

CHAPTER SIXTEEN

Martin drained his glass and glanced again at his watch:
8.50 p.m. and she was late. An hour and twenty minutes
late. Sauntering up to the bar, he ordered another drink and
settled down to wait. Maybe Harding had kept her back –
he'd give her another quarter of an hour.

He waited until a quarter past nine and then stepped outside to give Hercules a run before slipping behind the wheel
for the drive home. So much for the intuitive hunch that
said everything was breaking his way.

He saw the flashing lights through a break in the wind-
bowed poplars that lined his route home, saw them long
before he slowed down and joined the queue of glowing
brake lights waiting patiently behind the blue-and-white
police 'Accident' sign.

Martin groaned. That was all he needed.

Half a mile back the road had widened into a causeway
running a little above the wide, flat roads it bisected. The
verge to Martin's right gave way, just beyond the trees, to
a steep, grassy slope that ran down to a concrete drainage
ditch nine feet below the level of the road.

There was a motorcycle patrolman with a flashlight and a
reflecting orange jacket standing behind the 'Accident' sign.
Two police cars were parked across the oncoming lane, their
blue roof lights swinging a warning across the sky as a tow
truck reversed gingerly towards the lip of the road.

Martin reached under the dashboard for the small camera
and flash unit. Then he pulled his car in to the kerb and
sprinted towards the glow of harsh artificial light that
washed up onto the road. He held the camera to his ear as he
ran, listening, above the crackle of police radios and the

shout of half-heard instructions, for the hum of the electronic flash unit as it came on charge.

He slithered down, his leather shoes slipping on the long damp grass.

There was a battered blue Ford Anglia at the bottom of the ditch. The nose of the empty car was rammed against the shelving side of the drainage ditch, and the windscreen was spread over the buckled bonnet, scattered into the grass in a thousand glittering fragments. Firemen and police were working at the front of the vehicle, rocking and heaving it violently from side to side.

Martin raised the camera to his eye, felt for the button – and paused, eye pressed to the viewfinder.

Sandra Harris had an Anglia. He'd seen it parked outside the Graveline offices. A pale-blue Anglia. The flash went off.

'Hey – you!' The shout came from a burly police sergeant in mud-spattered uniform and Wellington boots who was tramping purposefully towards the reporter. 'What the hell d'you think you're up to?'

'I'm a reporter.' Martin reached in a pocket for his press card. 'I was just driving by. Saw the lights.'

The police sergeant sighed. 'That's all we bloody need.'

'What happened?'

The sergeant wiped a muddy hand across his sweating forehead. 'See for yourself: driver misses the bend, hits those two trees ... up over the bank ... ends up there.'

'D'you have a name yet?'

'Aye, we do.'

'What's the name?'

The sergeant shot him a baleful glance. 'You'll have me shot, you will.' He relented and unbuttoned a top breast pocket. 'Driving licence says she's a ... Sandra Maureen Harris, 178 Springfield Road, Hull.'

'On her own? In the car?'

'One's enough.'

'Badly hurt?'

'What d'you think? Broken arm – face is a mess, too. Ambulance blokes reckoned there's a chance of head injuries. Oh – and a broken leg sustained after the accident itself.'

'*After* the accident?'

'Firemen,' the sergeant explained quietly. 'Had to do it to get her out. Chop – clean as a whistle. Only way.'

Martin swallowed. 'Poor kid.'

'Poor kid?' scoffed the policeman. 'Bloody asking for it, if you want my opinion.'

'What d'you mean?'

The sergeant pulled out a dirty handkerchief, blew his nose loudly, inspected the result and then folded the handkerchief back into his pocket. 'Tanked up to the eyeballs, she was.'

'Drunk? How d'you know?' demanded Martin. She had been on her way to a pub, for Chrissakes, not coming from one !

'It's all over the bloody driving compartment – best part of a bottle of Scotch.'

'Mind if I take a look around?'

The sergeant looked back over his shoulder. His men had rocked the car out of the ditch, and two mechanics in greasy overalls were slithering under the car with a length of towing chain.

'Stay out of the way for now,' the sergeant ordered. 'Wait until they've moved the vehicle back up to the road.'

Martin pulled into the lay-by and skidded to a halt beside the telephone kiosk in a shower of dry pebbles.

His first call was to the hospital.

Sandra Harris was in intensive care. If her condition stabilized overnight they would operate in the morning to save the sight of her right eye.

Martin slammed down the phone and began flicking impatiently through the phone book, searching for Harding's number.

Harding, H., Clearmont View, Forest Drive, Anlaby.

Martin dialled and waited, drumming his fingers. He could hear the call ringing in. The bastard had had plenty of time to get home. Martin looked up as the tow truck rattled past with Sandra Harris's car chained behind, the buckled front wheels lifted clear of the ground. Cortège for a car.

'Hello?'

Martin pushed money into the box. 'Mr Harding?'

'Speaking.'

'It's Taylor, Mr Harding – Martin Taylor. About that secretary of yours, Sandra Harris. She was due to meet me for a drink tonight, but she never made it – but then, you'd know all about that, wouldn't you? I'm coming round.'

'Like hell you are,' exploded Harding. 'Who d'you think you're–'

The line went dead.

Harding replaced the receiver slowly. He revealed a length of gleaming white cuff as he reached for the glass of chilled white wine he had brought with him to the phone. He took a deep swallow. Dressed in dinner jacket and white shirt, he was playing dutiful host to a group of his wife's friends. Now it was the noise of their bright party laughter that pressed in around his ears so that he was unable to concentrate. He strode across the deep pile carpet and pulled the door closed. The voices receded as he returned to the phone, head bowed in thought. He glanced at his watch and felt a flutter in his stomach that owed nothing to the excellent Ardennes pâté he had just eaten.

The thing was coming apart at the seams.

'Harold? Is anything the matter?' His wife, immaculately coiffured, stood in the hall wearing a long lime-coloured evening dress and an air of attentive concern.

'No, nothing. Something's come up, that's all.'

'Will you be long?'

'No more than I can help,' he answered shortly.

'I do hope not. Peter and Mary say –'

Harding brought a heavy hand down hard on the delicate Georgian table, and his wine jumped. So did Mrs Harding. 'I don't give a bugger what Mary and Peter say! Now leave me be – I've got some thinking to do.'

'Of course, dear – whatever you say.' Startled, Beryl Harding darted back into the kitchen.

Harding waited until the door had swung to behind her and then reached into his wallet for the telephone number he had scribbled on a scrap of paper. He dialled the number that would connect him to a hotel in Hull and the man he knew as Connors.

Evans answered instantly: 'Yes?'

'Things are happening,' Harding said quietly, turning to watch the dining-room door. 'That reporter bloke's been on the blower again. Taylor.'

'What did he want?'

'Sounded bloody angry, for one. Said he was coming round to see me.' He paused. 'You been buggering about with my secretary?'

'What time's he coming round?'

'Now – about ten minutes. What do I tell him?'

'You tell him nothing.'

'He won't settle for that! Look – I've got a house full of dinner guests. Suppose he comes in here and starts spouting his mouth off –'

'You tell him nothing because you're not there. Go for a drive. Get out for an hour or two.'

'And what happens if he's sitting on my doorstep when I get back? Then what do I tell him?'

'He won't be.'

'But if he is?'

'I just said: he won't be.'

'He'd better bloody not be! This whole deal's going up the bloody spout – and that's your concern, not mine. So get that bloke off my neck or ...'

'Or you'll what?' asked Evans softly.

'Just get him off my neck, that's all. He's making me nervous,' Harding ended lamely.

'Relax,' crackled the voice on the end of the phone. 'Make your excuses and get away. Quick as you can. I'll be in contact soon.'

'What'll I tell –'

'You're wasting time. Move!'

*

To Martin's surprise Clearmont View was ablaze with lights, the driveway choked with cars. He reversed back into the main road, parked on the verge and walked up the fir-lined driveway, his feet crunching on the deep, well-groomed gravel.

He walked slowly, taking his time, peering carefully at the front of each car. The driveway gave on to a cobbled court-yard lit by heavy reproduction coach lanterns that flanked either side of the imposing entrance porch.

Harding did well for himself out of the spying business, thought Martin.

Some distance away, on the far side of the courtyard, stood a pair of garages. Martin stepped off the gravel, pushed through a hedge of damp young firs and, keeping to the shadows, began working his way round towards them.

Suddenly he froze. A figure loomed out of the darkness – hunched, crouching, sinister, rocklike. Martin peered closer and let out a sigh of relief. Bloody garden gnome. He patted its silly pointed head and, hugging the shadows, darted across to the next clump of bushes. From there he was able to step directly onto the courtyard.

Two garages, both with roll-top doors. One open. One closed. Martin turned the handle of the closed door and pulled it gingerly towards him. It tilted backwards.

Ducking down, he slipped into the garage. The smell of oil and petrol-soaked stillness mingled with the sound of his nervous breathing.

Martin stretched out his hands and stepped deeper into the darkness. His fingers encountered smooth enamel and a low, rounded roof. Sliding into the gap between car and garage wall, he continued his fingertip exploration. Mini. A second car – a wife's car.

He worked his way round to the smooth, undamaged bonnet. No dents. Headlights both intact. Round the other side and out under the door again.

The other garage was empty. Nevertheless, Martin walked the length of the empty car space before hunching down in the middle of the concrete floor and patting around with the tips of his fingers until he came upon a small pool of oil.

He sniffed his fingers. Imagination, no doubt, but the oil smelled as though it could almost be warm. There was something else too. He sniffed again and this time picked out another smell – carbon monoxide.

Martin stretched to his feet and wiped his hands on a handkerchief. Time to go a-calling.

Melodious chimes sounded deep within Harding's home. Martin rang again. Presently the heavy oak door swung open and a woman in a long lime-coloured evening gown stood in the hallway. Over her shoulder Martin could see bright lights, a party in progress. Music struggled towards him past a dozen different conversations.

'Is Mr Harding in?'

'No. No – I'm afraid he isn't.'

'I was due to meet him tonight.'

'Are you sure you've got the right night? As you can see, we've something of a party in progress.' Sandra Harris was fighting for her life from a hospital bed and there was 'something of a party' in progress.

'And he isn't here? For the party?'

'He was, earlier. You've just missed him. He was called away suddenly.'

I bet he was, thought Martin. He smiled pleasantly. 'Would you please tell your husband Martin Taylor called? I'll catch up with him later.'

With Hercules bouncing ahead, Martin struggled up the stairs. He keyed open the front door and then stepped outside again for the bottle of milk on the doorstep.

It was only then that he noticed the envelope which had been slipped under his door. It was a note from Suzy. She was working late downstairs, marking papers. She would see him in the morning.

Martin poured some of the milk into a plastic saucer, opened a can of dog food and then, when Hercules was snuffling happily to himself over in a corner, he walked into the living room to catch up with the evening paper.

While he had been talking to Turpin, chatting up the little sod from the Admiralty Hydrographic Department in Taunton, reading about intercept receivers at the library, chasing after Harding and looking at smashed cars, the Department of Trade and Industry's formal inquiry into the loss of the motor trawler *Arctic Pilgrim* had moved into its fourth day.

The day's evidence had scraped no more than a single column on the front page. Martin loosened his tie, kicked off his shoes and helped himself to a generous Scotch from the sideboard. He stretched out on the sofa. It had been a long day. He felt shattered.

The bulk of the day's hearing had been taken up with the evidence of those trawler skippers whose vessels had been closest to *Pilgrim's* last reported position. Counsel representing the *Pilgrim's* skipper, Harry Thomson, had spent much time questioning John Ryder, mate of the *Midnight Sun.*

Martin tossed the newspaper aside and rubbed his eyes. A little soothing music was called for. A bit of John Denver. A touch of the Rocky Mountain Highs.

He walked to the cabinet where he stored his records and reached down, stretching automatically for the record in its usual place.

It was not there.

Martin flipped through the albums. He had not lent it to Suzy, he was sure of it. Finally he found the album he wanted at the far end of the row – only that didn't make any kind of sense. Disorganized in many things, Martin kept his records and books tidy. It was one of the few systems he had. Consequently he clung to it, trusted it implicitly.

He placed the record on the turntable and then sank to the floor, back pressed against the cabinet, to study familiar surroundings with methodical, critical eyes. His gaze swept over the same old furniture, the potted plants and the loaded shelves. There. On the dresser. The little green travelling clock his mother had given him, the one he kept folded down into its case now because one of the hinges was loose. It was open, standing in its case.

Martin's scalp began to prickle.

He rose to his feet and crossed to his desk, his footfalls hidden by the music. Papers where they should be. Typewriter untouched. He tugged open the top right-hand drawer and scrabbled among the papers and cheque stubs. Looking for the negative.

It had gone.

Someone had been through his flat, turned it upside down. Harding? Was this where he'd been? A noise came from the kitchen. Martin ripped the stylus away from the record.

'Hercules?' There was no response, no familiar scrabble of young paws on the kitchen lino. Nothing to break the silence.

'Hercules? Is that you, boy?' Frightened now, Martin picked up a heavy glass ashtray and turned into the kitchen, arm raised. Then he dropped the ashtray with a crash and started forward.

The food Martin had set out for his puppy had been eaten, but it lay now as vomit laced with blood beside the saucer of milk. Beside the saucer, sprawled on his belly with one paw crumpled under him and the other trailing in spilled milk that ran away under the fridge, lay Hercules.

'Jesus,' Martin muttered, dropping to his knees beside the dog.

Hercules' eyes were almost closed; his shaggy chest was rising and falling in a series of shallow, nipped breaths. A trickle of milk ran from the corner of his mouth across his glossy coat and dribbled unheeded onto the floor.

Martin sank back onto his knees, cradling his animal. Hercules whimpered, his forepaws scrabbling ineffectually on the lino as he tried to respond to his master.

'Easy, boy, easy.'

Hercules coughed again before vomiting a little more meat and milk laced with blood. The effort seemed to exhaust him.

Martin laid Hercules carefully on the floor, reached for

his coat on the hook behind the door, lifted the dog onto it and wrapped the coat around him.

He lifted the plastic food tray and sniffed the remains of the meat cautiously. There didn't seem to be anything wrong with that. He opened the fridge and reached for the pint of milk he had brought in from outside earlier in the evening. And then realization dawned.

Milk was delivered in the morning, not the evening.

His pint for that day was still in the fridge, untouched. He held the bottle he had found outside up to the light. He studied it carefully and could just make out a faint brown tinge at the top of the milk – and a small, innocent little pin-prick close against the rim of the tinfoil cap.

Martin swore under his breath, scooped Hercules up in his arms, tucked the milk bottle under his arm and carried Hercules out onto the landing and down the stairs.

He hammered on Suzy's door. Music blared from within. Martin hammered again. A door opened on the landing below and Mr Hoskins did his leaning-through-the-banisters trick.

'What's all the noise about up there? Some people are trying to get some sleep.'

'Fuck off,' ordered Martin shortly. He continued his hammering, and, as one door slammed shut angrily, another opened. It was Suzy. She took in the dog in his arms and her eyes widened:

'What's the matter with Hercules?'

'He's been poisoned.'

'Poisoned? You're kidding!' She looked at his face.

'Let me in, will you?' asked Martin quietly. He brushed past her and closed the door with his foot.

Suzy turned on the lights in the hall. The music was very loud now. She went into the living room, and the music stopped abruptly. She returned to the hall looking bewildered.

'Poisoned? Are you sure?'

'Someone poisoned my milk – Hercules got to it first.' He held up the milk bottle. 'Exhibit A.'

'Why would –'

'It's this *Pilgrim* business, I think. I'll explain everything later. There isn't time now. Would you do something for me?'

'Sure.'

'Look after Hercules. Take him to a vet. See what he can do to help. Would you do that? Now?'

Suzy reached for her parka. 'Why can't you?'

'Please, Suzy, there isn't time. I'll explain things later – O K?' Martin put a hand on her shoulder. 'Now, listen – this is very, very important: where's your car parked?'

'Round the back.'

'Good. Use the back stairs. Bring the car round to the back door and carry Hercules out from there. That's the first thing. It's very important no one sees you carrying him out to the car.' Hercules whined suddenly, his head lolling from side to side. 'O K, boy, O K – take it easy.' To Suzy Martin said, 'Is that clear?'

She nodded, wide-eyed.

'Good. Second thing: see if you can find out what's in this.' He held out the bottle of milk. 'Only for God's sake be careful.'

'How could anyone? – I'm sorry. What do you want done with this?'

'You're the chemist. Isn't there somewhere in the university, a laboratory or whatever?'

'At this time of night?'

'Surely someone you know has a key? Call me when you've any news about Hercules, any news at all.'

Suzy zipped up her parka and picked up her car keys. 'Where will you be?'

'I'm not sure. Try upstairs first.' He leaned forward and kissed her on the lips. 'Thanks, Suzy.'

She took charge of the bundle in the coat and laid Hercules carefully on the hall rug. 'I'll call as soon as I've got anything,' she promised. Then she reached out a hand and touched Martin's cheek. 'Take care.'

'I will, don't worry. Just *you* look after *him*.' Martin patted his dog, muttered a few awkward words and left.

With his own front door closed behind him he poured himself another drink. He sniffed the glass suspiciously, caught himself at it and ran a tired hand through his hair. God, what a mess!

Martin bent forward, rested his head on his hands and tried to think.

By rights he should have made himself a cup of coffee, a cup of tea, even a bowl of cornflakes. Then he would have been lying on the kitchen floor. By rights. But he had been saved, saved by luck and a puppy who liked milk.

But if *he* had drunk the milk as he was supposed to, as they had every right to suppose he would, then he would have been found. One day later, two days perhaps, three at the outside, but he would be found. And if he was dead, then everything would be examined, from the contents of his stomach to the contents of his fridge. And the bottle of milk. Far, far better if he had simply been made to disappear.

And then it came to him. Perhaps that was their intention, after all: they would come back, clean up and clear away. Clear him away.

As Martin thought about that possibility it took root, hardened into complete, gigantic conviction. They would come back. He looked at his watch: 10.40 p.m. They would wait a while yet.

His first reaction was to run, his second to call the police. He did neither. Run where? Tell them what, exactly? Instead he forced himself to think things through a step further.

This was not Harding's style, he was sure of it. Harding might be behind it, almost certainly was, but Martin had been reporting for too long not to recognize the hallmark of someone who was used to getting his hands dirty. A professional.

The same someone, Martin thought suddenly, who could have turned over Mrs Millar's flat, started a fire or forced a car off an empty road.

Presently Martin went over to his toolbox, rummaged around and, after some thought, laid aside a heavy claw hammer, a reel of thin wire and a roll of insulating tape. Then he went to his bedroom cupboard, and hauled out his tripod, his camera and a few other bits and pieces.

Heart pounding against his ribs, mouth dry with fear, he began his simple preparations.

Less than one hundred yards away, Paul Evans felt across to the passenger seat of his Scimitar for the thermos of hot coffee his hotel had so thoughtfully provided. Working slowly in the darkness, he unscrewed the top of the thermos. The task would have been made easier if he had simply reached up and turned on the interior light above his head, but Evans did not work like that. He poured the coffee into a plastic cup and stirred thoughtfully.

All the while his eyes never left the second-floor windows of the block of flats opposite.

That light – there – that was from the kitchen, and that one there came from the bedroom. A few minutes earlier there had been one on in the living room, but that had now been extinguished. Evans sipped his coffee slowly and then held his luminous watch up to his eyes: 2330. There was no hurry.

Martin eased his cramped leg muscles and glanced about him for the hundredth time. The lights were on in the kitchen and the bedroom. The bedroom door was ajar.

The living room itself was in darkness except for the faint, inescapable green glow from the stereo. The room was silent save for the monotonous sound of the record stylus as it bumped round to the end of the record again. Martin made no attempt to turn it off. He stayed where he was, crouched down against the wall, lost in the shadows, hidden among the dark lumps of furniture.

Outside the night was quiet and traffic had slowed to the occasional car.

Martin began to feel faintly ridiculous, crouched behind his own sofa with a hammer in his hand.

An hour later, deafening in the hushed, laden silence, the phone began to ring – loud, strident, insistent.

Martin almost jumped out of his skin. Then, cursing

quietly under his breath, he settled down to count out each tone like a referee at a boxing match.

Across the city in an annexe of Hull University, Suzy Summerfield replaced the receiver, gathered up her parka and handbag and turned out the single light in the eerie, deserted building. Working alone, she had run the tests and isolated the chemical in the milk as gromoxone, a derivative of paraquat.

She walked slowly down the corridor. She had some other news too.

Across the stillness of the street Evans heard the phone stop ringing. He glanced at his watch, drew his coat closer and sank a little lower in his seat. Whoever had just called Martin had saved him the trouble.

Presently he put the thermos away, reached forward under the dash and pushed the two little retaining clips to one side. He jerked hard at the metal he found there, and the comforting weight of a pistol dropped into his waiting palm.

It was a 9mm Browning automatic which he had taken from the Army without telling anyone. He had reported it lost on an exercise drop in Thetford, Norfolk. He had stuck to his story, weathered the inquiry and returned a fortnight later to dig up the weapon he had buried in a field in a little oilskin pouch. He had filed off the serial number, and the weapon with its magazine of thirteen rounds had left the Army with him. Now it travelled around with him always. A little private insurance.

It would go with him tonight, just to make sure. He did not believe in taking chances.

He checked the load by touch as the Army had taught him, smacked the magazine into the butt, chambered a round from the magazine and applied the safety catch. Reaching up, he unscrewed the bulb of the interior light and eased open the car door. He stepped smoothly onto the road, closed the door softly behind him and walked into the shadows.

*

It was not a very loud sound, just the faintest of tiny scratches as Evans worked the lock with his special keys. Not a very loud sound, but all that Martin had been waiting for. Martin swallowed, shifted his grip on the hammer and rose to a crouch.

The front door eased open a crack, and a shadow fell across the kitchen floor.

Evans paused on the threshold, listening. He isolated and identified the regular, monotonous bump of the record stylus. That was good. He pushed the door wide with his foot and stepped slowly into the kitchen, pistol drawn and held straight down against his thigh, the old excitement burning his stomach.

Martin watched from the deep shadows, scarcely daring to breathe as he steeled himself for the moment.

The man paused on the threshold to the living room, feet away now. Martin sensed rather than saw the intruder turn towards the open bedroom door. Then the man stepped away from the kitchen into the shadows, lured by the light from the bedroom, pistol raised in both hands. It was working.

Martin shut his eyes and looked down at the ground. Evans's right leg brushed against the thin copper wire stretched between the leg of the cabinet and the camera tripod standing out of sight in the shadows. The wire came taut and triggered the flash unit of the camera.

As blinding light seared across Evans's wide, straining eyes Martin measured his distance, took a half step forward, raised the hammer and brought it down in a swift, scything blow that smashed into Evans's right wrist with a dull meaty *thwack!* The pistol spun away into the darkness.

Evans let out a low, feral grunt of agony, spun violently clockwise against the camera tripod and sent it crashing aside as Martin followed through with a wild, roundhouse kick that caught him a glancing blow on the shins.

Evans grunted again, lurched sideways against the dresser and sprawled backwards into the darkness.

Martin, the momentum of his attack almost spent, lurched forward and ran full tilt into a potted plant swept into his path with vicious strength. He toppled back against the sofa, lost his balance and then he, potted plant, sofa and all toppled over backwards with a splintering crash.

By the time he had struggled to his feet Evans was gone, hobbling through the kitchen nursing his bruised wrist. The door slammed behind him and Martin heard him pounding down the stairs.

Someone let out a high scream. Martin, galvanized by terror, started after the intruder. He wrenched open the door and took the stairs two at a time.

'Suzy!' he yelled. But the stairs were empty. When he reached the road it was deserted. The man had disappeared. Suzy was nowhere in sight.

Panting hard, Martin looked about him desperately, searching for movement in the darkness outside as he drew in great gulps of cool night air. Over to his right there was a sudden roar of an engine and the screech of rubber as a darkened car with no lights roared off into the night.

There was a groan behind him and Martin spun round. Then his face broke into a wide grin of relief.

The ever-inquisitive Mr Hoskins had stopped one in the teeth.

CHAPTER SEVENTEEN

Martin awoke with a stiff neck.

He was lying fully clothed, stretched out awkwardly in the chair he had pushed against the door.

He was still clutching his hammer.

He looked about him blearily and rasped a hand across the stubble on his chin. He felt awful. There was a deep, stabbing pain in his chest where the plant pot had struck him, and a taste in his mouth he did not even want to think about.

He pushed the chair away from the door and poked his head cautiously outside. No one shot it off. The landing was deserted; no one was stirring.

Martin trundled the chair back into the living room, and the havoc of the night before began to register through half-closed eyes: The sofa was still over on its back, the plant, its pot broken, lay among the cushions in a scattering of earth. The camera tripod was lying in a heap of stiff legs over by the far wall. One of his favourite pictures had been smashed and torn from the wall in its passing. The dresser had been swept clear of books and ornaments.

Martin scuffed through to the bathroom and began washing. As he brewed coffee in the kitchen afterwards, his thoughts ran over the night before. He would call down to see Suzy after breakfast. Meanwhile he ought to do something about the mess in the living room. He set to replacing the books on the dresser.

After two minutes' steady work he thought he heard a light step on the stairs outside.

Stomach churning, he lunged for the hammer and then remembered, far too late, that he had not bothered to lock the outside door. He slipped behind the thin dividing wall between kitchen and living room, raised the hammer once more and steeled himself for a repeat performance.

An impossible repeat performance.

He had hurt the man who hunted him, he knew that. Surprised and then hurt him. But not enough. Now he was back, outside, hunting trouble. And he probably had a gun. And this time there was no darkness, no stereo. There would be no surprise.

The kitchen door swung back slowly.

'Mart?'

Martin sagged back against the wall, the hammer dangling uselessly from limp fingers. Sick with relief, he stepped out from behind the wall. Suzy jumped.

'Mart? What's been going on?'

Martin stepped past her soundlessly and closed and locked the door. Then he took her in his arms and hugged her fiercely, drawing strength from her warmth and closeness. After a moment Suzy disentangled herself, her eyes straining past him into the living room.

'What's been going on? What is all this?'

He took her by the hand and led her gently into the chaos of his living room. 'I had a visitor, didn't I? Same gent who fixed the milk.' He sank down onto a chair. 'About four and a half hours ago, I think. He rubbed his eyes with the heels of his hands. 'God, I'm shattered.'

'He did all this? You mean you had a fight? Here?' she asked incredulously, eyes round like pennies.

Martin nodded. Suzy began picking up the pieces of broken pottery, dreading, in the sudden silence, the question she knew must come soon. It came now.

'He's dead, isn't he? The dog, I mean,' said Martin.

Suzy bent over the last piece of sticky glass and lifted it carefully, saying nothing.

'Isn't he?' he persisted.

'Yes.' Her shoulders started to shake and she came into his arms with a rush. She buried her head in his shoulder. The words, when they came, were muffled in his shirt. 'He'd ... he'd used gromoxone, part of the paraquat group, you know? Very efficient weedkiller. But on ... on a dog? It was horrible, Martin – horrible. By the time I'd found a vet who'd look at him, great ulcers were bursting at the ... at the corners of his mouth. The vet took one look and ... it didn't take a moment, honestly,' she finished in a small voice. She pulled away to look into Martin's face, her tears giving way now to anger. 'Who could do such a thing? What kind of a man?' She stood there silently, taking in the evidence of the kind of man it had been.

Martin did not bother to point out the obvious: that the milk had been intended for him. Presently he went into the kitchen and made coffee. While he was there and Suzy was in the living room, he scooped up Hercules' eating paraphernalia and dropped it quietly into the waste bin.

Marching back into the living room with cold-blooded cheerfulness, he sat down beside Suzy and told her, in as light a manner as he could manage, what she had missed during the night. He tried to make it sound like some sort of game almost, a prank.

By a little after ten they had finished cleaning up. With feminine ingenuity Suzy had found another pot for Martin's plant, the sofa was back on its feet, the broken glass from the picture had been cleared away and all the books were in order. Now Suzy was vacuuming the carpet while Martin squatted at the other end of the room checking the camera and tripod.

Suzy pushed the vacuum under the bottom of the dresser and felt something obstructing its progress. She turned off the machine, dropped to her knees and groped under the dresser. She drew out a heavy blue-grey pistol.

'Martin?' The fear in her voice brought Martin's head up with a jerk. Suzy was holding the pistol at arm's length like a distasteful exhibit at a biology class.

'Ah,' Martin managed sheepishly. He had not told her about the gun. 'I was wondering where that had got to.' He stepped forward and plucked the pistol from her outstretched hand. 'I'll take that.'

He walked through into the bedroom, dropped the automatic into a drawer and returned to the living room, brushing his fingers together daintily. 'Nasty, nasty things,' he mimicked. Then he stopped. Suzy looked furious.

'What's the matter?' he asked, innocently. Under the circumstances it was not a very wise thing to say.

'What's the *matter*? Christ, you've got a nerve! You've been chatting on as though you and this ... this assassin' – she spat the word out – 'just had a difference of opinion! You almost lulled me into thinking the poisoning was a mistake, too – and now that ... that thing! You never mentioned he had a gun, Martin. Not once! He really meant to kill you, you stupid bastard!'

'Now, Suzy –'

'Don't you "now, Suzy" me! I want to hear it again. From the start. And this time, you can leave out the jokes. I want to hear the truth, dammit!'

Later, as Suzy Summerfield and Martin Taylor lay happily together in each other's arms, Paul Evans lay alone on his hotel bed, grinding his teeth against the pain and staring up at the ceiling with bright, unblinking eyes.

He had not slept.

He had bandaged the bruise as best he could with strips torn from his spare shirt, but the pain had kept him awake until morning.

Evans turned his head slowly on the pillow. Twisting with awkward, agonizing slowness and using only the tips of the fingers of his bandaged right hand, he turned the face of the alarm clock towards him.

He ground his teeth at the pain. There was no need for the Colonel to know yet. There was still time. Besides, it was personal now. He lay back carefully on the pillows and mouthed the one word Taylor had thrown after him as he pounded down the stairs. Suzy. Suzy. Perhaps there lay another way.

Another half-hour. He would rest for thirty minutes more. Then he would move.

Suzy opened her eyes drowsily and shifted her weight

gently beside Martin so as not to wake him. She looked down on the warm sheets, at the unruly brown hair and the arm thrown across her warm, heavy breasts and gently brushed a strand of hair out of his eyes. She had very nearly lost him, she knew that now. And now, too, thanks to the nearness of the catastrophe, she realized what such a loss would mean to her. Presently she began, for the most selfish of reasons, to think of a way in which she might help.

Presently Martin awoke beside her. He glanced at his watch, groaned and swung back the sheets. He walked naked to the phone and began flicking impatiently through his contact book. Suzy watched him from the bed.

'Fielding, Fielding, P.,' he intoned under his breath. He found the number he was looking for and dialled impatiently.

'Hello, is that Mrs Fielding? Is your husband there, please? Thank you very much. I'll hold.' He covered the mouthpiece with his hand: 'What'd I tell you?' he whispered fiercely towards the bedroom: 'Taylor triumphs again – Hello? Mr Fielding? It's Taylor, Martin Taylor. Remember we spoke recently about –' He took the phone away from his ear and stared at it stupidly.

'He hung up on me. That bugger hung up on me!' he said incredulously. He paused, flicked through the contact book again and dug out another number. This time it was Harding's. He dialled that. There was no reply.

Puzzled, he dialled the office number. The call was answered promptly by a strange female voice. A replacement for Sandra.

'Mr Harding, please.'

'I'm sorry, he isn't available.'

Martin frowned. He hadn't yet even said who he was.

'When do you expect he will be?'

'Oh, not for some while, I'm afraid. He and Mrs Harding have gone away for a short holiday.'

'You're kidding!'

'I beg your pardon? Who is this calling?' asked the woman sharply.

'I'm sorry – it just came as something of a surprise, that's all. I was due to see Mr Harding today about a very important matter.'

'I see. He's gone away on the orders of his doctor for a short rest, so I understand. The strain and worry over the inquiry, I shouldn't wonder. Mr Moorby has taken over in his absence. Would you care to speak to him?'

'No, it's OK, thank you. It was a ... personal matter. Goodbye.' He turned towards Suzy. 'Fielding won't talk to me. Harding's left for a sudden holiday with his wife. Now, what do you suppose that all means?' Doors were shutting, and it was beginning to scare him.

'It means,' replied Suzy, wriggling out of bed and struggling unselfconsciously into tight jeans, 'it means the word is out. They're clearing the decks for action, I should imagine.'

'Thanks very much. What do you mean?'

'Has it occurred to you that you can't possibly stay here? That that man will be back? That it's only a matter of time before he comes through that door and starts papering the walls with you?'

Suzy pulled a sweater over her head, crouched down by Martin's mirror and began tugging a comb through her hair. Their eyes met in the mirror's reflection.

'I was having a little think while you were asleep. You remember you told me about that man Sam? Sam Spalding?' Suzy began to outline her idea. It was not a very good idea at first, but then Martin built on it and soon they had a plan.

Martin hunted out a pencil and began jotting down names as a sudden thought came to him: Sam Spalding's men in Royal Navy uniforms, the Under Secretary for Defence talking about Royal Navy personnel on merchant trawlers, that Royal Navy exercise – Squadex – that had been going on at the time *Pilgrim* disappeared ...

'There's something you can do for me, Suzy: find out through the Ministry of Defence what these ships are up to now. They're all Royal Navy. All were involved in that exercise, Squadex. If any of them are in port I might try and get a line on *Pilgrim* through them.' He shrugged and handed Suzy the slip of paper. 'It's just a long shot.'

'Uh-uh.' Suzy shook her head. 'Something wrong there.' Martin looked up sharply. 'What's that?'

'You said "I". You should have said "we". Reinforcements have arrived, remember?' Suzy grinned.

Twenty minutes later Suzy was gone. While she took the letter Martin had written over to the Three Mariners, Martin turned to his dressing. If all went well he did not have much time.

The flat seemed quiet after Suzy had gone. Martin looked down at the crumpled sheets. He missed her already.

Within minutes, or so it seemed, the lingering quietness of the flat had turned into an ominous, brooding silence.

He found himself listening anxiously to the little, normal sounds he usually took for granted. The creak of a door, a sound from one of the flats downstairs. Even his walls seemed to be watching, waiting, urging him to be gone, to hurry, hurry, get out. Twice he stopped what he was doing to peer down at the street – a white, frightened face at the window.

It was raining. People hurried by below, heads bent against the rain, eyes down to the pavement. Old men to the pub, children home to lunch, women to the shops for groceries. He turned back into the room, hurrying now.

He changed his mind. He took off the light shirt and neatly pressed trousers and donned instead a T-shirt, dark-blue turtleneck sweater, old jeans and tough rubber-soled boots.

He reached down his old kit bag from the top of the wardrobe and into this crammed underwear, socks and a couple of heavy sweaters. Then, holding the kit bag, he forced himself to walk slowly round the flat, choosing the necessities he would carry with him.

Hurry, hurry, hurry.

A razor from the bathroom. And a towel. Toothbrush. Paste. A small transistor from the bedroom. A powerful flashlight from the table.

Get out, get out, get out.

Tins from the larder, two paperbacks from the shelf. He went to his desk, opened the drawer and, fumbling in his haste, scooped out the cash from the little metal box. He glanced hurriedly at his fist. About thirty pounds.

Go on, go on, leave it – get out.

Press card and, almost as an afterthought, his passport. Parka off the hook behind the door. He was ready.

Out, out.

He hefted the kit bag, reached for the catch on the door – and hesitated. He crossed to the drawer and picked up the heavy automatic. He weighed it cautiously in his hand and then tucked it under his belt, beneath his parka in the small of his back.

Out.

'OK, mate – on your way.' Sam Spalding punched in the gears; the lorry gave a lurch and slowed right down as it crawled round the tight corner.

'Thanks a million, Sam.' Martin dumped his kit bag on the road, dropped off the running board and darted away into the shadows of a warehouse.

True to his word Sam had dropped him inside the docks beside the maintenance quay. Martin watched the lorry rattle into the distance, dwindle and then grow again as Sam turned and began to come back up through the gears towards him. Martin waited, holding his breath. There. Sam sounded the horn as he passed one of the trawlers in for maintenance and quota leave. Martin peered through the rain and wiped his glasses. *Harvest Maid*, it was. He raised a hand in gratitude as Sam rumbled past without a glance.

Martin waited a moment longer and looked carefully about him. No one was remotely interested in one more lorry and one more deckhand in dirty jeans walking along the wet quay hunched against the rain with a kit bag on his shoulder.

Martin walked nonchalantly up the gangway and dropped down into the well of the boat with a hollow thud. He stepped over a pile of welding gear, skirted the dismantled trawl winches, turned immediately to his right as Sam had told him to and stepped carefully into the darkness beyond the open companionway hatch.

Once out of the rain he dumped his kit bag at his feet, threw back his parka hood and listened.

Nothing. Silence.

He was safe. For the moment.

CHAPTER EIGHTEEN

Evans felt the lock snick back beneath the clumsy, probing fingers of his left hand. He pushed the door wide with his foot and flattened himself back against the wall. The door banged back. Silence. No sound from the flat, no welcoming shots from his own pistol.

He let out his breath in a controlled, soundless sigh. He had watched the Post Office messenger arrive with the telegram, and he had watched, too, this time from across the street in the newsagent's as the lad dropped down the stairs and crossed to his motorbike, buttoning the undelivered message back into the pouch strapped to his belt – which meant either that Martin was out and the flat was empty or that he was not answering the door.

It could mean something else, too. It could mean that Martin was in there, waiting.

Evans had considered involving the police or the Gas Board with some invented tale that would have sent unsuspecting strangers into the flat ahead of him with a legal excuse for entry, but had decided against it. There was no need for a more public involvement.

This way, his way, he would be able to resolve the matter privately.

And so the door was open.

Dropping to a crouch, he slipped his head round the door twelve inches above the floor. An instant later he pulled back, rose to his feet and leaned back against the wall. A moment passed.

Then, for the third time in twenty-four hours, Evans crossed the threshold of Martin's flat as an intruder.

This time there was no exploding flashbulb, no fight, no

hammer. This time there was nothing save the stillness of an empty room. Taylor had gone.

Taking his time, Evans began to search.

Half an hour later he helped himself to Martin's Scotch, dropped into one of Martin's chairs and put his feet up on Martin's coffee table. He had found very little.

He had not found the milk he had left on the doorstep, nor had he found the pistol Martin had knocked spinning from his wrist. He had searched under furniture, down the sides of chairs and behind cushions, and he had found nothing.

He had even turned out the waste bin in the kitchen. The discovery of the dog's discarded food bowl had solved one mystery even as he cursed himself for a fool as realization dawned.

What he did find, however, was a note from someone called Suzy.

He returned to the kitchen, rinsed out his glass and dried it carefully.

Evans was grinning mirthlessly as he let himself quietly out of the flat. Suzy.

Suzy replaced the receiver and frowned. Doing as Martin had asked, she had phoned the Ministry of Defence in London. The call had not been particularly helpful. It was not their policy to disclose fleet dispositions to ordinary members of the public. The little man was sorry, but there it was. Contact with officers and ratings aboard Royal Naval vessels would have to be through BFPO Ships. The advice gave her an idea.

Suzy lifted the phone again and this time went through to the Royal Navy at Portsmouth. A hesitant inquiry, a twisting of the heartstrings and she found herself talking to a kindly C P O who was prepared to help the girlfriend of a lovesick able seaman. 'Struth, he'd been one himself once, hadn't he? She used the ploy again on the phone to Rosyth and Greenwich.

Half an hour later only the frigates *Leander* and *Tuscan* and the logistic landing ship *Sir Tristram* remained unaccounted for. Ten minutes more and H M S *Leander* and the *Sir Tristram* were crossed off her list.

Which left only H M S *Tuscan*, 2,150 tons.

More phone calls. 'You might try Devonport, miss – most of the frigates are based there.' She tried Devonport. 'H M S *Tuscan*? She's out of the water, love. She's up in Barrow – Barrow-in-Furness. For repairs.'

'Repairs? What sort of repairs?'

'Hang on a second, love.' She heard papers being turned over and someone whistling tunelessly in the background. 'Here we are, then. Won't be a mo' ... *Tuscan* ... *Tuscan.* Yeah. Thought so. Buckled bow plating.'

'Buckled bow plating? What does that mean?' asked Suzy.

'Didn't your feller tell you? She's been in a bit of a scrape, old love, know what I mean?'

Evans was watching the door when the girl he had identified as Suzy stepped out onto the pavement. He leaned forward and started the engine. Then he paused, hand on the ignition.

Instead of turning left and walking round to the car park as he had expected, she crossed the road about thirty yards in front of him and vanished into the newsagent's.

Evans relaxed again, killed the engine and settled down in his seat to wait once more.

It was now eleven forty-five on Saturday, 8 June, and he had been watching and waiting outside Martin's block of flats since seven-thirty that morning. And before that, until 1 a.m. the previous night.

The girl had slipped out once before, two hours earlier, to do some shopping. Evans had followed her then, on foot, down to the market. Why she didn't ... There she was again, about to cross the street with what looked like newspapers under her arm. A nice looker, too. Long, strong legs and nice firm tits under that sweater, judging from the way they jiggled and bounced as she skipped across the road with a wide smile for the man in the sports car who had

215

slowed to let her across. Evans could see the man in the car making a meal of her as she gained the pavement and turned into the flats.

Another hour dragged by. Evans sat almost motionless at the wheel of his Scimitar, occasionally flexing the damaged muscles of his right hand. He grimaced at the dull, grinding pain that stabbed through his arm – as familiar, now, as toothache.

Evans's eyes flicked up to the door again as it opened. The girl again. This time she was wearing a parka and carrying a parcel under her arm. She turned to the left and walked quickly across to the row of lockup garages.

Evans brought the car to life and slipped painfully into first as Suzy's Mini paused, indicator flashing, and then turned right into Beverley Road. Evans let in the clutch and followed.

Suzy made slow progress through the Saturday traffic as she drove down Fernsway and cut across Porter Street and turned right into Hessle Road by the school.

To a fit man, such a shadow would have been simplicity itself. To Evans, however, it was a refined kind of hell. Hampered as he was by an injured hand that he was unable to favour for more than a moment at a time, the pain of constant movement brought the sweat to his forehead as he ground along in second gear, twisting and turning in and out of the stream of weekend drivers, striving to keep his station three vehicles behind the Mini.

Presently his difficulties diminished as, with fewer sudden halts, they snailed away from the prosperous commercial centre of the town, picked up speed and worked their way down Hessle Road and into the poorer residential neighbourhood with its terraced workers' cottages sandwiched in regimental rows between the main arterial road and the docks, wharfs, and ship and rail yards which had offered the scrapings of a wage to generations of Humbersiders.

The little green Mini turned abruptly left into Subway Street, drew in to the kerb and stopped. Evans, caught by surprise, muttered an oath and swung the wheel. He drove past without a glance, took the first turning on the right and rolled to a halt.

On foot now, Evans paced quickly back into Subway Street in time to see Suzy walk up to the main street and turn to her right. She still had the parcel. Evans broke into an awkward jog, his damaged hand held rigidly across his body.

Reaching the main street, he paused, looking swiftly to right and left.

She had gone.

Disappeared. Swallowed up in the haze of exhaust, the rumble of heavy traffic and the ebb and flow of pedestrians that thronged the cheaper shops.

He cast about him methodically, craning his head this way and that to peer between the lorries and the vans that thundered down towards the docks and the railway depot at Priory Yard.

One minute passed, another. Suddenly he had her again, coming out of the post office – a fleeting glimpse caught over the roof of a lorry.

This time she was not carrying the parcel.

Evans watched unobserved as Suzy crossed the street and walked easily towards him. He turned to the nearest shop window as she passed and then trailed her back to the Mini.

Both cars returned to the block of flats without further incident. With Suzy inside the building once more, Evans parked in a different place and settled down to wait for Taylor.

Suzy returned to the phone with an enthusiasm kindled by early success. She had decided to keep her discoveries to herself until she could present them to Martin personally for maximum impact. Besides, she was nowhere near a dead end yet. Now, after a moment's thought, she was on to the *Daily Telegraph* and their services correspondent.

Who, she inquired, was captain of H M S *Tuscan*?

More pauses, more suggestions, another string of phone numbers, and presently she had her answer.

Since September 1973 H M S *Tuscan* had been under the command of Commander Simon H. Jennings, R N. The private addresses of serving naval officers were never released. However, he could probably be reached through the wardroom of his parent shore base if he was not away at sea or on a course or on leave. The nearest naval shore base for a ship undergoing repairs at Barrow was H M S *Anvil*.

Half an hour crawled by. Evans drummed his left hand against the side of his thigh. Something was wrong. He could not shrug off a faint, nagging feeling of unease that built as the moments passed. He had missed something. Just then the train of introverted thought was derailed as he jarred his arm against the sill of the car window and swore aloud at the jolt of sudden pain.

A pity, that, because his instincts, usually, were quite sound.

Martin smeared his fingertips across the aimless little pattern he had been making in the condensation on the inside of the scuttle. Outside a seagull planed effortlessly in the wind and then darted, beak wide, at a half-submerged orange box. A drift of thin drizzle peppered the waters of the inner dock. Martin looked across the sluggish, oily water towards the gaunt, dripping warehouses that hunched, brooding, out over the water a few hundred yards away, and shivered.

He tugged up the zip of his parka and dropped back listlessly into a chair to pick up his novel once again, only to toss it aside a moment later, unable to concentrate. He glanced at his watch, dragged his kit bag from under the bunk and rummaged around for the last of the apples he had brought with him from the flat. He began munching, willing the hours to pass.

It was almost twenty-five hours since he had waved his thanks to Sam Spalding, twenty-five hours since he had seen a soul or spoken to anybody. For Martin, unaccustomed to the solitude of his own company, it felt like twenty-five years, lost in a limbo of his own choosing. He had become depressed and lonely.

Harvest Maid had not welcomed her trespasser aboard.

She was not, it was true, a big vessel, nothing to write home about, nothing to turn the head after, not in a port like Hull. Just another rust-streaked, salt-stained work boat, a narrow-beamed, middle-water sidewinder with a wheelhouse perched far aft, a forepeak set high in the bows and a long well deck that gave her just a pinch of freeboard whenever her holds were full.

Now she was just one among a dozen or so sidewinders moored alongside awaiting stores, or a crew, or a tide. Except that *Harvest Maid* was in refit, and that made her special. It also made her an empty ship, a still ship, a dead ship — a damp, dark, echoing hulk of a vessel with all the life gone out of her, sunk to the top of the ocean. Her crew were all ashore, her engines stilled; where there had been light and warmth and noise and laughter there was now nothing, just the cold and the chill and the silence which crept in between the plates of her steel sides to mingle with the smell of fish and diesel and the touch of grease, the smear of oil.

She was deserted, a place full of black holes that led down black, bottomless companionways and smooth, worn metal ladders to more blackness.

Feeling his way without a light and dragging his kit bag behind him, Martin had forced himself to press deep into the bowels of the vessel, slipping and stumbling in the darkness until he came to the tiny mess deck aft.

The eating area was lit by pale natural light from the two outboard scuttles, and in their inadequate illumination he saw dirty green curtains, an old dartboard on a nail by the bulkhead, and a table and two benches bolted to the steel deck. There was a stainless-steel serving hatch leading through to the galley. A chipped mug with a broken handle lay in the scuppers.

Behind the mess deck Martin had found two cabins, each with four bunks. He had chosen a bunk under the open porthole, laid out his sleeping bag and settled down to read one of the novels he had brought with him in a strange, alien silence that coiled his stomach into tight knots of tension. He had found it impossible to concentrate and had started at the slightest unfamiliar sound.

There were lots of strange, unfamiliar sounds.

In mid afternoon he had made a stealthy tour of the ship. The galley yielded a tin of sardines, a jar of pickles and half a stale loaf; the logbook on the bridge told him he was a trespasser on the property of Spencer Trawlers Ltd; and in the mate's cabin he discovered a four-week-old copy of the *Sun* and a much thumbed copy of *Mayfair* magazine which he took back as plunder to his bunk.

As the afternoon light began to fade he had squatted beside his kit bag and, with some trepidation, dug out the pistol.

The weapon had lain in the palm of his hand, heavy, dark, gleaming slightly with the sheen of oil. Once, many years ago at a cadet camp, he had been shown how to fire a revolver. A champion shot he wasn't. Six rounds they had given him – and all had vanished into Norfolk's flat, loamy countryside with a dry unflattering remark from his instructor.

Martin had turned the thing this way and that and then, taking scrupulous care, begun a series of cautious experiments.

That had been yesterday. Today was Saturday, and after a frightening, sleepless night alone in the deserted creaking vessel, propped up in his sleeping bag with the pistol under his pillow, Martin reckoned he had got the hang of the gun nicely.

He glanced at his watch once more and rose to his feet. He weighed the pistol in his hand, shoved it into his pocket and made for the companionway.

Now, at last, it was time to pick up the parcel Suzy should have left for him at the post office.

*

Evans was still watching, still waiting outside Suzy's flat.

He watched idly as an old man on the pedestrian crossing turned with a feeble little wave to thank the traffic that had slowed to let him cross.

Poor old sod, thought Evans as the old man hobbled up onto the pavement and limped down the street. As he watched, the old man patted his pockets, drew out an envelope and dropped it carefully into the pillar box outside the chemist's before turning to retrace his painful steps.

Suddenly Evans snapped to full alert. He craned across the steering wheel and stared at the red pillar box as though Martin himself was hiding within.

Leaning forward, he gunned the engine to life with sudden, violent anger. With a screech of rubber he mounted the pavement, sheared across the oncoming traffic and turned to a blare of angry horns. How many post offices had they passed on the way down to the docks – two, three? Why go all that way just to post a fucking parcel? He saw the answer in a blur of shop windows. It was a drop! It was written in startled eyes caught in rearview mirrors as, hand forgotten, pain ignored, he trod on the accelerator and scythed through dawdling crowds back towards Hessle Road.

Nine minutes later Suzy banged the phone down on the receiver, swept her leather handbag off the chair, slammed the front door and bounced down the stairs to her car, thrilled with excitement.

She had just discovered that Commander Simon H. Jennings R N had been relieved of his command on 22 February, and was now a patient at the Royal Naval Hospital, Frankfort Gate, Bradford. Suzy had discovered something else too: the Royal Naval Hospital at Bradford specialized in the treatment of psychiatric disorders.

Someone was holding up the queue.

Martin, two customers back from the counter, looked about him nervously and willed the sweet, dear, dawdling old woman in the dark coat to get her bloody postal orders and go! He felt exposed, vulnerable, in such a public place.

Half a year crawled by. The woman moved at last and the man in front registered a small parcel. Then it was his turn.

'I'd like to collect a parcel, please. Poste restante.'

'Your name, please?' asked the serious young man in glasses.

'Taylor. Martin Taylor.'

'One moment, please.' The young man turned to the back of the post office, and Martin stole a quick, furtive glance about him.

The post office was busy. There were two queues snaking towards the counter, but Martin found little comfort sinking among such a crowd, hiding from a man he would recognize only by a damaged hand.

Glance at a face, look at a hand. Glance at a face, look at a hand. Martin told himself that he was jumpy, that the bloke was probably flat on his back in some hospital, yet still his eyes travelled restlessly, looking at the faces, looking for the hand swathed in bandages.

The clerk was returning from a rear storeroom, clutching a bulky brown parcel. Martin heaved a sigh of relief.

'Here you are, sir.'

'Many thanks.' He tucked the parcel under his arm, picked his way through the queues and emerged once more onto Hessle Road. Thank Christ that was over! With a lighter heart now, he turned to the right and mingled instantly with the crowds of Saturday shoppers.

He was thinking of the girl as he turned down Filton Road and picked out, poking at the sky over the slate rooftops, the tips of the cranes that were his landmark. Almost home now.

Sharklike, the long snout of the yellow Scimitar cruised slowly around the streets, pausing at a junction here, stopping suddenly for half a minute there as Evans tried to cut Taylor's trail. Eyes lost in shadow, hands resting lightly on the wheel, Evans peered closely into faces and shops and down streets, searching for one man with a parcel on a busy Saturday afternoon.

He slowed almost to a halt, indicated he was turning right and swung the wheel. The long, narrow engine cowling poked curiously down into Filton Road. Fifty yards, a hundred, a hundred and fifty, each covered with just a whisper of rubber on tarmac as he crawled along at a speed only slightly faster than a fit man can walk.

He saw the parcel first. Evans accelerated carefully, closing the distance.

He dropped back a little. He had him cold. He glanced quickly in the mirror. The road was empty of traffic.

He could attack, turn right at the bottom and be away before anyone had even begun to look for a number plate. He moved his left hand to the gear lever and slipped in the clutch.

Then he paused. Why hurry? Better to hit him when he knew where he had been holed up, make a proper job of the business once and for all. Almost reluctantly his hand slipped off the gear lever, and the clutch re-engaged. He could afford to wait. He had him now.

Martin turned left at the bottom of Filton Road into West Dock Avenue.

Evans crept round after him, forty yards behind. Easy does it ... The bloke was wide open, unsuspecting. He didn't look to right or left and he never once so much as glanced over his shoulder.

Evans grinned a little grin and settled down to enjoy the stalk. Easy as knocking off clay pigeons. Or Micks down in Rossville Flats.

There was a level crossing ahead. Martin stepped between the rails even as the tracks began to tremble and sing and the bells began to sound. He hurried across.

Too late, Evans trod on the accelerator and the car spurted forward. Pleasurable anticipation had blunted his reaction time and he screeched to a halt two feet from the tracks as the barriers dropped with a crash, chopping across the road before him. He pounded the steering wheel with his good hand and swore soundlessly as the first of the wagons rolled past.

It was a long goods train, twenty-five wagons long. Evans knew because he counted.

CHAPTER NINETEEN

The brooding, dripping silence that pervaded the lower deck with a chilling, unnerving monotony was broken by a new sound, an alien sound – the crackle of wrapping paper. In the small cabin aft, Martin was tackling Suzy's parcel.

At other times and in other places he might have worked at the knots, saved the string and folded the paper neatly away for a next time. Now he tore wantonly at the careful wrappings in his impatience to re-establish contact with the world that waited for him beyond the dark, friendless tomb of the deserted vessel.

Suzy had done him proud. There was a lump of something heavy wrapped in tinfoil that turned out to be fruit cake that was still warm in the middle; there were tins of fruit, some bars of chocolate and a bundle of fresh clothes wrapped in another pair of jeans, together with a roll of newspapers and some post that had been delivered to his flat. Best of all, there was a letter in Suzy's handwriting tucked into the leather case of a small metal hip flask.

Martin beamed like a lantern. Depression evaporated, loneliness slunk to a far corner. It was Christmas and his birthday all rolled into one. He decided to celebrate. Tucking the pistol under his belt, he padded through to the mess deck on silent feet and listened intently for a long moment, eyes staring through the steel deck plates above his head. Then, moving quickly, he risked one of his infrequent brew-ups on the galley stove.

He used the stove sparingly. The hiss of the butane gas masked the silence that, for all its frightening disadvantages, he had come to recognize as his greatest ally : while it lasted he had a flawless, foolproof warning system. But each time he used the stove or ran a tap, the advantage swung away, instantly and impartially.

Back in his cabin with a mug of hot sweet tea, Martin fished out his penknife, hacked himself a massive wedge of fruit cake and sprawled out on his bunk to read Suzy's note.

The hip flask, Martin read, was a present. He laid the letter aside, unscrewed the top of the flask and sniffed. Praise be – cognac ! He raised the flask in a toast and took an incautious swig that left him spluttering for breath in a welter of cake crumbs and fiery spirit. Recovering, he poured a more modest amount into his tea and settled down once more with Suzy's letter.

His face was dirty, lined with strain and flecked with stubble. Suzy's letter could do nothing about the dirt or the stubble but, as he read the warming, private words, the lines of strain softened into a smile.

His post contained the usual round of circulars and bills, but hidden among the khaki buff envelopes of petty official-dom he spotted the cheerful pale blue of an airmail letter. It was from a chain of magazines in Houston, enclosing details of the forthcoming oil conference in Trondheim. Nice work, if you could get it. He turned to the newspapers to catch up on what he had been missing.

'Waves the Size of Houses,' announced the back-page headline story about the inquiry. Martin took another bite of cake and began reading. Presently his chewing slowed and he sat back, vaguely puzzled. He flicked to the front page of the newspaper and checked the date – Saturday. Today. That suggested the story had been gleaned from evidence submitted to the inquiry the previous day, Friday, 7 June.

He read on. The story was full of climatic conditions, the effect of wind and waves, sequential wave patterns and recorded examples of damage related to wave height and water mass. There was bugger all about the discovery of the lifebuoy, yet Martin was certain the lifebuoy evidence had been scheduled for that day's hearing. It would make more than a paragraph, for God's sake – it was all they had.

Sea state, wave height, lag time between one crest and another, visibility, weather forecasts for early January in the Barents Sea area ... Then, suddenly, tucked away down towards the bottom of the column:

Written evidence relating to the discovery of the life-buoy, found off the north coast of Norway on 5 March, was submitted to the Inquiry by H. C. Hockling of the DTI on behalf of Dr D. C. Dowdall of Polperro, Cornwall.

After examining the bulk of the written evidence in chambers Chairman Mr M. Armstrong-Carpenter told the Inquiry: 'The highly technical nature of the report effectively precludes any constructive analysis of its findings by Counsel, who, while admirably qualified in Marine Law, are, perhaps, singularly unqualified in matters relating to Marine Molecular Biology.' (Laughter.)

Thanking Dr Dowdall for what he referred to as 'meticulous micro-biological detective work,' Mr Armstrong-Carpenter went on: 'I realize such a report should, strictly speaking, be laboured over for many hours by an Inquiry such as this. However, let us not lose sight of our primary objective: to resolve the matter relating to the disappearance of the Motor Trawler *Arctic Pilgrim* and to bring to a speedy close the period of suffering and anxiety endured by the bereaved.

'I have decided, after much deliberation, that, in an Inquiry related solely to one vessel's disappearance, an exhaustive dissection of such a specialized work as that of Dr Dowdall by anyone less than another expert in the same field would be counter-productive to the best interests of this Inquiry.

'The relevance of such scientific evidence, relating as it does to diatomic and planktonic growth on a lifebuoy discovered twenty-five days *after* the vessel's disappearance, must, in any event, remain problematical. I am satisfied that Dr Dowdall's evidence cannot add materially to our investigations.'

An objection to such irregular procedure from Counsel for the Dependants was overruled. The Inquiry continues on Monday.

Martin tossed the paper aside, appalled.

He sat for a long time without moving, staring unseeing at the drab, peeling bulkhead opposite, feeling nothing but a great contempt for the reporter who had written the article. A reporter who had taken down all the facts in wearying, unimaginative detail, spelled all the names right, got all the titles down correctly and missed what was happening right under his nose.

Two hours later, an open tin of peaches at his elbow and a pair of the skipper's binoculars pressed to his eyes, Martin stood in the shadow beneath an open scuttle, the binoculars resting against the circular rim of the porthole as he studied the phone booth with extreme care. There lay his way to Professor Dowdall.

It stood on the quay opposite, a small oblong of glass and cheerful red paint, pygmied in the shadows cast by a line of gaunt warehouses. Six hundred yards, he judged – seven hundred at a pinch.

The gate snicked shut behind her as Suzy walked up the garden path, her handbag clutched to her side. She felt awkward, nervous, uncertain. When the curtain moved in the bay window downstairs her mouth went dry and she wanted to turn and flee. What was she doing here? She still did not really know what she was going to ask the woman she had driven sixty miles to see.

The Royal Naval Hospital at Bradford had refused point-blank to disclose any information about one of its patients. Indeed, the hospital's senior nursing officer had seemed extremely surprised that Suzy Summerfield – a civilian – even knew of the hospital's existence. Yes, a Commander Jennings was staying at the hospital, but she must understand that any further discussion about a patient or his condition was both unethical and an unwarranted intrusion. Suzy was not a hard, intrusive, insensitive woman. She was not even a journalist. Moral sympathy instantly aroused, her veneer of investigative nerve had promptly evaporated. She had apologized lamely and almost run back down the marble steps to the sanctuary of her little Mini.

What would Martin do? What would he expect her to do? The questions had arisen unbidden to the top of her mind as she reversed her car across the gravel, and there they had remained, two prodding little gremlins clamouring for attention. She had ignored the nagging voices for ten minutes and then found herself pulling in at a phone kiosk. Perhaps Jennings had a wife. Perhaps they even lived nearby. One last try, she promised herself – a Martin Taylor long shot. And if that did not work – as it wouldn't – then she would call it a day and go home, gremlins satisfied.

There was a Jennings in the phone book, inevitably. 'Jennings, S. H., Lt. Comdr.' The address was over in Dewsbury. It had not been far to drive.

'Damn you, Mr Taylor,' Suzy muttered weakly as she pressed the doorbell. The door opened almost immediately.

'Mrs Jennings? I called earlier ...'

'You must be Miss Summerfield. Won't you please come in?'

'Thank you.' Suzy stepped over the porch and found herself in a narrow hallway. She could smell cooking from the kitchen, and a pair of rugby boots hung by their laces over the banister rail. The house had an air of raffish neglect. Somehow Suzy had expected commanders in charge of warships to live in grander surroundings.

'We'll go into the lounge, if you like,' offered Mrs Jennings calmly, leading the way.

'Fine.' Suzy was racking her brains for more to say, for something that would make an ally of this stranger.

'Do sit down,' said Mrs Jennings graciously in the voice Suzy knew she used when entertaining her husband's superiors. In the light from the standard lamp Suzy detected that Mrs Jennings, seemingly in her middle thirties, would normally have been a pretty, vivacious woman, strung taut by a natural tension that would serve to heighten her air of vitality. But there were rings under her eyes, and a strand of hair had come loose from the neat bun behind her ears. There was a brimming ashtray on the arm of her chair

229

which Mrs Jennings now tried to remove from sight.

'Filthy habit.' She laughed sharply and chucked the ash into the empty grate. Some blew back into the room to settle on Mrs Jennings's skirt. She brushed it away with quick, nervous movements. This is awful, thought Suzy desperately. I should never have come – never.

'You said on the phone you wanted to ask a few questions about *Tuscan* and my husband, Miss Summerfield. I suppose I should ask you why, although quite frankly I've been in such a daze these last few weeks –'

'Mummy! Mummy!' A boy in school uniform erupted into the living room. 'Those batteries don't work! You said you'd get me P-fours and you've got P-fives instead! You promised! Now I'll –' He noticed the guest for the first time. 'Oh. Sorry.'

'Hello,' said Suzy, sitting back in her chair.

'I do apologize. This is Mike.'

'Hello, Mike,' said Suzy.

'How do you do? Mummy, what am I going to do? They won't fit.' A grubby hand held out four small flashlight batteries.

'Oh, dear,' said Mrs Jennings, a hand pulling at her hair. 'I'm so sorry, Mike.' She glanced at her watch. 'And the shops and shut now. It'll just have to wait until tomorrow.'

'Oh, Mummy – you promised. You promised you'd –'

'Perhaps I can help,' offered Suzy, seizing her chance. 'I've got some bigger batteries in the car. Why don't you use those? I think they're P-fours. In fact, I'm sure they are.'

'No, really, we couldn't possibly –'

But Suzy was already on her feet, grateful for the interruption, the breathing space. When she returned from the car Mrs Jennings was juggling pots frantically in the kitchen. Suzy handed the batteries to Mike, who scampered upstairs.

Mrs Jennings emerged from the kitchen wiping her hands on an apron. 'There was no need for you to do that, Miss Summerfield, Mike is quite capable of –'

'Please – call me Suzy. No one's called me Miss Summerfield since I had a visit from the tax inspector.' She smiled. 'Oh – and why don't I talk to you in there?' Suzy gestured towards the kitchen. 'You're obviously busy. I can chat to you while you work.'

'Are you sure? You see, it's Mike's night for model-making and I promised I'd ... Well, if you're sure. You'll have to excuse the mess,' she threw back over her shoulder as they picked their way down the hallway. -

Gradually the ice broke into little pieces as Mrs Jennings made supper for her son. There was a framed picture on the working surface of a younger Mrs Jennings in a bright summer frock standing proudly on the arm of a young naval officer at some formal occasion. Suzy warmed towards the woman, and presently, quite naturally, she was standing there beside the sink in an apron, helping with the dishes.

Suzy told Mrs Jennings gradually about Martin Taylor and about the *Arctic Pilgrim* story. Mrs Jennings nodded absently.

'I remember reading about that. Awful story – simply awful. Simon was up there, too, at the time. I expect you know that.'

'I knew *Tuscan* was on exercise up there, yes. Was your husband still ... still in command then?'

'Oh, yes. He was having a whale of a time, by all accounts.' The note of bitterness was quite pronounced. 'He'd only been in command – what – four months? Five? A ship of his own. He was like a cat with two tails. Then he came back, and for some reason ... some reason ... I don't know, he just ... went ... to ... pieces.' She turned away, bowing her head over a scrap of handkerchief.

'Look, it's none of my business, none of it. I had no right –'

'Oh, no – it's all right, really. I get like this occasionally. You must forgive me. Do you know –' she whirled round, tear-filled eyes blazing now with anger – 'do you know, Suzy, no one from his ship has so much as been to *see* Simon – or me, for that matter – since all this happened.

231

Not one person! It's as though ... as though ... it all just never happened. But it happened, all right – oh, yes. God knows what it was, but they broke him. They broke him as sure as you're standing there.'

'They?'

'Their high and mighty Lords of the Admiralty.' The bitterness washed into her eyes now. 'Whoever it was that turned a fit, dedicated naval officer with the world at his feet into a ... a ... a cabbage. I can't think of another word for it.' She choked off into another bout of sobbing, and Suzy's arms went impulsively around her thin shoulders.

'Do they tell you what is actually wrong with your husband?' Suzy asked gently.

Mrs Jennings sniffed. 'Oh, they've got some fancy name for it. Acute psycho something or other. It's depression, that's all, they tell me. He could snap out of it tomorrow ... or ... or it could take another six months. Either way he's finished, finished with the Royal Navy.'

'Can I ask what happened – I mean, did he –'

'No, I don't mind.' She gazed off into the past, a wet plate forgotten in her hands. 'He came home on leave as usual, only right away I knew something was wrong, not as it should be. Usually Simon is so ... so attentive, so full of fun, you know? Only he virtually ignored me. He snapped at Mike – something he's never done before – and spent hours and hours just sitting in his study, staring out of the window, brooding. Nothing I could say, nothing I could do, seemed to make any difference. I just couldn't break through to him, do you understand what I mean?'

Suzy nodded dumbly.

'That went on for – I don't know – a couple of weeks? Ten days, certainly.' Mrs Jennings dried her eyes, and her words came more fluently now as she began to share the burden she had carried alone. 'He never used to eat, he didn't even bother to change out of his pyjamas. He used to get up mid morning and lock himself away in his study for hours at a time. And all the time ... all the time his leave was just slipping by Then, three or four days before he was due to go back – I forget just how many – I heard voices in his study. I thought at first he was talking to himself, but he wasn't, not in that sense, anyway. He was talking into ... into a tape recorder. Then, the day before he was due to report back aboard, he just went to pieces. I heard him sobbing ... sobbing. In there. I went to him.' Mrs Jennings looked up with heavy, haunted eyes. 'I'll never forget it as long as I live. He'd changed into uniform, you see. Only he'd taken a razor blade and ripped off all the gold braid and cut off all the buttons. He just sat there with braid and bits of his cap, his buttons, heaped in his lap, with the tears just running down his face and with that tape recorder just hissing, hissing in the background.'

'I'm so sorry, I had no idea.'

'Luckily Mike was away at school then. I called the doctor, and Simon ... Simon went away.' The voice ended in a whisper.

Suzy studied the plate she was drying. 'Mrs Jennings –' her voice was very low, very controlled – 'I want you to know how much I appreciate you taking me into your confidence. It can't have been easy.' She paused. 'Now I have to ask you something that I expect, I fully expect, you to say no to. But I'm going to ask it all the same, because my man – the Martin I was telling you about – has put a lot of himself into this *Arctic Pilgrim* business. Not as much, I'm sure, as your husband, Simon, but everything he knows, everything he has. I just have a feeling that what happened to your husband has got something to do with what happened to that fishing boat. Don't ask me to –'

'You want to borrow that tape, is that it? You want to listen to Simon's tape?'

'I don't ... That is, I ...' Suzy floundered, taken aback. She pulled herself together. 'If you'll let me – yes. I'd like to take it away, play it once and then return it immediately. If you feel you can trust me I'd like to leave you my phone number so that if at any time you changed your mind, you could –'

Slowly Mrs Jennings tugged open a kitchen drawer and removed a cassette. She stood there quietly, weighing it – and Suzy – in her hand. 'I've meant to listen to it myself, oh, a dozen times. But somehow it's been too ... too painful, you know?'

Suzy nodded. 'I think so.'

'I must have it back, you understand,' said Mrs Jennings finally, holding out the tape.

In Hull, the yellow Scimitar drew in to the kerb and stopped. Evans pulled the map towards him and spread it out across the steering wheel. He had to be in there, somewhere.

In *there*.

For the hundredth time he studied the box of land blocked off by Hessle Road, the Freightliner Depot, the river and the Boulevard. He glanced up at the clouds as the first rain began to spatter the windscreen and folded the map away impatiently. There was an easier way. He spun the car round in a tight circle and began to drive back into the town. Towards the girl's flat.

It was forty minutes later, and in Dewsbury Mrs Diana Jennings was having second thoughts. That tape was private, it wasn't for anyone else to hear. And what was stopping it from being copied – not by Suzy – she trusted her – but by that man Taylor, or by anyone else – copied or transferred onto another tape. And then another. Suddenly she saw her actions as betrayal – betrayal of her husband's innermost torment. She hurried to the phone in the hall and dialled the number Suzy had left her. The phone was answered almost immediately.

'Look, I've been thinking,' she rushed. 'I'm sorry, but I'd rather you didn't hear what was on that tape. It's private, personal – I should never have agreed to lend it to you. I don't see really that it can have any relevance to your trawler, Suzy. Can I have it back? Straight away? I'd sleep so much easier. I am sorry –'

'It's not Suzy, actually –'

'Oh. Well. Can you see she gets that message, please? I don't want her to play the tape. Can she return it to me as soon as possible? Tell her I'm very sorry but it's really the only way. It's Mrs Jennings calling. She'll know who I am.'

'Right-oh, Mrs Jennings. I'll pass on the message.' Evans replaced the receiver.

Suzy clattered up the stairs and let herself into her flat. A cup of tea and a bite to eat and then she'd sit down and play that tape; hear what Commander Simon H. Jennings had to say for himself. A pound to a pinch of salt there was *something* there that would shed some light on what was going on. Not bad sleuthing for a day's work, she thought happily. Martin would be pleased. She hung her parka on the hook by the plant stand and started towards the living room. All it had taken was a bit of audacity at first and then a little bit of patience and –

A man was sitting in her living room.

Sitting in her favourite chair, stirring a cup of her tea. He looked up and smiled pleasantly.

With a sudden, terrible jolt of fear Suzy knew who he was.

'Who're you?' she managed with a small voice gone suddenly dry. She swallowed. 'What are you doing here?'

The smile didn't waver. The stirring of the tea and the silence continued.

'Who let you in here? This is my flat! How dare –'

'Now take it easy, Suzy.'

She let out an involuntary gasp. 'How d'you know my name?'

'It is Suzy, then. That's a relief.' He continued to sit there – calm, cold, terrifying with polite, latent menace. 'It would have looked pretty poor if I'd broken into the wrong flat, wouldn't it? Quite lower the tone of the neighbourhood.' Beneath the smile Evans watched her closely, watched her eyes grow wide with fear as she considered and then discarded the possible options for a swift retreat. A bright

235

one, this. A thinker. Brave, too. But a woman – with a woman's fears, a woman's levers. The technique that just hinted at ugly threat might yet be sufficient. Mentally, Evans shrugged. He didn't much care either way.

'Broken in? Look, I don't know what you're after, but if you're not out of here in twenty seconds ...'

Evans shook his head tiredly. Maybe it wouldn't be enough, after all. He'd heard it all before, both in training and on operations.

'What'll you do, Suzy? Call in the police? Be sensible. Come on, sit down.' He gestured to a chair.

Suzy hung back as though she knew the chair was mined.

'Sit.'

Eyes rabbit-wide, Suzy sat.

'Shall I tell you what you'll do? You'll have a nice cup of tea and then you'll tell me where Mr Sunshine has been hiding himself.'

'Mr Sunshine?'

'Your Mr Taylor. The hero of the hour who at this moment is hiding somewhere, leaving you alone.'

Suzy flushed.

'And then, when you've told me what I want to know, then and only then I'll wash up this cup and saucer and tiptoe away very, very quietly. No fuss, no mess and – especially important, this, Suzy, as far as you're concerned – no pain.'

The tape, thought Suzy suddenly. He mustn't get hold of the tape.

'What are you going to do to him?' she asked, dull-voiced.

'Your Mr Taylor?' Evans shrugged. 'I just want to talk to him, that's all – straighten out a few things.'

'I don't believe you. You're going to kill him. You bastard.'

The man leaned forward and the smile froze into bleak granite. 'I don't care if you believe me or not. What you think, what you suspect, doesn't matter any more. You're out of your depth, Suzy. Now –' he gestured at the kitchen behind his shoulder – 'why don't you make yourself that cup of tea? Then we can have our little chat.'

Suzy got up slowly, clutching her handbag.

'Oh – and there's just one other thing. The tape. Mrs Jennings wants the tape. I said I'd look after it for her. For safe keeping.'

'The tape?' Suzy managed bravely. 'What tape? I'm afraid I don't know what you mean.' The lie was stamped across her face.

Evans saw it and shook his head sadly. 'Don't give me grief. She phoned about half an hour ago. I said I'd pass on the message. Go on, love – make that tea.'

'Oh,' said Suzy, defeated. She went into her little kitchenette and began working, her stomach fluttering with fear. As she dug into the tea caddy an idea came to her. She glanced over her shoulder. The man was studying a row of books on a shelf.

Presently Suzy went back into the living room, the teacup rattling the saucer. She hated herself then for the tell-tale betrayal of her weakness, her fear.

The man looked up. 'Don't worry – nothing's going to happen to you. I mean, you are going to help me, aren't you? After you've finished your tea.'

'Damn your fucking tea!' Suzy flung the cup and saucer towards him and stepped swiftly to where she kept her stereo equipment, her tapes and records. A little anger was called for now – a little fear and anger. It wasn't hard to find. 'You repulsive bastard,' she whispered as the man wiped at the tea stains that had splashed against his legs. 'You think you can push people about just because ... because ...' She raved on, and all the while her hands were busy below the level of the chair's head-rest and out of sight of the intruder.

Now the man rose, stepped over the broken crockery and walked softly towards her. 'You've finished? Come back here and sit down. Sit down or I shall hurt you. Sit down. Now.'

Suzy fell silent. Arms dropped weakly to her side, and she did as she was ordered.

'That was silly. What you don't yet seem to have grasped –'

He hit her.

He brought his left wrist up and across, smashing the back of his hand across her jawline as she leaned forward. Her head flew up in a cascade of rich chestnut hair as she fell sprawling over the far side of the chair. She moaned softly as little drops of blood from her gashed lips dripped silently onto the carpet.

A gentle hand pulled her back into the upright position. Evans offered her a clean handkerchief solicitously.

'There is no need for further pain,' he said softly. 'I need two things from you – both I know you can give me. First: where is Martin Taylor? Where is he hiding? Second: I want that tape. I want it now. The police, your Martin Taylor, even the Seventh Cavalry – all are beyond reach. It is just you and me now. Be practical. Tell me what I want to know. Further pain is both unnecessary and pointless.'

With small, trembling fingers Suzy held out a tape cassette. Evans inspected it briefly.

'Thank you, Suzy.' He squatted down beside her and, with soft fingers, brushed a strand of hair out of her eyes. The hair was damp from her tears: 'Now –' the voice became silken – 'where is Martin Taylor? Where is he hiding?'

'I ... I don't know.' Her tremulous defiance hung in the still air, a fragile thing that would not withstand more than one gust of wind. Suzy sensed that that wind was about to blow. She moaned, turned her head aside and closed her eyes. Let it pass – please, God, let it pass.

'Suzy, Suzy – I can cause you such distress!' Slowly Evans's hand reached out and cupped her breast. After a moment his fingers moved to the top button of her blouse and rested there. 'Pain? You want pain? I can cause you pain. Humiliation and degradation – those too. Ask yourself: is it really worth it? Is it?' The blouse fell open, and Suzy's breasts spilled forward. 'And very nice too,' murmured Evans. 'Isn't Martin a lucky lad?' He weighed them absently, and his fingers pressed gently, a housewife choosing oranges.

Suzy closed her eyes tighter still with the shame of it and died inside as she felt his fingers still upon her. The feeling in her breasts increased until she moaned aloud with the heavy pain of it.

'Just tell me. Tell me where he is.'

'I've told you – I don't ... I don't know,' she gasped.

'But you do, you do,' insisted Evans quietly, squeezing.

'No ... No ... I ...'

'And I've told you: I don't believe you.' He released her breast and stood before her once more. Another silence. And then another vicious backhander to the face that catapulted Suzy across the chair and onto the floor. There was another blow after that and then more humiliation as slowly, strip by strip, Evans peeled away the woman's self-respect, her defiance, her courage. Finally:

'He's ... he's on a ship,' she sobbed.

CHAPTER TWENTY

The last strains of Mussorgsky's *Pictures at an Exhibition*
drifted across the small cluttered sitting room and faded
into the old curtains and the piles of books and dusty documents.

Over by the window Dr Dowdall stirred at last in his
cane chair and rose slowly to his feet. His wife had loved
that piece of music, and they had listened to it often.

The doctor shuffled over to the wireless and turned it off.
Then he returned to his seat and resumed his sightless staring out across the tumbled crags and choked gullies to the
village below.

It had become a custom of his, this sitting by the window,
looking from his vantage point down over the hills and the
slate roof of the schoolhouse as the sharp outline of church
and gravestone – her gravestone – blurred in the lengthen-
ing shadows of dusk. Usually these long moments beneath
the window were restful, peaceful times of recollection and
tranquillity, but it was a tranquillity that eluded him now,
its place taken by a slow, alien anger which had burned
within him for days.

He thought for a moment, trying to remember the last
occasion when he had felt so ... so *agitated*. His precise
mind isolated the moment exactly to a time, eighteen months
ago, when a perfect stranger in a large motor car had
knocked on his front door and offered him, outright, a
monstrous cash sum for his cottage.

Then he had been able simply to slam the front door. It
had taken him some while to recover. He imagined, moodily,
that it would be some little time now before he could put
this other matter behind him. It was all most upsetting.

He had been working late in the shed as usual, running a series of tests on two of his old favourites, *Fragilaria islandica* and *Navicula tripunctata*. So engrossed had he become in the delicate infinite world of diatoms, so absorbed in the business of slides and formalin, that he had missed the click of the garden gate as it opened. He realized he had a visitor only when a shadow fell across his workbench. He jumped involuntarily. A little of the cleaning alcohol spilled across the specimen slide he had just prepared so laboriously. The doctor pushed old-fashioned spectacles up onto his forehead and peered up at the stranger with undisguised annoyance. He did not particularly welcome visitors at the best of times: well-dressed young men who arrived unannounced and without knocking in the middle of a delicate experiment began at a disadvantage that could very well prove insurmountable.

'Who are you?' the doctor demanded pointedly.

'Dr Dowdall?' The young man smiled with a poise the doctor instinctively distrusted.

'That is correct. What do you want?' The doctor wiped his hands on an old tea towel and straightened painfully.

'My name's Yates, Dr Dowdall. I'm from the D T I.' Both facts were hardly accurate, but they would undoubtably satisfy a scruffy old man like this.

'Then I'm surprised they don't insist on better manners. Are you in the habit of walking in on people unannounced?'

The young man smiled blandly and with a certain genuine amusement. 'I did ring. I rang several times, in fact. You were probably busy. I saw the light from the road and decided to come down and see you. Forgive the intrusion, but I've just driven down from London and it would have been a pity to miss you. Wasted journey.'

'I trust it is important?'

'Of course.' He stepped a little farther into the shed and leaned nonchalantly against the edge of the doctor's workbench.

Dr Dowdall hurriedly moved precious test tubes out of

harm's way as the man leaned back and crossed his arms comfortably:

'It's about that report you submitted to our people. That report regarding the lifebuoy.'

'Indeed?'

'Yes. As you may or may not be aware, the inquiry is now in full swing, and any day now that report of yours will be submitted in evidence.'

'I had heard something of the kind.'

'Oh?'

'From the newspapers, you understand. We're not entirely isolated down here. We do get the newspapers. We've even learned to read them occasionally.'

The young man smiled uncertainly. 'I didn't mean to imply –'

'Oh, but you did, don't you see? You did. Never mind, go on.'

'Well ...' he began, thrown momentarily by an old man he had been too ready to consign to senility. Better take it a bit easy. 'I am instructed, first of all, to pass on the Ministry's thanks and appreciation for all the painstaking work which went into its compilation ...' The hollow, insincere words rolled on and then trailed away, leaving a strange silence.

Dr Dowdall frowned and bent over his microscope. 'The Balance of Payments must be looking up,' he observed idly, studying a specimen intently.

'I beg your pardon?'

'I had no idea that the nation had so much money to spare we could afford to send someone all the way from London to Cornwall just to pass on by word of mouth a few words of ministerial congratulation which could just as easily have been sent by letter or the telephone.' He looked up sharply. 'There must be another reason for coming all this way.'

The man's poise slipped a notch as he came off the workbench and unfolded his arms. 'I am instructed merely to pass on that message of thanks and –'

'Ah!'

'– and tell you it would be appreciated if you now considered the lifebuoy matter closed. London feels the safest course to avoid any further controversy regarding this matter would be simply for all concerned to say nothing. We are prepared to say that you are indisposed, away on holiday. It would be greatly appreciated if you, in turn, said nothing which might inflame public interest in the *Pilgrim* inquiry in general and your findings regarding the lifebuoy particularly.'

Dowdall considered all this for a moment in silence, his old, bent fingers resting lightly on the twin focusing rings of his microscope. 'I'm not altogether clear what you mean. If called upon to elaborate upon my findings, I shall, naturally –'

'I think that would be rather unlikely.'

'Oh, you do, do you?' He rose to that, the Old Master challenged by the young apprentice on his first day at work. 'Well, I consider it highly probable, young man – highly probable.' He sat back on his stool and wagged a swollen arthritic finger at his vision. 'My report – which, no doubt, you have not bothered to read – suggests that, wherever else that lifebuoy may have spent the last three months, it was definitely *not* in water with a saline content of more than eight per cent. The presence of large amounts of *Nitzschia subtilis*, together with a profusion of *Fragilaria islandica*, suggests, to the *trained* eye at least, that –'

Yates interrupted softly. 'You miss the point, Doctor. Let me make the position crystal clear: your report, admirable and thorough though it undoubtedly is, has caused a certain ... confusion in London. Your conclusions, in particular, suggest a chain of events which our people in London, for reasons in the national interest, do not, at this stage, wish to pursue.'

'National interest – what national interest?'

'I am unable to elaborate. Let me just say it is for this reason that your report will not now be released to the body of the public inquiry and that, consequently, there will be no opportunity for any lengthy cross-examination. That is why I am confident you will not be called upon to elaborate upon your report. That is the situation.'

He paused as the doctor digested first his words and then their implication. The old man felt suddenly confused and rather unsteady on his feet.

Yates mistook the doctor's silence for acceptance, and he went on with more confidence. 'However, it is not impossible that you will be approached by counsel, by members of the public, the press – that sort of thing. If that happens, then my instructions are to suggest you say nothing, nothing at all; do not allow yourself to be drawn into a situation which, ultimately, can only work to your disadvantage.'

Dr Dowdall pulled a grubby handkerchief from the sleeve of his cardigan and began polishing his spectacles. He cocked his head to one side, and the weak, inflamed eyes regarded the younger man with the same owlish intensity he reserved for the diatoms that swam about on his specimen slides. 'Among all those fancy words, young man, you are suggesting my report will be suppressed – is that what you have come all this way to tell me?' he asked softly.

There was a silence. Somewhere below them in the bay an outboard motor buzzed into life.

'If you like – yes.'

'Why?'

'I don't know. I'm just the delivery boy.'

'And what will happen to my report – my conclusions?'

'I really have no idea.'

Dr Dowdall's shoulders slumped fractionally beneath the threadbare cardigan, and he shivered. Perhaps it was the cold, sweeping in from the sea. 'So all that work was for nothing – it'll just be brushed under the carpet?' His voice quivered slightly.

Yates glanced at his wristwatch and straightened the knot of his tie. 'Now I really must be getting back.' He moved towards the garden and paused, hand on the door. 'Good night, Doctor – and do think on what I've said.'

Yates closed the door behind him, and Dowdall listened

without moving as the brisk, crisp footsteps receded up the path and the metal gate catch clicked shut.

Long after the snarl of a powerful engine had dwindled away to the north-east Dowdall sat at his workbench, experiment forgotten, his logical, cloistered mind grappling with the unfamiliar cross-currents of fear, indignation and anger.

No one had ever spoken to him like that before. The roughhouse tactics of intimidation, however subtly administered, were new to him. Far into the night his brain tugged this way and that as he struggled to come to terms with the realization that all his careful, painstaking work had been for nothing, that the accuracy of those careful conclusions had been brushed aside for some darker political expediency.

He worried most, however, about inaction, about a silence, his silence, which, while it lasted, perpetuated a dishonest act that somehow brought together a lifebuoy, a phial of freshwater diatoms and the lives of a missing trawler crew.

Now it was early Saturday evening and he was no nearer a decision about what action he should take. His confusion was compounded by the certain knowledge that inaction was, in itself, an act of professional betrayal.

Dr Dowdall sighed and struggled to his feet. It was time, he supposed, for his supper. He sighed once more. Cooking, like smiling, dangerous young men in well-cut suits, was something he had come to actively dislike.

It was Mr Hoskins who came to the rescue. Twice in the last hour he had twisted his long neck up through the banisters to listen to the long, raking sobs that came from the girl's flat above. His argument had been with that noisy reporter fellow upstairs, not with the girl, who a few months ago had helped him hang a pair of new bedroom curtains. Finally, he tiptoed up the stairs and peered in through the door that stood slightly ajar.

The girl was distraught, lying curled on one side by her record player, a series of livid bruises on her face, her clothes torn, her hair dishevelled. Once Mr Hoskins had been a keen member of the St John's Ambulance Brigade. Now his training came to the rescue. He covered her with a blanket and reached for the phone.

Twenty minutes later Suzy Summerfield was in hospital and under sedation. The doctor turned down the hem of the sheet and stood for a moment regarding his patient.

'Bastards,' he muttered.

Martin flattened himself into the deeper shadows of another warehouse and paused to catch his breath, the brickwork rough and uneven beneath his fingers.

Somewhere off to his right a hooter sounded mournfully in the darkness. Behind his back, past the bulk of the warehouses and the high perimeter wall with its icing of jagged, broken glass, a bus wheezed on its way towards Pickering Park. The wind moaned gently around the high buildings and raised a rattle of shroud lines against aluminium masts.

Martin held his wrist up to his eyes and studied his watch carefully: 9.45 p.m. If Sam Spalding was right, then he was safe from the night watchman for another fifteen minutes at least.

That should be time enough. He was just over halfway, he reckoned. Halfway and so far not a sound of discovery.

The docks were quiet now – quiet, empty, deserted. Hugging the shadows, Martin had rounded the bottom of the dock basin and begun a series of quick, darting rushes up the left-hand side of the quay, flicking between the deeper pools of shadow cast by the string of offices, warehouses, fish markets and workshops that lined the western end of the dock.

To his right now there was the narrow frontage of dark, greasy cobbles cut by the gleaming sunken tracks of the dock railway. He could just make out the edge of the quay and the twelve-foot drop to the still, oily waters of the inner dock, shimmering like rich velvet in the dappled stern-head lights of a dozen trawlers tied up alongside.

Martin slipped a hand behind his back and adjusted the heavy pistol he had tucked under his belt. Time to move.

Judging his moment, he pushed away from the safety of the deeper darkness and sprinted soundlessly across the cobbles to his next landfall.

Out in the open past the corner of that warehouse stood his objective – the telephone kiosk. And his biggest problem.

It was brilliantly illuminated from within, the only source of light for yards around. To Martin the kiosk looked as conspicuous as a lighthouse. Anyone using the phone would be outlined against the glass for every moment of the call.

He stood in the shadows fingering the coins in his pocket, putting off the moment of maximum exposure. He looked about him one final time and then stepped boldly out into the open, crossed to the kiosk and pushed open the narrow door.

Fumbling with his coins in his haste, he dialled Harding's number from memory and waited as the seconds crawled by. He looked about him with wide eyes, fighting the urge to run.

Brrr – brrr. No reply. Harding's still away.

Right. Enough. Out into the darkness, the *ting!* of the bell ringing in his ears.

Martin waited another full minute in the enveloping, healing darkness, a pile of coins clenched tightly in his left hand. Then he was back inside the kiosk, dialling directory inquiries.

'Which town, please?'

'Polperro, Cornwall.'

'And the name?'

Presently, four hundred and ten miles to the south-west, an elderly Doctor of Marine Biology struggled to his feet and shuffled through to the hall to answer the strident summons of the telephone.

The long, lean snout of the Scimitar slid silently across the intersection and paused, sniffing for the scent of its quarry.

Inside the vehicle Evans sat in darkness. There were no

lights outside, no glow of illumination from the instrument panel within. Evans sensed he was close. He sat motionless, the pale milky glitter of steady eyes the only outward sign that within lurked a dangerous, watchful predator.

His eyes were drawn almost immediately to a small oblong of golden light about three hundred feet away to his right. Evans leaned forward across the empty passenger seat, flipped down the catch on the glove compartment and reached inside for the binoculars. He raised them to his eyes and fiddled impatiently with the focus. The image sharpened.

Presently a small smile of anticipation began playing round his lips. He lowered the glasses, and then the car rolled silently forward.

'I'm extremely grateful, Doctor ... Yes ... Yes, indeed, and I'll look forward to receiving your letter on Monday ... I will, yes. Many thanks once again for your help ... And to you. Goodbye.' Martin slammed down the receiver with a joyous crash and erupted out of the stale little booth into the cool night air.

Much of what the doctor had told him – first with reluctance and then with a strange, growing enthusiasm – had been too technical for Martin to follow, but the gist of it had been simple enough.

Martin's mind swam with the doctor's words, making him careless so that, as he began to retrace the steps he had taken with such care, such elaborate, ridiculous caution, he walked quite openly. The doctor's report on the lifebuoy – that had been deliberately suppressed at the inquiry. His conclusions, had they been revealed in public, would have indicated quite clearly that the lifebuoy, while genuine beyond doubt, was almost certainly a plant, a red herring. It was a blind, dropped into the water off Slettnes Light no more than an hour, possibly two hours, before it had been found by that Norwegian fisherman.

Evans pressed down decisively on the accelerator. The Scimitar lunged forward.

248

CHAPTER TWENTY-ONE

And if that lifebuoy had been a plant, then the man who had found it, that Arnt Whatsisname ... Arnt ... Arnt Jacobssen had in all probability –

It was a tiny sound, the merest whisper of rubber on cobbles. But it was enough. Martin spun round. He stared, shackled to the quay, as the dark lean shape rushed out of the night towards him, gathering speed with every foot of its whispering advance. Black out of blackness.

Evans hit the lights then, all the lights.

The little figure grew rapidly in the centre of his windscreen, a puny hand thrown up to ward off the blaze of lights. Evans grinned wolfishly, grinned because this time Taylor was too late, much too late, a lifetime too late.

It was death Martin saw bearing down on him out of the darkness, and he recognized it as such with utter, bleak certainty. He moved above himself and watched from a distance as Martin Taylor stepped leaden-legged away from that lean, questing snout, a slow, heavy hand reaching for the pistol in his belt.

The car swung effortlessly, remorselessly towards him.

Ten feet. Five. Evans raised a hand in derisory dismissal and spun the wheel. There was a bump against the near-side front wing, the doll-like figure flicked aside, the wheel straightened and the road ahead was clear, picked skeleton-clean by the bright twin cones of his headlights.

In those last closing seconds before impact Martin had managed another half-step away from the car towards the edge of the quay. It was not much of a step, as steps go, but it was a step that saved his life. He was plucked off his feet, spun round and then tossed, arms flailing, over the edge of the quay before the injury to his left leg had the time to turn into a scream of pain.

Martin felt himself falling backwards, arms windmilling wildly. It seemed to take an age to fall the twelve feet between the edge of the quay and the rusty side of the trawler to the waterline. He hit the oily dark waters shoulder first and disappeared below the surface, twisting down into the deep darkness and grazing his injured leg against the pitted, slimed steel of the vessel's hull. He opened his mouth to scream away the pain, and greasy water poured into his mouth, down his throat and into his lungs. He gagged, sinking lost towards the filth of the dock floor.

He began to fight.

He lashed out at the water with his hands and kicked out with both legs, the pain ignored. It was the ooze and the slime which terrified him – that and the blackness, the darkness of the grave, of oblivion. He was sinking deeper and nothing could save him. Then, through the panic that was killing him more surely than the water itself, Martin realized his kapok-lined parka was smothering him, dragging him down and keeping him under with its sodden weight.

With blind, frantic fingers he struggled with the zip. It came free at last. He struggled out of the coat and pushed it away. As it sank beneath him an empty sleeve brushed against his legs. The lingering caress of a corpse.

Lungs bursting now, Martin kicked for the surface, kicked for life itself. Up and up he drove, up through the darkness until he could hold his breath no longer. Farther still he went until finally, a micro-second before his lungs burst to flayed ribbons within his chest, he surfaced, a greasy cork on a sea of black oil.

For long, dangerous seconds he just lay there, wallowing among the potato peelings, the tins and the cardboard boxes, sucking in great whooping lungfuls of air. His eyes stung with Christ knew what and his hair was thick and sticky with diesel. The stench of fish and fuel oil mingled decisively with the contents of his stomach, and, without warning, he vomited painfully into the water.

250

Evans turned the yellow Scimitar at the end of the quay and, lights blazing, drove slowly back along the cobbles.

Martin badly needed something to hang on to. Although his left leg felt as though a shark was feeding on the end of it, it was the cold that was doing the real damage, gnawing away at his vitals, chewing at whatever reserves of strength he had left. It struck upwards savagely from the dock floor, flattening his lungs and making him draw breath in narrow, pinched little gasps. Martin shook his head, spat away the taste of vomit and diesel and began a cautious dog paddle down the length of the trawler.

The scuttles were high out of the waterline, beyond the reach of his clawing fingers. There were no rope ladders, no lines hanging down over the side. Martin wiped a hand over the grease that covered his face and willed his eyes to pierce the gloom ahead.

He turned in a slow, painful half-circle and propelled himself slowly towards the quay wall six feet away. His fingers groped at the smooth, slime-covered granite as he searched for purchase. Nothing, just nothing . . .

He looked up fearfully. The part of the trawler which showed above the quayside was bathed in a harsh, wavering light. For a second Martin did not understand, then realization dawned and a new coldness stabbed at his belly. He searched with desperation for cover, but he was trapped in a narrow oblong of oily water, trapped without a handhold or a hiding place. A rat in a barrel. One downward glance, one beam of a flashlight . . .

He could hear the car's engine quite clearly now. The acceleration ceased and the noise settled to a quiet, even murmur.

Pushing a half-submerged orange box out of his way, Martin paddled clumsily on, his fingers scrabbling along the greasy wall, his eyes searching desperately.

Evans hefted the flashlight and got out, leaving the car lights blazing across the deserted trawler. He played his flashlight down on the water. It was a powerful beam, and he took his time: debris and grease, old bottles, rusty tins,

a few timber spars, an orange box and – there was movement, over there to the right! Evans flicked up his flashlight and impaled a large water rat on the end of its beam,
frozen in the act of nibbling at a piece of rotting cabbage.
The beam moved away and began quartering the water
slowly, carefully, missing nothing. A minute passed and
then –

'Oi! You! What d'you think you're up to?'

Evans swung round. An old man on a push-bike was
cycling slowly towards him, a large metal flashlight hanging round his neck on a piece of string.

'I'm looking at the boats.'

'At this time of night? Get on with you,' scoffed the
night watchman, swinging an old leg over the saddle and
dismounting beside the Scimitar. He peered into the car
and then stepped closer to turn the beam of his flashlight
into Evans's face. Evans screwed up his eyes and turned
away.

'How'd you get in here, anyway?' demanded the old man
suspiciously.

'Through the gate,' Evans answered shortly.

'And which gate would that be, now?'

'The one back there.' Evans gestured vaguely. 'Don't
worry – I'm on my way.' He sauntered past the old man,
closed the car door and drove slowly away.

The old man shook his head, turned off his flashlight and
climbed slowly back onto his bicycle. He cycled away, the
chain clanking against the chain guard.

Martin waited as the *clank-clank-clank* diminished into
the night, and offered up a silent prayer to all night watch-
men. Holding his breath, he ducked from beneath the half-
submerged orange box and paddled slowly and with much
pain round to the stern of the trawler, where he clung to
the thick mooring lines, gasping with relief and trembling
with exhaustion.

Sunday was a day of rest. Definitely.

It had taken Martin fifty-five minutes to drag himself

back to *Harvest Maid* and another twenty minutes to edge along the narrow unlit companionway and down the two steep steel ladders to the mess deck and the tiny cabin aft. There he collapsed, fully clothed, onto his blankets to sleep the clock around until 11 a.m. the following day.

Martin at last rose shakily to his feet. Leaning heavily against the top bunk for support, he unbuckled his belt and gingerly peeled down his damp, stinking jeans.

He swore weakly, fearfully: from hip to mid shin the outside of his left leg was a mass of violent bruising, a wondrous rainbow's hue of purples, yellows and blacks that matched the spectrum of his own pain. He bit his lips and began a feather-soft examination of the damage along the line of the bone.

The skin was broken in many places; angry red scabs oozed blood and lymph where he had pulled his jeans away from the dried grazing, but, miraculously, the bones seemed intact beneath the crustation of dried blood and filth from the dock.

He flexed his leg experimentally and moaned aloud as the strained muscles took his weight. He waited for the waves of pain to recede and then slowly managed first one step and then another, clinging to the bunk above for support.

Like a drunk ricocheting from one lamp standard to another, he hauled himself painfully up to the bridge, where he ransacked the small wooden first-aid cabinet for dressings. On his way back to the cabin he caught sight of himself in the reflected light of the scuttle. His hair stood up in dark, oily spikes, and his face was smeared dark with oil. The stubble on his chin showed through like iron filings, and his eyes were inflamed, sunk in deep, dark holes. If this was the face of a man who was planning another inconspicuous journey to the post office tomorrow, then he would have to do something about his appearance.

Hunting around, he found a plastic washing-up bowl in the galley and a corner of dried soap in one of the heads. He ran cold water into the bowl, shuffled back to his cabin, dug out his towel and a change of clothes and, stripping naked on the mess deck, began washing himself slowly from head to toe.

Evans turned off the tap and groped outside the shower curtain for a fluffy white towel, his body glowing pink from the piping-hot water. He towelled himself dry and noticed that his hand was a little less painful, that it had regained a little of its dexterity beneath the swollen, discoloured bruising. The enforced activity of the previous twenty-four hours had prevented the muscles and tendons from stiffening completely, so that already he was able to hold small things between the tips of his fingers.

He dressed and then stood in front of the long mirror, combing his wet hair. The line of his mouth hardened as he reconstructed once again that exact moment of impact, trying to recall precisely his first, elusive impression as the car tossed the doll-like figure aside and swept on down the quay. A kill or not a kill?

His frown deepened as the conviction grew that he had not killed.

And that worried Evans, worried him a great deal.

To whom had Taylor been talking for so long – Harding? No chance. Harding was away out of reach on the south coast somewhere. Fielding, the mate?

No matter. Evans adjusted the knot of his tie and reached for his jacket. It was just possible that before he had got to the girl in her flat the two lovebirds had arranged another drop at that post office, another supply of home comforts from the little lady. Evans scooped up his hotel key and made for the door. If they had arranged another drop, then, if Taylor was still alive, he'd be there to collect, he'd be there if he had to crawl in on his knees.

And so, therefore, would he.

For the remainder of that morning Martin lay quietly on his bunk, zipped into his sleeping bag, an ear cocked fearfully for the step that meant discovery, naked now without the gun he had lost in the dock. He started often, heart pounding, eyes flying wide with fear, nerves frayed ragged by the two attacks on his life and the brooding stillness of his surroundings.

In the middle of the afternoon he shuffled up to the bridge and sat for long hours in the shadows, watching the approaches to the mooring through borrowed binoculars. No one came, and he was left alone with his thoughts and the cry of the seagulls as they wheeled above the dock looking for scraps. By the time lights began to flicker on in the town beyond the dock wall Martin had identified a few of the missing pieces to his jigsaw.

They were pieces which seemed to point away across the sea to northern Norway.

Martin hadn't the courage to risk the stove again, so supper was a bizarre mixture of cold baked beans, peach slices and fruit cake washed down with a generous pull at Suzy's flask. Then he retreated within the quilted warmth of his sleeping bag and read once more the letter from Houston inviting him to attend the oil conference in Trondheim. Trondheim was a long, long way from North Cape, but it was still a damn sight closer than the bottom bunk in a trawler moored alongside St Andrew's Dock – and the air promised to be a little healthier into the bargain ...

Martin fell into an uneasy, troubled sleep.

He was haunted by the memory of that thin, drawn face screwed up against the glare of the night watchman's flashlight. As Martin turned, smiling, to thank the old man, his saviour shot out a thin, bony hand and dragged him backwards with him into the darkness. Fighting free, Martin struggled upwards towards the light as a seagull with oil on its feathers began to peck hungrily at his own sightless, rotting eyes.

Martin awoke, sweating. He tore free from the shroud of his sleeping bag and stumbled to the scuttle, where he pressed his forehead up against the cool glass and gazed at the lighter sky above. Presently he pushed the vivid nightmare aside and thought deliberately about the good news, about the contents of that letter from the doctor he would collect in just a few hours' time.

He returned to his bunk and snuggled down into the warmth of his sleeping bag. He shut his eyes. His use of the post office was one card, at least, he had managed to keep close to his chest.

Martin awoke on Monday morning to the moan of wind in the rigging and the steady patter of rain on the steel deck above his head. The skies were low and leaden, the rain bouncing high as needles on the cobbles of the quays beyond as men hurried reluctantly to another working week, their coats pulled high over their heads.

It rained throughout the day's early morning, and Martin's spirits sank as, huddled alone on the bridge, he watched and listened to the work going on around him. He was an observer only, on the outside, a part of nothing except this personal, nebulous investigation which seemed, just then, to be a matter of little consequence to anyone but himself. He did not feel like a champion of the finest traditions of British journalism. He felt isolated and scared.

In London, Colonel Francis Mann-Quartermain was alone also. There were people with him, but he was alone, marked apart by the finality of his private meeting with Sir Peter Hillmore.

Sir Peter had told him that, after much thought, he had decided he had no alternative but to ask for his resignation. He expected to find it on his desk at the end of the week. There was to be no appeal, no redress, no publicity. Out of touch with the subtleties and nuances of the world he moved in, Mann-Quartermain was a dangerous anachronism, Sir Peter said quietly; he had exceeded authority, abused trust, distorted power. Now he was to go. He could couch his resignation in whatever terms he chose; the real reason would remain a private thing between them. In return for the silence of his departure, Sir Peter would see to it personally that pension rights and the Civil Service gratuity remained unaffected.

A dangerous anachronism. Mann-Quartermain looked about the old, familiar office with a sense of near-panic. It was still his. Until the end of the week. He lit his pipe with trembling fingers. Then what would he do? Where would he go?

Shortly before 3 p.m. Martin laid the binoculars aside. He would need some kind of walking stick to help him along and, ideally, a coat of some description to replace the expensive parka he had left at the bottom of the dock. He solved both requirements surprisingly easily: there was an old yellow sou'wester on a hook behind the sliding door leading from the bridge to the tiny radio shack and an old broom handle which he discovered in an engine-room locker.

Taking his money from his kit bag, Martin limped slowly along the dark companionway towards the well deck, the faint tap, tap, tap of his stick echoing hollowly against the steel walls in the confined darkness.

No one paid any attention to the yellow-oilskinned figure who limped slowly down the quay and out of the dock gates in the heavy rain. As he shuffled along Martin peered about him ceaselessly, bitterly aware that only luck had saved him last time, luck and an empty upturned orange box. Each time a car approached he shrank back into a doorway and let it swish past before resuming his halting, painful trek towards the Post Office.

Soon his dark hair was plastered wetly over his eyes, his only dry pair of jeans was soaked below the knee, his left leg throbbed with hot pain and his body was clammy beneath the waterproof folds of his borrowed sou'wester.

He limped on determinedly, a pilgrim figure in a faded yellow oilskin with, unbeknown to him, the initials of the garment's owners stencilled across his shoulders: S T L.

He turned left into the main road and stepped into the travel agent's. He emerged a few minutes later to limp slowly along the main road towards the Post Office.

The water streamed unchecked down the sloping, streamlined windscreen of Evans's Scimitar. Every so often he reached forward and turned the windscreen wipers on. The glass cleared obediently for a moment, the wipers stopped and the rain hammered across the toughened glass once more. Once, twice, a hundred times Evans had reached forward automatically to the wiper switch, but, characteristically, he was not irritated by monotony or repetition. He was, simply, waiting. He had been there all morning.

He looked through and past the yellow-oilskinned figure – it was not what he was expecting. But then he noticed the stick, and that made him lean forward for the wiper switch once more. The windscreen cleared.

The stick drew attention to the limp. The limp drew attention to the legs and the legs to the face under its mop of dark, wet hair, hunched low against the driving rain.

Evans swore under his breath and reached for the door handle. He'd hardly dented the bugger! He swept his coat off the back seat and dodged quickly across the busy street just as Taylor turned in at the revolving glass door of the post office.

'You've a letter for me, I think – poste restante,' Martin said quietly to the girl behind the counter. He felt weak and a little sick from the effort of walking. He gave her his name, and she moved to the row of pigeonholes behind the counter.

Pray God it had arrived – then he could be off, away, out of this, away from the rain and the bloody trawler.

'Here you are, Mr Taylor.' She held out a fat cream-coloured envelope with spidery green writing on the outside. Martin took the envelope, mumbled his thanks and limped towards the revolving door. He patted the envelope against his palm, rejoicing in the weight of solid information. The old professor had been as good as his word. An ally, an ally at last!

From outside the post office Evans had watched Martin at the counter, had seen him take delivery of a fat envelope. He chose this moment to intercept him. Evans stepped to the revolving door just as Martin approached from the other side. Martin pushed with his free hand and then, dimly aware someone else was trying to step into a different segment of the revolving door from the street, he paused politely and glanced up.

Evans pushed the door to set it in motion. Automatically he had used his right hand. He winced with the pain and turned a little to his left to favour his good hand. The shift of position seemed unnatural, awkward. An alarm bell shrilled in Martin's head. He jerked back to study the man through the glass. Their eyes met and locked, inches apart. Recognition was mutual, instantaneous.

For a moment both men froze into immobility. Martin moved first. He lunged forward, thrusting his full weight against the door. It moved forward no more than a foot, but it was enough to shut off Evans's retreat back into the street. Martin pushed again, hard, and saw the man grimace as he was jammed against the wall by the force of the door behind him.

Martin pushed yet again and squeezed out onto the pavement and then, seeing his opportunity, turned and jammed his broom handle into the turnstile, locking the doors momentarily. Without a backward glance he turned to his right and hobbled rapidly away down the pavement, pushing his way through the slow-moving pedestrians, breathing hard.

Evans put his shoulder to the revolving doors, and the broom handle broke with a brittle snap. He pushed into the post office now, and an old lady stood between him and the door in front of him.

'Out of the way – move!' he ordered, pushing past her into the door and out again into the street. He looked to his right, saw a flash of yellow oilskin about twenty yards ahead and, breaking into a run, plunged headlong after his quarry.

The range closed rapidly as Evans overhauled Martin in a macabre race of the disabled. He could read the letters quite clearly on Martin's shoulders now – S T L. Where the hell had he got the jacket? Feet flying, Evans had the answer almost before he had posed the question. He lengthened his stride in his anger. Martin glanced over his shoulder, saw that the range was closing rapidly and knew he would never be able to outdistance the man with two good legs. He turned and ducked into the first large store he came to.

It was a big supermarket. Pushing past the patient queues, he thrust deep among the shoppers with their laden metal carts. An empty cart appeared in front of him and he swept it up, stripped off his tell-tale yellow oilskin, dropped it into the metal basket and forced himself to adopt the slow, shelf-searching dawdle of the other customers.

Mindlessly he began filling his basket with food from the shelves, his laboured breathing drawing curious stares as it sawed across the plastic Musak and the background whirr of the cash tills.

Martin stole another glance behind him and saw Evans closing. They were separated now by a dozen metal baskets, a dozen struggling housewives.

Evans passed a metal circular bin offering steak knives at a fantastic discount price. He paused and slipped one of the razor-sharp knives quietly under his jacket.

Martin turned at the end of the corridor of laden shelves and began moving past the cold meats towards the front of the store, his mind working on overdrive as he tried to think ahead.

The exit sign beckoned in a far corner. Martin cut across the store towards it, pushing his laden cart ahead of him like a bobsleigh.

His speed was his undoing. Evans noticed the sudden movement and moved smoothly through the crowds on a course that would intercept.

Martin glanced back, saw the tall head bobbing through the brightly lit corridors of plenty and turned deeper into the maze of bargain offers and never-to-be-repeated reductions. Evans dutifully followed, and a plan, a wild, improbable plan began to form in Martin's mind.

At the next intersection he made a show of turning into

one particular avenue of shelving. Once the shelves hid him from view he bent low and, ignoring the curious stares of the women nearby, doubled back on his tracks.

The simple ploy worked. Evans took the decoy and turned down the same corridor. Now they were walking slowly towards the front of the store in parallel, separated only by a single stack of shelving. Martin waited as Evans peered ahead, obviously puzzled, looking this way and that, searching for his quarry. Martin knew he had only a matter of seconds.

Twenty paces ahead, a delicate pyramid of tins, each one balanced precariously on another, pointed improbably at the ceiling.

He hurriedly topped up his cart with a random selection of heavy jars and packets and then, just as Evans drew level with the pyramid, Martin, with a strong, sudden flick of his wrists, pushed the heavily laden cart sideways across the highly polished floor.

The cart smacked broadside into the neat pyramid of tins with a solid, meaty crash that sent the whole structure toppling gloriously sideways. Evans threw up his hands, skidded on a tin and went down on his back as they thundered down around him like shrapnel.

Bedlam. Shrieks and screams as managers, assistant managers and shop assistants flocked importantly to the scene of the disaster. Martin didn't wait. As shoppers crowded round and choked the gangways he was off, limping fast down the store and out into the rain.

He hurried. All he had bought himself, he knew, was a lead, a head start, a tiny piece of time.

Luck, just for once, ran with him. A black cab had just stopped at the pavement to disgorge a couple of elderly ladies beside an antique shop. As they paid, a young man stepped forward and leaned in at the front passenger window.

Taylor hobbled up. 'Do you mind if I take this one? My leg...'

'What? Oh, right you are, Chief – it's all yours.'

The young man held the door for Taylor, who swung stiff-legged into the cab and smiled his thanks. The man slammed the door, and the cab pulled away.

'Take me down to the docks, will you? St Andrew's Dock.'

Martin sat back, tore open the letter from the professor and quickly scanned the pages of neat, laborious notes. It was there, all there.

He stuffed the letter into his pocket and directed the driver through the dock gates and down to the quay to *Harvest Maid*.

'Wait here – I'll be five seconds.' Martin hopped out of the cab and limped over the cobbles and down onto the cluttered well deck of the trawler.

It was speed that mattered now.

Evans was sprinting hard, the coattails of his jacket flying out behind him as he splashed through the puddles. He spun into the phone booth, snatched the receiver off the hook and flicked rapidly through the phone book.

S T L – Spencer Trawlers Ltd – 18 Trafalgar Square – Hull 2875.

He dialled. His call was answered.

'Spencer Trawlers Limited. May I –'

'This is the harbour police. I want to know which of your trawlers is in port. Right now.'

'Well, er ... let me think,' began the receptionist uncertainly. '*North Maid* – she's down in Grimsby. *Sea Maid* – she's off around Iceland somewhere, I think –'

'I'm not after those that are away. I want to know which of your vessels are here. In Hull.'

'Well, none of them are.'

'None?'

'Not really, no.' She paused. 'There's *Harvest Maid*, of course, but she's in for a long refit at St Andrew's Dock and –'

'*Harvest Maid* – she bloody would be,' muttered Evans. He erupted out of the phone booth and began running back towards his Scimitar.

*

Martin rolled up his sleeping bag, tucked it under his arm and turned to the cabin door. He paused and looked back. It wasn't much, but it had been home, a refuge. He dropped his kit bag at his feet and patted his pockets for paper and pencil. He dug out a pen, but his notebook was now at the bottom of his packed kit bag. He fumbled in his pockets and dragged out one of the pamphlets he had taken from the travel agent. He paused and then scrawled on the back: 'I borrowed a few things – no stars for B & B – the cooking's lousy.' He weighted the note with an empty tin and crammed two five-pound notes into the tin. Then he banged the cabin door behind him and limped hurriedly back to the taxi.

Martin dropped into his seat and slammed the door.

'Kermington Airport,' he ordered.

The Scimitar rolled to a halt beside *Harvest Maid* nineteen minutes later. Two minutes after that Evans was in the small cabin aft, reading Taylor's stupid bloody note scribbled on a timetable of flights from Amsterdam to Oslo.

Evans screwed the note into a ball of paper and flicked it out of the scuttle. He pocketed the five-pound notes and ran back to his car, his heels clattering on the metal deck plates.

CHAPTER TWENTY-TWO

The urgent, height-seeking roar of the engines eased to a slow, steady rhythm as the Fokker Friendship flattened out of her climb and swung round to the south. Martin peered out of the window and watched as the coastline slid by below.

The illuminated red square above the flight-deck door was extinguished, and the captain's regulation voice assured nervous passengers they could smoke if they wished. There was a small release of tension. Seat belts snapped up and down the cramped cabin. Presently a young hostess in a tight brown skirt passed along the aisle taking passengers' orders for drinks with a wide, practised smile.

Martin ordered Scotch and forced himself to relax. He had caught the 4.30 p.m. with minutes to spare, thrusting his way to the tail of the queue of sober-suited businessmen at passport control and raising a frown of annoyance from the executives as they took in his dirty jeans and damp, uncombed hair.

The Scotch arrived and Martin settled into his narrow seat, his bruised leg thrust out awkwardly in front of him. He pulled out Dowdall's crumpled letter. There was a line or two of opening pleasantries and then:

I already had to hand the Admiralty Materials Laboratory report on hydrostatic pressure damage to the lifebuoy. The report showed that the lifebuoy had never been below a depth of sixty-six feet and that, if it had ever reached that depth at all, it had done so only for a matter of minutes, perhaps seconds, rather than days or months. AML concluded that, since the lifebuoy had absorbed only 1/40th of its potential maximum, it had not been subjected to pressure of any sort and that, in all probability, it had been floating on the surface. I concur with those findings.

Martin turned to a fresh page of neat, spidery writing:

In my turn I was asked by Dr Isaacs (an old friend and ex-pupil of mine) to do the following:

1. Ascertain if the lifebuoy had ever been attached to the *Arctic Pilgrim* and, if so, for how long and at what depth;

2. Ascertain if the lifebuoy had been drifting and, conceivably, for how long;

3. Investigate any other avenues which might be of value in giving some indication as to where, how and why *Arctic Pilgrim* sank.

My first action was, naturally, to examine the lifebuoy for myself. There were no obvious signs of damage or crushing; on the contrary, the lifebuoy appeared almost new. A greenish coloration was noticed on the grabline and I decided to begin my experiments by washing this greenish matter gently from the line. I took further washings from the lifebuoy surface, particularly from the areas around the eye holes through which the grabline passes.

These washings I divided equally. Half were stored in formalin for future reference (I have them still) and half were cleaned by a variety of established methods to remove the organic cell contents. These were then examined under my microscope.

The washings from the lifebuoy contained diatoms -- specifically: marine, brackish and freshwater diatoms. Of that there is no doubt.

The most significant aspect of the lifebuoy flora is its composition, that is, not only for the species it contains but also for those which are absent. I expected to find deep-water diatoms − plankton species such as *Chactroc-cros* or *Rhizosolenia*, all species which produce enormous populations in Arctic waters, and yet *these were absent*.

I made another discovery which showed itself on a representative cross-section of all planktonic growth described below. Despite the youth of such development − I will touch too upon that a little later on − I found evidence of stunted mutant growth: the embryonic beginnings of rogue genus development usually encountered around the *site* of radio-active disturbance. Taken alone, this discovery would be somewhat alarming; taken in conjunction with the absence of flora whose presence I would normally have taken for granted, I find the whole most unsatisfactory.

Another notable absentee is the genus *Melosira*. This produces vast numbers of cells which are some of the first to swarm in the spring waters of the Arctic. Again, no species of *Melosira* were observed in the material examined.

Through the long Arctic night when there is no light, growth and development is halted and does not commence until the amount of solar energy incident upon the sea has reached a critical value – something in the region of 0.100 cal. per cm² per min. By the end of February and the beginning of March, this area is exposed to something approaching eleven hours of daylight in any twenty-four-hour cycle. Diatoms of whatever size literally burst into life. It is truly amazing to witness.

The lifebuoy was discovered in an area where the Continental Shelf runs very close to the shoreline. I would expect characteristic, deep-water plankton to be thriving in enormous, clouding masses in such an area. It is inconceivable, to my mind, that an object could have been in such waters for such a period – two months – at such a time without there being some physical evidence of contact with the more common and tenacious groups of deep-water marine diatoms mentioned above.

The diatoms I did discover were of the species which attach themselves by means of mucous stipes to either floating objects or hard substrates – usually rocks, cliffs, quays, harbour walls or pylons situated between the rise and fall of the tide.

They are not planktonic. They do not float. They are entirely supported and are inevitably found in conditions of reduced salinity. Salinity count in the area of discovery is a high 34.5%. This was most unusual.

Then I thought that perhaps the lifebuoy had been inadvertently cleaned – this would account both for its condition and, perhaps, the paucity of marine growth. I duly contacted Norway and was told most emphatically that this was not the case. Upon reflection, I accept this: even if it had been cleaned, it is extremely unlikely that one particular species would have been removed by random cleaning in preference to any other; if the lifebuoy had picked up floating surface diatoms from deep water it is inconceivable they would be removed by the handling of the lifebuoy yet leaving intact those picked up in the littoral (shoreline) zone.

The hostess walked by with a swish of tight skirt, and Martin ordered another drink.

He stopped reading and stared for long minutes at the clouds below. He reached for his notebook and began to read the letter again, this time underlining the salient points with a red pen.

If I now look to the age of the growth on the lifebuoy, what do I learn? Of the eight dominant species all were in the process of early colony formation. The most advanced was the relatively short-chained links of *Fragilaria islandica*, but even here the chains were only twelve to fourteen cells long and most were only half that length, giving a maximum growth-time of seven days.

The suggestion that the lifebuoy was first blown inshore and *then* carried out to sea was investigated, as was the possibility of tidal drift. The wind blows from the north and west at that time and the tidal flow at that time of year was towards land throughout the relevant period.

Taylor turned to the last page of carefully written notes.

So – what are my conclusions? They are these:
1. The material recovered from the lifebuoy consisted of a population of diatoms representing marine, brackish and freshwater species. These diatoms were invariably distorted by rogue genus development.
2. The species consisted mainly of forms that live in mucous colonies attached to hard substrates usually associated with the shoreline;
3. The paucity of growth suggests the lifebuoy had not been long in contact with the developing fauna;
4. The almost total absence of deep-water plankton as well as benthic species indicates that the lifebuoy had most probably: (a) never been far from shore; (b) never been

submerged for any length of time and (c) been floating in relatively shallow water.

I hope the enclosed can be of some help to you in your inquiries.

WILFRED R. DOWDALL (DR)

'More ice, sir?' asked the hostess with a bright smile.
'Pardon?'
'Would you care for more ice, sir?'
'No ... no, thank you.' Martin laid the letter gently aside. Thank Christ, Dr Dowdall had kept it relatively simple. Even he could grasp the drift of the man's findings – and it was dynamite, thought Martin excitedly, enough to blast that inquiry off its complacent backside. Suddenly he wanted to share his excitement, his discovery, with Suzy. He would give her a call from his hotel when he arrived. With her technical training, maybe she'd extract even more from Dowdall's letter.

But Suzy was in no mood for puzzles. As Martin flew steadily northward Suzy was in a deep, drug-induced sleep, her system's healing agents working flat out to mend the damage done by a man whose mind was already twisted beyond repair. A woman police officer sat patiently at her bedside, notebook in hand. Poor kid, thought the WPC, she looks as though she's really been through the wars.

Twenty-five minutes later the warning light went on, the engine note changed, the seat belts snapped shut and the Fokker Friendship began the long, gentle glide down into Holland's Schipol Airport. There Martin would transfer to the SAS DC-9 which, after a refuelling stop at Oslo, would carry him the two hundred and fifty miles further up the coast to Trondheim.

Evans locked the Scimitar, took the grip lightly in his hand and strode towards the main terminal building at Leeds Airport. He flicked a glance at his watch and pushed impatiently through the swing doors into the main concourse. Taylor would be landing about now. Evans had arrived at Kermington Airport just as the flight closed. He had watched, impotently, as Taylor limped hurriedly across the wet tarmac to the small twin-engined aircraft – an incongruous, scruffy figure in dirty jeans among the suits and the smart attaché cases.

Evans had lingered until the aircraft lumbered up into the murk and disappeared. Then he had returned to the reservations counter to be told that the only way of getting to Amsterdam that day was to drive to Leeds Airport fifty-five miles away to the west.

Racing back to the hotel to pack and settle the bill, he found a message waiting for him in his pigeonhole behind the reception desk: 'Ring London immediately.' Instinctively Evans knew it had to mean bad news. Something had changed; the restrictions were on again, the political constraints. He tore the paper into four and watched the pieces flutter into the wastepaper basket. It was too late for that now, much too late. He was committed.

Evans drove to Leeds in just over the hour.

Now he paid for his ticket by cheque and took his place patiently in the passenger lounge. The flight would be called at 5.15 p.m., takeoff was 5.45, arrival at Schipol 7.20. Weather along the route was clear. Characteristically, Evans did not fume at the delay. Indeed, he drew a certain comfort from the little formalities of international air travel: people who use airports sign forms, buy tickets, book flights, use taxis, make inquiries. He would pick up Taylor's trail at Schipol, no trouble.

Martin had fifty minutes to wait before he could board the SAS flight to Oslo and Trondheim. After changing sterling into guilders, he grabbed a carton of freshly brewed coffee and a hot pastry and limped through to the airport barber shop, where he treated himself to a haircut, a wash and a shave. Then to the SAS information counter, where he made a hotel reservation in Trondheim for that same evening and spent a further five minutes working out route connections for the trip north from Trondheim.

Finally he crossed to the airport Post Office beside the

escalators leading to the arrivals lounge and copied onto a Telex form the message he had blocked out in rough on the flight from Hull. Addressed to Pinkerton Publishers, Inc., 1009 Southern Boulevard, Houston, Texas, it read:

YOUR CONFERENCE OFFER ACCEPTED. SUGGESTION: IN VIEW NORWAY'S DECLARED INTENTION EXPAND EXCLUSIVE ECONOMIC ZONE TO TWO HUNDRED NM EARLY AUTUMN, THIS NOW UNPARALLELED OPPORTUNITY SUBMIT TIMELY THREE THOUSAND WORDER BACKGROUND EEZ EFFECT RE US/NORWEGIAN OPERATIONS NORTHERN NORWAY. OIL CONFERENCE STARTS MONDAY SO HERE ANYWAY. CAN COVER BOTH STORIES PINKERTON EXCLUSIVE. IF IDEA APPEALS, PLEASE CABLE FUNDS SOONEST. REPLY C/O HOTEL EIKEN, TRONDHEIM, NORWAY. REGARDS. MARTIN TAYLOR.

Martin paid for the Telex, gulped the last of the hot coffee and hobbled across to the departure gate just as the last call for Flight 664 to Oslo, Trondheim and Bodø was announced over the public-address system in English, Dutch, Norwegian and German. Allowing for time-zone changes, Martin reckoned the Telex would reach Houston at 12.30 p.m. Central Time.

A petite dark-haired hostess with enormous brown eyes smiled sympathetically as Martin hobbled towards her with his boarding card.

'Have a pleasant flight,' she smiled, tearing his card in half. Martin stepped with relief onto the conveyor belt which would carry him out to the blue-and-white Scandinavian DC-9 he could see through the glass at the end of the terminal.

Fifteen minutes later he was airborne.

Evans, too, was up in the air. His Trident touched down at Schipol five minutes later than scheduled, at 7.25 p.m. It took him ten minutes to buttonhole a helpful KLM schedules officer, who consulted their computer before confirming with a smile that yes, certainly, a Mr Martin Taylor – British passport number C 323735 – had indeed boarded the 7.25 to Trondheim via Oslo. He was sorry, but no, there were no further flights to Norway from Schipol that evening. First flight in the morning was at eight. In the meantime, might he suggest the Hotel Imperial just a few minutes' walk from the terminal?

Next morning, it took Evans a carton of two hundred king-size cigarettes to jog the memory and win the whole-hearted co-operation of the fat little taxi-fleet controller who sat by his microphone in the wooden shack beside the low terminal building of Trondheim Airport.

Although it was early June, the windows were closed and a powerful electric fire turned the radio room into a hothouse. The man was sweating freely in his shirtsleeves, and dark damp patches showed under his arms as he tore open the packet of cigarettes with short, stubby fingers. He lit the first cigarette with the stub of another of a cheaper brand and inhaled hungrily.

He threw a switch on the console and spoke rapidly, calling up first one cab and then another, ringing the city in seconds as he hunted down the inquiry. He turned to Evans with a gap-toothed smile of confidence. 'One minute – one minute only. I have Trondheim – here.' He tapped the palm of one pudgy hand.

He was as good as his word. Before the first cigarette had burned down to its filter he was leaning forward, listening, as one of his drivers reported in. In the background Evans could hear the snarl of traffic. The controller turned back to Evans, his finger holding down the microphone key.

'This man you are looking for – he is young, *nei*? With a long bag, a bag like this.' He indicated a long sausage-shaped object. 'And his leg? His leg was not good?'

Evans nodded.

The controller nodded agreement and terminated the conversation with his driver. He swung round in his chair to face Evans, and the chair groaned its protest as he leaned back and linked his hands behind his head. 'One of my men took such a man to Hotel Eiken last night.'

'Hotel Eiken?'

'In town – perhaps twenty minutes away. Not, certainly, one of the best hotels, but good, comfortable, *ja*? You want to go there, meet your friend?' He smiled a crafty smile. 'I order you a taxi?'

Two hundred cigarettes did not, Evans discovered, stretch to include the hire of a powerful Volvo station wagon which swept him along the flat modern motorway towards the town of Trondheim itself. They made good time as the young driver picked a path through the string of laden lorries that thrummed along the road beside the vast, glittering expanse of Trondheim Fjord to their left with its scattering of jaunty, brightly coloured fishing vessels. To Evans's right, lush green pasture was dashed with the small bright blooms of early flowers which in turn gave way to the coarse scrubland of alpine, snow-flattened vegetation leading through the belts of pine, spruce and birch to the soaring snow-tipped mountains beyond.

Evans sat back in his seat, enjoying the drowsy warmth of the morning sun through the car windows, watching the brightly painted fishing boats bobbing to their own reflections in the deep icy stillness of the fjord. It was his first time in Norway, and the picture postcards do not lie. He relaxed temporarily into the role of tourist.

Not unnaturally, then, he paid little attention to the stream of oncoming traffic and none at all to one particular dark-blue Volvo that flashed past seven miles outside the city limits.

But in the boot of that rapidly vanishing Volvo lay a long, sausage-shaped kit bag, while in front, behind the driver, huddled in a vast new parka with more zips and pockets than he knew what to do with, sat Martin Taylor.

Martin was in good spirits. He had slept soundly between clean sheets for the first time in days, and the nightmare world of hiding and waiting was behind him; he had awakened to a knock on the door and a telegram from Houston backing his trip to northern Norway and infor-

272

ing him that twelve hundred dollars had been cabled to the National Bank, Trondheim, in his name.

Martin had wolfed breakfast and gone shopping. Hence the fleece-lined parka, a suitcase full of new clothes and a small battery-operated tape recorder that fitted neatly into a side pocket.

He glanced again at his watch. The flight northward would leave in twenty-five minutes. Once again he was in plenty of time. He did, however, have one small, nagging worry. Suzy. He had tried to call her twice the previous evening. He had tried both their flats and received no reply. He shrugged. It was probably nothing. If time permitted he would try again from the airport.

Evans's taxi ride into town was not a complete waste of time. He was able to confirm with the hotel receptionist that the man calling himself Martin Taylor had settled his bill no more than an hour ago and had then left by taxi for the airport.

No, he had made no phone calls, but yes, he had sent one telegram during his short stay. Certainly they had kept a copy – they were required to do so by law; he himself had translated the message into Norwegian for the English visitor. The old man frowned and fingered the frayed cuff of his cardigan. It was against regulations to divulge the contents of any message to a third party, but (he accepted the cigarette readily and slipped the packet into his pocket with only a moment's hesitation), since both gentlemen were from the same company, where was the harm? Regulations, regulations, everything was controlled by regulations these days. Some must have been made to be broken.

The limping Englishman had sent a short telegram to Arnt Jacobssen, skipper of *Kingflud II*, Vadsø.

The green-and-white D H Otter twin gave another sudden, sickening lurch towards the ground, and Martin clutched involuntarily at the armrests of his seat.

There was a stifled moan of fear from the portly German

tourist seated behind him, and Martin closed his ears to the rest. If the woman kept to form there would be the sudden splutter of airsickness and a muttered prayer for salvation.

Martin wouldn't be sorry to get down again, either.

The small Widerø aircraft carried its full load of sixteen passengers, and its sturdy, stumpy propellers seemed to be chewing hard at the air to remain airborne. There were clouds not far below, thick, fleecy clouds that scudded by almost at arm's length. There were mountain peaks, too, many mountain peaks, each with its collar of glittering snow and ice flecked by the silent racing shadow of the tiny aircraft as it skimmed up the prickly spine of Norway.

The aircraft bumped and then sagged into another air pocket, and the engine note changed. The cabin curtains swayed to one side, and Martin, leaning out into the aisle, watched the young co-pilot reach up to the cabin roof and adjust the throttle levers.

The engine note sweetened and the Otter banked steeply to port. The nose dipped. Another landing ahead. The wing tip scythed through a wisp of cloud, and a moment later the cabin interior was plunged into ominous gloom as the cloud enveloped them completely.

The farther north they had travelled, the lower they seemed to fly. It was almost, mused Martin deliberately, as the German tourist started again, almost as though the North Pole itself was sucking the aircraft down into the ground. Amsterdam to Oslo had been flown at a civilized 27,000 feet; Oslo to Trondheim, 22,000 feet, Trondheim to Bodø, 16,000 feet. Then it had begun to get interesting as they changed aircraft and clambered into the cramped little Otter for a series of short, birdlike hops up the coast to the north: Svolvaer, Leknes, Stokjosen – each stop a ten-minute affair followed by a short takeoff, a steep short climb, a moment or two of sweet level flight and then another steep, dizzying spiral down to some remote hamlet lost in the vastness of water, ice and tundra, humbled in the lee of some huge snow-worn mountain.

A few clapboard houses, a dirt road along a rocky coast-line, a knot of waiting, waving people. Then the screech of rubber on tarmac, a puff of wet spray whipping past the windows and the burble of idling engines. Mail handed down, mail handed up. Passengers out, passengers in. A wave of farewell from the man standing beside the little red fire tender. Seat belts fastened and then up again. And down again, buffeting up the long coast of Norway.

CHAPTER TWENTY-THREE

The bright flags of a dozen nations whipped and fluttered in the breeze. The flags, together with a scattering of immature, slender young birches planted out among the smooth rocks, softened the harsh exterior of the modern three-storey Turisthotell.

Inside, there were thick rugs scattered on the highly polished wooden floor, and an enormous stone hearth dominated one end of the reception area. In winter the place would be warm and cosy, a haven from the knife-edged wind and the snow-laden darkness of a savage Arctic winter. Now, with the log fire unlit and the sun streaming through thick double-glazed windows, the hotel exuded a faint air of neglect, a fighter resting between bouts.

Kirkenes is a mining town, a winter town. Now it was caught out by the distractions of a summer which it knew would never last and which, consequently, it could never take seriously. With unconscious loyalty, the town's largest hotel reflected that attitude exactly.

But the staff were welcoming enough, the bedroom taps kept their promise and there was a telephone in each room. From his window on the second floor Martin looked out over the sprawl of high wooden houses and shops that led down between the two shoulders of smooth snow-capped rock to the mouth of the fjord. The sun was warm on his face, and across the road the balcony of the old people's home was crowded.

Carried to him now on the crisp breeze came the rattle and *tonk-tonk-tonk* of a donkey engine as a bulk ore carrier down by the quay wallowed under a rust-red cloud while it took aboard the takings of the town's largest employer, the Sydvaranger Mining Company.

Martin turned away from the window and sprawled across the bed for the telephone. It seemed to take an age for the call to ring in the flat all those miles away in Hull. Martin pressed the phone against his ear, willing Suzy to answer. Where the hell could she be? London again? The university? Staying with friends? All were possible, he told himself, pushing his concern to the back of his mind once more. It was time he contacted Arnt Jacobssen, the skipper who had found the lifebuoy.

The hotel operator connected him with the main shipping offices in Vadsø thirty miles to the north across Varangerfjord.

While he was waiting for the call to come through Martin rolled onto his back and studied the printed notice framed on the wall.

Where other hotels list in-house fire precautions, Turisthotell Kirkenes offered a copy of the royal decree of 7 November 1950, which spelled out the ground rules for behaviour this close to the one hundred and twenty-five miles of shared border with the Soviet Union. It was illegal to fire shots at people, animals or objects on the Soviet side of the frontier; it was illegal to behave in an insulting manner towards the Soviet Union; it was illegal to photograph the Soviet Union; it was illegal to talk to or otherwise communicate with the people on the other side of the border without permission from the Norwegian Border Commissioner; and so on.

His call came through, and with the help of the hotel operator Martin asked if *Kingflud II* was in port. Where might he contact her skipper, Arnt Jacobssen?

Kingflud II was at sea.

She had left harbour – would he wait one moment, please? – she had left Vadsø harbour early that same morning. No, they did not know when she would return – one day? Two? Perhaps three? It depended upon the weather. Upon the fishing.

Martin rang off and lay back on his bed.

Jacobssen must have left soon after receiving his telegram. He could be away for days, perhaps even weeks. Still, he

had to return sometime, and in the meantime Martin had ?
legitimate reason for being so far north: the oil story for
Houston.

He reached for the phone. Presently he was speaking to
the local editor of the *Kirkenes Finmarkposten*, Kjell Bølset.
They talked briefly. Certainly he could call in. It was always
a pleasure to meet a foreign journalist.

Bølset had assured him it was a short downhill stroll to
his office behind the quayside. He must have done it on
bloody skis, thought Martin grimly as he turned past a
snowmobile repair shop and saw the newspaper office and
printing works before him. His leg ached fiercely.

He was shown up a short flight of stairs and limped
along a corridor to a light, open-plan office area with four
desks, a number of typewriters and telephones and a Telex
machine that chattered away unheeded over in a corner.
Tall glass windows at the far end of the office overlooked
the floor of the printing works, and there was a low book-
case beneath another window loaded with a profusion of
plants and ferns.

A pretty fair-haired girl in her early twenties sat at one
of the desks working over some notes, and a portly balding
man in his late forties was watering the plants beneath the
window from a small green watering can. He looked up as
the door opened, laid the watering can carefully aside and
glanced at his watch.

He smiled. 'Mr Taylor?'

Martin nodded and limped forward. The older man
squeezed out from between the desks and came towards him,
hand outstretched. Martin shook the limp hand firmly, and
Bølset waved him to a chair opposite his desk. Martin sank
into it thankfully.

Bølset made a show of clearing the papers from his desk.
'Some tea?'

The girl took the hint and rose gracefully to her feet.
Both men watched her cross to the corridor. Bølset fitted a
cigarette into an ebony holder, struck a match and regarded
Martin quizzically over the flame.

'And very nice too,' approved Martin.

Bølset smiled and waved the match to and fro until it went out. 'Also, she is fluent in English.' The smile widened.

'A requirement for the job?'

'A help, most certainly. Here everything is either marine or industrial. When important things happen, they happen in English. As a good Norwegian, I find that regrettable, but ...' He shrugged his shoulders and wiped a speck of ash off his sleeve. He leaned forward across his desk. 'So – to business. How can I be of assistance?'

'I write sometimes for some American oil magazines: who's drilling where and for whom, expectations and explorations, deep-water technology ...'

Bølset nodded and inhaled deeply. He had met such men before.

'With the recent talk about plans to increase Norway's Exclusive Economic Zone from twelve to two hundred nautical miles, my people are a little concerned about long-term drilling prospects above latitude sixty-two degrees.'

'And you would like to – what is the expression – pick my brains?'

'Pick your brains, yes. Yes, I would.'

Bølset blew a long feather of smoke towards the window. 'You have come at a very ... sensitive time. I do not mean that I cannot help you, only that the help I am able to give may be of a rather limited nature, ja? Let me explain: to understand what the people of Norway want and what they feel, it is necessary always to consider first what is happening between Norway and the Soviet Union.'

'You mean the N A T O thing?'

'The N A T O thing?' Bølset looked up. 'Always, as you say, there is the N A T O thing, but no, I do not mean that. I refer rather to the delicate stage of Norwegian–Soviet negotiations regarding oil and the Continental Shelf boundaries to the east of where we are sitting. We are prospecting and they too are prospecting, all the time. Ah, Bridget –' he broke off gratefully as the girl returned with a tray of tea things and a platter of locally cured salmon on brown bread.

'Two things you must first consider,' Bølset urged through a mouthful of smoked salmon. 'One, the Russians are running out of oil, just as we in the West are. Within the next nine or ten years ...' Bølset talked on fluently and Martin made notes as he talked.

Presently it came to Martin that he might be able to draw Bølset more closely to matters of a non-economic, military nature. He tried first with a question about Soviet attitudes towards the three-hundred-mile 'security zones' surrounding the rigs and offshore installations farther to the south.

Bølset gave an evasive reply and passed on smoothly to discuss the sovereignty problems surrounding Spitzbergen as though the question had never been asked. Martin was embarrassed, puzzled – and then a little angry. The man was so obviously competent in matters relating to his own part of the world that it was inconceivable he would be ill-informed about matters relating to Norwegian security on this, Norway's front line.

Several minutes passed in more oil talk, and then Martin tried again, this time directing the thrust of his question towards published Soviet fears that N A T O would put Barents Sea oil platforms to clandestine military use by turning them into listening platforms which would monitor naval traffic in and out of Murmansk. This time his question registered with a flicker of alarm before it was turned away with another vague remark. Then they were off again, with Bølset talking now about Norwegian policing operations and the two-hundred-nautical-mile offshore limit. Bølset prattled on, and gradually the atmosphere changed as his answers became more clipped, his responses more guarded to Martin's sharpening questions.

Martin reached across the desk and helped himself to the salmon. Watching closely, he began to pose another question. 'There's something which I don't suppose you can help me with but I'd like to ask anyway.'

'Oh?' A gate clanged down in front of the eyes.

'It's to do with N A T O.' Martin paused and there was silence.

'Please go on,' Bølset managed at last. The girl had stopped typing.

'It's about a trawler that vanished out of my home town, Hull – oh, back in January sometime, it must have been. Ship called the *Arctic Pilgrim* – vanished just off here with all her crew. They never found a thing.'

'Oh? I would hardly think that would be a NATO matter,' remarked Bølset. 'Why do you tell me this?'

'Or, rather,' Martin continued quietly, 'they did find one thing. They found a lifebuoy with the ship's name written all over it in big letters so that even a blind man would see it was from the *Arctic Pilgrim*.'

'So? So they found a lifebuoy? I do not find that in the least strange. What are you saying? You come here asking me about oil and very soon you –'

'Did you know about the ship? About the lifebuoy?'

'Certainly I did not. Why should I?'

'Biggest search these parts have seen for years and the editor of the local newspaper knew nothing about it? Nothing?' The words crackled across the desk like counsel accusation.

Martin reached into an inside pocket and withdrew a newspaper clipping. 'If you knew nothing about it,' he said softly, 'then someone's writing your newspaper for you when you're not looking.' He laid the piece of paper carefully on Bølset's desk. 'I found this in my hotel.'

Bølset studied the newspaper clipping for a long time. It was a short story about the discovery of the lifebuoy.

Bølset lifted his eyes. 'Please, you will leave now,' he said huskily.

Martin Taylor left.

He had limped a few yards down the road and was looking in vain for a taxi to take him back to his hotel when he heard his name being called.

He turned to see the girl walking quickly towards him, her coat billowing open as she walked.

She smiled uncertainly. 'Mr Taylor?'

'What the hell was all that about? I've come a bloody long way to be told a pack of lies by some –'

'Don't be mad at Kjell, Mr Taylor. It's just that you frightened him a little.'

'I frightened him? He's meant to be a bloody newspaper editor. Look, all I asked him was –'

'I know what you asked him! All *he* knows is that a strange Englishman comes to talk to him about oil and very soon all he wants to know about is the security situation and a missing boat.'

'And the man's a bloody liar! You saw the story! You heard what –'

Her voice rose. 'He is not a liar!' People passing by turned round. The girl lowered her voice and laid a hand on Martin's sleeve. 'Please – may we go somewhere and talk? I am known here, even if you are not.' Her smile robbed the words of offence.

They walked on and turned into a coffee shop. The girl led the way between empty tables to a booth at the back. She exchanged greetings with the waitress and ordered coffee for them both.

'So what *was* going on back there?'

The girl sighed and cupped her hands around her coffee cup. 'Kjell Bølset has not been here for very long. He is still – what is the expression? – finding his legs?'

'Finding his feet, yes?'

'Finding his feet. He came here from Trondheim five or six weeks ago. There he was industrial correspondent. So this job, as editor, is better. He is still very ... anxious, very new, yes? He was not here when they found that lifebuoy you talk about, so when he says he knows nothing about that, it is true.'

'OK – but why wouldn't he talk in general terms about the security situation? You can't get away from the bloody word up here: notices in the hotel bedrooms, tanks at the airports, bunkers set in the side of –'

'It begins a year, two years ago. In those days I was new to newspapers and the man here was Erik, Erik Stabburs. It was very different. Erik was not like Kjell, not at all. Erik was ... was ...,' She tapped the side of her nose expressively.

'He was investigative?'

'*Ja* – he was, as you say, investigative. For a long time he wrote stories for the paper that were not kind to the situation regarding not just the USSR but Norway also. You remember Powers? That American flyer Gary Powers?'

'The U-2 pilot? Shot down by the Russians a long while back?'

The girl nodded. 'That man, yes. It was Eric who disclosed that Bodø had been used as a stopover base for U-2 flights over Russia from Pakistan long before Powers was shot down and captured. The stories were good and always, always correct, *ja*? But, for some reason, Erik's position became –' she hunted for the right word but it eluded her – 'uncertain.'

'There was pressure, do you mean?'

'We never knew for sure, but yes, we think so. It would, after all, be a simple thing for the military to suggest to Trondheim that for reasons of national security, Erik should ...'

'Investigate somewhere else?'

'Like that, yes. Erik was transferred. There was no trouble. One week he was there and the next he was on holiday and pouf! Kjell Bølset was in charge with his little watering can and his plants. And so now the newspaper is full of news about the mine and about what the mayor said about the winter roads and about the fishing and' – she smiled without bitterness – 'it is not the same since Erik left.'

'Do you know where he is now?'

'But of course! Across the fjord – in Vadsø.'

Martin hitched a lift into Vadsø with the bearded, cheerful young fisherman who had sat beside him on the ten-minute flight across Varangerfjord.

The aircraft had been almost empty; the long-suffering green-and-white Widerø Otter twin had carried just Martin, the fisherman, a young woman in a head scarf and an old man with his arm in plaster and a bottle of gin under his coat. It had been mid evening, yet the fjord below shone in the warmth of the golden sun as the aircraft swooped down towards the small airport scratched from the narrow ribbon of land between the lower slopes of the mountains and the rocky seashore.

The young fisherman dropped Martin off beside the quay with a cheerful wave and drove away – and, for the first time since leaving Hull, Martin felt loneliness close in around him.

There was the sea in front of him, lapping innocently against the low harbour wall. Somewhere out there in this same sea not so long ago, Johno had died; beyond the moored fishing boats and the empty fish market, thirty-six men had gone to their deaths. Because of that and a few tenuous links, a few phone calls and a few slices of luck linked to stubborn obstinacy and a handful of coincidences, here *he* stood in this remote little fishing village far above the Arctic Circle, more than a thousand miles from home.

Vadsø had been an old whaling port. Now fishing boats bobbed to their moorings while, beyond, upright wooden homes were crammed between the sea and the ice-flecked rolling tundra. Up on a hill overlooking the town Martin could make out the stark round white domes of some kind of radar installation that hung, huge and menacing, to dominate the skyline with sinister brooding silence.

There was a roar overhead and the Widerø aircraft flew over the village and banked round towards Kirkenes. Martin shivered in the sudden silence, sat down on a bollard and tugged Dr Dowdall's letter from an inside pocket. He felt a wave of affection towards the old doctor he had never met as the clear, uncompromising letter gave him confidence; this was where it would end, this was where the answers lay.

He stowed the letter away and walked past the heaps of bleached whalebones that still littered the quayside to the tiny glass-fronted harbour master's office at the end of the quay, where he spent five minutes checking on Arnt Jacobssen.

Kingflud II was still at sea, but the weather was changing. A storm was on the way. It was thought likely *Kingflud II* would be in first thing the following morning. Martin thanked the harbour master. And where might he find Erik Stabburs? He clumped back along the wooden jetty.

Half an hour later he stopped outside a small wooden house at the end of a cul-de-sac of identical homes hugging the eastern edge of the village and looked down at a pair of oil-stained suede shoes sticking out from beneath a battered red Volkswagen. A transistor radio was balanced on the seat of a child's tricycle beside the car. Martin bent down and turned off the radio.

'*Hva er det?*' from beneath the chassis.

'Erik Stabburs?'

'*Ja?*' The oil-stained shoes were withdrawn, there was a grunt, a muttered oath, and then a grease-smeared face appeared below the sill of the driver's door. Eric Stabburs was a little older than Martin, with piercing blue eyes and a thick blond beard trimmed close to his chin. He was handsome, striking.

Stabburs regarded the stranger critically and rose lithely to his feet. 'Can I help you?'

'I'm an English journalist. Martin Taylor. I'd like to talk to you.'

'To me?'

'If you're Stabburs – yes.'

Stabburs considered this and then nodded. 'I'm Stabburs. You're a long way from home.'

'Yes, I am. A long way.' Martin paused, curiosity getting the better of him. Finally: 'How did you know I was English?'

Stabburs broke the ice with a rich, deep chuckle. 'A Norwegian would never pronounce my name as you did.'

Taylor laughed his relief. It was going to be all right. This man was going to help him. 'Then I apologize. How should I pronounce it?'

Stabburs came to a decision. He smiled. 'Forget it – it's Erik, anyway.' The two shook hands warmly. Erik Stabburs turned to regard his car with disgust. 'You understand cars? Volkswagens?'

Martin shrugged. 'Not a clue. Sorry.'

'Me too.' Stabburs slammed down the bonnet in defeat. 'What the hell? Let's go on up to the house – we can talk in there.' He tossed Martin the radio, swung the child's trike under his arm and led the way up the gravel path. They climbed some wooden steps, pushed past a glass-fronted sun porch and went into the hall.

There were boots, bicycles and overcoats heaped in domestic confusion inside the front hall. Stabburs shoved the trike into a corner and pushed open the door into the living room. Two flaxen-haired children were seated on the floor in their dressing gowns watching TV, and a blonde-haired woman in her late thirties was seated in an arm-chair, her legs drawn up under her as she sewed a button onto a small shirt.

She turned round naturally as the door opened and then tried to rise to her feet as she caught sight of the stranger. Erik Stabburs stepped behind her chair, smiled down at her fondly and pressed her back into her seat. She smiled at Martin uncertainly.

'Ulrika, this is Martin Taylor, an English journalist. He has come to talk to me. All the way from England.' He winked broadly at Martin as the woman smiled a welcome.

'I am pleased to meet you.'

'My wife, Ulrika. Those two over there are Myer and Ingrid,' said Stabburs. He spoke over their heads to Martin. 'I think we had better talk out on the porch, *ja?*'

He led the way out onto the glass-fronted sun porch. 'My office,' he explained apologetically. 'Here I can work quietly. You will observe? The lock on the door – and the view?' He gestured proudly. The lock was not particularly impressive, but the view certainly was. From his seat Martin could look out across the whole length of the fjord, down to the open sea.

'We can talk here without interruption,' suggested Stabburs, sitting down on the bench opposite Martin. There was a sudden crash from the living room and a babble of voices, suddenly stilled. Stabburs got up and closed the door. 'Almost without interruption,' he temporized. 'So – tell me, why have you come to see me?'

'I was in Kirkenes – I went to see Kjell Bølset. There I met Bridget. She told me I should see you. I went to see Kjell about oil activities in northern Norway. I write about oil, for magazines – American magazines, mostly. Kjell was not very ... helpful. The girl was. She told me to come and see you.'

'About oil? Bridget told you to see *me* about oil?'

'I came up here to do a story about oil; I came up here about something else too, about a more sensitive matter. Kjell was helpful about the oil, that was fine. But he was not prepared to help me at all about ... the other thing. The girl, Bridget, she overheard my talk with Kjell, and afterwards she told me to come and see you.'

'About this "other thing"?'

Martin nodded. 'Four months ago a fishing boat, a trawler, vanished out here' – he gestured beyond the wide window towards the open sea – 'off North Cape. She came from my town, Hull, you see. She disappeared completely. Nothing was found – no wreckage, no bodies, nothing. Until, two months later, a month ago, they found –'

'A lifebuoy. I remember! The lifebuoy was found by a man from this village. Out at sea. It belonged to the *Arctic* ...'

'*Arctic Pilgrim*. That's it, yes, it did. I want to talk to the man who found it. I believe the lifebuoy was a plant. A red herring. Are you with me?'

Stabburs frowned. 'A red herring?'

'A red herring, put there to confuse people. I think *Arctic Pilgrim* was on some sort of intelligence mission – in fact I'm damn sure she was.'

Stabburs pulled out a pipe and lit up slowly. 'And that is the real reason you are here, that you have come all this way?'

Martin nodded.

'Whom are you writing this story for – not your oil magazines in America?'

'Hardly.'

'For whom, then, do you write such a story?'

'Christ knows. I just want to find out what happened, that's all. My father was one of the crew.'

Stabburs puffed gently at his pipe. Plumes of fragrant smoke rolled silently against the glass doors of the conservatory. 'So – it is personal also,' he said at last. 'One moment, please.'

He got up and vanished into the hall. He left the door ajar, and Martin heard numbers being dialled on the telephone. Presently Stabburs began talking softly in Norwegian.

Martin gazed out across the fjord until he returned.

'O K – I just talked with Bridget. About you.' Stabburs smiled. 'It was as you said.'

Martin relaxed. 'So you believe me, then?'

'Believe you? Believe what?'

Martin leaned forward earnestly. 'I covered the straightforward sinking and that was that – except that attention settled on a letter no one seemed able to find, written by one of the crew at sea to his wife and posted back in England by the mate who'd been taken ill and later taken off the ship at Tromsø. I found the letter – or part of it – in his wife's flat after she'd been killed in a fire.'

Stabburs shrugged. 'And that's suspicious? It does happen.'

'Sure, it happens – but it got me wondering: day before she could have given evidence at the inquiry? Hell of a coincidence. Still, as you say, it happens all the time.' Martin paused. 'There was a lot of talk in Hull of getting together an expedition to come up here and look around for wreckage. A lot of people, ordinary people, saw that as a way of doing something positive to find out what had happened. The idea caught on. Money poured in. Then two things happened pretty much together: they found the lifebuoy with *Pilgrim*'s name plastered all over it, and the little bloke Silvers, the bloke who was trying to organize the expedition, was suspected of being a crook, and, what with the lifebuoy *and* his court case – well, the expedition idea just fizzled away.'

'And the man who organized the expedition?'

'Silvers? Killed himself the same day he was found guilty of receiving stolen goods. I bumped into him in a pub only hours before he committed suicide. Pissed out of his mind.' Martin pointed at a glass. 'Drunk. A couple of days earlier he'd been knocking on my door saying it was a put-up job, that he'd been framed.'

'Framed?'

'Made to look as though he was guilty when he wasn't.'

Stabburs nodded and puffed at his pipe. 'And you? Did you think he was ... framed?'

Martin considered for a long moment. 'At the time? No.'

'And now?' asked Stabburs quietly.

'Now? Now I'm not so sure. In view of what's happened since then, it's certainly possible.' He thought of the fight in the flat, the attack on the quay, the days spent hiding on the trawler, the chase in the supermarket. 'Anything's possible.'

He told Stabburs the full story. '... One thing led to another. Eventually I spoke to a night watchman who remembered being ordered to look the other way when some special equipment was put aboard a boat called the *Venturer*, the *Arctic Pilgrim*'s sister ship, owned by the same company. He identified the gear without any trouble as E W – electronic warfare – equipment.'

'You did well,' commented Stabburs quietly.

Taylor shrugged. 'I worked at it a long time, that's all.'

'And the inquiry? That was arranged, too?'

Martin sighed again, tired of the whole business. 'Fixed? Told to look in a certain direction? To hurry things through by a certain date? Who knows?' He reached into his jacket pocket. 'This is a report on the plankton growth on the lifebuoy written by the marine biologist whose work was totally ignored by the inquiry. None of this came out in court. Not a word. Said it was too technical.'

Stabburs reached across for the letter. 'May I read this?'

'Help yourself.'

Stabburs read the letter from Dr Dowdall.

'Søren!' Stabburs swore suddenly.

'What's the matter?'

Stabburs slapped the letter. 'This – this here: where he writes about what he discovered? About the ... the "seat of radioactive disturbance?" ' He pronounced the long words with difficulty.

'What about it?'

Stabburs leaned forward. 'We have here, near Vadsø, a little village – Kiberg.' He turned down the corners of his mouth. 'It is little, ja?' Martin nodded. 'I have a friend in Kiberg. Nils Gitlesen. He is the doctor of Kiberg. A good man. We drink beer together sometimes, ja? A short time ago he comes here, to this home. He is worried. We talk and he give me information – information like this.' Stabburs then told Martin about Iversen, Elvaag, Scroeter and Borgssen, the crew of the fishing vessel Nijdar. He spoke, too, about the fishmonger and the other nine cases of contamination.

'Did your friend, this doctor, report what he found?' asked Martin.

'Ja, ja – he made his report.'

'And?'

'What can I say? Nothing happened. I wrote a story – and that was never published. I made some telephone calls. I spoke to the radio people. Gitlesen, the doctor, my friend? He tells me that very soon the people from Vadsø come and talk with him. Then, one day, more people arrive. Tests are done along the shoreline – here and at Kiberg. Myer, my own son here, he comes home from school one day and tells me he sees men on the beach with their funny suits and their machines. He asks me why they are ... how do you say? vacuum-cleaning the shore. I tell him it is nothing.' He shrugged. 'What do I know?'

'Did you ask the authorities? Did you check further?'

Stabburs made a sour face. 'I am not inexperienced. Yes, I checked. And I find out? Nothing. Zero.' He held up a circle made by fingers and thumb. 'Here, many things not released. Everything comes under "security". No formation is available. It is often so nowadays. Everyor too ... too ...' He quivered his hands expressively. 'Each time a Soviet submarine goes by out there' – he jerked a thumb towards the sea – 'half Norway holds its breath. There are many, many Soviet submarines. We are not a very courageous people.'

Stabburs read on and then folded Dr Dowdall's letter in half and handed it back to Martin. 'It is very, very detailed.'

'Too detailed, some would say.'

'And none of this came out at the inquiry?'

'Not a word. It was never submitted in evidence.'

'But there is no doubt at all about what your Dr Dowdall is saying! He means to say your lifebuoy was ... was ...'

Martin smiled at the other's agitation. 'That the lifebuoy was a plant? Yes. That is why I want to talk to Arnt Jacobssen. He found the lifebuoy.'

'How can I help?'

'You know the people, the area. Do you know Jacobssen? Does he speak English?'

Stabburs shrugged. 'He can, yes. When he wants to. Here everyone speaks English – when it is in their own interests to do so.'

'Then I expect Jacobssen will speak only Norwegian.'

Stabburs grinned. '*Ja* – I think that is possible.'

Martin glanced at his watch and put the thoughts of these last few minutes into words. 'May I use your telephone to call England? I'll pay for the call.'

'Please.'

Martin rose and went to the phone. Allowing for time-zone changes, it would be about 9 p.m. in Britain. He dialled through and presently heard the phone ringing in Suzy's flat. The thin distant sound brought with it a pang of loneliness. There had to be an answer this time.

But there was no answer. He dialled his own number, and again there was no reply. He now dialled the university.

There was no reply from there either. Martin racked his brains for the name of one of Suzy's girl friends he had met at a party recently; the one who had once shared a flat with Suzy. Christy ... Christy Mason? No, no ... Christy ... Manson. Yes. That was it. Christy Manson. Over in Danson Lane somewhere. Through to international inquiries, and presently, in Hull, another phone began to ring.

'Yes?' A girl's voice with loud music in the background.

'Is that Christy? Christy Manson?'

'Speaking. But you sound miles away. The line's terrible. I can hardly –'

'It's Martin Taylor – Suzy Summerfield's boyfriend. D'you remember? We –'

'Martin! We've been trying to reach you! Where are you?'

'Norway. I'm trying –'

'Norway! Wow – what are you doing there? We've been going mad just ...' The line wavered and faded.

'Hello? Hello? Christy? Can you hear me?'

'... hospital since yesterday. It looks as if somebody –'

'What's that? Hospital? Start again – I missed that.'

The line suddenly came clear and it was as though Christy were standing at his elbow. 'I said, Suzy's in hospital. We were trying to reach you. Hello?'

'Yes, yes, I heard what you said. Suzy's in hospital.' Stunned, Martin's voice was flat, without intonation.

'In hospital – that's right. She's not seriously hurt, though – just a bit.'

'What happened, for God's sake? Was she in a car smash?'

'No, no – nothing like that. Somebody broke into her flat and beat her up. Suzy's shocked, of course, but they say she'll be O K in a day or so.'

Martin felt his stomach grow cold. Then he was aware of a sullen, molten anger that grew from his shoes and threatened to engulf him completely. This was his fault, his fault ...

Christy was still talking, the words far away, seeping to

him through a mist of reproach and bitter, black anger:
'... neighbour, a Mr Hoskins. He phoned the university.
We've been trying to reach you all day.'

'O K, O K – I've got all that. Where is she? Where is
Suzy now?'

'Hull General Hospital. Er ... Ward Four G, I think it is.
But you'll have to –'

'Thanks, Christy. Thanks a lot.' The line went dead.
Martin stood by the phone staring down at his hands. They
were shaking.

Erik Stabburs laid a hand gently on his shoulder. 'Martin?
Something is wrong?'

Martin looked up. 'Suzy. That bastard got to Suzy. He
hurt her.' Suzy had featured in the story he had told the
Norwegian journalist.

'I am sorry,' Stabburs said simply. 'Is she badly hurt?'

'I don't know,' Martin muttered. 'I have to find out.'
Presently he was back on the phone calling the hospital.
He went through to Ward 4G.

'My name is Taylor. I'd like information on one of your
patients,' he said shortly. 'Suzy Summerfield. A Miss Suzy
Summerfield. She's a friend of mine. I understand she was
admitted sometime yesterday.'

It was dark in Ward 4G. The night nurse was sitting alone
at a small desk between two rows of darkened beds. The
desk was lit by a single shaded lamp. She was solely responsible for the lives of thirteen patients for the next eleven
hours, and the tiny muted buzzing of the phone beside her
starched sleeve had interrupted solid study for her finals.
Now was not the time for progress reports.

'I'm sorry, I'm not at liberty to divulge that sort of information over the phone. You'll just have to check with the
ward sister in the morning,' she said, more shortly than she
intended, as she bent low over the phone so as not to dis-
turb her charges. She fully expected Mrs Heath in bed five
to die sometime in the early morning, and, in truth, she was
a little frightened. She was just nineteen.

Martin detected something of the girl's youth over all

those miles. 'Look, Nurse, I'm calling from Norway. I can't call back in the morning.'

'I'm sorry, Mr Taylor. We're just not permitted to give information to anyone other than close relations.'

'Jesus,' muttered Martin with exasperation. 'Look, Nurse – I'm going to marry the girl, all right? Will that do? Is that close enough?' The announcement took even Martin by surprise. He examined the statement objectively and found no flaw therein.

The young nurse was not made of stone. In fact, she had just recently become engaged. And he was calling all the way from Norway.

'Wait a moment, then, I'll see what I can do.'

Martin waited impatiently until the voice came on again. This time it was calm, professional. 'Yes – here we are. Summerfield, Susan. Admitted eight forty-five p.m. yesterday to H G H. Cuts, abrasions, bruising and shock. Evidence of sexual assault although not of penetration –'

'No!' cried Martin involuntarily, screwing his eyes against the pain.

'She was sedated and left to rest. She's going to be all right, Mr Taylor, don't worry. All she needs is rest.'

'Did she say what happened?'

'Hardly – she was unconscious when admitted. I was on duty then, but she –'

'Unconscious? Jesus wept –' Could it get worse?

'She's over the worst now,' soothed the young nurse. 'Is your first name Martin, by any chance?' she asked shrewdly.

'Yes, yes it is. Why d'you ask?'

'We know quite a bit about you, in that case, Mr Taylor.' There was warmth in the voice now. 'Your girl's been talking about you quite a lot. In her sleep, you understand. Your ears should be burning. She thinks the world of you.'

Martin glowed with a sudden private warmth. 'What has she been saying – about what happened, I mean? Did she say who attacked her?'

'No – no, she didn't. She just kept saying something about someone taking the tape, some tape, and about collusion over something or other. I'm afraid she wasn't very coherent. She was under sedation. Hello? Can you hear me?'

Martin had been scribbling silently. 'Yes – I'm still here. What about the police? Are they doing anything?'

'They've popped in every so often to see how she is. They'll be back in the morning to take a statement. She should be much better by then. All she needs, as I say, is sleep and rest.'

'And you're sure she'll be all right?' persisted Martin anxiously.

'You can never be certain, Mr Taylor,' said the nurse with a caution older than her years, 'but off the record: yes. I think she'll be fine in a day or two.'

Martin nodded his relief. 'Good, good. Thanks a lot, Nurse – you've been marvellous.'

The girl smiled in the darkness. 'I'm glad I could help. I hope you'll be happy together.'

'Yeah – so do I,' said Martin. He rang off.

In Hull, the nurse replaced the receiver and, alone in the darkness, crossed the ward to help Mrs Heath die with as much dignity as possible.

'I'm going to need your help again, Erik, OK?'

'If there is anything I can do …'

'There is. I want the number of your World Health Organization headquarters here in Norway. Where would that be? Oslo? Trondheim?'

'Oslo. I have the number, although at this time of night …' began Stabburs doubtfully.

'There'll be a night crew – a duty press officer. He'll do for a start. And if I don't get any joy there I may need you to prise open a few doors in Norwegian, OK?'

'I will get the number,' said Stabburs. The English journalist had diverted his fury into taut, professional efficiency. Stabburs felt almost sorry for the unsuspecting duty press officer who was about to walk into the path of his

determination – a sheet of paper with the word 'STOℓ'
printed on it in tiny letters held in the path of a thundering
train.

'*Ja? Hva gjelder det?*' The voice in far-off Oslo sounded
sleepy, casual. Another call from a provincial newspaper
asking for details about the whooping-cough outbreak in
Ostersund. Put down the coffee, reach for a pen. Nothing
too strenuous. This was the quiet shift.

'Good evening. My name is Taylor. I'm a British journalist
working in your country. Do you speak English?'

'Of course, Mr Taylor. How may we help you?'

'Good. I want some help. Could you confirm that your
people have been doing littoral tests along the shoreline
around Kiberg and Vadsø? I know –'

'Mr Taylor, may I suggest you call back in the morning?
It would be much easier to deal with your request then. The
files, you understand, are –'

'I see,' said Martin quietly. 'And what is your name,
please?'

'My name is Gadsen, Mils Gadsen. You had better –'

'Thank you. And the name of your superior? Your
department head?'

'Mr Liefsen is the director of the bureau, but I hardly
consider –'

'Then you listen carefully, Mr Gadsen. I will ring you
back in five minutes. If you are not prepared to help me,
then I shall personally call your Mr Liefsen first thing in the
morning with the express purpose of nailing you to a bloody
cross. Do I make myself clear?'

'Mr Taylor, there is really no need . . .' began Gadsen with
a squeak of alarm. Jesus, why did *he* have to get all the
crank calls?

'Five minutes, then.' Martin looked across at Stabburs
and grinned wolfishly as he replaced the receiver.

Stabburs rolled his eyes towards the ceiling. 'Now I *know*
the real reason you come to work in Norway.'

'Why?'

'Simple. You have no one left to offend in Britain.'

The five minutes passed.

'What is it that you wish to know, Mr Taylor? I have the file on our monthly activities before me now. It is not exhaustive, you understand, but perhaps you will find what you want.'

'Right, then. First, is it true that your people have been doing tests along the Vadsø–Kiberg coastline?'

There was a rattle of papers. 'Kiberg ... Kiberg ... Kiberg–Vadsø. Yes, that is so. Between February the seventeenth and February the twenty-second, shingle and marine growth samples were removed from the littoral zone between Kvalneset–Kiberg and the area Pasvik–Pasviknakken to the east across Varangerfjord. Does that satisfy you, Mr Taylor?'

'It'll do for a start. Tell me: why were the samples taken at that time – from those specific locations?'

There was a pause. 'The World Health Organization takes sample readings from any number of different locations. It's part of our constant monitoring process. The same too is done in your country.'

'Yes, but why there?'

'There is no particular reason – except perhaps that there is much maritime activity off our northern shores. Incidents of pollution are not as infrequent as we would like.'

'You're telling me that those samples were taken from that area at *random*?'

'To the best of my knowledge I understand that to be so, yes. There is nothing before me to suggest otherwise.'

'Will you wait one moment?' Martin covered the mouthpiece with his hand and had a whispered conversation with Stahburs. Then: 'Those tests were not conducted as a direct result of certain ... ah ... discoveries made by the Vadsø Medical Centre?'

Gadsen sounded puzzled, irritated. 'Mr Taylor, what is the purpose of this inquiry? You have –'

'And those tests? What did they tell you?'

'You have a degree in marine biophysics, Mr Taylor? A doctorate, perhaps?' Gadsen sniped safely from behind cover. 'It is too complicated a business to –'

'Try me,' suggested Martin shortly.

Gadsen sighed. 'Very well.' He paused. 'Minute traces of gamma radiation were detected among the various small marine organisms that populate the littoral zone of that region. These varied in strength from just a few M R – a few millirads – to the equivalent of Roentgen Absorbed Dose twenty-five–thirty at the extreme upper limits.'

There was silence while Martin scribbled the details on a pad Stabburs had thrust towards him. 'What you're saying, then, is that your scientists *did* find traces of mild organic disorder along your northern coastline? And that this disorder was induced by some form of radioactivity?'

'Along *parts* of that coastline, yes. That disorder was more pronounced in the area Pasvik–Pasviknakken. To the east.'

'And what did your people learn from that?'

'Learn? What do you mean?'

'Where did that lead you? What were your conclusions?'

Gadsen gave a short laugh. 'You have much to learn about our country, Mr Taylor, much to learn. Look at the map! You tell *me* where that led us.'

Martin tried to picture the area. 'Over the border? Over the Soviet border?' he hazarded.

'Correct! Over the Soviet border at Grense-Jakobselv.'

'So?'

'So our investigations stopped, Mr Taylor! That is what happened. They stopped on the border. It is the usual thing.'

'The usual thing? You mean it has happened before?'

'Not often – but, yes, it has happened before.'

'Is there no kind of provision for scientific co-operation between Norway and the Soviet Union in matters of this kind?'

Again there was that short laugh. 'Are all you British so naïve, Mr Taylor? No, there is no "provision for scientific co-operation", as you put it. We just have to – what is your phrase, Mr Taylor? – we just have to ... to lump it.'

'So what happened to your investigation? What about your conclusions?'

'Our conclusions? They are still under investigation.'

Martin felt the conversation begin to revolve into

porridge. 'Will those conclusions be released? Made public?'

'I could not say.'

'OK, then. To come back to my question: no one at WHO has tied those discoveries of organic disorder to incidents of severe sickness among the people of Kiberg itself?'

'I have just told you: the matter is still under investigation. It is not for me to say.'

'But you don't think so?'

'I repeat: the matter is under investigation. It would be improper for me to –'

'Thanks very much!' snarled Martin, slamming down the phone in his frustration.

Stabburs was at his side with a can of cold beer. He gave it to him along with a wry I-told-you-so smile. 'So? Now you see? When matters of public concern in Norway come up against matters of national sensitivity, national security, there is, as the Americans say, no contest.' He slapped Martin on the shoulder and turned into the living room. 'Come. I must watch the news on TV. The children are with Ulrika upstairs. It is quiet here now. We will have a few beers, ja?'

Martin followed him into the living room, and as he tumbled down among the cushions and the little homely touches his thoughts suddenly switched to Suzy, the woman he would marry, and the man, far away, who had assaulted her: '... sexual assault but no evidence of penetration'. And all because she had chosen to side with him. Martin leaned forward over the cushions, took a deep swig of the cold beer and forced himself to concentrate on the distractions of the Norwegian commentator and the clip of news film about mineral deposits. Stabburs sensed his mood and jollied him out of it with a running commentary. Martin unwound a little and watched the pictures, his mind still tugging occasionally at what that nurse in Hull had told him Suzy had been trying to pass to him. It must have been important, very important; at the very surface of her subconscious – something about tape, the tape and somebody being in collusion with somebody else. But what tape? And collusion over what?

'Hey – those are our ships,' Martin exclaimed, sitting forward. News film shot from a helicopter showed a group of three trawlers plunging through heavy seas surrounded by a cloud of wheeling seagulls. The red ensign at the stern was clearly visible. The nets were out and men were working on the trawl deck. Gleaming in their yellow and red waterproof suits, they paused in their work to look up and wave at the helicopter as it clattered overhead.

'Ja, ja – they are your ships. Those boys are going home now,' supplied Stabburs from the sofa.

'Home? But I thought the ban on those fishing grounds was still in force?'

'It was, ja. It was. But not now. Five, six days ago it was finished. The British ships, they are waiting, just outside. As soon as the ban is over – zut!' He made a cutting gesture with his free hand. 'They come in. They fish. Now they go home.' He gestured at the television and remarked, 'Those boats, they too come from your town. From Hull.'

Ulrika returned from putting the children to sleep upstairs. She ruffled her husband's hair, smiled at Martin and collapsed into her chair with a theatrical groan. Stabburs handed her another can of beer, and presently, in deference to their English guest, they began to talk in English about their children, about the day's triumphs and setbacks. Martin envied them their unity, their clanship. He thought again of Suzy.

Presently, however, he was giving their conversation only half his attention, because something was still nagging at his brain. It had to do both with the boats he was watching on television and with the words Suzy had moaned to him from her hospital bed. If he could only put the pieces together ... But it was useless: the more he worried at it, the more elusive the strand became.

Ulrika was talking. '... and Nikol, she was on the bicycle. She came around the corner like so ... ach ... I do not know how it was that the driver of the truck missed striking the little girl. He crossed the road and almost there was the collision. Nikol, she of course was –'

'What did you say?' said Martin sharply, snapping to full awareness.

Ulrika looked startled. 'I am sorry. I was telling to Erik only that the little girl of our ... our neighbour –'

'No, no – I'm sorry. I meant after that.'

Ulrika looked puzzled. 'I said they almost have the collision. Do I use the bad word?'

Martin smiled. Because the way she pronounced it, the word sounded not like 'collision', but like 'collusion'. A different word altogether. Suzy's word.

'Not at all, no. You used the right word. "Collision" is fine. Just fine.'

'Javisst. Takk.' Dr Nils Gitlesen replaced the receiver slowly, ran a heavy hand through his thick hair and pushed himself up from behind his desk. He crossed wearily to the metal filing cabinet over by the far wall, reached inside the top drawer and rescued a bottle and three glasses.

'Whisky? For medicinal purposes, naturally.'

Martin and Stabburs both nodded. Dr Gitlesen gave a tired smile. It was an old, tired joke, but then he felt old and tired. Too tired, really, for many more questions. Even from these two. Seated before him now in their bulky parkas, the two journalists had driven thirty-five miles to the small wooden-walled clinic at Kiberg. The man they had come to see banged the bottle down on his desk and slopped amber liquid into the three glasses.

'That was Vadsø Medical Centre.' He sighed. 'Piers Iversen died half an hour ago.' He raised his glass and threw off the Scotch at a single gulp.

Martin and Stabburs exchanged glances.

'And are there any ... any more outbreaks?' Martin asked.

Gitlesen rapped his wooden desk top and shook his head. There were no more reported outbreaks. It looked as though, at last, the worst might just be over.

'And that makes it – how many?' asked Martin softly.

Gitlesen rubbed tired eyes and glanced briefly at the ceiling. 'Three dead, two seriously ill and eleven now recovering satisfactorily,' he intoned automatically. Vadsø had, at last, taken his warnings seriously. But reaction time had been slow – and for three of his patients that was all the delay death had needed.

'And Iversen was one of the crew? Of the *Nijdar*?'

Gitlesen nodded. 'One of four. Elvaag too is dead – he died five days ago – and both Scroeter and Borgssen are ill. I worry particularly about Scroeter. But ... he is in Vadsø now, so perhaps he will be O K. Who can say?'

'You were saying? Before the phone call?' Martin prodded gently.

Again Gitlesen ran a hand through his hair. 'Saying? What was I saying? *Ja, ja* – those fellows on the *Nijdar*: they tell me how it happens, *ja*? They needed a few kroner, you know? But – if the fishing ban continues they will have no money. So? So what do they do? It is obvious: at night and without the lights, in their little boat, they go fishing. I know, I know.' He held up a hand to stem an imagined flood of criticism. 'There was a ban. So what? There have been bans before. How do you tell that to men like these? They *know* these waters. And they need the money. To have the money they must catch a few fish. It is simple.'

'What reason were they given for the ban?' asked Martin.

Gitlesen shrugged. 'Who needs a reason? The recent storms, the bad weather, the loss of your trawler.' He shook that mane of thick hair. 'But those reasons would mean nothing to men like these.'

Martin leaned forward and tapped the letter from Dr Dowdall that lay on Gitlesen's desk. 'The lifebuoy he mentions there, the poisoning of those fishermen, that shoreline: what would cause that kind of ... of contamination?'

Gitlesen dragged the bottle towards him and slopped more Scotch into his glass. He rammed the cork home and tossed the bottle to Stabburs, who caught it deftly. Gitlesen spun the fluid around the bottom of his glass, hunched over his drink and said quietly, 'That is my question also. What would cause such sickness? Martin, do you have any ideas?'

Martin twisted in his chair, and the wood creaked in the silence. 'Well, I'm no expert, but –'

'In these matters none of us are expert,' conceded Gitlesen.

'Well, then, yes – I do have an idea. It comes from asking the question from a little further back: to have radioactive contamination you need to have a leak of radiation, and to have that – well, you need something for the radiation to leak *from, ja*?' In his tiredness Martin allowed the intonation to creep out unconsciously. 'That could be from a nuclear power station, or a nuclear laboratory, or from nuclear waste, or a –'

'A nuclear missile,' Stabburs finished for him.

Martin nodded. 'Or a nuclear missile. Now, there are no nuclear power stations around here, no fast breeder reactors, no laboratories that I know of and not that many nuclear bombs lying around in a corner somewhere.' The room was quiet now. 'But there are nuclear missiles. Hundreds of them.'

'Missiles?'

'Out there. Out at sea. On submarines.'

'Yes, but certainly they –'

'You asked if I have any ideas. My idea is this: I think there was an accident, a collision between the British trawler I was telling you about – the one that was snooping, spying – and a Soviet submarine. I think that the Soviet submarine was damaged in some way and that there was a leak of fissile material from the submarine's nuclear weapon load that seeped into the sea.' Martin paused and looked up at the thoughtful young doctor. 'That's what I think.' Another thought suddenly struck him. 'It would also explain the need for a fishing ban. They'd want to keep people away from a contaminated area. Did the men from the *Nijdar* tell you exactly where they had been fishing?'

'I did not ask,' the doctor confessed. 'Only that it was away there – to the east.' He gestured vaguely and there was a long silence.

'Well, you've heard my idea,' said Martin finally. 'What do you think? Nils? Erik?'

Gitlesen nodded. 'That is what I think also,' he said simply.

Stabburs nodded in his turn.

Someone was shaking him by the shoulder. Martin awoke blearily. Stabburs was up and dressed. Martin peered over the window sill, and a thick fog blanketed his vision. Stabburs threw open the window.

'Listen!' Stabburs beckoned, thrusting his head outside into the raw morning.

Shivering in his underpants, Martin crossed barefoot to the window and stuck his head outside. He could hear nothing.

'Do you hear it?' asked Stabburs.

Martin strained his ears. The wind changed direction, and Martin detected the steady *tonk-tonk-tonk* of an engine. A marine diesel engine. They looked at each other.

'Jacobssen,' breathed Martin. 'He's back – Jacobssen's back!'

CHAPTER TWENTY-FOUR

Evans heard it also. It was the sound he had been waiting for.

He propped his elbows against the back of the chair in his hotel room and once more quartered the quayside and the approaches to the fish market through the binoculars.

Taylor would be along soon; he would be drawn, just as he had been drawn, by the distinctive sound of the engine. He would be along soon – he would bet Taylor's life on it.

It was not easy to follow the progress of the fishing boat as she nosed her way up the fjord in the mist. With each gust of gentle wind the throb of her engine beat against the damp timbers of the quay, now close at hand, now far away.

Visibility was down to fifty yards, and the rain fell lightly in shifting curtains. The tang of windblown sea salt hung heavily in the air. Twenty minutes slipped by. Half an hour.

Evans's eyes flicked away from the glasses. A heavy lorry rumbled past below his window in a mist of fine spray as a red Volkswagen swung left across the slip road and bumped steadily across the wooden timbers of the jetty towards the shipping office.

He watched incuriously as it parked against the chained-off lower section of the quay. The doors opened. He was looking for one man on foot, not two men in a car, two men in parkas who pulled up their hoods, thrust their hands deep into their pockets and then ran hunched against the rain towards the glass doors of the shipping office.

Only, one of the men ran with a limp.

Evans flicked up the glasses and they locked onto the limping figure. Like cross hairs.

*

They would find *Kingflud II* moored behind the fish market – that was his custom; Jacobssen always liked to moor there. Stabburs thanked the old man behind his desk, and they set off down the quay, their heels clumping purposefully on the wooden jetty.

Evans crossed the road and moved silently after them, his rubber-soled shoes making no sound as he flitted between the parked lorries and the fish baskets that littered the jetty.

It was low tide.

The first they saw of *Kingflud II* was the masthead light, gleaming at them through the mist like some pale Hallowe'en mask. Martin and Stabburs looked down at the boat. Back at the inquiry, Martin had imagined her tall, proud, substantial – yet here she was, smaller than he had pictured her, with that raised sheer and that square high wheelhouse aft. Her derricks were swung inboard and her hatch covers were off. Pale yellow light washed out of the open hold, but there was no sound and no one in sight. Martin and Stabburs paused – and then they heard the clang of a shovel against steel.

Stabburs pointed to a weed-slimed ladder bolted to the jetty and gestured 'After you' to Martin.

Martin began climbing slowly down to the deck. Stabburs was close behind.

Evans slipped behind one of the wide steel girders that supported the roof of the fish market, wiped the rain from his eyes and eased the slim, razor-sharp quarter-inch carpenter's chisel to a more comfortable position under his belt. The presence of the second man complicated the situation. Until *his* role was clear, he would bide his time, wait. He watched intently as Martin paused at the bottom of the ladder, crossed to the open hatch and looked down.

There was a man below in gleaming yellow oilskins shovelling salt onto a bed of mackerel. As Martin watched he scooped a slithering armful of fish out of a huge wooden bin and slapped them down on top of the others. He dug his shovel into a heap of salt crystals and began sprinkling the salt over the catch.

Martin leaned out over the hatch. 'Jacobssen – Arnt Jacobssen?'

There was no response as the man bent to his work, the powerful yellow shoulders glistening in the light from a lamp clamped to the bulkhead beside him.

'Jacobssen!' shouted Martin.

The man looked up. Forty-five, fifty, with a wide, powerful frame, sparse sandy hair that glittered with beads of sweat, and a belly grown on beer. He was panting as he held up a thick arm to ward off the rain which lanced across his eyes like bright wet needles.

'Ja?'

'I'm Martin Taylor. I sent you the cable. The telegram.'

Jacobssen hesitated and then, without a word, returned to his shovel and the business with the salt.

'Jacobssen!' shouted Martin again. The man stood back from his shovel and looked up impassively.

'I've come to talk to you – I want to ask you some questions,' Martin shouted. 'About the lifebuoy. About the lifebuoy you found.'

Jacobssen hawked, spat on the deck and scooped up another armful of fish.

The anger rose like bile in Martin's throat. There was a wooden ladder in one corner of the hold. He swung his leg over the rim of the hatch and began climbing down.

The hold was small and stuffy. It stank of fish and diesel. Martin waited silently while Jacobssen sprinkled more salt. Then he grabbed the shaft of the shovel and tore it from Jacobssen's hands.

Jacobssen swung round, eyes blazing. Martin, half a head shorter than he, stood his ground defiantly. He tossed the shovel aside.

'I'm the man who sent you that telegram. About the lifebuoy you found from *Arctic Pilgrim*. You found a lifebuoy, remember? A lifebuoy?' He made a circle with his hands.

Jacobssen turned away and bawled something to Stabburs in Norwegian. Stabburs climbed down and joined them in the cramped little hold.

'He says he doesn't understand you. Are you mad? What do you want?'

Martin turned to Jacobssen and looked up into his eyes. 'Tell him I'm here about the lifebuoy he found. Tell him I've come all the way from England to talk to him about the lifebuoy.'

Stabburs translated. Jacobssen listened and then his eyes slid away as he began to reply in Norwegian.

'What does he say?' demanded Martin.

'He says of course he remembers finding the lifebuoy, but that is all that he remembers. It was a long time ago and –'

'Crap. It was a month ago. And what? And one lifebuoy looks much like another?' Martin shook his head briefly. 'More crap.' He stabbed a finger at Jacobssen. 'You tell him this lifebuoy was special – very special – and I want to know who gave it to him. Who gave it to him to find.' He watched as the words brought fear to Jacobssen's eyes so that before Stabburs had finished translating he was interrupting.

'He says no one gave it to him. He found it at sea.'

'Where at sea?'

'He doesn't remember.'

'Far out? Close in? Where?' snapped Martin. Stabburs translated.

'He doesn't know.'

Martin reached slowly into his coat pocket for Dr Dowdall's letter. He waved it gently between finger and thumb. 'Tell him I don't believe him. His story stinks. Tell him he's a liar.' Martin paused deliberately. 'A fucking liar, OK? Tell him that, will you? Now.'

Jacobssen looked like thunder. Stabburs looked alarmed. 'Martin? Are you sure? I mean ...'

Martin put the letter away. 'OK – leave it be. You're right. We'll not get anything more out of this oaf.'

He tossed Jacobssen his shovel, and the two journalists climbed back into the fresh air and up the slimy ladder onto the jetty. Stabburs dusted his knees and the two began to walk back towards the car.

Evans moved silently after them.

'And that is all?' asked Stabburs incredulously. 'That is all you ask of Jacobssen? But we discovered nothing! No information!' He tugged at Martin's sleeve. 'Come – we go back,' he announced decisively. 'This time, in Norwegian –'

'No, that's not all,' growled Martin without turning round. He grabbed Stabburs's sleeve and pulled him along. 'Did you notice anything back there?'

Stabburs frowned. 'What sort of thing?'

'Like the crew, for instance.'

'Crew? There was no crew.'

Martin banged him on the shoulder. 'Right. No crew. Not a crewman in sight. Now, maybe it's different in Norway, but back home everyone turns to to help unload the catch. Everyone. I've never heard of a skipper doing all the work himself.'

Stabburs caught the mood. 'No, no! You are right! There would be three, possibly four men also on a boat of that size.'

'Right. Three or four men. Only where were they? He wasn't taking any chances. He was hoping that when I found he was at sea, I'd go straight home again. And if I didn't, and I did come round asking awkward questions, everyone else would be safely out of the way.' He paused, thinking. 'Do your men here have to belong to a union? Seamen's union, something like that?'

Stabburs nodded.

'And where would that office be? The union office?'

Stabburs pointed to the shipping office a few yards ahead. 'Shipping office, union office, weighing office, weather office – it is all of these. It is quiet today only because of the mist, the warnings of storms.'

They went inside to the old man behind his high, old-fashioned desk. Presently the old man pulled a worn, stained ledger towards him and began running a dirty thumbnail down a list of names. The two journalists had the name and address of one of *Kingflud II*'s younger crew members.

Following the old man's directions, they walked back to the main road and turned down a narrow alleyway between two rows of cheap clapboard houses. Downtown Vadsø. They picked their way carefully down the debris-strewn alley, studying door numbers.

A wooden exterior staircase ran up to a green door on the first floor.

Martin stepped round the overflowing dustbins and climbed the stairs to number 35. There was no bell and he hammered on the door. It shook flimsily. Voices within were suddenly stilled.

Stabburs came up behind him and they waited. The door opened cautiously. A little girl of five or six in a red cardigan that was too big for her stood in the doorway sucking her thumb and regarding them gravely. Stabburs hunched down beside her and spoke to her softly. Then he ruffled her fair hair and stood up as the child turned and scampered away into the gloom, calling shrilly for her father.

Stabburs turned to Martin and nodded. 'It is OK. He is inside.'

They stepped over the threshold and walked down a gloomy uncarpeted hall into the main living room. There was a loaded clothes-horse standing by the gas fire. Two small boys sat on the sofa playing with empty cigarette packets. The room was damp and cheerless. A kitchen led off the living room. From here a young man in vest and trousers watched them nervously as they stepped into the room.

'*Ja? Hva glelder det?*' He had been shaving in the mirror over the sink and one side of his face was still covered in soap. His Adam's apple bobbed anxiously as he came through from the kitchen wiping the soap off his face, as though the only people who hammered on his door were the collectors and the reclaimers and the rent people.

Stabburs stepped forward, and all three shook hands. As Nilssen cleared the two boys off the sofa and offered the journalists a seat, his wife came in from the kitchen. She too carried that pinched, drawn look, the universal hallmark of poverty. She was older than he and her hair was drawn back, held by an elastic band. She was heavily pregnant.

She wiped her hands on an apron and shook hands politely before sweeping the children before her into a back room.

As they sat down again and Stabburs began talking, Nilssen's first look of anxiety eased into one of careful watchfulness. But there was still the tension, a tension that matched the long earnest face and the dark smudges beneath the eyes.

Stabburs turned to Martin. 'Petar Nilssen says he speaks a little English – a little only. Perhaps, if you talk to him slowly?'

Martin leaned forward. 'Thank you, Petar. I'm sorry I don't speak Norwegian. I don't know what my friend has told you, so I'll start at the beginning, OK?'

Nilssen nodded jerkily and swallowed, as though the wrong response could cost him his head.

'It's OK – there's nothing to worry about. I just want to ask you a few questions, do you mind that?'

'Please – you ask me.'

'We've been down to the docks. We saw your boat – *Kingflud* II. How come you're not down there? Why aren't you working, unloading the catch?' Martin spoke idly, as though he were just passing the time.

'Skipper Jacobsen says OK, we work good. He give us ... holiday. Every man has holiday today.' Nilssen smiled for the first time. When he smiled he looked about eighteen.

'Good trip? Good fishing?'

Nilssen nodded warily.

'How long have you been with Jacobsen? With *Kingflud* II?'

Nilssen held up two fingers. 'Two year.'

'Were you with him when he found the lifebuoy four weeks ago?'

There was a pause. Nilssen glanced up at his wife standing listening in the doorway. Finally: 'Yes. I sail with him.'

'What happened?'

A silence grew. Nilssen looked unhappy. He turned Stabburs and spoke in Norwegian.

Stabburs turned to Martin. 'He says they were out fi

and they found a lifebuoy. They brought the lifebuoy back to port and handed it to the authorities. That is all.'

Martin turned to Nilssen. 'Where did you find it? Where did you find the lifebuoy?'

Nilssen shrugged, his eyes on a stain on the arm of the sofa. It was obvious he was holding something back.

Taylor waited. 'Who was on the bridge? Who was at the wheel?' Martin grasped an imaginary wheel as Nilssen looked up.

'I hold the wheel.'

'And you have no idea where you were?'

There was another miserable silence. It was Martin who broke it. 'Let me tell you why I ask.' He was close now, very close. 'The ship *Arctic Pilgrim* – she came from my home town. I want to find out what happened to her – to the men, the fishermen. Men like you. Understand?'

Nilssen nodded.

'I already know she was doing some kind of work for the military. I know, too, that the lifebuoy that your skipper found spent the time immediately before it was found lying in some harbour or freshwater river somewhere, OK? It had never been in deep water out at sea – not for more than a few hours, anyway. It just isn't possible.'

He reached for Dowdall's letter. 'This is from a British scientist who examined the lifebuoy,' he continued softly. 'His report confirms that the lifebuoy could not possibly have been at sea for very long.' He paused. 'So what did happen out there?'

Nilssen had been watching Martin. Now his gaze wavered. He sat back and ran a hand through his hair and groaned softly. Martin said nothing. Nilssen twisted round to look at his wife. Suddenly she began to talk. Stabburs listened intently as she began to argue with her husband.

'What's she saying, for Chrissakes?' Martin whispered to Stabburs.

'She says you are a good man. You are looking for the h and he should help you. How would she feel if he – – had vanished at sea like the men from your town? It has gone on for long enough. He should tell you what he knows.'

It was the woman who broke into halting English. 'Mr Taylor?' Martin nodded. 'Petar – he is a good man. He did not want to do what Jacobssen said, but Jacobssen was skipper and Petar ... Petar was ... crew, you understand?' She looked about her and gestured at their few belongings. 'Here in Vadsø, it is not always so easy to get work. And, for the little ones, Petar needs to work. So when Jacobssen say to Petar, Petar, you say nothing; Petar – he says nothing.'

The woman shuffled round to stand beside her man, a protective hand on his bare shoulder. 'Only to say nothing is difficult. It is better that we talk.'

'Thank you.' Martin turned now to Nilssen. 'Will you tell me about the lifebuoy? You didn't just find it, now, did you?'

Petar Nilssen shook his head. 'Five weeks ago Jacobssen ... he has the trouble with the ...' He rubbed fingers and thumb together.

'Payment? Money? Payments on the boat?' prompted Martin.

Petar nodded. 'Ja – everyone knows. Things are difficult for Jacobssen – for the crew. One day, Jacobssen, he is called away. To Kirkenes. It is very important, he says.' Nilssen shrugged. 'Soon, all is O K once more. We have diesel, we have supplies, and Jacobssen, he pays the crew as before, ja?'

'So what happened about the lifebuoy?'

Nilssen smiled without humour. 'That is a simple thing. A man comes here, one night, to the boat. Jacobssen is told: go to a certain place. We go to that place. We find the lifebuoy. Jacobssen is very pleased. We pick up the lifebuoy, we make the report as we are told and we come back. That is all.'

'Do you know why Jacobssen was ordered to pick up the lifebuoy?'

Nilssen shrugged again. 'I do not know.'

'Where was that place – the place where you picked up the lifebuoy?'

Nilssen thought for a moment. 'Twenty-three, twenty-four hours' sailing from Vadsø.'

'To the east or the west?'

'The east.'

'You are certain?'

'Yes. We were heading east. Into the P Z.' Nilssen pronounced the letters in the Norwegian fashion, and Martin looked to Stabburs for clarification.

'The prohibited zone. The area of the fishing ban announced by the Soviet Union. The one they just lifted.'

'So the lifebuoy *was* picked up from within the P Z?' Martin asked.

'I am almost sure, yes.' Suddenly Nilssen looked up. 'The charts ... Jacobssen keeps them –' he turned to Stabburs for a word – 'he keeps them folded. Small, like so. It is not necessary that both our position and the prohibited-zone line are shown at the same time, yes?'

'I'm with you.'

'I remember one thing. Jacobssen had been very angry with me before that day because I put coffee on the chart – I put coffee mug on the chart. It leaves a ... a mark on the chart – like so.' He made a circular movement with his hand.

'A rim mark, you mean?'

'*Ja.* The lifebuoy – she is in the middle of this ring. I remember this because it is curious, *ja*?'

'You're sure about that? No other coffee marks? Just that one rim mark?'

Nilssen nodded emphatically. 'Jacobssen is old sailor. He never mark his charts.'

Martin considered this: 'Tell me: afterwards, after you picked up the lifebuoy, did you – did any of you – have any sickness? Headaches? Things of that sort?'

Nilssen looked puzzled, and Stabburs had to translate. Nilssen's brow cleared immediately.

'*Ja* – for a day or so only, that is all. We all have a little sickness, but it soon passes. It is the weather, yes? She is very bad that time.'

'And one more thing,' said Martin. 'Tell me – where does Jacobssen keep those charts of his?'

They clattered down the exterior staircase, walked down the alley and turned back towards the quay and *Kingflud II*.

Neither looked behind them. There was no need. But had they done so they might have seen a man in a dark-blue turtleneck sweater leave the shadows behind the staircase and set off in pursuit.

Kingflud II was deserted. Jacobssen had left, and the hatch covers had been pulled roughly into place. The tide had turned and the boat now rode a little higher up the jetty.

They paused at the top of the ladder for a moment, the damp striking up into their bones. Somewhere out in the fjord another vessel pounded by, the mournful wail of her foghorn smothered in the folds of damp mist. The quay was empty, deserted. The rush of traffic and the warm press of people a few hundred yards away seemed another world, a lifetime away.

Martin clapped Stabburs on the arm. 'Come on – let's get on with it.'

They dropped down the greasy ladder. Leaving Stabburs as uneasy sentry at the bottom of the ladder, Martin made for the wheelhouse. He climbed the short wooden ladder and turned the brass handle. It was locked. He peered through the fanlight. The door on the other side of the wheelhouse was locked, too.

Martin glanced furtively about him, turned slightly on the top wooden step and rammed his padded elbow against the fanlight scuttle. It gave with a little tinkle of glass, and he reached through and slid the catch.

The wheelhouse was small, compact and spotlessly clean. Coffee mugs jammed behind a wooden batten below the Clearview screen, brass-capped wheel, echo sounder and V H F radio, sloping chart table at the back of the wheelhouse with, below, a chest with drawers of various sizes. A chart chest.

Martin looked about him, uneasy in the role of burglar. Through the brass porthole at the back of the wheelhouse he could see Stabburs standing at the bottom of the ladder.

Martin began to hurry as the worms of fear began to wriggle. He tugged open a drawer at random: sweaters neatly folded, hand-bearing compass still in its box, a bundle of signal flags.

He opened another drawer: books on navigation, shackles in an empty biscuit tin, a flare pistol and a box of cartridges.

And another drawer: neat coils of light fishing line, more sweaters smelling of the sea – but no charts. So where were the bloody charts?

Martin had overlooked the thinnest drawer of all, right at the top of the chest. He felt a surge of relief as it ran smoothly towards him at his touch and *there* were the charts, all neatly folded and numbered, just as Nilssen had said they would be. Now, the chart should be ...

Stabburs banged his hands together and stamped his feet. It was cold doing nothing. A thought came to him then and he paused: in the eyes of the law, of course, he certainly wasn't doing nothing; he was aiding and abetting or some such thing, and if the harbour police happened to come along now, he would find it difficult to –

He jumped as someone hailed him from the top of the ladder. Then he relaxed. At least it wasn't a policeman, thank God. He smiled back uncertainly as the man in the dark-blue sweater gave him a cheerful wave and began climbing down the steel ladder towards him.

Nilssen had been right, dead right.

There was his prohibited zone, the area covered by the recent Soviet fishing ban. And there was the single coffee stain made by Nilssen's mug: that was where the lifebuoy had been picked up, well within the prohibited zone, as Nilssen had said.

O K. Martin forced himself to shut off from his surroundings and concentrate on finding the flaws in the logic of his reasoning. It was time he took it all one step further:

Suzy had discovered something in Hull. 'Collusion' referred in fact to collision. *Arctic Pilgrim* had been sunk after hitting, colliding with, something. That was what Suzy had been trying to tell him. He'd buy that.

At the same time *Pilgrim* sank, *and in the same area*, there was a radiation incident, a leak of radioactivity. The two incidents had to be connected. This was endorsed by Dr Dowdall's examination of the *Pilgrim* lifebuoy, by the mild effect of contamination upon those who handled the planted lifebuoy before it had been cleaned, and by the effects of illegal fishing within the contaminated area upon the crew of the *Nijdar* and those who handled and ate the fish they caught.

A phrase Erik Stabburs had used once kicked suddenly into his mind: 'Each time a Soviet submarine goes by out there, half Norway holds its breath.'

Maybe, just maybe, *Pilgrim* collided with one of those Soviet nuclear submarines. Maybe the submarine's reactor, its power plant or its missile load had been damaged in some way. The fishing ban would have been imposed to restrict public access to the contaminated area, to let the Russians clean up in private.

And, thought Martin, it followed also that the area of contamination, the area of the fishing ban *and the area of the collision* were one and the same.

It further follows, thought Martin rapidly, that if I now unfold this chart to its full size, like so – the chart crackled in the stillness – then the area of contamination should coincide both with the area of official search all those weeks ago and with the rough location of *Pilgrim*'s last reported position.

Martin stared, his mind spinning.

Because the areas *did not* coincide. Not at all.

Realization dawned – and the enormity of the deception took his breath away.

The official search had been terminated thirty, forty miles

to the west of the area of contamination, of *Pilgrim*'s last position, and no trace of her had been found despite all the technology, the sophistication.

Because that was the way they wanted it. *Arctic Pilgrim*, in their eyes, in somebody's eyes, had become just another battle casualty.

So they'd just gone through the motions. For the folks back home.

There was a sudden noise, and Martin's head whipped up. He laid the dividers aside and beckoned impatiently. Stabburs was standing at the wheelhouse door.

'I –' Stabburs gave a little cough. Martin felt a tingle of terror as Stabburs toppled slowly backwards, eyes up to the sky, and crashed out of the wheelhouse down to the deck below.

'Erik!' yelled Martin.

Lunging at the door, he looked down at the deck. A man in a dark-blue sweater was bending over the still body, wiping a thin chisel on the back of the Norwegian's coat. A widening red stain showed just above Stabburs's shoulder blades. The wheelhouse door banged in the breeze, and Evans looked up, full into Martin's eyes.

For Martin, the shock was profound, catatonic. He was speechless, anchored to the deck plates by the totality of the surprise.

Evans rose from a crouch, the thin-bladed carpenter's tool held delicately in his right hand. He stepped smoothly over the body, crossed to the ladder and began climbing slowly, his eyes never leaving Martin's face.

Martin backed into the wheelhouse and slammed the door. Only that wouldn't stop him, wouldn't slow him down for more than a second. Only a weapon would do that – a weapon. He had to have a weapon.

But there was nothing, nothing. Then he saw the boat-hook resting over against the door, but even as he moved towards it the man outside was pushing at the wheelhouse door. It opened an inch, two inches, before Martin got his boot to it and kicked it shut. The catch clicked shut for an instant, and Martin threw all his weight against the flimsy door. He leaped back just in time, reaching for the boathook, as the bright tip of the chisel thudded again and again through the marine ply. Martin's outstretched fingers could just reach the boathook; he grabbed it and jammed it between the Clearview screen and the chart table.

Evans pushed silently at the door. Immediately the pole of the boathook began to bend. Martin stared, hypnotized, as he backed towards the far door, his fingers scrabbling blindly, frantically, at the lock.

The boathook gave with a splintering crash, and Evans lunged into the wheelhouse, hunting hungrily for him with wide, scything sweeps of the chisel.

Martin scooped up a neat row of reference books and hurled them into Evans's face. The man did not even falter. He ducked, warded off the books with one hand, dropped into a crouch and came in low with the chisel.

Martin, near to panic now, lashed out wildly with his foot. He missed as Evans swayed back easily out of reach and raked his shin with a long, slicing slash of the chisel. Martin cried out as he felt the warm blood gush into his sock. But the door was free now. Before the man could step forward Martin whipped open the door and tumbled the six feet or so down to the deck. He landed awkwardly on all fours and moaned aloud with the pain. He began hobbling aft, specks of blood from his shin dribbling crimson onto the dark, seasoned timbers of the deck.

Where to hide? Where to go? The question ran round and round inside his brain, but no answers came, just the question. Always, always the question. Where to hide? Where? Where? Think, Martin! You want to live? Then think!

He glanced over the side. Dark, oily waters slid by, and his courage deserted him. Not that way. Not again. Not over the side. Where, then? Where?

The hatch covers were in place, but they were not battened down. Martin stole a glance over his shoulder. Evans was hidden from sight by the edge of the wheelhouse.

He had seconds now, only seconds, as the germ of a plan took frail root.

Most holds had internal hatches through to the crew's quarters so that sailors could inspect the shift of cargo in heavy weather without removing the hatches. If he was quick he could be down the hold, through the hatch and up *behind* Evans before he realized he'd been outmanoeuvred. But he would have to move fast. He would have to move now !

Martin hobbled towards the hatch, threw his leg over the rim and squeezed down into the darkness. He climbed down the ladder, down into the stinking hold, pausing at the bottom to look up at the triangle of pale light that was the sky. He listened. There was no sound. He felt something sticky beneath his fingers and sniffed his own blood.

He turned away and blundered blindly forward into the crate of fish Jacobssen had been working with. His outstretched hands slipped over slimy fish heads and entrails.

He moved to his right, and something went over with a loud clang. Jacobssen's shovel. He stooped, felt around for the shovel and picked it up. Casting from side to side ahead of him with the shovel, he worked his way steadily towards the back of the hold until he came against the smooth steel of the bulkhead.

Starting from his extreme left, he felt his way along the wall of the hold, feeling in the darkness for the hatchway that would lead him to safety.

The wall was smooth and solid. There was no hatch.

There was no access aft. Unless he could regain the deck before Evans followed his spoor of blood to the ladder, he was trapped. He began to hobble painfully towards the ladder.

He was reaching out to grasp the bottom rung when the triangle of light above was blocked and a dark shape swung nimbly onto the ladder and began to climb down silently towards him.

Martin tried to still his laboured breathing in the stifling darkness of the hold. His eyes were accustomed to the darkness, while those of the man on the ladder were not. The advantage, such as it was, lay for the moment with him. He must use it. To beat the man who had assaulted Suzy. The thought gave him sudden courage.

He watched as the hands came down the ladder, peering for the glint of light on metal that would be the chisel. That was the hand to go for.

There was the merest flicker of light at the left wrist, and as the man reached the bottom and paused to collect his bearings Martin stepped forward and grasped that wrist tightly with both hands. The man tried to wrench free, but Martin was ready. He jerked the arm towards him, spun the man round and cracked the wrist sharply against the edge of the ladder. The chisel tinkled away into the darkness and the two men locked together with a grunt.

Evans kneed Martin viciously in the groin, but Martin, anticipating the move, twisted away suddenly and raised a foot against the bulkhead behind him. The man's sour breath was full in his face as he pushed away from the bulkhead and propelled them both backwards into the darkness.

Evans's knees caught against the rim of the fish bin, and the two fell backwards into a sliding, stinking sea of fish. Dead eyes gleamed coldly in the darkness as they rolled and slithered together.

Martin had released Evans's hand as they fell, and now Evans chopped hard at Martin's neck with his left hand before he got both arms around Martin's chest and began to squeeze in a vicious bear hug. Martin gasped. He felt as if he were caught between two contracting steel bands. He rolled to right and left, sobbing for air.

They rolled over and then over again, slipping and sliding on dead fish before Martin was able to work an arm free and batter weakly at Evans's head. No good. He was suffocating.

He tore at the man's hair, but Evans countered by burrowing deeper into the thick folds of Martin's parka. Martin lashed out with his legs, but nothing could shake the steel bands crushing his chest.

His fingers ripped and tore at the lobe of one ear. As

Evans's head came up to shake off the troublesome distraction, Martin clenched his teeth and plunged one rigid thumb deep into Evans's right eye. There was a moment of resistance against muscle and living tissue, and then his thumb sank deep within the wet socket.

Evans's arms came loose and he moaned deep down in his chest. The noise grew and bubbled into a scream of agony as Martin lashed out, wriggled free and slithered over the edge of the fish bin. He fell panting on the salt-strewn deck, whooping breath into starved lungs.

There was the slip and flop of wet fish onto the deck beside him, and Evans slithered blindly after him.

Martin crawled towards the ladder, his fingers scratching at the salt on the deck. He dragged himself forward, pursued by that laboured, pain-racked breathing. If only he had a gun. A gun. A pistol. A flare pistol. In the drawer of the chart chest in the wheelhouse. If he could only ... He lunged at the ladder and hauled himself upward. One rung, two, three – he was almost clear – then Evans had wrapped his arms around his legs and was trying to drag him down. Martin locked one arm round the ladder and chopped viciously at the head below with the other. He felt over the sweaty domed head and then rubbed the salt he had been clutching over the hole where the eye had been.

Evans screamed. Both hands flew to his face. Martin kicked free and scrambled, panting, up the ladder towards the light.

He rolled over the lip of the hold and began hobbling down the deck towards the wheelhouse. Ten yards, fifteen, and Evans had not yet appeared. Twenty yards. A hand appeared over the rim of the hatch.

Martin threw himself up the short ladder and scrambled into the wheelhouse on his knees. Now where, where ... He began pulling at the drawers in his haste, his panic. Sweaters and fishing line, books and pencils ... The flare pistol. His hand closed greedily on the butt while, trembling, his other hand tore at the cardboard carton of cartridges. He crouched down fearfully, his eyes flicking to the empty doorway. Five seconds, that was all he had, five seconds, four ... The cartridges spilled loose inside the drawer as Martin heard that hideous wet panting drawing nearer. His fingers shook as they closed round a cartridge and slipped it into the chamber. He snapped the breech shut and dropped onto the floor, the pistol held out in front of him. He thumbed back the heavy hammer with a loud click as Evans's head appeared above the ladder.

Evans was smeared with entrails and glittering fish scales. Sweat rolled down his face, and the damaged eye rolled obscenely against his cheek. Martin steadied his wrists against the deck, sighted carefully down the wide barrel and pulled the trigger. There was a sharp, flat report.

The flare hit Evans in the throat.

The force of the charge at the base of the cartridge snapped his head back and severed his larynx. It picked him up, propelled him away from the ladder and then dropped him onto the deck with the white phosphorus flare still spluttering in his throat. He lay there, spreadeagled on his back in a widening pool of blood, his limbs twitching spastically.

Martin coughed in the sudden silence, waved away the acrid smoke that filled the wheelhouse and lurched to his feet, the flare pistol dangling forgotten at his side.

He tottered to the wheelhouse door and climbed stiffly down to the deck to stare down at the twitching, smoking body whose fingers opened and closed emptily, clawing at the life that seeped away. Taylor sank down to his knees almost in supplication as the body twitched again.

'Die, please – why won't you die?' he said, the tears running down his cheeks.

The flare spluttered and died. Presently, and in his own time, Evans died, too.

Whole minutes passed with Martin hunched beside the body of the first man he had ever killed. Reaction took him then and he began to shake violently. He felt the nausea rising, crossed to the rail and vomited painfully over the side. He roused himself finally and returned to the corpse. He searched the body awkwardly for a name, for documents, an identity. He found none. He did, however, find a cassette. One tape cassette.

More minutes passed and then he stumbled to the other side of the wheelhouse to where Erik Stabburs's body lay.

He cradled the Norwegian's head in his arms and rocked gently to and fro, his pain a physical thing now because this man had been his friend; this man had trusted him and this was his doing, his alone.

The Norwegian stirred, his eyes flickered open and then closed again. Relief rolled over Martin like warm honey.

Stabburs coughed awkwardly. 'Did you ... did you get the man?' he whispered huskily.

Martin nodded, unable to speak.

'Yes,' he managed finally. 'Yes, I did.'

CHAPTER TWENTY-FIVE

Martin's ears were popping. He swallowed as he slipped the catch on the folding door, stepped out of the cramped toilet and picked his way back to the front of the aircraft. He had been acutely aware of the stench of fish and the stains on his clothes from the moment he had boarded the lunchtime flight from Kirkenes to Narvik. Still, he had done the best he could with a wet towel and the airline's nailbrush. The rest would have to wait.

'Excuse me, please,' he repeated, stepping carefully over the legs and baggage of the other passengers as he settled back into his window seat. He had been on the S A S D C-9 aircraft for an hour. Kirkeness, Vadsø and the corpse of the man he had killed lay far astern. Erik Stabburs was back there, too, recovering in the hands of the young doctor.

Martin reached down between his knees and pulled his tape recorder out of his hand luggage. He dug out the tape he had taken from the man's body and studied it quietly for a moment, weighing it in his hand. There was no writing on the cassette, so he slipped it into the machine, turned down the volume and held the tape recorder to his ear. A time for answers: he depressed the 'play' button: a guitar began to play the opening chords of a popular song and a male voice began to sing about the love he had left behind. Martin depressed the 'forward wind' button, and the tape jibbered forward. To more music. Puzzled now, Martin flipped the tape over and played through that side also. With the same result.

Songs, just songs. There was not a word or a message from Suzy or anyone else. Martin sat in thought for long minutes as the aircraft thrummed westward. The message had to be there, then, he decided: in the words. He took out a pad and a pencil and began to listen carefully to the words of each song.

He arrived back in Britain fourteen hours later at nine minutes to ten B S T on 12 June.

At eighteen minutes past ten the telephone rang in the foyer of the Conservative Club, Albemarle Avenue, Leeds. A red-coated usher took the call and conferred with the bemedalled master of ceremonies. The M C moved discreetly between the laden, glittering banqueting tables and stooped solemnly beside the dinner-suited elbow of the guest of honour at the top table.

'A telephone call for you, Sir Peter,' he murmured above the orchestra and the tinkle of expensive crockery and dinner-table small talk. 'I am told the matter is urgent.'

'Very well. I shall come directly.' Sir Peter Hillmore patted a starched napkin to his lips, laid a hand lightly upon the shoulder of the guest to his right, murmured a line or two that left them smiling and moved silently to the telephone in the curtained alcove beyond the wide doors.

'Yes?'

'I do apologize for the interruption, Sir Peter. Duty desk here. It's that man Taylor, sir. You left instructions you were to be notified directly he re-entered the country.'

Sir Peter studied his nails. 'He's back, is he?'

'Just arrived, sir. London Heathrow Terminal Two. Arrived at twenty-one fifty-one on a flight from Narvik, Norway.'

'Is he travelling alone?'

'Yes, sir.'

'And where is he now?'

'Under observation, sir – believed to be making for King's Cross Station for the night sleeper back to Hull.'

'Very well. Keep me informed. I'm staying here overnight at the Royal. Once he's seen onto a train, contact me again. Let me know his estimated time of arrival. Oh, and I want local Special Branch notified. They're to pick up his trail and report directly to you. You can reach me on the vehicle net. Is that understood?'

'Understood, sir.'

A little later that same evening Colonel Francis Mann-Quartermain phoned through to the duty office. Banking on the fact that, true to his word, Sir Peter would not yet have processed the mechanics of his dismissal, he told the duty officer he had an urgent message for the head of S I S. Where could he reach him? The duty officer scratched his head.

'It's a little awkward, actually, sir,' he confided. 'He's up north. Leeds. Guest of honour at some function or other. Can I take a message, sir?'

'D'you know where this function is taking place?'

'If you'll just hang on a moment, sir.' There was the rustle of papers in the background. 'Here we are: Conservative Club, Albemarle Avenue, Leeds. He's staying overnight at the Royal. Won't be back until tomorrow evening.'

'Many thanks.' Assuming Sir Peter had kept his discoveries to himself, there was just a chance that ... What have I got to lose? thought Mann-Quartermain mirthlessly.

Shortly after midnight he made another phone call. The number he dialled did not connect him to the Conservative Club or to the Royal Hotel. It connected him, instead, to the man Dr Dowdall had recently found so intensely annoying.

Yates.

The British Rail breakfast was the only good thing about the interminable train journey northward. He had missed the night sleeper and spent weary hours at the station waiting for the first train north. Now Martin felt tense, dirty and tired – and with each clack of the rails his gnawing concern for Suzy's well-being bit deeper.

He was off the train and running before it had screeched to a halt. Through the barrier, into the first taxi and off to the hospital, his bags heaped on the seat beside him.

'Bloody hell,' muttered the man from Special Branch, taken unawares by the hurrying figure that darted through the ticket barrier. Still half asleep but coming awake fast, he tossed the newspaper aside, let in the clutch and set off in pursuit.

'Hang on a minute, driver, will you?' Martin hobbled up the wide staircase, his parka flapping open around him. He limped hurriedly towards the reception desk.

'Ward Four G?'

'May I help you?' asked the sister. Half-drowned seamen, distraught fathers-to-be, mothers of road-accident victims – she dealt with them all.

'Ward Four G: is it through here?'

'I'm sorry. Visitors are not permitted into the wards until between two and three-thirty this afternoon.'

'Oh, I see. Well, I'd like to inquire about ... about a patient.'

'Then perhaps I can help you,' suggested the sister. 'Name, please?'

'Taylor. Martin – Oh, her name? You mean her name? Sorry. It's Summerfield – Suzy ... er ... Susan Summerfield. Ward Four G.'

'Let me see, now. Ah, yes – the young woman. I'm sorry –'

'Sorry?'

'Yes. I'm afraid you've had a wasted journey. She's been discharged. She went home yesterday afternoon.'

'Thanks. Thank you very much.'

Martin wheeled round to limp rapidly down the stone steps to the taxi. 'O K, driver – we're going back towards Beverley Road – and step on it, will you?'

'Here we go again,' muttered Special Branch as the taxi shot away into the traffic. Why couldn't he get the easy ones?

Sir Peter Hillmore's dark-blue Rover was two miles east of Castleford when the red light on the leather armrest began to wink urgently once more. He laid his papers aside and reached for the handset. 'Yes?'

'Duty desk again, sir. That man Taylor. He's on the road again. Just left the hospital.'

'Understood. Keep me informed. I should be in Hull at –'
Sir Peter glanced at his Rolex – 'eleven at the outside.'

Sir Peter pressed the button, and the armoured glass sepa-
rating passenger from driver slid down with a whine. 'Move
it along, driver. Hull in ninety minutes.'

The head nodded imperceptibly, the glass window whined
up and the heavy car began to surge past humbler traffic as
Sir Peter settled back and took up his papers once more.

It had become his habit to submit twice-yearly reports on
his department's activities to the Conservative Leader who
was now in Opposition. Such action, of course, was highly
irregular and would be regarded as an act of betrayal by his
elected superiors. Sir Peter shrugged. He did not see it quite
like that – and, besides, since he always personally delivered
the single copy of the report to the man's private address in
Eaton Square, there was no risk of discovery. Over the
months Sir Peter Hillmore had come to treasure the hour or
so they spent together talking quietly in the panelled study
with its fine books and polished grand piano. Sipping old
French brandy and discussing events, trends and future
strategy, Sir Peter was reminded of the crucial importance of
his role, of his proximity to the proper conscience of a once-
great nation.

Now he was putting the finishing touches to the latest
report.

It was nine pages long, each page written in careful longhand. Sir Peter turned back to the beginning. There, halfway
down the first page and neatly underlined in red ink, was
the one word 'TROJAN'.

The Department's activities in the first quarter of the
year [he read] were complicated by an unforeseen development regarding the TROJAN programme set up by you
and me in the autumn of 1970 . . .

Sir Peter nodded at that, recalling how they had pushed
the programme through Cabinet and then watched with
satisfaction as their trawlers began steaming home with
intelligence gathered at a fraction of the cost of more flam-
boyant NATO surveillance programmes.

I need not remind you that the winter series of NATO Arctic Exercises have presented us in the past with opportunities for TROJAN deployment we have not been slow to exploit.

In recent months Soviet reaction to Own Force activity on these Arctic serials has become noticeably more overt. Consequently, our opportunities for real EW gain have become enhanced also.

You will be aware too that, with the Vladivostok accords scheduled for later this year, our need for hard MRV intelligence has become pressing – particularly with regard to the new SSN-8 missile.

Just prior to Christmas, Naval Intelligence received information suggesting Soviet naval forces intended to subvert SQUADEX to their own ends and resume SSN-8 testing during that same time frame. This, one presumes, would be to test NATO reaction time to launch signature.

This rumour, presented first by SOSUS, was endorsed by ILLIAC IV. SOSUS, you may recall, furnished us with the firing frequency of the new SONY A-B Soviet underwater nuclear mines. Be that as it may, SOSUS indicated that SSN-8 test firing was about to resume.

Accordingly, the British trawler, *Arctic Pilgrim*, in her role as an EW support vessel, was deployed in the area.

On station, she began to monitor predetermined frequencies without incident. She began to record 'Delta' transmissions and signal pulse widths. Her sonar was active also.

Almost immediately, however, her sending capability was itself jammed by powerful Soviet shore stations. This was not unexpected.

Although she was therefore 'deaf' to all incoming signals, the attention she was receiving – particularly from those Soviet shore stations – suggested that, once again, we had deployed our slender resources to maximum effect.

No harm leaving that in, Sir Peter considered. He turned the page.

Arctic Pilgrim was on station two and a quarter hours. Under conditions prevailing at the time such a duration is not considered to have been excessive. As far as we have been able to determine, everything was going to plan.

As is my custom with EW missions of this nature, I placed myself in Control HQ (Northwood) at a position whereby all incoming signals would be seen by me alone and where I could impose direct unit-code contact between myself and Trojan Warrior (trawler escort [RN] under attachment). This, again, was standard procedure.

At 1414 ZULU we began to monitor strong signals' interference followed at 1450 ZULU by Code Purple print-out from ILLIAC IV via satellite link.

This told of an alarming and unforeseen development: Field Trojan's monitoring frequency was building against both the frequency of the Soviet shore stations and that of the SSN-8 test signature she was monitoring. Field Trojan, the Soviet jamming stations and the SSN-8 test signature were combining to produce an harmonic around 23.6–24.0 GHz. In other words, the audio waves on these frequencies were combining – mounting one upon another like waves in the sea – to ascend the frequency scale *without being programmed to do so.*

This harmonic was ascending towards the firing frequency of the chain of Soviet SONY A-B seabed nuclear mines.

Each unit, in isolation, was unaware of its interaction with the other two. That information was held only by ILLIAC IV and was passed, by ILLIAC IV, to myself only at Control HQ (Northwood).

As I have shown, Field Trojan was subject to broad-band jamming. She could not be contacted on any frequency, while the consequence of SONY A-B being armed and then fired unintentionally with SQUADEX units deployed within range was, of course, too serious to contemplate.

I had already positioned a vessel to act as EW Support within operational distance. The ship was the Frigate HMS *Tuscan*, Commander Simon Jennings RN commanding. In view of the situation described above I took, Sir, the following action. I hope you will feel that under the circumstances ...

Sir Peter Hillmore read on as his car swept him towards Hull and a tenacious reporter he had never met called Martin Taylor.

Martin dumped his kit bag on the landing, wiped his hands down the front of his parka and took a deep breath to still the thumping of his heart. Then he rang Suzy's doorbell.

There was no reply.

He rang again.

After an interminable moment he heard timid movement within. He swallowed nervously. The door opened a cautious inch.

'What do you want?' asked a small voice. There was the glitter of a door chain that had not been there before.

'It's me – Martin,' said Martin, his voice thick with an emotion he distrusted.

'Martin!' The chain rattled and the door opened a further tiny crack. The chain was new and so, too, were the bruises and the dark shadows under her eyes. But the smile was the same crooked smile she had smiled for him before.

'Martin! It *is* you! Oh, Martin!' she cried. The door went back with a crash and that smile washed out of the flat onto the landing and bathed everything in its incandescence. 'Oh, Martin, Martin ... I've missed you so,' she whispered huskily into his neck. 'God, you'll never know ...' The words choked off into warm tears as she hugged him fiercely to her, never to let go.

Martin felt the tide rise and burst within him also. 'I've missed you, too.' He choked, the tears coursing down his cheeks with the truth of it.

They stood there until Martin heard a cautious step on the stair behind him. He spun round to see Mr Hoskins advancing towards him menacingly. Mr Hoskins recognized Martin with a sour look as Suzy called out happily. 'It's all right, Mr Hoskins – it's all right, really. He's come home. He's back.'

'So I see,' said Hoskins, trying to hide the hammer behind his back.

*

Half an hour passed, yet still they moved everywhere together, as though afraid a break of physical contact would dissolve forever the newfound spell of their happiness. Suzy was trying to make coffee with one hand while clutching Martin with the other. It was not a very easy thing to do.

Once again they both started talking at once. They stopped, and then Martin said with a smile, 'Did they tell you you were chatting to me in your sleep? All about collisions and something about a tape?'

'The tape!' A hand flew to her mouth.

'Don't worry,' said Martin. 'It's here.' He tapped his pocket. 'I got it back.'

'Martin? But how did –' Ugly realization dawned and Suzy held up a slim hand. 'I don't want to know, Martin. Not yet.' Martin had not pried into the details of the attack, and, for her part, intuition warned Suzy that questions about Norway would only lead to more pain, more harsh truths. 'Tell me later. Anyway –' she turned to the tea caddy – 'that's not the important one.'

'Now she tells me!' groaned Martin as he thought of the hours spent making notes on the aircraft back from Norway. 'What happened to the one *you* were talking about?'

'It's here – or it should be,' said Suzy, emptying tea bags onto the kitchen table. 'I switched them when that ... that man wasn't looking. Here we are!' She held the tape aloft triumphantly.

'What's on it? It's that collision you were talking about – the one between *Pilgrim* and the Russian submarine, am I right? Of course, once I'd realized   What's the matter?'

Suzy was frowning, the milk jug poised over their cups. 'A Russian submarine? A Russian submarine and *Arctic Pilgrim*?'

'That's right. You said –'

'The only collision I know about involved a frigate. A British frigate. H M S *Tuscan*.'

'What are you talking about?' demanded Martin, as all the neat little pieces fell apart in his hands again.

'Remember those boats you asked me to check on? The Royal Navy boats that had been on that exercise –'

'Ships. The Royal Navy calls them ships,' Martin corrected automatically. What the hell had been happening?

'Ships, boats – what's the difference? Anyway: you know that exercise? Squadex?' Martin nodded. 'Well, H M S *Tuscan* was one of the ones on your list – only suddenly, half-way through the exercise, she had to return to port for repairs. She left the exercise area on February the eighth.'

'Did she, by Christ! What sort of repairs?'

'I'm just coming to that: she'd damaged her front, her bows. In a collision.'

'How did you find out all this?'

'I phoned up and asked. They were really quite helpful,' said Suzy with a self-satisfied smirk. She enjoyed Martin's look of pained professionalism.

'You phoned them up? And they *told* you? Just like that?'

'More or less. Oh, and there's more. Know what else I found out?'

'Tell me.'

'The captain of H M S *Tuscan* was relieved of his command as soon as his boa – ship returned. I went to see his wife. She told me all about it. She's very bitter. The poor man had a nervous breakdown about something that happened on that trip.'

'What, for Chrissake?'

'How should I know? It's on the tape.'

'And you haven't heard it yet?'

'I've only just come out of hospital, Martin, and ...' She paused.

'And?'

'I haven't any batteries,' Suzy ended in a small voice.

Martin laughed for the first time, it seemed, in years. 'Come on, Woodstein.' He picked up the tape, grabbed his coffee and led the way upstairs to his flat.

Sir Peter Hillmore's Rover slid to a halt against the kerb. The driver got out and crossed casually to the battered pale-green Capri on the opposite side of the road. Special Branch wound down the window with difficulty.

'He's in there. Second floor. Arrived about forty minutes ago.'

Sir Peter Hillmore's driver nodded curtly and returned to the Rover. Sir Peter glanced at his watch. There was plenty of time. He was not expected back in London until the evening.

'We'll give him a while longer. See what transpires,' Sir Peter decided, reaching for *The Times*. 'Keep an eye on that door.'

In the pale-green Ford Capri, Special Branch reached for the *Sun* and turned to page three.

The tape began to hiss quietly:

'These last few days ... they've been pretty bloody, actually.' Cough. 'Start again: I ... I don't know why I'm talking to ... to myself like this. Perhaps it'll help me see things a little ... a little clearer, straighten things out. It's just that I can't ... I can't seem to *see* things, to think things, events, past a certain point. Everything just seems to go blank ... void.'

The voice was hesitant, self-conscious, a looking-over-the-shoulder-at-the-door sort of voice, as though the very act of confiding into a machine branded his disorder as incurable, the actions those of a man already lost.

'Diana ... well, she's tried to help, of course – she's been marvellous. She's tried to understand, tried to talk about it, but I ... I can't ... I can't stand that. It's not her fault, nothing to do with Diana – but she wasn't *there*. How ... how can she help? How can anyone help who ... wasn't there? It's just me. Inside me, my head. I've just got to got it out, that's all. Then it will be better. Easier.'

The voice took on a firmer note, an edge of resolve. 'What I've decided to do is just talk the thing through, from the beginning, as it happened. See if I can't make progress. I don't think I could ... I can ... face going back, d'you see? Not there. Not now. Not as I am.

'Call sign Trojan Warrior – that was us. R N unit for E W support attached. Things seemed to go well – for a while, anyway – working out on the flank of the exercise area. Weather was pretty rotten, of course, but then it's always bad up there. Nothing ... nothing unusual about that No, no – everything seemed fine. Until ... until that signal. That started it – that was the one. "Captain's Eyes Only: Shut down for nuclear and close with Field Trojan. Immediate." A little ... a little *unusual*, perhaps, but nothing we ... nothing I couldn't handle. It wasn't as if they were ... testing me, was it? Not then, not on my first command.

'I can't recall all the ... all the details ... Oh, yes: Northwood again – "Close Field Trojan visual by fourteen fifty-five. Urgent message follows." Visual! But ... but they knew our position! Knew it better than we did! They must have known we couldn't get there in time, they must have!'

Suzy clutched Martin's hand tightly across the table. 'Poor man, he –'

'Sssh.'

The tape ran on and as they listened the voice dropped to a whisper. 'We were making progress, but it ... it was obvious we were never going to close the distance, not in that time, with those seas. It just wasn't on. Then the intercept signal: "At own discretion disable by SSM or gunfire if in Captain's opinion unable effect alongside manoeuvre by fifteen-oh-two." Jesus God ... how could we go alongside? What was I to do? Disable by missile or gunfire? One of our own ships, our own trawlers? Why? Why?'

Suzy glanced at Martin, her eyes wide with horror and disbelief as Martin began to learn that the Royal Navy had murdered his father. Martin was looking down at his hands, his face quite white.

The tape ran on remorselessly: 'I ... I signalled Northwood, called up a repeat – I couldn't ... couldn't believe it! It was too extreme, too fantastic! Northwood confirmed. No delays, no checks, just: "Execute Immediate. Advise when task completed."'

The tape ran on silently for one minute, perhaps two. Martin never moved. He sat in utter silence, looking down at his hands. Finally the voice continued, quieter still:

'I thought we had missed at first – it was too far for gunfire, and in those . . . those conditions anything could happen. But as we drew closer I could . . . I could see this dull-red glow in the sky reflected off the belly of the clouds over . . .'

'Bastard – bastard – bastard,' said Martin, his fist pounding slowly against the table with great force.

'. . . God, I never . . . I mean . . . I don't remember how long we took to close – forty-five minutes . . . an hour? Presently I could see the ship quite . . . quite clearly. She was low in the water, sinking. The missile had hit for'ard of the wheelhouse. All of her paintwork had been scorched by the blast, her fo'c's'le deck was ragged, torn away, and I think . . . I think she was on fire somewhere down below the waterline. Yes, yes, she was, I'm sure of that. We ran on through the rain and the mists to pick up the . . . the survivors . . .'

'You . . . you . . .' Martin felt that his head would crack with the sorrow, the impotent, blazing anger of it.

The voice paused now, as though considering something carefully. 'It wasn't until . . . until we cleared the ship's blind side that radar saw her. We should have seen her earlier. Why didn't we? Why didn't we see her earlier? It was a . . . a submarine, surfacing, close by. The trawler's echo must have masked her completely, so that instead of . . . instead of two returns there was just . . . just one. We . . . we came round through the mist and . . . and there she was, her decks coming awash one hundred, one hundred and fifty metres off the trawler's beam. God, she was big, huge. Hotel Class – forty-four hundred tons.'

'Your submarine,' whispered Suzy, with a hand to Martin's arm. Martin nodded and bent forward, listening as the voice became animated with the memory of action vividly recalled:

'I saw the men then – the survivors. My survivors. Some were already in the water, just lying there, still, floating, not moving. One . . . one was on . . . on fire. God, oh, God, what did I . . . ? Others . . . others were clinging to the super-structure, yelling, shouting in the wind and the storm for the rafts and the boats that had been blown away with the blast. I ... I was watching. It was ... very horrible.' There was a catch to the voice now, and then a muffled sob. 'A few were trying to ... to swim towards the submarine, to safety. I remember ... I remember thinking: Oh, that's all right – she'll lower her nets, put out some boats and pick them up, save them. But she didn't. Why? Why didn't they lower nets, do *something*? They could have helped easily, so easily. I could actually *see* the captain on the sail, on the fin, watching the men in the water. Men with wives ... with families, little children ... children like Mike ... Oh, God – why? Why did I do it?' He was sobbing openly now, the pain of guilt, of conscience, sawing across magnetic tape. 'We ... we could hear the men in the water yelling for help, crying out, as the cold got to them – they *knew* they were dying if we didn't help them quickly! Yet he did nothing. *Nothing!* And when ... when I tried to move in and help, that *bastard* Russian, he ... he just manoeuvred his ship between us. I moved – and he moved. I moved again – and he moved, blocking, always blocking. I couldn't get close enough to ...'

'Martin!' exclaimed Suzy. 'He's ... he's murdering them!'

The tape continued. 'There was nothing I could do. Nothing! I ... I looked through the glasses, and he ... he waved at me. He *waved*! They said ... they said afterwards I was shouting, shouting ... I don't remember. I don't remember any of it; I just remember the men dying – dying in the water ... I don't remember giving the orders – there's nothing left now about the collision, nothing! Perhaps ... perhaps it was an accident, ramming the submarine like they say I did. I don't remember. All I see ... all I see is the men, the men in the water, shouting, calling, pleading for help, their arms moving slower and slower and ... and I did nothing to help them. Nothing ...' The words ended in prolonged sobbing.

'Stop it, Martin. Turn it off, please,' begged Suzy, her hands over her ears. 'I can't take any more.'

Martin reached out slowly and stilled the agony of Commander Simon Jennings R N.

And there was a long silence.

Suzy watched Martin anxiously, her own distress eclipsed by a deeper concern for the man who had just learned that his father had been murdered on the high seas by callous, deliberate neglect. Martin sat staring at the table saying nothing. Prepared for loud, blind anger, she was frightened by this dark, brooding silence.

Martin looked up slowly, dragging a hand through his hair. 'So that was the way of it. I told you, right at the start, there was something funny going on, didn't I?' Suzy nodded. 'But that,' Martin continued, 'that's ... monstrous, horrific! Why? Why go to all that trouble just to – to what? To sink their own boat? It doesn't make sense. It doesn't make any sense at all, dammit!' Martin smashed his fist into the table and gazed with mild disinterest at the raw, bleeding knuckles. He stood up and zipped up his parka carefully.

'What are you going to do?' asked Suzy gently.

'Do? I'm going to see a man about a bloody trawler – that's what I'm going to do! Mr Harding, Mr sodding Harding, the man who gave Johno a break!' The door slammed behind him and Martin dropped downstairs.

Martin's Renault was followed as it turned into Beverley Road. They made quite a convoy: the Renault, Sir Peter's Rover and the Special Branch Capri.

And, behind them all, a white Triumph 2000.

Martin turned into Filton Street and drove down towards the river. Almost at Harding's office now, he was deep in thought. This time he knew what he was going to say, what he was about to demand. And then, when he had all his answers, then and only then he would get on the train to London and –

A dark-blue Rover surged past and cut in ahead with a sharp blast on the horn. The Rover slewed across his path, and Martin jammed on the brakes. A door opened and a young man in a dark suit was walking briskly back towards him.

'What the hell d'you think you're playing at?' demanded Martin angrily. 'You damn near had me –'

'Sorry about that, Mr Taylor. Would you get out and come with me, please? Gentleman wants to talk to you. In the car.'

'Are you out of your –?'

'If you don't mind.' The driver opened Martin's door and stood there firmly. 'Your vehicle will be quite safe.'

'What's this all about?'

'Please – the car.'

Martin walked cautiously towards the rear door of the Rover. It opened and a well-dressed man in his mid sixties leaned across with a disarming smile. 'Mr Taylor? Won't you join me?'

'Is that an order – or an invitation?'

'A little bit of both.' Sir Peter smiled. 'Come, now – there is no need to worry. Please.' He gestured.

Martin hesitated a moment longer and then got into the back, noting the registration number. And a fat lot of good that will do me, he thought, putting the pieces together rapidly, his heart thumping out his nervousness.

'This wouldn't have something to do with *Arctic Pilgrim*, I suppose?' he said as casually as he could manage.

The other nodded.

'And where do you fit in, Squire?' Martin asked. 'Graveline Trawlers? Another company? Government? D T I?' He tapped the leather briefcase on the seat beside him. 'Government, at a guess – yes?'

'You're very observant, Mr Taylor.'

'I'm also in a hurry, so what do you want?'

'We understand you've been taking rather a special interest in the disappearance of ... *Arctic Pilgrim*,' began Sir Peter, testing the water.

Martin nodded. 'You could say that.'

'Might I ask why?'

Martin gave a harsh laugh. 'Why? Because my old man was on that ship – that's why ! And because I ...' He shook his head in exasperation. 'Look, I don't get it : I mean, what is all this? You must know what I've been up to or you wouldn't be here. I'm not a complete fool. What do you want?'

'Tell me: your investigations – have they been ... ah ... successful? What have you discovered? Please – I would be very interested to know.'

Martin groaned, suddenly tired of the whole rotten business. Suzy was right – it would bring nothing back.

'O K.' He sighed. 'Arctic Pilgrim – she wasn't just fishing, right? She was ... she was spying too. She was carrying intercept receivers to spy on the Russians.' Martin ran a hand through his thick hair. 'Don't ask me how, or where – she just was. And that ... that lifebuoy? Discovered after she disappeared? It was a plant, put there to thwart a search of the Norwegian coastline, O K? Now, I may be leaving out whole chunks of the story, but I'm tired and that's the gist of it, all right?' And it's all you're getting, he thought. You can read the rest for yourself in neon lights after I've written the story.

Sir Peter was used to weighing men, and he considered this one sitting beside him now. There were dark rings under his eyes, and his dirty, creased trousers stank strongly of fish – but there was a hard determination around the mouth and the set of his shoulders that suggested he would not easily be deflected. 'And what did happen to the ship?' he asked. 'Did your investigations tell you that? Do you have any idea?'

Martin smiled without humour. 'I've an idea, as it happens, yes.'

'Oh?' Sir Peter waited patiently.

Martin sat back comfortably and folded his arms. 'She was sunk,' he said quietly, clearly. 'Not by the storm, not by an accident, not even by the Russians. She was sunk by us: by the Royal sodding Navy. By surface-to-surface missile.'

Sir Peter blinked rapidly and studied the lock on his briefcase. Good God, the man really had done his homework. Long moments passed before he looked up. 'I see I must congratulate you, Mr Taylor. You really are most determined. Or imaginative. Tell me – what makes you think it was sunk by the ... by the Royal Navy?'

'I don't think – I know.'

'How do you know?' demanded Sir Peter.

Martin shook his head. 'You're not getting me that way. I suspect you know what really happened – you wouldn't be here if you didn't. You know whether I'm telling the truth or not. We both do.' There was a pause and then Martin asked, 'So just where do you fit into all this? Do I get a name?'

'I'm just a civil servant,' murmured Sir Peter.

'But an important one,' observed Martin. 'They don't give armed drivers and Rovers away with luncheon vouchers.'

'Armed drivers?'

'Smiling boy.' Martin jerked a thumb at the man standing casually by his car. 'His jacket flapped open when he got out.'

Sir Peter held up a finger. 'Another point to you.'

Martin shrugged. 'I've put in a bit of practice over the last week or so. I seem to attract men with guns.' Sir Peter nodded without surprise, and Martin felt a jolt of fear. So he knew about that too. 'Your doing, was it?' he asked calmly. 'The bloke with the gun? Here and in Norway?'

Sir Peter shook his head emphatically. 'No – but it was *my* responsibility, and that makes it my fault. It was never supposed to happen, never. The operation was completely unauthorized. There will not be a repetition as far as –'

'Unauthorized operation? That sounded a bit military.'

'Just a title, that's all.'

'So tell me: what is the purpose of this ... this little meeting?' Martin waved a hand around the interior of the Rover.

'I wanted to meet you – to see the man who's been causing our people so much ... inconvenience.'

'Our people?'

'The department I work for.'

'And that's all you'll tell me?'

Sir Peter nodded. 'I'm afraid so.'

'I could trace the number plate.'

'You could not trace the number plate.'

'Oh. Well, you've run me off the road, you've had a good look at me. What's supposed to happen now?'

Sir Peter looked directly at Martin. 'Drop it. Forget it –

drop the whole thing. In your own best interests, Mr Taylor, forget it ever happened.'

Martin exploded. 'Drop it! Forget it! My father is murdered on a trawler, someone tries to kill me a couple of times – and damn near succeeds – he beats up my girlfriend and causes Christ knows what suffering to hundreds of innocent people, and you say drop it! You're off your trolley, whoever you are! What kind of a fucking reporter do you think I am? Putting aside my personal involvement for a moment, do you *really* expect I'm just going to walk away and say, "Fair enough, old top, you win – I won't write a bloody word?" Do you? Write it? You'll be able to read the bloody thing in neon lights by the time I've finished!' Martin stormed on recklessly. 'The public has a right to know that this sort of thing is going on! What about the wives, the families of the men who were drowned, murdered – what about them, for God's sake?' He sat back angrily.

'Like most of your generation you think we are at peace, I suppose?' said Sir Peter quietly. 'You think – if you think about it at all – that as long as the bombs aren't actually *falling* everything is fine? You are wrong. We are at war now – we have been at war since the very day your sort of war ended, but it is a war of intelligence, of knowledge. Your kind of war, the kind that kills by the thousand, by the million, the one that is somehow respectable because it has been "declared" like some sort of shooting season – your kind of war is averted by this knowledge. Do I make myself clear?'

'I'll let you know if you lose me,' said Martin, his words hiding a stirring of sympathy for the thrust of the older man's reasoning.

Sir Peter went on. 'Forgive the parable, but there are two men, each in a little darkened room isolated from the other. In their ignorance they fear each other, each wondering what the other is plotting, but very soon they learn that, by turning on the light and peering over the wall, they can see what the other man is like, what he is doing; they can see that he is not plotting to take over their room after all, that the giant of their mind is just a man after all – and so fear goes away, imagination becomes rational and there is a return to stability. That is a kind of security, would you not agree?'

'I follow what you're saying, yes,' said Martin, seeing for the first time where the man's conversation was taking him.

'You, with your story, your search after truth, your "The Public Has a Right to Know" – *you*, right now, *you* have the power to put us back into the darkness of that little room, do you see? Go ahead with your story and what will you achieve? Really? Oh, you'll be able to puff and boast about your scoop, your tenacity, your precious journalistic integrity –' he made a careless gesture of dismissal – 'and you will have given "the truth" to a handful of people who no longer need it, to a handful of people who are just beginning to adjust to their loss. But you will build *nothing*. You will achieve *nothing*.

'What *harm* will you do? What will you destroy? I shall tell you : all the work, all the effort that has gone into one of the most successful intelligence programmes since 1945 will be wiped out, wasted. The programme relies on Cabinet support, and that will be stopped – of course it will. The programme will be buried forever. The flow of vital intelligence will stop.'

'You seem to have conveniently forgotten about –'

'Wait. Let me finish. "The Public Has a Right to Know",' mocked Sir Peter Hillmore. 'The wail of every beer-soaked hack from Glasgow to Salisbury; a talisman for intrusion. But you aren't a hack – you are a journalist of intelligence, of integrity. Yes – *Arctic Pilgrim* was carrying out an intelligence mission. Yes – she was spying on the Russians. Yes – she was sunk by the Royal Navy. I admit all these things to you here, in this car. But tell me : do you know *why* she was sunk? *Why* she was spying? Do you?'

Martin shook his head.

Sir Peter snapped open the locks on his pigskin briefcase and drew out the file he had been studying in the car earlier.

He removed the top two pages and then handed Martin the section headed 'TROJAN'. He covered the report briefly with his hand.

'I am going to tell you – rather, I am going to let you read for yourself. But before you read these pages, I beg you to ask yourself one question.'

'What's that?'

'"What good will it do? What will it achieve?" Publication of your story – even if you get it past the "D" Notice people – will achieve nothing. The programme will be stopped, the work will be wasted. Your father was one of those killed on *Arctic Pilgrim*. I am sorry, I am genuinely sorry – but nothing you or I can do will change that. Write your story, bask in your moment of journalistic glory, and the cause he unwittingly died for will be wasted, wiped away, forgotten. Nothing positive will be achieved. You want to be effective? To take a positive decision, make a contribution? Decide *not* to write your story, not to publish.' Sir Peter shifted a little awkwardly. 'You'd better read that report.'

Martin did so.

He sat over it a long time, absorbing the impact of its message. Several times he looked up to ask a question. The anger had gone now and had been replaced by a quiet, thoughtful intensity.

The first time: 'You. You ordered *Tuscan* to fire that missile?' And Sir Peter Hillmore nodded.

And again: 'These ... these "clinics"? The man who attacked me, tried to kill me in Norway?'

Sir Peter nodded again. 'Strictly free-lance. Acting to orders I knew nothing about and would never have sanctioned, I promise you.'

And finally: 'And Harding? What does he get out of it?'

Sir Peter Hillmore shrugged. 'Not a lot – five or six thousand a year.'

Martin laid the report aside slowly and looked directly at the man whose arguments, whose revelations, had turned his determination into such turmoil. 'I can't say ...' he s finally. 'I won't pretend it makes no difference, all this, because it does. I need time, time to think. Can I contact you in a few days?'

Sir Peter smiled. 'Nice try, but I think I'd better contact you. I'll call early next week.'

Martin made to get out of the car. He paused. 'Do you need my number?'

Sir Peter shook his head. 'Don't worry, we'll be in touch.'

'I don't bloody doubt it,' muttered Martin with a touch of his old cynicism. He got out and walked slowly back to his car.

Sir Peter's Rover turned back into Beverley Road and was soon picking up speed on the motorway heading back to London. It had been a long trip, all told, and presently Sir Peter dozed in the back, lulled by the comforting rush of rubber on tarmac. The driver also relaxed, his thoughts in London and not on the road behind. Thus neither noticed the white Triumph 2000 that stayed five or six cars behind, shadowing their progress at a steady sixty-five mph.

The Rover stopped at a service station outside Mansfield at lunchtime. Sir Peter and his driver went in to lunch together as the Triumph drew up quietly in a space nearby. While Sir Peter and his driver were inside, the driver of the Triumph worked quickly with the pliers and the package that looked like a thermos bottle, so that when Sir Peter returned to the car the Triumph was already further down the motorway, parked beside a phone booth.

Forensic evidence later established that the bomb had been placed against the rear off-side wheel arch and that it had contained nine pounds of a distinctive explosive stolen earlier that week from a construction site in Coleraine, Northern Ireland.

As the pall of black smoke rose into the sky and the first of the sirens wailed across the afternoon towards the smoking wreckage, Yates punched money into the phone and spoke briefly into the receiver.

'Those Irish pigs have been throwing their bombs about ʼr here again,' he said cheerfully. 'Dreadful business.'

'They'll deny it, of course. It's just another sign of the times we live in,' agreed Francis Mann-Quartermain sadly.

Two days after Sir Peter's funeral Stefan Ilya Rokoff, all smiles and beams, arrived at the office of Colonel Francis Mann-Quartermain. The Colonel, he knew, would be in a good mood. Just two and a half hours earlier the Colonel had been summoned by the Prime Minister.

Stefan Rokoff smiled at the pretty young secretary and, with gallant gesture, handed her the rose from his button-hole as he waited for the Director of S I S to spare him a moment of his valuable time. He was in no hurry. Not any more.

The findings of the inquiry into the loss of the Hull motor trawler *Arctic Pilgrim* were published six weeks later: 'The Motor Trawler *Arctic Pilgrim* had been overwhelmed by heavy seas and had capsized with the loss of all hands. There was no evidence to suggest negligence or neglect on the part of any of the parties concerned.'

Marcus Armstrong-Carpenter got his M B E. Three months later, however, he was becoming dangerously talkative. He was killed that same winter in an unfortunate car accident outside Rugby.

Because negligence was never established at the inquiry into the loss of the vessel, damages could not be awarded to the dependants. Each therefore received a maximum settlement of £3,200, of which £2,000 came from the life-insurance plan run by the company and the remainder was made up by contributions from the Lord Mayor's Fund, the Fishermen's Trust and the Trawler Officers' Guild. The Hull Chamber of Trade generously donated enough money to wipe out all outstanding instalment-plan agreements left behind by the crew of the *Arctic Pilgrim*.

Officially, the *Arctic Pilgrim* matter is closed, and for all Martin Taylor knows, the body of the man he killed still lies beneath the Vadsø jetty, its feet wrapped in five fathoms of chain.

One windy autumn afternoon Martin Taylor sat at his typewriter, and presently Suzy heard the clatter of typewriter keys:

For Norman Fullerton, 23 March 1969, was a special day. On that day, at the age of twenty-seven, he began to ...

More about Penguins
and Pelicans

For further information about books available from
Penguins please write to Dept EP, Penguin Books Ltd,
Harmondsworth, Middlesex UB7 0DA.

In the U.S.A.: For a complete list of books available
from Penguins in the United States write to Dept DG,
Penguin Books, 299 Murray Hill Parkway, East
Rutherford, New Jersey 07073.

In Canada: For a complete list of books available from
Penguins in Canada write to Penguin Books Canada
Ltd, 2801 John Street, Markham, Ontario L3R 1B4.

In Australia: For a complete list of books available from
Penguins in Australia write to the Marketing
Department, Penguin Books Australia Ltd, P.O. Box
257, Ringwood, Victoria 3134.

In New Zealand: For a complete list of books available
from Penguins in New Zealand write to the Marketing
Department, Penguin Books (N.Z.) Ltd, P.O. Box 4019,
Auckland 10.

SKYSHROUD

Tom Keene with Brian Haynes

The certainty of instant nuclear retaliation has helped preserve a fragile international stability. But now the Head of United States Air Force Intelligence is convinced that the concept of Mutual Assured Destruction – MAD – is finished.

General Clarke Freeman believes the Soviets are perilously close to perfecting a Charged Particle Beam Weapon, an infallible defence against nuclear missiles. Safe from retaliation, Soviet global control is only the press of a button away. Yet while General Freeman talks, no one is listening – and already the clocks on project Skyshroud are unwinding remorselessly . . .

and coming soon

EARTHRACE

Tom Keene

THE WORLD IS HIT BY A RECESSION. AND A SMALL AFRICAN COUNTRY HOLDS A KEY TO ITS FUTURE . . .

Tasamanga is a small, parched patch of Africa ravaged by drought, famine and corruption.

Earthcom is a British-based multinational plucking minerals from Tasamanga's poor earth.

Peter Garrick and Anne Leonard are relief workers in a land where dried milk saves lives. Now they are caught up in Earthcom's reign of terror and a new East/West scramble for Africa as satellites make prospecting easy – and espionage and sabotage essential.